INVASION

ROBERT TREGAY

TTP
THE TREGAY
— PRESS —

INVASION

On the 2nd of September 1939, after the outbreak of war with Poland, Germany sent an assurance to Norway in these terms:

The German Reich Government is determined in view of the friendly relations which exist between Norway and Germany, under no circumstance to prejudice the inviolability and integrity of Norway, and to respect the territory of the Norwegian State.

(Extract)

PROLOGUE

Drøbak, Norway, 10th of October 1939.

The air so cold, the snow so deep, the fjord so black.

Twilight gathered. Alexander Brann stood high above the town, facing north, his eyebrows frosted hard. Violent storms had funnelled down the Narrows these last few days, and a blanket of snow covered the landscape. Now, the last of the squalls were spent and a frozen, deathly calm descended. In the town below, the people huddled around their fires. Ice formed in the harbour and along the rocky shores. No winter in living memory had begun so early and with such venom. It suited Brann well.

Slipping below the skyline, he picked his way through deep snow, a length of rope coiled over his shoulder, a spade in his hand. He entered the forest and lumbered down the old fisherman's path towards Hallangspollen, a remote branch of the main fjord where a thin bank of mist enveloped the water, filling the rocky coves and drifting onto the steep, bouldery beaches. Perfect, he thought, as his grip tightened around the shaft of the spade; no one would be here, not in this desolate place where the shadowy light of the gloaming had taken hold, where the air was unmoving; sharp, like a huntsman's knife.

Continuing through the mist he reached a large, moss-covered rock, then paced thirty strides into the forest where he found his tree, marked by a freshly-cut notch at waist-level. Kicking away the snow around the trunk, he stared down at a broken surface of stony, frozen earth. Below lay his prize, his first win in the war to come, gilded by the prospect of a clutch of 20-Mark gold coins. Easy money, too easy. He'd do it for nothing. He grabbed his spade, then jabbed at the hard clods until, grunting in satisfaction, he broke through to a layer of dark, more pliant clay.

Brann never tired. Not him. He took a break, looked around and listened as the eerie chill of twilight captured the forest air. A tree nearby creaked and a thin shower of snow fell away from high above. Across the water, a wolf howled. Tentacles of mist spread up from the fjord, like ghosts creeping through the trees. But nothing frightened Brann, not the forest, certainly not a dead body – an amusing thought. In the end, terminating the man's mission had been simple, like a forest tree yielding to his cross-cut saw. Now, the Brit was waiting for him, stock-still, like a King's Guard at the palace. "Sorry, my friend," he muttered; "should have been back earlier, but the weather...you know how it's been."

Clearing more of the soft earth and pulling away stones and broken roots with his forester's gloves, he slowly exposed what was hidden two days ago, well wrapped and tied with twine. All was as it should be except, clearing the last of the earth, he saw the spade had ripped the sacking, revealing the left-side of the corpse's face and cutting the skin below its lower lip.

Dropping onto his knees, he peered down in the failing light. Fair hair and high forehead, a blooded, twisted nose; the skin a terrible, pallid grey, old and battered and bleached of its colour as if it were a porcelain doll, but somehow gone soft, then frozen again. The eyes, still half open; opaque, specks of earth like freckles over the faded blue. He leaned closer. His breath pumped out, the cloud dissipating in the cold air, merging into the gloom of the forest.

"Not up to much, were you?" he muttered.

But something was missing. Groping inside the sacking, he found what he sought. They must have been dislodged by the spade. Now he could place the cheap, wire-rimmed spectacles in their rightful place. There was no need to deprive the man. Not now.

"You were an idiot," he whispered, his head on one side, his fingers feeling the contours of his victim's face, the back of his huge gloves wiping away a smudge of earth on the cheek and flattening the fold of skin torn by his spade. "You thought you could outwit Alexander, didn't you? Thought you were invisible, safe; like an old elk, creeping out from the forest into the mire. But the wolves had gathered, watching your every step. So you were a dead man from the day you returned. And here's a tip," he whispered into the dead man's ear. "No one wears a new sealskin coat working the boats. Not around here."

Using his thumbs, Brann snapped the broken nose, wiped away the bloodstain and finally wrapped a length of sacking around the head, tying it with twine from the pocket of his coat. He ran his hands over the contours of the corpse's face again, slowly, systematically, checking the spectacles were straight, glancing occasionally over his shoulder into the mist; it was still empty and silent, just another creak high in the canopy. A few snowflakes drifted down between the trees. It would soon be dark.

Lifting the frozen body, he passed the rope beneath it, looping it twice. It was surprisingly heavy, the patches of ice maybe, the damp sacking. He stood and looked down, the body neatly wrapped, the earth brushed off.

"No more squealing," he whispered, "...not that you could; not now, and not where you'll be going."

With a final look back, he pulled the rope over his shoulder and dragged the body a short distance towards the shoreline, carefully avoiding sharp boulders and tree stumps that might snag the sacking. Breathing heavily, he followed the edge of the forest across rocks and frosted grasses and then, skirting a jumble of bleached driftwood strangely fulgent in the failing light, he reached an isolated, ramshackle boathouse. He dragged open the doors, leaving the body lying against a wedge of soft blown snow nearby. With a brief smile, he ran his hand along the gunwale of his old fjord-boat and glanced into the advancing darkness. Then, grunting with the effort, he dragged the boat into the frozen, vaporous air.

Stopping at the edge of the fjord, he cleared a space in the stern of his boat, then hauled the body down the beach and carefully lifted it inside. As he pushed away with his oars, scattered patches of wafer-thin ice broke up and crackled as he manoeuvred between the rocks, heading through the mist towards open water.

He hummed as he rowed, tunelessly. But no one heard. Fog drifted past, dense and liquid, an empty silence but for the familiar tinkle of water slipping by and dripping off the blades. Far off, a foghorn moaned. Revelling in a few powerful strokes of the oars, he breathed out, stretching the corners of his heavy mouth.

Shipping the oars off Skarholmen, the last of the islands where the waters dropped off into a deep trench and the big fish lay, he allowed the boat to drift, the mist dissolving, the darkness impenetrable, the fjord soundless. After a short rest, he leaned forward onto his knees to check the package, lying with a heap of fishing gear on the bottom boards. It had been worth taking time to prepare the rocks, so the ropes would hold; a body could easily slip free and float to the surface. But no one would ever find the Brit, he would make sure of that.

A pointless man: a British spy, a fool sent by fools. He had spoken when the end came, revealing some worthless snippets. Maybe, Alexander, you should have been more patient, got more out of him? Brann pondered the question. No, the man was useless, empty-headed and he didn't have the stamina, did he?

In the darkness Brann waited: to be calm, focussed. Wiping away the wet on his face he listened for any sound alien to the fjord. Just a gentle sloshing from the hull of the clinker-built boat. He would relish the moment, etching it into his memory. With a hand on the gunwale to steady himself, he took hold of the rope and dragged the package towards the edge. He checked again through the sacking that the spectacles were just so, then gave one more pull so the body slipped over the edge and into the water; slowly, carefully, just the faintest splash, the boat rocking, then settling again. He let the body slide, little by little, into the blackness of the fjord, the weight of the stones pulling the rope steadily through his hands until it ran out, the ragged end flicking across his gloved hands with a dull slap.

He peered over for a final look. Just a few ripples remained, caught in the light of the crescent moon as the last of the mist drifted away.

Then everything was still.

As he returned, he started to hum again, a forester's song. Louder this time. Because a thought entered his mind. They'd replace him, wouldn't they, the Brits? They'd send another useless spy.

Part One
BENEATH THE DOME OF A NORTHERN SKY

In 1934, the construction contract for an advanced heavy cruiser was placed with Deutsche Werke, Kiel. Named 'Blücher', the German warship was launched on the 8th of June 1937. After more than two years of fitting-out and initial sea-trials, she weighed anchor at Gotenhafen at 0800 hours on the 7th of December 1939 and sailed east to conduct speed trials and fuel measurements.

Later the same day, nineteen hours out from the Tyne Commission Quay, England, the Fred Olsen liner, 'Black Prince', sailed into Skagerrak, the stretch of water separating Denmark and Norway. Warned of possible danger from hostile shipping, her captain, Finn Wichstrøm, hugged the rocky coast of Norway until he could turn north into the main channel towards Oslo. Among his passengers, sailing on a one-way third-class ticket, was a young student, Thomas Waldemar Galtung.

ONE

It was too late for regret: he had made the decision. Or rather the decision had been thrust upon him, 'choice' a mere illusion.

From a cold and empty deck he watched rocky islands slip by as daylight faded, the steady thrum of the ship's engines offering some comfort as the stormy North Sea was left behind and the fjord closed in. Ahead, a single star shone for a moment, beckoning northwards and granting a safe passage to Oslo, before it flickered and disappeared behind dark, ragged clouds. It was then that his mind drifted, as it often did, back to Oxford some six weeks earlier, the day everything had gone to hell. He'd been standing beneath the trees by a bend in the river, waiting to meet his tutor for his doctorate research.

But the professor never arrived.

What followed he played, over and over, like a film in his mind. It had begun as a perfect autumn day. A few figures were ambling through the mist by the river, singly or in small groups; lovers and friends, hangovers and thinkers, silhouettes against the glare of the early morning sun. One or two he knew, and they'd exchanged a few words. Overhead, a heron had floated, skimming the trees and dropping slowly towards the Cherwell until it was lost from sight. He'd glanced at his watch and waited, delaying the smoke he'd promised himself, but his new Peterson, bought the previous day at a tiny tobacconist on Cornmarket Street, had remained ever since in his jacket pocket, unused. It was then that a tall man, long-legged and very thin indeed, had appeared, standing by the bench the professor always took as his own.

"Thomas Galtung?" the thin man said.

"Yes," he replied.

"The professor has been delayed and sends his apologies. I am an old friend of his." He took a step forward, his hand extended. "Biggeloe, John Biggeloe. The professor says you share his passion for the ice age." He smiled, unconvincingly, with colourless lips, so thin they barely existed.

"Indeed," Thomas had replied, too polite to have refused the hand-shake. He looked at Biggeloe: the professor's friend certainly was thin, gaunt even, as if his head had been covered in ancient tissue-paper glued down over a bony skull. Worse, his appearance carried little of the geolo-gist, even a geologist from Government with a research grant, if there were such a thing. A mathematician, perhaps? It was impossible to know.

"You must wonder who I am," Biggeloe said, airily; "why I'm here, talking to you?"

Yes, Thomas had wondered, but all he had mustered in response was an ambivalent thrust of his hands into the pockets of his thick corduroy trousers, a gesture of defiance which had not passed Biggeloe unnoticed, even as he looked away.

"You've been waiting for a letter from Edgington, the landowner?" Biggeloe said. "Has it arrived yet?" He clearly knew the answer, so Thomas simply shook his head and waited to see what Biggeloe's true purpose might be.

"It's an important site, yes?" Biggeloe had looked him in the eyes.

"To me, of course. There's a sequence, glacial and interglacial. Cold, then warm, then cold again."

"... and therefore more than one ice age," Biggeloe had interjected.

"Yes; maybe four. But the evidence is weak and I'd like..."

"...to prove it convincingly."

"You seem to be ahead of me, Mr Biggeloe."

"Perhaps, but Edgington's letter will be delayed. I'm sorry."

Thomas could still feel, all this time later as night consumed the fjord, the heavy lump that had settled in his gut at that moment; the feeling that a brick wall had appeared between his life in Oxford and Biggeloe's designs for his future.

"Unfortunately, the war has...intervened," Biggeloe had said, pursing his lips.

"You're involved?" Thomas muttered, clear now that his research project was dead and there were other matters at stake. "Involved in the war I mean? Conscription? Everyone's talking about it."

"Maybe," Biggeloe replied. "But for you, there are various ways this can go."

"One way. You mean there's one way this will go?"

"A walk? It's a beautiful river." Biggeloe had set off, then stopped and looked back. "We have little time," he said, his voice suddenly harsh, his lips barely moving. "I have a mission. It requires someone with inge-nuity and bravery; an inquiring mind."

"I'm not available, sorry." Thomas still remembered his exact words, 'not available', and had been surprised, looking back, at the resolution he'd conveyed in the tone of his voice. "I'm unsuitable for what you have in mind," he said, "and you'd regret it." He'd waited a moment and then added: "You recruit spies, right?"

"You grew up in Norway, outside Drøbak?"

"Drøbak! I haven't been there for years."

"It's a strategic location, the key to the defence of Oslo, and there-fore Norway."

"I don't see how I can help."

"Physically very capable, yes? You ski. Handy in the ring. You can climb. Handle a boat. At home in, what shall we call it? Weather. The north."

"So?" whispered Thomas.

"So we'd like you to be interested..." Biggeloe had said without a pause. He'd flicked a fallen leaf aside with his dusty brogue and added, "...unless you'd prefer the navy."

That was the moment, thinking back from the freezing deck of *Black Prince*, that Thomas had known for sure he was confronting forces beyond his own narrow world. There had always been rumours in Oxford, a few jokes amongst his friends about who would be 'recruited'. But recruited to what? No one knew and, anyway, 'they' chose linguists, mathematicians, geniuses, so it was said. Who would want a geologist, and not an especially clever one at that?

"The *Courageous*?" Biggeloe had lifted his eyebrows. "Heard of her? Torpedoed in September in the Western Approaches with the loss of over five hundred men. Terrible. Well, *Courageous* has a sister ship, needing recruits, so I'm told. *Glorious,* that's her name. Could be that's where the navy needs you to be. Can't say, don't work for them myself. Lots of call-up papers going out, though."

Biggleoe's voice had dropped to a rasping whisper, his head thrust slightly forward, his eyes fixing Thomas in a firm stare.

"Or you can help us," he'd said; those exact words. "Keep an eye on events in Norway. Eyes and ears. Home ground for you and safe, safer than the navy. And maybe, best of all, you can continue your research. A site's been identified for your fieldwork; even better than Edgerton's river terraces, so I'm told. You'd have a tutor, too, in Oslo, another professor. You've read a few of his papers apparently."

And now the fjord narrowed and Biggeloe faded. Thomas leaned against the icy railings, the hard north-westerly whipping up white caps and froth on the black water below. Far away, the first lights of the capital appeared. In the last of the daylight he watched shattered clouds hurry along beneath the starless dome of a northern sky. He shivered all over as bitingly cold gusts raced across the open decks, cutting through his wet clothes. Or perhaps the trembling was fear, a dread of an unknown life ahead?

Black Prince followed a narrow channel for the final miles up the fjord. Twisting around rocky islands, past Thomas's hometown of Drøbak and the secretive inlet of Hallangspollen, the ship churned the deep waters of the Narrows, the brooding, steep-sided cleft in the mountains guarding the gateway to Oslo. He drew a long deep breath, struggling to make sense of too many emotions, the landscape rekindling distant memories from childhood. Ahead lay the brightly lit quay at Vippetangen and Oslo's myriad diamonds of light, a city at peace held gently within its timeless ring of mountains. Never, as *Black Prince* settled against the quay, with the terror of the North Sea behind him, had he savoured the prospect of firm land so much. And never, as the ambiguities of his mission hovered like a malevolent spectre over his life, had the future seemed so uncertain.

"Name, please," came an officious voice.

Thomas waited with the other passengers as a young orderly, smartly dressed in a black uniform, came into view.

"What's this?" Thomas inquired.

"Passenger list. Name please, come on, snow coming."

His name duly ticked as he left the ship, he took a few steps onto the granite and ice, his body so cold he could barely walk. The first outliers of a snowstorm swirled and kicked, caught in the eddies around the fortress at the back of the quay. Picking up his cases, he headed for the outline of a well-lit building which, he hoped, offered shelter and warmth, a chance to read the street map of the city. And then, through the battering of the wind, he heard a voice from close behind, on his shoulder: "*What's the weather like in London?*" It was an English voice, with a northern drawl, care-worn, with an air of familiarity, a thrust of expectation in the question almost whipped away by the wind. He turned to look and the snow stung his face. A figure walked briskly by, just a shadow. "*Not as cold as Norway,*" he stuttered.

"Follow me, not too close," said the shadow, striding ahead towards the city.

Only once in his childhood had Thomas visited the capital: a day out for his eighth birthday — weeks of saving for his parents — a visit to a park with sculptures of entwined, naked bodies; an hour at a café; a passing inspection of the National Theatre... all memories which had faded as the years passed, like a postcard left on a windowsill.

As they turned into Myntgata, the silhouette of a great stone edifice briefly showed and was then lost to the storm. "Norges Bank," said the shadow, slowing. "If you're short of cash, it's the place to go. More in there than you'll get out of us."

Another five hundred yards, and the shadow stopped, his voice raised against the wind. "Rådhusplassen. Take the Drøbak bus;

shouldn't be long. Here's some money, in case. We'll probably meet again, although the future never quite knows itself." He stepped away, then looked back as if a final thought had crossed his mind. "Forget what they taught you back in old Blighty. They're all new to it, you know, never been in the field themselves. All you need you learn for yourself. And then you hope for luck; good luck, that is." He dipped his head and disappeared into a swirl of snow.

Thomas found the bus stop on the edge of Kontraskjæret and joined a small queue that had begun to form, each person head down against the driving wind. Nearby was a kiosk emblazoned with the day's headlines: *Norway Confirms Neutrality in Finland War*. But nowhere else were there any tell-tale signs of the conflict engulfing Europe. Here he was, standing in a bus queue with ordinary Norwegian people in a country at peace. For the first time since it all went to hell that day in Oxford, everything around him was normal.

Before long, the Drøbak service arrived and Thomas felt a rising feeling that, out of the mess, there could be some hope. Nodding at the driver and then the conductor as he passed through the bus, he waited and watched the other passengers heaving their cases onto the luggage rack. An old lady struggled to reach and a young mother, holding a child, placed her free hand under the case and gave it a decisive shove. The old lady's eyes shone and Thomas felt relief wash over him like a warm wave.

In the seat in front sat a fair-haired girl travelling with a small, gold-coloured case, as if she were returning home from a weekend away. As she turned her head sideways to follow an old couple joining the bus, his mind was instantly taken back to Marion, the love of his undergraduate years in Oxford, who had returned to Deal and moved on. It had been the biggest mistake of his life: an impulsive and reckless offer to marry her after so few weeks which, of course, she rejected, being cautious and solicitous by nature, the very qualities which had attracted him to begin with. Now, he felt sure, he would never see her again.

Leaving the city, the bus crept through the night, its headlights picking out the snow exploding out of the darkness. Every now and then they stopped at pull-ins with red-painted shelters serving small groups of farms and once or twice larger towns, each time Thomas watching people alight or climb in as the journey progressed. An old man, maybe a farmer, wrapped in a snow-covered sheepskin coat, grunted as he passed by. Their eyes met for a second, a warm and friendly exchange. Thomas might have known him once, he and maybe other passengers as the night bore on.

Ticking off the landmarks as Drøbak drew closer, the country became familiar. The snowstorm had eased. Soon they would be passing the long track leading up to the Bell House, the small farm where he grew up. Only now had this prospect become real; only now could he hear his father, sat at the kitchen table, a little askew, coffee cup in hand: 'We are the luckiest people alive, Thomas. The animals, some land, good grass, plenty of wood. You, your mother, me. We don't need more than that.' It seemed long ago, but only in the last year or two, as he thought back, had he grasped that the family had been poor, struggling to find enough to eat in the bad years when spring droughts would hit milk production or when the barley rotted, unharvested, laid flat by late summer storms. Then, he had sat with his parents, sharing their tears and despair about the winter to come.

It was dark and still and the storm had blown out. Drøbak could not be far away. They slowed, and he pressed his face to the window and cupped his hands to cut out the light from inside the bus. There was still nothing to see, just the odd field-fence or tree picked out by the headlights, but his memory played out his daily trip to school many years ago, when they would stop at the layby where he would now disembark and a few children from outlying farms would jump aboard, throw their satchels onto the rack and immediately begin squabbling and scrapping for the few remaining seats. It was above this layby, at the top of a track leading up through the fields, that he could still picture a small, white house tucked into the edge of the forest beneath a high, rocky crag. That house, now empty, was Stensrud, his new home and it reminded him that no connections were left of his old life hereabouts: not his parents nor the old farm, not any friends from school that he might still know; not even Klara and the Holmbekks, who once took him in but would now have no reason to remember he even existed. Neither could he count as a friend the old man who once lived at Stensrud, who he saw a few times from the bus, toiling, bent over in his garden. But they had never actually met.

The bus arrived and the driver pulled on the lever to open the front door. Thomas nodded to him, stepped into the night with his cases and watched as the bus turned into the road to begin its long descent into town, the snow-covered fields glowing a yellowy white in the narrow beam of the headlights. As it pulled slowly away, Thomas gazed at the remaining passengers lit up inside and wondered about each of their stories and who might meet them when the bus drew to a stop in town: the fair-haired girl with the golden case was still there, and the old farmer in a sheepskin coat; two women who had joined the bus at Nesset were manoeuvring a case from the overhead rack and readying themselves for arrival; a man wearing a trilby pulled down over his eyes had slumped in his seat, and seemed half-asleep; and a young couple who had sat opposite Thomas for much of the journey were still balancing a game of chess on their knees and, with a few pieces still on the board as he'd left the bus, there seemed little hope that a final decisive move would resolve the game in time.

The bus had gone. It was still and dark. He made his way up the track, deep in snow, towards his new home, Stensrud.

———

After a night of broken sleep, he awoke, groggy and disoriented, recoiling at the damp sheets and the musty smell of old wool pelts that covered the bed. An unsettling thought had invaded his dreams, over and over, and it continued to play in his thoughts in the morning. During his training he had overheard a discussion between Biggeloe and his superior.

'He's not a natural, you know that,' the senior man had said. 'Unsure of himself, thinks too much.'

'True,' Biggeloe had replied. 'But there's a gap to fill.'

Pulling the curtain aside, Thomas looked into the darkness. A ghostly reflection showed in the glass, lit by candlelight: a grey, exhausted man framed by the window. '*A gap to fill...*' he murmured. He let the curtain drop and glanced over his shoulder as a sharp creak in the roof timbers split the damp air. He shivered — the cold or the fear, he was unsure — but he stayed in his room, sitting on the edge of the bed, watching the flicker of the candle, waiting for the silvery glow of sunlight to squeeze through a gap in the curtains to signal the start of another day.

TWO

The scent of old woodsmoke and the discovery of some faded copies of the local newspaper, *Akershus Amtstidende,* which everyone used to call *Amta,* should have been a comfort, a connection to his former life. But, as Thomas wandered Stensrud's limited confines after a dismal night, it was not like that. The small windows, low ceiling and massive wood beams, which imbued the place with its cave-like quality, rather shrouded him in sadness, reminding him of what he had lost. His old home was never empty, not like this, and never cold.

But he was not someone prone to self-pity. It was best to act and, in any event, the cupboards were bare and he was hungry. Dragging on a jacket, and after exploring the grounds around the hut, he headed through a hand-fashioned gate made of hazel sticks towards the break in the forest he had spotted that morning from his bedroom. A faint glow of morning sunlight showed through the treetops.

Later, after working his way up through the forest, he passed an isolated farm, Torsrud, a smallholding occupied, he recalled, by an old man called Severin Nordby. A friend of his father's, Nordby was reputedly a strange and eccentric loner generally known as 'Mad Nordby'. Pictures from the past formed in his mind: competitions amongst his schoolfriends to invent and play out the most gruesome version of the man, even though Thomas was sure few had ever met him; he was just a legend living high up in the forest, all alone.

But not quite alone, for the boys at school were also captivated by the story of Marta, the *Silver Girl Ghost*, the rumoured lost sister of Mad Nordby who had apparently vanished one day, reappearing on occasion as a glittering apparition that floated noiselessly across the farm. Thomas glanced back at Torsrud, half expecting to see her, hovering in the shadows on the edge of the forest or drifting over the snow and passing through the barn's wooden walls. But she was not at Torsrud today. He shivered and raced on towards the ridgeline.

The forest was empty; no one else would choose such a route to town. So, a while later, it was surprising to see a figure lumbering towards him; a large man, heavily clad in a forester's jacket, an axe over his shoulder.

"Morning," said Thomas. "A fine day to be out."

"That it is," said the man, and they exchanged a few pleasantries.

"Perhaps we'll meet again," said Thomas.

"You never know," the man replied, with a brief smile that stretched still further his broad face, dark with several days' stubble.

Thomas waved and the man lifted a hand and nodded, and they went their separate ways.

Arriving at the ridgeline minutes later, at a high point he'd never visited before, a steep-sided rock outcrop was silhouetted against the sky; half natural like a Cornish tor, half man-made like a small fort. Walking up to it, he saw a weathered wooden sign lying in a cleft in the rocks, its post rotted away. The place had a name: *Steinborg*. From here, a vast panorama opened up, laid out like a map, revealing the great sweep of Oslo fjord, extending to the capital through the Narrows to the north and to Denmark far to the south. Below, as he'd hoped, was Drøbak, where a few scattered houses were visible, suggesting there'd be shops nearby and the supplies he sought. He dared to feel a twinge of hope that some normality would come of this new life.

Picking a line downhill, he eventually reached the northern limit of Storgaten — the main road through the town. Here, a low building to his right caught his eye: a general supplies shop and grocer, *Svensens*

Handel, a name he faintly recalled from childhood, but had never visited and had forgotten until now.

"I'm stocking up. Empty shelves at Stensrud," he explained to Ivar Svensen, a man of average height, somewhat rotund and wearing a faded blue apron. Thinning, mouse-coloured hair running grey, a heavily coloured face and a prominent lump on the side of his nose, the man was every inch what he expected shopkeepers to look like, Norway and England alike. Handing over a buying list on a crumpled sheet of paper, he also requested two packs of Wills Cut Golden Bar, ready rubbed, from the shelves behind the counter.

"Stensrud, you say; old Larson's place," said Svensen, glumly. "He died." His ample jowls shuddered as he conveyed this nugget of bad news. Scanning the buying list, he dropped a bag of oats onto the counter with a thump. "You're from around here? I can tell."

"Yes. Then I went away."

"I can tell that, too. But you don't just go away; you go *somewhere.* England, right?"

Thomas shrugged. "I'm back here, that's what matters. I'm a student."

"No students 'round here."

"I study deposits from the ice age."

"New one on me," said Svensen, his suspicious eyes narrowing as his pencil totted up the order on the side of a cardboard box. "No glaciers in Drøbak," he muttered. "Anyway, how come you weren't enlisted back in England? You lot have been at war for three months."

"Lucky, I guess."

"Handy coming back, though?" Svensen grinned, sarcastically. "There's no general call-up here, so you'll be alright. Mind you, the politicians here are useless: not prepared to defend the country, don't want to offend the bloody Führer, I don't know...so they do nothing, despite the fact the place is crawling with Nazi spies." He stopped, seeming to ponder his sweeping assessment of the defence of Norway. "Could equally be you lot who want to take us," he added.

"The British?" said Thomas. "Hell, they're not my lot."

"Don't you worry, I'll keep it to myself." He winked. "Anyway, I'm up there, doing my bit. Kopås battery. Sergeant." He jerked his head upward to the fjord-side above. "Everyone knows, so it's no state secret. And see that," he said, pointing to a glimpse of the fortress through a gap in the houses across the road. "Whoever comes up this fjord thinking they can take Norway will have a hot welcome from us. Those guns out there, they fire 28-centimetre shells: huge, bigger than you can imagine. Made by Krupp, you know: German. That means they work and the Nazis will wish they hadn't sold 'em to us," he exclaimed, theatrically. "And if it's not them — the Nazis — that try it on, it'll be the same if it's the Brits. Tell 'em that. Tell 'em we've got some bloody great guns, pointing down the fjord. And none of you will get past us."

————

As Thomas returned to Stensrud, the light was already falling. Within a day of arriving in Norway he seemed to have aroused in Svensen quite the opposite reaction to the one Biggeloe had planned: '*You'll drop back into Drøbak as if you'd never left*,' he'd said. To be regarded with suspicion in the place of his birth was bad enough, but these worries had now accumulated on top of *the gap to fill*. He replayed the tone of Biggeloe's voice: there had been a conviction to it. But what gap? He should have asked.

A blue-painted table had been placed by the window. He dragged across a chair and sat there, taking in the view. His hand drifted to his Petersen, but it still didn't seem right, not now. Smoking a pipe was for gentler times. Through the window, he observed the work of the sun casting an orange flush over the tops of the trees. It reminded him of a small painting in an aunt's house in Cornwall, the only oil he'd ever seen, except for a house full of them at the Castle, Klara's home. Then the sun faded and the minutes passed and night began to dissolve the snow-covered fields and the sawtooth horizons of the spruce forest. Battered clouds raced by, black against the dwindling light in the sky. The wind moaned and whistled under the eaves and rattled the bare birch trees in the forest. He felt a shiver of unease. Picking up a wedge of wood lying by the stove, he shoved it under the door — there was a lock, but it wouldn't stop a flea.

Night finally fell and he dragged closed the thin curtains, unable to stay a shiver of fear which coursed through his exhausted body. How he yearned for his old life: his parents, his friends in Oxford, his research and the prospect of an academic career and a settled life. What was he doing here, a barely trained spy – not even a spy, just eyes and ears – shunted into a role he felt no connection to? The optimism he'd felt high on the ridgeline had dissolved away, replaced by a rumbling anxiety: the uncertainty of the gap to fill, the precariousness evoked by Svensen of being an outsider in his own country, the irrational fear evoked by the wind, as if it were alive and braying, a hunter knowing its prey was all alone in an old, creaking cabin.

THREE

Winter rolled across the capital, pitiless and uncaring, wave after wave of blizzards cascading off the mountains and prowling through the streets. Everyone suffered from the intense cold and the draughts which crept through the gaps in their wooden houses. At Norges Bank, the central bank of Norway, snow piled high against the granite walls and, inside, the temperature fell.

Worst of all were the corridors and storerooms at basement level, where Matthias Holmbekk, Senior Clerk (Gold Reserves), stood by the service entrance, rubbing the frost from a tiny security door window. Peering out over Kirkegata, the street connecting the cathedral to the wharves of Vippetangen, he pondered on the mystery of why he had been required for this particular task: waiting, freezing and, as so often for the clerks, the last to know if some important event were to take place. The bank was now closed at the end of another busy week and, just a few steps away, Nicolai Rygg, the Governor, paced silently.

"Never known a winter like it, sir," Matthias ventured in an unsuccessful attempt to open a conversation. The Governor remained mute. Matthias selected a Lucky Strike with cold, shaking fingers. He lit up and took his first, warming draw and resumed his vigil at the window. Next to him, leaning against the basement wall, was his finest black cane, a genuine antique with real silver ferrules and ebony insets. Smoke drifted up and his mind wandered, recalling the joy of his children's laughter and the lush summer meadows of his small family farm. He should have been grateful, content with his lot; he knew that. But the resentment always returned at moments like this, when the unjustified gulf between himself and the man pacing the concrete behind him — in fact all the senior bank staff — was laid bare, year after year.

The clock, high on the wall behind the Governor, ticked the minutes away. Matthias's cigarette burned out and he squeezed the last embers onto the lobby floor under the leather sole of his finely-polished shoes. Again, his eyes swept the empty street through the falling snow and, once more, his hand slid to his silk-lined pocket, searching out his Luckies. Like a movie star. Like Gary Cooper. But now there was no time for the smoke he still craved.

"Headlights," he said, uneasily, glancing over his shoulder.

Outside, a large car stopped beneath a streetlight. Three figures in long black coats emerged, tottering against the wind, moving through the shadows until they came closer, a small pool of light outside the basement door picking out the wire-rimmed glasses of the instantly recognisable Johan Nygaardsvold.

"The Prime Minister, sir, plus two others." Matthias's hand moved quickly, fumbling with a cluster of keys fastened to his belt and snapping back two black, outsized bolts. A flood of sharp, frozen air and a roar of the snowstorm accompanied the Prime Minister as he hurried in.

"All set?" Nygaardsvold boomed, striding past Matthias and vigorously shaking the Governor's hand. Moments later two more black coats eased their way through the half-open door. Only then did Matthias recognise them: Oscar Torp, Minister of Finance; Halvdan Koht, Foreign Minister. In front of him now were four of the most powerful men in Norway, an experience few could ever boast. Turning back to the service door, he locked up and rammed home the bolts, then hurried to join the group as they disappeared into a dimly lit corridor.

Matthias was no longer these days embarrassed by his limp, accepting his God-given limitations when a turn of speed was called for, so now he walked a little askew to gain momentum from an extra twist of his hips, his cane beating rhythmically on the tiled floor to match his pace. *Tap...tap...tap...tap.* Soon, he caught up with the Governor and his guests. After two more security doors, they stopped at a small flight of stairs, preceded by two guards who seemingly appeared from nowhere.

"Before we meet next week," he pushed forward to hear the Governor say, "I've arranged for you to see it all first-hand." They descended the stairs and entered another long, wide corridor. Part way along, on the left side, the Governor stopped in front of a massive door finished in dark-coloured bronze and decorated with rounded brass studs.

"Mr Holmbekk?" the Governor said, lifting his ample eyebrows, his instructions always so polite.

Setting aside his cane and fumbling in his pocket, it took a few seconds for Matthias to find what he sought. "Left-side, sir," he said, holding up a modestly sized key. "Yours is right."

The Governor moved half a step to make space for his clerk, one of the most revered officials in the eyes of all the junior staff. Matthias turned his key at a nod from the Governor. He heard the two familiar clicks. The Governor then drew a black notebook from the inside pocket of his jacket and entered a code using the knurled brass dial positioned just above the two keys. A heavy, muffled clunk sounded from deep inside the door. Matthias would love to have known that code, to be given the responsibility. But the lack of trust was soon forgotten. Never had there been a day like this: the Prime Minister, just a step away. He could just feel the warmth of his breath. *The Prime Minister breathes, just like you and me*: he would relate the story to his children.

At another nod from the Governor, Matthias stepped forward and turned a small brass wheel, drawing back the five massive bolts which secured the door. Then, taking hold of a brass handle, barely larger than the latch on his own barn door at home, he leaned back, emitting a faint grunt, and the huge door opened. He was now the one man in the bank entirely familiar with the small, windowless room they would now enter. His finger hovered over the light-switch. He silently counted, his emotions cannoning between guilt and the thrill of keeping them waiting. One second, two, five then six. In the gloom of his vaults, he was looking the Prime Minister in the eye. Seven seconds and he flicked the switch. The lights, faltering at first, lit up Matthias's world. He stood, facing the four men, desperate to contribute, to risk a few words...to be on equal terms, for a moment.

"Welcome," he said, "to the most important room in Norway."

———

Fragments of mist hung over the forest and shrouded the fields, the landscape drained of its colour in the early morning light. The previous evening the telephone had rung at 2100 hours, exactly. Thomas had let it ring, as the shadow had instructed, ten times, and had picked up and then replaced the receiver. Two minutes later it had rung again. He let it ring twice and picked up. A man's voice.

Karoline, I didn't wake you, I hope?

"There's no Karoline here," he had replied.

Ah, my apologies.

It was difficult to sleep after that exchange. Today he would meet his Norwegian contact. It could have been him at Vippetangen; he didn't know. The shadow never gave himself a name. Crashing down the narrow stairs, Thomas brewed a pot of bitter-tasting coffee and sat at the blue table by the window, trying to calm his nerves.

Dressing quickly, he rapidly disposed of breakfast, closed the door on Stensrud and waited for the Ås bus, which later dropped him off at the Norwegian College of Agriculture on the edge of town. After exploring the campus, he climbed the stairs to the administration department to begin arrangements for his new academic life.

"We've a nice system set up for you," said Ingrid Tveter, the administrator for post-graduate studies. "Your tutor's well organised — a famous geologist, he is." Quite unlike what Thomas had expected from an administrator, Ingrid was young, smiling and enthusiastic, her expressive hands surrendering an envelope with, she said, over twenty papers representing his initial reading material.

"He's also found me a research site here in Norway," said Thomas, "near some roadworks, apparently, not far from where I live." Ingrid smiled again and he sensed himself looking away, embarrassed and unable to believe she would be interested.

"Here's your library pass," she said, still smiling. "Valid for a year. I'll take you there — the library. It's in a separate building, the best in the country for agriculture and related subjects. Lots of space for reading, specialist journals and a few rooms for private study and tutorials, too."

Ingrid, her soft shoes padding quietly on the hard floors of the library, proved to be a most considerate guide. He looked at her as she strode ahead, the sway of her hips, the lift of the hem of her blue polka dot dress, the way she threw her hands out when she walked. There was an affinity in her voice. They could even have been at school together, perhaps a year above or below...he must ask her one day. Then she turned and said: "Geology," as she pushed open a door on the top floor. "Just a few shelves. It's linked to Oslo University, and it's well stocked with books and journals. Its main role is to support the teaching of agriculture, but I think it'll be an ideal base for your research and, of course, I can obtain any other books you want. Now, let me show you the tutorial rooms. You book them through me."

At the back of long lines of bookshelves was a corridor, off which were perhaps ten doors, all closed. Each was numbered. She consulted her schedule. "Your tutorial is Room 7 at half past four. You can use the library whilst you wait, of course." She smiled again, turned in a single sweeping movement, and disappeared between the high bookshelves.

Room 7 was lined in dark wood panels and along one side were shelves and rows of books, annals of something, a society of some sort. Thomas sat down and waited. Sometime later, a man walked in and closed the door. "What do you make of the library?" he asked.

"Excellent for the Ice Age."

Thomas took a deep breath and waited. The northern drawl was familiar: Vippetangen, the shadow.

"I'm Pendleton; that's all you will know about me. Welcome again to Norway. Or should I say welcome back. I hope you're settled in, if that's possible in this miserable winter."

Thomas nodded. He placed his hands on his lap to stop them rattling on the table.

"Everything you achieve in your mission will be funnelled through me," said Pendleton. "We might meet here again. Or we might not. Never ask the receptionist in Admin about me or get into a conversation. Just collect your papers and leave. Try to avoid conversing with students; anyone for that matter."

Pendleton was nervous, his eyes flitting from Thomas to the door. His appearance could be described as anodyne, the sort of man you would pass in the street and not bother to look at. Rather small, thinning mid-brown hair a little too long over the ears and collar, a hangdog face reduced by gravity, dark under the eyes, about forty years old. He could have been a not-very-successful salesman except, underneath his drawl and a hint of depression, there was an immediate clarity in his thinking, a vigour and ruthlessness in the way he spoke and an intense wariness in his eyes: the look of a rat waiting for the pounce of the cat in the dimness of the grain store.

"I was briefed to ask you how I should pass on information," said Thomas.

"We arrange the next meeting each time we meet. If I need to see you here unplanned and urgently I will telephone you — we'll use a new coded exchange each time at 2100 hours, which you must memorize and never write down. This arrangement should be secure, but if either of us is under duress, we make a single change to the script, which will also change each time we meet."

"So I need to be at Stensrud at 2100 hours each evening?"

"You won't be anywhere else, will you. Not at the dances..."

"But if I am?"

"Don't be, unless it's essential for your mission. If you are away I will telephone again next day, same time. And remember, you must not travel with any notes, plans or photographs. You must memorize everything. Your identity must be that of a student, a researcher, working from home and this place. Between our meetings you must attend the library for legitimate study at least once a week, each time for at least two hours, up to the whole day depending on bus times. Go shopping in Ås, if you want. Get a part-time job for extra cash. Anything normal. Keep an eye out for anyone you believe may be following you, but don't look nervous or use evasion tactics. Just act normally. Try to be here on different days each week, so there is no pattern. When we meet, you must also study, before and after. And one more thing. Don't get friendly with the staff here and don't wear distinctive clothes; you're just a bookish, commonplace student. Shouldn't be difficult for you, eh?"

Pendleton stopped at that point and let out a long, almost soundless sigh. Thomas wondered who he really was and what had drawn him into a world of espionage. Maybe he was at home in that world, found it exciting, rewarding in some way, although it didn't appear that way. Maybe he hated whoever he was working against, the Nazis?

"What if the bus isn't running or for some reason we lose contact?" said Thomas. "Or I have bulky documents, impossible for me to store in my head?"

"I've set up a dead drop. You can use it to pass on plans or notes, or if you need to contact me. The signal is a turn of a metal finial on the corner of the Hansen enclosure at the cemetery. I'll give you the details now, before I leave. It will be checked twice daily.

———

As the bus ground back along the Drøbak road, Thomas tingled at what he had been through. It had felt unreal and it confirmed in his mind that he was entirely unsuited to life as a spy. He looked out at the sun, a silken disc glowing behind a grey blanket of cloud. Snow hung off the trees like a Christmas fantasy. Norway was at peace. But underneath this façade, he was required to become part of a different world, a shadow world and a life of intrigue and uncertainty. And, now that his role as a spy, of sorts, had taken on at least a mantle of reality, another question trickled through him: Where do my loyalties lie? Am I spying for the British against the Norwegians, or helping the British protect Norway in the event of a German invasion? Both possibilities seemed to be true.

It all depends what will happen next.

———

Thomas's trip to Ås had yielded a treasure trove of ice age research material and he chose to start with the most interesting of the papers handed over by Ingrid Tveter: the Report of Committee on Glaciers, published in April that year in the Transactions of the American

Geophysical Union. Its author, the Dutch-born American geologist, François E. Matthes, had recently introduced the idea of the Little Ice Age, the most recent period of mountain-glacier expansion. A succession of exceptionally cold winters in Europe from the Medieval period until around 1850 had excited Thomas's interest. It might help validate his hypothesis that the Ice Age might not just be a single event; the climate could fluctuate in cycles.

He took a sip of coffee, a pencil in his right hand. In the corner of his notepad, he wrote the date, 12th of December 1939. Looking up, he gazed out of the window and once again became absorbed in the world as it was long ago. He looked forward to a few hours of reading, a little normality, but knew in his gut it would not last.

FOUR

A cold mist settled over Bremerhaven. Carl Westervik leaned on the rusty railings of *S.S. Martina*, wrapped in a thick civilian coat and a heavy wool hat. He lit a cigarette, a shiver of excitement running through his muscular frame. Two cranes loomed overhead, already removing from the hold a consignment of grain, a quantity of sawn timber and a variety of tinned and specialist foods from Norway. He watched as wagons were loaded and, later, as they were dragged away by a squat steam locomotive, its wheels screeching, black smoke belching from its chimney and drifting over the quay.

Once the crew had left the ship, and as the dock cleared of stevedores, an Abwehr agent clattered up the steps from the lower deck and handed him several documents to sign, confirming the unloading and onward transportation of the shipment in the name of Nordic Trading A/S. Westervik folded the papers and secured them in his case. He then took a taxi to the railway station and bought a return ticket to Berlin.

Arriving at Lehrter Bahnhof late that afternoon, he headed for Schöneberg where he found a cheap hotel off Potsdamer Strasse. Then, the following morning he followed the Landwehrkanal and entered a discrete doorway at 76/78 Tirpitzufer, the headquarters of the Abwehr, the German military intelligence service. After being searched, his docu-

39

ments were checked and he was guided towards the office of Oberst d. G. Freytag von Loringhoven, head of Abwehr II, the sub-section responsible for intelligence gathering and sabotage in foreign countries.

Westervik had stood out as an ideal agent for undercover work in Norway. At a young age his father, German by birth and blood, had been killed on the Western Front in the Great War, a loss intensified by the injustices heaped upon Germany in the post-war years. Hyperinflation during the Weimar Republic destroyed his family's wealth and his own substantial inheritance, cementing the bitterness he felt approaching his adult life.

After basic military training, he was recruited to a secret espionage unit in 1935. In one more step, as Germany asserted its independence in Europe, he joined the Abwehr in 1937, playing a small part in the Anschluss of Austria and, in October 1938, commanding a unit which helped secure Sudetenland for the German Reich. It was there that he absorbed the value of political chicanery, subterfuge and unconventional action in support of military objectives.

It was just weeks before Westervik's next break came, a move facilitated by his mother's Norwegian-Swedish heritage and a childhood spent speaking both German and Norwegian at home. He was placed by Wilhelm Canaris, head of Abwehr, under deep cover in Norway, a precautionary move that would prove increasingly visionary. Now, a year later, he was well established in the country.

A week after arriving in Berlin, Westervik returned to Bremerhaven. Over his shoulder he lugged a heavy canvas bag filled with another batch of handguns, a scoped rifle and ammunition. Norway would no longer be the Abwehr backwater it had been. The year spent in laying the ground would provide the perfect platform for the most daring of plans already forming in his methodical mind.

He boarded *Martina* and settled down to share a brandy with the captain, Günther Hartman, excited and content with the prospects ahead. His plan, he hoped, would go down in history as one of Germany's great military successes, achieved with just a handful of men, perfect guile and supreme planning.

First, though, his instructions were to identify and remove any hostile players, which were most likely to be the British.

———

The Castle, as it was commonly called, grew out of a steep-sided rock two miles inland from Drøbak. It was approached by a spiralling drive winding up through pine forests and drifts of birch and had been the home of the Holmbekk family since its construction by Nils Holmbekk in 1874. A gothic fantasy with turrets, sheer walls and castellated walkways, the Castle was more properly at home in the Scottish Highlands or Bavarian mountains than in Norway. But that was the eccentric genius of it: a fantasy castle set in traditional Norwegian farmland and forested knots, lands extending as far as the eye could see.

Christian Holmbekk had managed the estate for the last two years following the death of his father, Magnus. Finding a break in the steady falls of snow that had blown in that day, Christian left the Castle and eased the Type 230 Mercedes, in black over grey, into his parking spot at Lehmanns Quay. He climbed the steps for a meeting with Egil Alvestad, his harbourmaster, who had been appointed twenty years ago to oversee rent collection, leasing arrangements, landing and onward transport of fish catches, local ferry movements, ship repairs and launching, and various work connected to coastal freight movements. There was little that happened on the fjord that Egil didn't know about.

Christian glanced over the empty quaysides as he pushed open the heavy door to the harbourmaster's office. "We should have had three shipments of timber going out to Rotterdam this week," he said, as they sat down at a small table by the stove. "And the last of our barley and oats to Harwich."

"All cancelled," said Egil, a terrible gloomy expression painted on his face.

"It worries me, the war losses," said Christian, frowning as he consulted his notes. "*Arcturus, Gimle, Primula*: all Norwegian cargo ships torpedoed by German U-boats in the North Sea, with lives lost. Just in December to date. These tragedies kill business; everything stops. To make it worse, insurance premiums are through the roof."

"Anything in the open seas is fair game," said Egil, closing his blue-covered book of shipping movements out of Drøbak. "Only trade from here to Bremerhaven is still safe, plus routes into the Baltic and down to Kiel."

"What do you suggest we should do, Egil?"

"There's only one option. We switch to German-registered shipping companies and expand trade with Germany. And sell our own fleet."

"Perhaps. But it'll take time, finding new markets in Germany. As for selling the ships, no: there'd be heavy capital losses. The banks would call in the loans as soon as we sell the assets...and what would we get for them? Next to nothing. No, it's too late. We'd never find buyers, anyway, except for scrap. Who would want to buy a ship only to see it sunk the next day?"

Egil muttered and shook his head. "Sorry sir, I..." He shrugged. "I really don't know what we do."

Christian made his way back to the car. He had no solution, either. The snow had started up again, driven by a freezing northerly funnelling down the Narrows. As he opened the driver's door, a young man walked past, his head half-buried in a large hood and scarf, wandering as if searching for his destination.

"Can I help?" asked Christian. "You look lost."

The man stopped and turned towards him.

"It's alright, thank you," he said. "Just refreshing memories."

As the visitor turned to continue his perambulations, a jolt ran through Christian's body.

"Thomas?"

FIVE

S now fell like a hazy dream, day after day settling deeper and subsuming the colours and textures of the landscape, weighing down the skeletons of the forest trees until, finally, they cracked with a ghostly, mournful cry.

Thomas's mind drifted back to his childhood. He treasured just one photograph of his family: a small, framed print discovered amongst his mother's belongings. *The Bell House, 1929* was written in pencil on the back: his father's hand, just before he died. Father stood proud in that photograph, his broad, strong body, his best Sunday clothes. And his mother, before she sold up: smiling and happy. They had lived their lives: worked, laughed, worried and now they were just a memory, shades of grey, chimeras, lying there behind the glass. *And I, Thomas, am the only one who cares, the only one alive.*

————

With some trepidation, Thomas prepared for his visit to the Castle to see the Holmbekks again. It made no sense why Christian, or Herr Holmbekk as he always as a child called him, should want to see him again. There was no family connection with the Holmbekks and they were separated by a gulf in wealth and status. His friendship with Klara had been transitory — just a few years when they were young. Nevertheless, he hoped, despite his fear of rejection or of making a social *faux pas*, that she would be at home today.

He knocked twice and stood back, removing his hat and running his fingers through his unruly thatch. The door opened and there was Christian again with his lively crop of fair hair, expressive eyebrows and sky-blue eyes.

"I honestly thought I'd never see you again," said Christian, beaming. "Such a wonderful surprise."

Ushered into the hall, Thomas was greeted by Sigrid, Christian's wife. "Christian hopes you'll stop for lunch," she said, "although I can't stay on myself."

Thomas looked around. Nothing had changed. The huge painting of Sognefjord still dominated the hall and, in one corner, there was the old, carved wooden cabinet, decorated with the initials of Christian's family line beneath the initials 'OSSH'.

"OSSH?" said Thomas, turning back to Christian.

"Made for the wedding of Ole Sivert Sivertsen Holmbekk, 1793 – my great great grandfather," said Christian, leading Thomas into the Great Hall, where two people sat, their faces glowing in the light of a vigorous open fire. They stood to greet him.

"You remember Agnes, my great aunt?" said Christian, as a slightly built, grey-haired woman with a neatly proportioned face and wire-rimmed glasses rose to greet him.

"Maybe when I was a boy?" said Thomas, embarrassed by his uncertainty.

"Well, I remember you," said Agnes, her smile a warm welcome. "And yes, I'm great aunt to Matthias, too, of course," she said, glancing at a thin, reserved-looking man with dark brown hair and a clipped moustache.

"Agnes is the family historian; our expert on the Holmbekks and all our secrets, foibles and poltergeists," said Christian, laughing. "And Matthias, my cousin, our resident banker and guide on all matters yellow and glittering."

"He means gold," said Matthias, half rising from the chair and nodding with a hint of pomposity. "Not mine, of course. I work at Norges Bank, in charge of the gold reserves."

The door opened and a portly, grey-haired lady appeared carrying a large tray laden with afternoon tea.

"Toni, I remember," said Thomas, thrilled to see her again.

"Of course you do. She's been with us for nearly forty years," said Christian. "Nanny, housekeeper and loyal friend of the family. Now, let me think," he said, turning to Thomas. "You left in June 1931. I can't believe it. And look at you now. Tell me, what brings you back to Norway?"

"Research, related to past climates," said Thomas. "It's scientific work, a bit academic I suppose, er, not very interesting."

"Past climates?" said Christian, sceptically. "How on earth can anyone research that around here?"

Steeled from his encounter with Svensen, Thomas was better prepared this time to address questions of this sort, but it was to no avail.

"It's beyond me," concluded Christian, smiling, "but it's impressive, nevertheless. Well done."

After lunch, discussion turned to events in Europe. "Norway's neutrality won't count for much if they have a go at us," Matthias said, not at all as reserved as he first appeared. "Look what the Nazis have done in Czechoslovakia, helped by the Brits. The Brits! They helped the Germans steal Czechoslovakia's gold. Can you believe it!"

"Really?" said Thomas, shocked at the idea.

"It's true, though the Brits won't tell you that," said Matthias. "Or that they want to control Norway as much as the Nazis do."

"I can't imagine that's true," said Thomas.

"Norway is just a prize," said Matthias. "We'll see who gets us first — the Nazis because they want us, or the British to keep them out."

At that point, a young woman rushed into the room and, like a bee, came to a halt in the middle of the group and spun around. "It must be Thomas; they said you'd be here," she said, her voice clipped and to the point. "Really, I might not have recognised you, it's been so long."

"I knew it was you the second you walked in the door," said Thomas, smiling.

"We must meet up," she said, "but, sorry, can't stop now. Late. Off to Oslo."

"Klara..."

But she had gone, the staccato clip-clop of her boots fading as she crossed the hall. The front door slammed shut and the room went quiet. Those briefest of impressions conveyed, unmistakably, the same girl he had once known; small in stature, but tough, decisive and confident. She hadn't changed, he felt sure.

"And a mind like a racing car," said Agnes, as if she could read Thomas's thoughts. "Impatient, always questioning whatever anyone says," she added with a conspiratorial edge.

"Usually her father," added Christian, smiling thinly, his voice tinged with a sense of despair.

"You usually deserve it," concluded Agnes.

————

Every day was cold and the snows heavy and frequent, the hours of daylight becoming so short they seemed to pass into night again almost as soon as the orange glow of sunrise appeared, if it were to be seen at all. Thomas took the bus into town and walked north along Storgaten towards Drøbak church and its fine cemetery. He arrived as an eerie fog drifted off the fjord. Years had passed since his father's funeral, and he had never since visited the grave. It was cowardice, he knew, and guilt. He pushed open the gate. It squeaked, an uncertain, metallic protest. Shuffling a short distance through uncleared snow, he reached the grave and took a deep breath. "Forgive me," he whispered, his eyes fixed on the simple granite headstone, tears falling and freezing onto his face, in sadness, shame and regret. With his gloved right hand he pressed against the cold stone, reading the words his father had become.

GUDMUND GALTUNG
*25-6-1879 + 10-4-1929
ELSKET OG SAVNET

After standing for a while by the grave, a sense of calm returned, and he let his eyes scan the misty cemetery. Quickly, he picked out the Hansen enclosure, a seemingly forgotten collection of graves and memorials where Pendleton had located the signal for a dead drop: a finial on the corner of the metal fence closest to his father's grave. Checking he was alone, he saw that a flower motif on the inner face had acquired a dash of new paint. He turned it so that the newly coloured flower faced out, towards his father's grave, and then headed for the church.

On the left side of the porch was a winding staircase, as Pendleton had said, leading up to the organ balcony, which was a majestic space overlooking the nave. Even on this dark and unforgiving afternoon, a few dedicated worshippers were scattered across the painted wood pews. It took Thomas just a few seconds to squeeze behind the organ and find, buried in the inner workings, a wooden box fixed to the floor but with a lid which could be turned to reveal a space inside. For anyone who chose to look in this dusty place, the box would have seemed just part of the structure, no longer functional, or perhaps a cast-off dumped there years ago, and jammed in. Here was Pendleton's dead drop, and he deposited a map of the fjord showing the fortress, the town and the Narrows, with various defensive structures clearly marked.

Leaving the church, he ambled for a while around the cemetery and explored the water's edge. Fog smothered the fjord and his mind was taken back to the *Glorious*, the warship he would be serving on if he were not here. It was hard to imagine what his role might have been on such a vast fighting ship, so ill-suited he felt himself to be, not only to spying, but to the discipline of military life. Yet, if he were serving on that ship, he could at least hold his head high, just being there, like all the other young recruits. Here, as he thought back to his first dead drop, and the information it contained, it was hard to throw off the sense of cowardice which washed over him, wandering as he was through the trees in safe, neutral Norway.

The light was already falling and it was time to return to Stensrud. As he closed the cemetery gate again, trying unsuccessfully to minimise its disapproving squeal, a short figure appeared at the church porch. It was the vicar, standing quietly, seeming to contemplate the end of another day. Thomas approached and greeted him. Digging deep into his pocket, he found some coins and placed them into grateful hands. "For the cemetery," he said.

Turning to leave, he stopped as the vicar drew him back with a gently spoken question: "Forgive me, but I was watching you. He wasn't your father, was he?"

Thomas nodded.

"I thought so. You went away afterwards, with your mother?"

"Yes."

"You're Thomas. I can hear it in your voice: just a hint of England. We rarely see anyone born outside Drøbak here, you know; not normally, not at the church, although..." The vicar looked up, as if searching the heavens to help jog his memory. "There was someone," he said, slowly, "like you and your mother...with a tinge of an English accent. He first attended church in...not sure...early September maybe... He came a few times..."

"And is he still here?"

"I don't think so, not at the church, at least," said the vicar, smiling. "He was a working man, on the boats, I think. I only exchanged words once or twice, then I never saw him again. Nice man, though, good-natured I thought; fair hair, blue eyes, like you."

"You don't recall his name?"

"No, unless...maybe. Yes, Haugen, he was called. I remember that because I have an old aunt with that name. No relation, of course. But... I never knew his Christian name."

"And you haven't seen him since?"

"No, not since the autumn; just before the snow came in bad and caught us out. Early October, wasn't it?" He smiled again, lifting his hand in a brief wave and disappeared back into the church.

SIX

The short December day would soon be done and night would fall again over Oslo fjord. Captain Günther Hartman guided *Martina* through the channel between the outer forts of Bolærne and Rauer. There were dangerous rocks, small islands and narrow sounds to navigate, and constant changes of course. He stepped out onto the starboard bridge wing, a flurry of snow stinging his eyes. The glow of daylight had disappeared behind the mountains and the small port of Drøbak lay ahead, its lights showing off the starboard beam. Ahead, in the dusk, lay the Drøbak Narrows. Not bad, he thought, and returned to the bridge. "Slow ahead," he commanded into the voice pipe. "Steer oh-five degrees."

"Oh-five degrees, sir," confirmed the helmsman. "Steady on oh-five degrees."

Hartman preferred to avoid a nighttime passage of the Narrows, the great cleft where the fjord is squeezed between forbidding, forest-covered mountains. But tonight would be an exception. "Steer oh-three five degrees." He waited; then, into the voice pipe: "Dead-slow ahead."

The triple expansion steam engine turned lumpy as it slowed. Wipers squeaked as they worked to clear snow settling on the wheelhouse windows. *Martina* rolled as she swung across the waves.

"Two minutes to rendezvous," said Hartman. He returned to the bridge wing and braced himself against the railings. It was a relief to leave behind the muggy air of the bridge, to feel the sharpness of the weather. He squinted, his eyes scanning the night. Wind from the north, force four. Snow, heavier now. The water, jet black, flecked with small waves. The light falling.

A door opened below, spilling a shaft of light into the falling snow as Westervik, clad all in black, made his way out to the main deck. He looked up towards Hartman, briefly raised an arm and then drew a balaclava over his head.

"Engine to idle. We'll hold this position," said Hartman into the voice pipe. The ship drifted slowly forward and then settled, pitching and rolling. Snow, heavier now. The wind, rising, shrieking through the halyards and around the derricks, reflecting the madness and the thrill of being at sea, a northern sea, often dark, always lethal. Never go overboard: you would die in minutes.

Below, Westervik clutched the starboard railings in his right hand, his left holding the large bag which had come aboard with him at Bremerhaven. Hartman again scanned the twilight. He pulled his thick woven hat further over his ears and kicked at the snow settling on the deck. Force five now, pushing him south, too fast; the rendezvous five minutes late.

Then, a light showed from the fjord. Hartman returned the signal — three flashes — and looked out towards the town, trying to gauge the shoreline, which was barely visible despite the lights. They had minutes to spare as the ship was driven relentlessly towards the land.

A shouted voice, faint against the wind. "Martina!"

A small fjord boat, with one man aboard, pulled out of the gloaming and into sheltered water on the lee side. Two crewmen dropped a hanging ladder and several fenders over the side. Westervik lowered his canvas bag over the railings, took one look back towards the bridge and disappeared down the ladder.

"Get on with it," muttered Hartman.

But without delay the boat departed, the man at the oars rowing hard, out into the wind, then north eastwards until Westervick had disappeared into the darkness. Hartman, satisfied with the transfer, returned to the warmth of the bridge. His job was done: Westervik had been safely delivered.

"Half ahead," he said. They were moving again; it was always dangerous to drift. As they picked up speed he altered course, and *Martina* swung northwards. "Steer three-three-oh degrees."

Outside, another squall kicked up and, within minutes, was lashing the old ship as she plodded up the fjord with her cargo of auto-parts, domestic products and German foodstuffs towards the Drøbak Narrows, and then Oslo.

———

The rumble of *Martina's* engines quickly faded into the stormy night. A heavy, snow-laden wind funnelled down the Narrows with a deep whistling sound, lifting spray off the waves and freezing it onto Westervik's sealskin jacket. The oarsman pulled hard and confidently; he knew these waters and soon found shelter in a secretive branch of the fjord north of the town.

"Hallangspollen," the oarsman said. "We're out of the worst now."

Westervik watched the oarsman as he guided the boat through the darkness. Alexander Brann: a huge man, immensely strong and calculating. Often morosely quiet, he hid well a capacity for extreme violence, yet often found fragments of mirth in moments of stress. These were good qualities, when they could be controlled. And with generations of German antecedents on his father's side, Brann was loyal to the ideology of National Socialism.

"It's good to see you again," said Westervik. "Impressive, finding the ship on a night like this."

"It's nothing," replied Brann.

"Hartman knows this fjord, too," said Westervik, trying to disguise his chattering teeth. "You'll meet him one day if we can coax him away from *Martina*."

Sitting stationary in the stern on an icy wooden thwart, the cold was seeping into Westervik's bones. He pulled his collar tighter and rubbed his gloves to scrape off the ice, though the waves were no longer breaking over the sides of the boat. The boat swung left, then right, and

Brann, like a machine until now, stopped rowing. They glided through still water, almost silent but for the crackling of breaking ice, and finally crunched against a beach. It was by now so dark that barely any detail of the surrounding land was visible.

Shipping the oars, Brann stepped into the shallow water. He dragged the boat a short distance up the steep beach, took a torch from his pocket and lumbered towards the outline of a boathouse which emerged in the narrow beam of light. Westervik hitched his bag over his shoulder, jumped onto the slippery boulders, and followed Brann up the beach. It was calm here, almost windless, strangely so after the storm on the fjord, yet strong winds still raged through the trees high up above the cliffs of Hallangspollen and could be heard as a faint whistling, far away.

Westervik felt simple relief at returning to dry land. He watched as Brann turned the key to open a large, rusting padlock and remove a heavy metal bar used to secure the boathouse doors, which he dragged open. Once inside, Westervik carefully placed the canvas bag onto a stack of sawn timber. Under the light of his torch, he extracted a heavy rolled blanket laced several times along its length. He calmly untied the bundle to reveal a scoped rifle and a box of cartridges wrapped separately in waxed paper.

"I'll take the rifle," he whispered. "The rest as planned."

"Do we have a date yet?" said Brann, closing the boathouse doors.

"No. But it won't be long," responded Westervik, removing a glove and shoving his right hand into his pocket. Fumbling, he found what he sought. "Here, a thank-you from Berlin, for a job well done," he said, as he dropped a number of coins into the pocket of Brann's coat. "Gold."

He looked again at the dark profile of the heavy-footed giant. You may look clumsy, he thought, but you're thorough and reliable. "One last thing," he added. "I picked up a snippet from Svensen, the shop-keeper, before I left for Berlin."

"Handy."

"He's an old windbag, but he's useful, so I often call in; buy some-thing and just let him talk. He was puffing on about a new tenant, a student, in a cabin called Stensrud, on the Ås road."

"I know it," said Brann. "What's his name?"

"He never said. Anyway, this tenant, he's British, English, whatever, but Svensen says he's also Norwegian; local, a Drøbak kid." He watched as Brann turned over in his mind this new development, clearly engaged by the idea of someone new on his patch.

"He's a mongrel," Brann said, eventually, a smile slowly growing and electrifying the bristles across his broad face, "one who likes the deep, fresh waters of our fine Norwegian fjords."

"You may have got it in one," said Westervik, "but we don't know, do we? I'll check him out."

SEVEN

The government ministers hurried through a heavy fall of snow and slipped into Norges Bank through the service door. Following the Governor, they took a steep, narrow staircase past windows guarded by steel bars and entered a timber-panelled room on the second floor, at the centre of which was a massive oak table.

Arriving last, Matthias closed the door, set his cane aside, and took his place at a small table behind the Governor's chair, the place where the note-taker always sat. A sheaf of lined paper, two pencils, a pen and a bottle of black ink were neatly laid out. He drew the paper to the middle of the table, loaded the pen, and waited, glancing through the high window at the snow being spun around in the tempest outside and lit up by the lanterns overhanging the bank's front entrance. After an exchange of pleasantries between the Governor and each of his visitors, the parties settled down, silent and still, each participant waiting for the Prime Minister to open the meeting.

The Prime Minister (PM) tapped hard on the great table and invited the Governor (Gov) to set out his plan. Matthias's pen hovered over the notepad, his ears alive to every word.

"Early in the year," said the Governor, "the larger part of our goldreserves — one hundred and twenty-five tons — was transported to

America in view of the risks of war. But fifty tons were retained," he said, tapping the table with his forefinger in time with his words. "That was the gold you saw in the vaults." Taking a deep breath, he drew himself up and eyed the Prime Minister. "My recommendation is simple. The prospect of war coming to Norway is far greater than it was. It would be a dereliction of our duty not to move the last of our reserves out of the country, to safety...and to do so immediately."

Matthias, his pen moving fast over the notepad, recorded the Prime Minister's reply.

PM: The law will not permit the movement of any more gold out of Norway. In addition, the idea is politically and economically unacceptable. It would be too great a threat to our neutrality.

"Neutrality!" exclaimed the Governor, Matthias now struggling to keep up with what would turn into the most epic verbal engagement he had ever heard. "We are backing both sides: Nazi Germany with its Swedish iron ore and the British Empire with our merchant fleet. We are dancing on a pinhead and it will not end well."

"Maybe, but with respect, Nicolai, that is not for the bank to judge and, as I said earlier, moving the gold out of Norway at this point in time would cause financial panic, instability and even a run on the Krone if it became public knowledge...which it inevitably would. This is the Government's position." The Ministers nodded support. "I'm sorry."

Matthias gazed out through the window, the snow still spinning violently in the storm, lit up in the patch of light. He was unconvinced by the Government's case for neutrality; Nazi Germany would not be so easily appeased. Maybe the British, too, had eyes on Norway, for their own reasons — to keep Germany at bay? He suspected the gold really was at risk if war came to Norway, as the Governor had argued, yet he could not imagine it all being sent overseas, leaving panic and financial chaos...and himself with empty vaults and a meaningless job. It seemed an impossible decision for anyone to make. He realised that he would have no idea, if he had to make a rational decision himself, how to weigh the two opposing arguments.

Instead, there was another factor which swayed Matthias's thinking. As long as the gold remained in the vaults, fruitful possibilities remained for his own enrichment. This, if the decision had been his, would have carried the day.

The Prime Minister stood and a scraping of chairs on the wooden floor followed as his ministers rose too, and collected together their papers. The meeting was over, the gold would stay and Matthias could withdraw to the clerk's room, to await instructions.

————

Standing alone with the meeting notes clutched close to his chest, Matthias gathered his thoughts. A single pool of light shone onto his typewriter, a sheet of headed paper curved over the roller. The door opened.

"The fools," the Governor grumbled, striding into the room. "Mr Holmbekk, if Nazi Germany attacks us, they will come straight for this bank, heading for our gold. And do not imagine for a moment there will be a polite request to buy it at a fair price."

"Sir?" said Matthias, unsure of how he should respond, if at all.

"They will just walk in here and take it. But we will prevent it. We will concoct an escape plan for our gold."

"Very good, sir," Matthias whispered, though he had no idea what such a plan might entail.

"We will save it, just as the Poles did. Hit on all sides by Germany and Russia, the whole country overrun in a blitzkrieg. But they got their gold out, all of it. Over eighty tons. A brilliant operation."

"I had no idea," said Matthias.

"We can learn from them. We will prepare the gold for a rapid getaway. And you, Mr Holmbekk, will be responsible for a plan to make it happen; a plan that is invisible, just a rearrangement of some boxes in the vaults."

Matthias smiled at the prospect of the Governor's idea. The gold, it seemed, would stay in the vaults. But there would also be a plan for its escape. A perfect outcome. And it slowly dawned on him what the Governor had in mind.

"A stock-take, sir, so to speak, so it appears that nothing out of the ordinary is taking place?"

"Precisely, Mr Holmbekk, excellent." The Governor brushed his fingers down his neatly clipped moustache. "You will have work to do. The gold will be repacked into smaller boxes, easy and fast to move and load. And you will prepare a new set of registers, with each load leaving the vaults to be matched with a particular, numbered lorry. The work will be carried out in secret; nothing to raise any eyebrows. Just you, quietly plugging away. Your instructions will come from me and me alone."

Matthias's mind quickly filled in the details. "Two tonne lorries, sir; that's what I suggest. Easy to secure and anyone can drive them. And in an emergency...not too prominent."

"Very good. How many?"

"Twenty-five to thirty."

"Good, but of course we can do nothing in advance in relation to transport," said the Governor. "Just the telephone numbers of the transport companies kept with the registers. And we keep an eye on them to ensure they'll still be there when we need them."

"Now, the coins, sir..." said Matthias, warming to the Governor's plan. "We're still buying British sovereigns, as they become available, so we need some flexibility before the last of the registers are finalised."

"Very good," said the Governor. "So we keep a few kegs open so they can be filled with the new sovereigns. Yes?"

Matthias thought for a moment. "Yes, and the new sovereigns should all be assigned to the last lorry. It will be well within the two-tonne limit. This will give us the flexibility to conduct a final audit of the last lorry and update the registers on the day...if needs be."

"Good." The Governor drew himself up. "And Mr Holmbekk..."

"Sir?"

"If the moment comes, we will save Norway's gold."

EIGHT

Thomas squinted as the first flecks of snow raced out of a grey Arctic sky. It was the winter's shortest day and a vicious north-westerly scoured the landscape as angry clouds consumed the mountains far away, one by one. He pulled tight his silk scarf and felt his senses sharpen, a whiff of fear running through him as he pushed on through the forest towards the ridgeline.

He knew important questions must now be answered, about himself and his mission. Below was a barbed-wire fence between two tree-covered knolls. This was the edge of Kopås, the battery above the town he had located by Svensen's flick of his head a week or so ago. Lower down, the wire disappeared beneath a drift of blown snow. It was an open invitation to report on the battery and its role in defending the Narrows. The storm, he hoped, would provide the cover he needed.

Minutes later he crossed into Kopås. Once inside the military site, he left his skis behind and crawled to the top of a rocky whaleback, the coarse granite scratching at his clothes, the cold of the raging storm and flying crystals of ice creeping through to his skin. In his imagination, in front of him a line of guards emerged, all pointing rifles at his head. Every part of his body shook.

He gulped in the cold air, his heart pounding. From here the battery, or part of it, was now visible: a gun emplacement with a rounded concrete roof, the barrel pointing down the fjord. Still no guards came to challenge him. Fearful of a trap, he pressed on.

As he edged forward, wading through deep snow and crawling from rock to rock, more artillery structures appeared, camouflaged by the steep terrain, snow and scattered trees. A truck moved slowly along a track cut into the hillside below, the sound of its engine carried on the wind. Further on, by a drift of birch trees, he picked up a trace of wood smoke and cooking. He lifted his nose. Again, the same smell. Coffee, fried eggs, maybe. Upwind, there must be barracks and a soldier's mess.

This was Kopås. Combined with the cannons on Oscarsborg fortress, here was Norway's main defence against a seaborn attack on Oslo. Any invader could only succeed by forcing the Narrows against this defensive line.

Steadily, he worked his way around the barely defended boundary of Kopås battery, noting gun emplacements and ammunition stores. As the minutes passed he relaxed and fear drained away. His hands had stopped shaking — enough to write legible notes and produce a plan of sorts in the shelter of his jacket. Satisfied, he returned to the rocky whaleback, bending forward into the north-westerly still racing in from across the fjord. He looked down at the water: battleship grey laced with flashes of white and darker smudges where the squalls churned fiercest. Soon, the fjord was blotted out; the storm's fullest fury was yet to come. He pulled his hat down and leaned into the blinding, racing snow.

Only then did he hear the shout, muffled by the hissing wind. Peering over the top of a rock, he picked out a faint, moving shape: a soldier wading upwards through deep snow. There were more agitated shouts. He saw a soldier raise his gun and heard the sharp crack of a rifle shot.

With seconds to decide, he could either capitulate or flee.

Move! He jumped and then slid painfully down a coarse rock, falling up to his waist in soft snow. Making it to his skis, he looked back, imagining a guard already on the rocky whaleback, his rifle raised. But still no figure appeared. Fumbling in panic with the bindings, he dragged his skis up through the deep snow to the surface, his heart pumping so hard he felt his body would explode. But he was now skiing back between the rocky knolls.

Precious time had been lost fixing his skis and progress was desperately slow but, after a while, he began side-stepping up a steep gully towards higher ground. Within seconds he was exhausted. He looked back. The wind screamed across the hillside, the snow a white blur. Then, one by one, at least a dozen faint and intermittent grey figures came into view.

This was a decisive moment in his life. Press on or give up. Live or die. He decided to risk a final effort to make it to the safety of another gully that was opening up ahead, deeply cut into the fjord side. Once there, it would be easier to escape. Ten seconds to go...five. His lungs, his legs, arms, everything screamed with pain. One step up, a half step sinking back, each time draining energy as he dragged his skis through the powdery snow. But he was almost there.

At that moment a shot sounded through the storm and the rock in front of him shattered with a sharp crash. More shots followed in quick succession. A bullet cracked the air, close. He ducked and kept going as a shot hit a rock just above his head, then several struck the snowbank to his left. As he finally lunged into the gully, a bullet clipped his rucksack and struck a boulder next to him, shards of rock scattering, one piece hitting his left thigh. He looked down in disbelief, almost frozen by shock, barely able to move as a patch of blood emerged around a rip in his breeches. He dragged the stone, sharp like an arrowhead, out of the bloody wound, and cried in pain.

He had decided to risk crossing the wire, but it was too late to worry. He would outrun them, beat them on skis. The guards were a long way down, giving him time to recover his breath, to think more clearly and plan his route up the rocky slopes that were emerging at the head of the gully. At first, they looked no worse than any other crag falling away to the fjord. Scale them and it would take him to an area of denser forest higher up, where the cover was better. But the closer he came, the more it began to shake him. Frighteningly high with jagged spikes of rock and sheer faces covered with tongues and rivulets of ice, it appeared an unclimbable precipice; a dark, intimidating wall of terror. He was trapped in the gully between the barbican ahead and the pursuing soldiers behind.

But there was no alternative. Fixing his skis to his rucksack he looked up, pulled in a long breath, then started to climb, picking a line with good footholds on broken ledges of rock and making height quickly. It was not so bad: plan a line and stay clear of the ice. Don't rush, stay calm. Around him, snow swirled in eddies and the wind shrieked through the pinnacles above.

Minutes later, he stopped as a frightening obstacle emerged. The route he had mapped in his mind was no longer clear and an unclimbable overhang closed off the way ahead. He scanned the rock-face for an alternative.

Breathing heavily, he cursed. To bypass the overhang to the right was too exposed, the rock smooth and icy. It was impossible. He shrank back, shuffling his feet to feel more secure on the narrow ledge he had been forced onto. Go left: it was the only option.

Move by tentative move, he crept across a shoulder of rock until he reached a broad platform. From here he could see the full extent of the gully below...and the fearful height of the precipice. He shivered in raw fear, then lifted his head and began to climb.

Now well above the relative safety of the rock platform he continued to make height along a line of broken rock between a vertical black scar spattered with snow to his left and a horrible, slippery sheet of ice running down the side of the overhang to his right. On a small ledge part way up, he looked down again; the guards were still out of sight behind the cliff. But he felt sick at how high he now was, how exposed to a rifle shot if he were seen and, worst of all, because he had reached a point from where it was impossible to return. It was ahead, up the cliff, or nowhere.

Breathing deeply to calm his shaking hands and ease the knot in his guts, he started up again, carefully selecting each handhold, each foothold, trying to find the safest line. For a while he made good progress, but the act of climbing became increasingly hard as he gained height. He was now exposed to the full terror of the storm, his fingers freezing, his body failing, his energy exhausted.

INVASION

A deep slot above him had opened up, with water seeping from cracks and freezing into icy streams. Now without shelter of any sort, his position caught the full force of the storm, threatening to tear him off the rockface. From here, he looked down to the gully where he had started, far, far below, and into the turbulent fragments of cloud sweeping up the side of the fjord.

A rock, disturbed as he climbed, suddenly broke away and clattered and bounced off the rock ledge below. His whole body shook. He looked up again. The rocky slot appeared to lead to the top but seemed unclimbable. Would his failing strength allow him to make the attempt? Again, there was no option but to go on. Gaining height up a narrow crack made of loose shards of rock, he squeezed into the slot. He pushed and wriggled higher, wedged in, bending his body to ease himself up, his hands barely working.

He urged himself on in that crack in the rocks, opening and closing his grip, trying to make his fingers work for a few minutes more. Exhausted, he inched his way up, each small gain a victory, each push taking him closer to his goal.

At last the top came into sight. He glanced down again. Still the guards were nowhere in sight. Looking up, he could see that the rocky slot he had been climbing ran out just above his head. The way to the top was short...but perilously smooth and icy with patches of thin, wet soil. He looked back again, then up. There was once again no choice: he had to keep going.

Hugging the surface, finding every small ledge and crack, he inched up that terrible, slippery slope, certain that one small mistake, one moment of bad luck, would lead to an unrecoverable fall.

Part way up, a narrow crack appeared between the ice-covered rocks: relief for his searching fingers. A juniper, itself clinging to the cliff and thrashing wildly in the wind, gave a welcome, if precarious, handhold. Then, finally, the thick roots of a pine tree provided him with support, a hold which no self-respecting rock climber would ever press into service, but which played its part, and he slumped over the lip of the cliff, shaking with fear and cold, the snow driving past him.

He was up. Standing, he glanced back down the cliff and into the gully, then turned and pushed on into a nearby area of dense pine forest. A wave of relief swept through him. He would escape.

After a short rest and, keeping to rocky ground and trodden tracks in the snow to disguise his route, he eventually made it to the ridgeline, where he stopped behind a low mound of rock. Up here, the wind was now so strong it was difficult to stand. But it had a benefit: he glanced in satisfaction as snow raced and sizzled over the surface, quickly filling his boot prints.

Steinborg stood silhouetted against the sky, grey on grey, not far away. He fixed his skis and pushed hard across an open area of stunted forest, then diverted from it into a block of dark spruce where the snow lay thinner on the ground. Once again, he removed his skis. Dead branches scratched at his face as he forced a way through, but he was clear and heading downhill towards safety. He stopped and listened for any sign of the chase from the higher land behind. All he could hear was the storm and the furious thumping of his own heart.

There was one trait above all others Thomas trusted in himself: his ability to read the land, to find his way, to follow his nose: *å gå dit nesen peker*, as his father used to say. So, he knew where he was, despite never having travelled the dense forest before. He slowed down and worked out a bearing to take him down to the Drøbak road.

Eventually, the forest opened up and scrubby willows and aspen appeared, with deeper snow underfoot. He looked up into the canopy. The treetops swayed and the wind high up bellowed and whistled, but the storm was abating and down here it was calmer. Again, he stopped to listen. Nothing. His heart still raced and he felt his leg wound pounding. He pressed it to check, but the blood had stopped flowing. Whilst not a serious injury, his breeches were ruined and he felt a flash of annoyance at the waste.

Nearing Stensrud he felt himself relax. It was over; he had survived. Walking on through the forest he heard the sound of a car. The Drøbak road: almost there. He drew a deep breath and blew out through his teeth, mimicking the storm. Never had he felt such relief.

As he stopped by the road, another sound emerged. He crouched behind a large boulder, completely still, and listened. Nothing. He listened again, straining to hear what had first alerted him. There was something, a sound, very faint and intermittent...perhaps it was just the wind in the canopy? He waited. No, he was now sure, frighteningly sure. From higher up, carried by the wind, came the faint sound of voices.

And one other noise: *the baying of dogs.*

NINE

After taking the train to Oslo and exploring the Palace Park, Westervik took time to admire the changeover of the King's Guards. He then slipped into a small café bar nearby, run by a discrete German couple, Hans and Louisa Schmidt. They had for some time been in the employ of the German military intelligence service, the Abwehr. Westervik was joined in a secluded backroom by Walter von Elverfeldt, who entered via a back route off Grønnegata. An impeccably dressed military attaché, von Elverfeldt was outwardly answerable to the German envoy in Oslo, but his true command lines were direct to the head of Abwehr II in Berlin.

Westervik had been on edge all day, but the familiarity of the room helped him to settle: its sparse brown wood furnishings, the yellow glow of the wall lights and windows of frosted glass brought memories of the bars of his youth in rural Bavaria.

"You look well, Carl," said von Elverfeldt, offering him an R6. "Berlin is pleased with what you've been sending us."

Westervik took a long draw, releasing a hazy spiral towards the high ceiling, stained brown by decades of cigarette smoke. "Thank you," he said. "You should now have a good picture of Oslo's outer defences on the fjord. The fortress may look impressive, but it was built in the

1890's and the guns are old, slow to load and undermanned. The other batteries have smaller artillery and should be easy to pick off. The underwater barrier to the west of the fortress is still in place; there's no way through there."

He glanced at von Elverfeldt out of the corner of his eye and shifted in his chair. "That leaves the Narrows," he added.

"Which we must hope stays open," said von Elverfeldt. "Yes?"

"Quite. Fortunately, there are no moves to close off or mine it, and no sign of any reinforcements on the fortress. I keep in touch with several of the gunners through the local men's club; I'm hosting the next meeting at my home and expect a good turnout. Plenty of aquavit will loosen tongues, it always does."

"Norges Bank?"

"Nothing new. The Banking Hall is of no interest; no gold or high denomination currency is held there, only daily cash. The currency and gold vaults are in the basement; you have the floorplan. The people managing the gold reserves are tight-lipped. The most senior clerk lives near Drøbak, but he's a loner, a bugger to get to know — very wary. I think, when it comes to it, we just secure the building as a first objective and force a way in. If we get to Oslo quickly, with surprise on our side, they'll never get their gold out in time."

"Excellent. Anything you need?" said von Elverfeldt, allowing Westervik time to enjoy his R6.

Westervik took another deep draw and looked at the attaché. The man was always so polite, friendly and helpful, but it was difficult to feel truly secure. "Couple of things," he said. "At some point I need to sell more commodities, to keep Nordic Trading active."

"I'll arrange it."

"Second, it would help if one of your people could check the passenger lists for arrivals in Oslo from Britain. I'm interested in the period one week either side of the seventh of December."

"Haugen's replacement?"

Westervik nodded. "Probably, but I'm not sure."

"Name?"

"I don't know. But I believe he's half British, half Norwegian in some way, posing as a student. There can't be too many of them sailing the North Sea to Norway, not now. I need a date, port of departure, anything else you can dig up, please. But mostly, I need a name I can play with."

"Very well, I'll see what I can do."

Westervik offered the briefest of smiles by way of thanks, disguising his sense of frustration in the way intelligence was managed by the Reich: it was scattered, it seemed to him, amongst the organs of state by design, so no one could ever have the full picture, know who to trust or accumulate too much power.

"There's one other issue I want to raise," said von Elverfeldt. "A new Norwegian police surveillance outfit was set up in thirty-seven. *Politiets Overvåkingssentral* they call it: Police Surveillance Centre. It's run under the Oslo police chief, Kristian Welhaven."

Westervik waited, half anticipating what might be coming.

"Until now their attention has been on internal security: gypsies, leftists and so on. There's a new focus now: foreign infiltration. They're recruiting more local agents across the country."

"Drøbak?"

"Very likely," said von Elverfeldt. "Watch your back."

Westervik thrummed a brief tattoo with the fingers of his left hand on the dark wood of the table, his mind immediately unsettled. It was far more than watching his back.

Trails of smoke rose above the two men and dispersed as a grey mist. Hans Schmidt, a rather grey and gaunt man, and now at least seventy, walked silently from the back of the bar and placed a brandy in front of each of them. He nodded and retired, closing the door.

"One more development..." said von Elverfeldt. "Back home."

"Go on," said Westervik.

"Quisling has been in Berlin recently. He met the Führer twice, arguing for more Nazi-Norwegian cooperation, with National Samling in charge of Norway of course. I can't imagine the Führer accepting that, but Quisling's been effective. There are now German eyes on the strategic importance of Norway."

"About time."

"There's more. The Führer has just ordered the preparation of a study for the occupation of Norway," said von Elverfeldt. "The information you've already gathered has been invaluable. And Carl, your role will be central to the plan if it proceeds."

"I see," said Westervik, leaning forward, looking von Elverfeldt in the eyes. He needed to measure the trust in what was being said. "But there's only so much I can do alone," he said. "I've secured local support but will need intelligence operatives if this turns serious — Abwehr people with military training."

"The omens are good," said von Elverfeldt.

Westervik drew deeply on his R6, calming another flutter of nerves he felt in his guts. All the months of groundwork could now be playing out.

"Just keep up the good work, Carl. Focus on the fortress and Kopås: the main defensive line, the military issues." His voice dropped to a whisper and he glanced around the room. "It means action, seeing through your own plan. And if Haugen's replacement turns up and gets in the way — if you have any concerns that he might disrupt the main event..."

Westervik knew what was coming.

"Eliminate him."

———

Thomas listened again, straining to be sure, crouching lower amongst the trees. He willed himself to think clearly. A familiar stretch of road lay in front of him. And Stensrud was just minutes away up the hill.

But he could not outrun the dogs.

Frantically trying to work out a solution, he looked left along the road and heard a faint rumbling noise mixed with the rush and whistles of the storm. A shape emerged over the crest of the hill. A large vehicle, then another, and several more. A line of military trucks approached. The lead vehicle stopped and several soldiers jumped out into the rush of driven snow. Then, another vehicle stopped and disgorged more soldiers, spreading out over the fields and into the forest. In a few minutes armed men would be released close to where he stood, and that would be the end of it. If he ran back into the forest, he would meet the dogs following his tracks from Kopås. He was trapped. He could run, head south or east, but the dogs would track him down. Cross the road and he would be on open land. Shot as he ran.

The game was up.

But as he watched the military convoy come closer and more soldiers emerge, another vehicle crested the hill, a grey outline in the driven snow, the familiar deep growl of its diesel engine cutting faintly through the hiss of the storm. The bus. From Ås or perhaps Oslo. It didn't matter which; there was only one destination: Drøbak; down the hill and away from here.

Suddenly he was clear. Tracking back into the forest he ran down-hill, dodging between the trees, ducking under branches, jumping ditches and fallen, rotting tree-trunks half-hidden by drifts of snow until he emerged, panting, at the next bus-stop. Oppegårdstjernet.

From the edge of the forest he looked back up the road, desperately hoping the bus would be there. And it was. He could see it clearly, its wipers swinging at full speed. It was now ahead of the stop-start of the military trucks.

Thick scrub, thrashing around in the wind, grew between the forest and the wooden shelter on the bus-stop, providing good cover. As the bus approached, he stepped into the road and held out his hand. Jumping on board, he threw his skis onto the floor, swung his rucksack into the luggage rack and slumped into a seat on the third row back. Inside the bus the air was warm and stuffy, the windows steamed over and the sounds of the storm outside muted. Breathing a sigh of relief, he placed his hand on his chest, feeling his heartbeat, barely able to believe he hadn't yet exploded.

"Drøbak centre," he wheezed to the conductor, dropping some coins into his hand.

———

Late that night, after sheltering in Drøbak church, he walked in darkness back up the hill and out of town, the fresh snow squeaking beneath every step. The storm had passed, replaced by still, intensely cold air. Lights from distant houses and farms sparkled in the darkness.

Overhead, he picked out Orion, the hunter. The Milky Way ran through the sky, like a glowing drift of smoke, lit by a million stars.

"Hell," he murmured, looking down at the plate-sized spread of congealed blood on his breeches. Damn near killed...*by my own side...*

Yet, mixed with exhaustion and fear, was an abiding sense of satisfaction: a sense of relief. He had, as he'd hoped when he set out for the ridgeline that morning, begun to play his part, to assuage his lingering sense of cowardice...to feel, for a moment, alongside the men of the *Glorious*.

TEN

Several days passed, empty and without ceremony or any recognition of Christmas. The fear of a knock at the door receded as Thomas dared to think that was the end of it: he had escaped the dogs and who knew what else through sheer good fortune. Never had a passing bus been so welcome, but the risks he had taken could not possibly justify the meagre output for British Secret Intelligence, or even his modest leg wound and ruined breeches.

Gradually, the Kopås Incident as he thought of it, faded and his mind turned to his meeting with Pendleton, which would bring a tumultuous year to some sort of conclusion, for better or worse. It was New Years' Eve, as a poster for a student party reminded him. He walked into the administration building at Ås and found Ingrid, who gave him an especially warm smile — at least, he thought so. She handed him a new set of papers from the Norwegian professor. Thomas returned the first batch and thanked her, lingering just a moment longer than was necessary. "You'll be in the library, today?" she asked.

"A short while, maybe," he replied, flicking through the papers. And then she said:

"It's interesting, what you study. I read one or two of the papers, the easier ones."

He looked up. Ingrid was a mirage. "And your subject, what's that?" he asked.

"Rather different. The gothic novels of English nineteenth century literature."

"Dracula...?"

"Yes, but there's more to it than that. I'm studying for a doctorate. This is just a part-time job," she said, glancing towards the main library door.

"Live burials, stakes through the heart, dark and ruined castles," he said, smiling. "It's hard to associate that with you."

"Never judge by appearances." She shrugged and began shuffling the files behind the reception desk.

"Sorry," he said, as he set off down the corridor, replaying to himself his ignorant summary of the gothic world.

After some pretence at reading in the library, he knocked on the door of Room 7 and, with a mixture of relief and fear, greeted Pendleton with a short nod.

"Churchill wants a more active British presence in Norway," said Pendleton with no hint of preamble, his eyes wary as if searching for the enemy amongst the bookshelves. "We need more intelligence on the military situation in the Oslo fjord."

"Which is already waiting for you at the dead drop. Damned near got myself killed doing the job, so you'd better appreciate it."

"Good. Which brings me to the fact you're unarmed. Strangely, you don't seem too bothered. You should be."

"I'm not a one-man army. That was my briefing," Thomas said sharply. "Just eyes and ears. Sick joke."

"Not my decision, what you are. Never mind, you'll find some personal protection tied to the underside of your privy when you get back. It's the same as you trained with apparently: an unmarked, Belgian-made .32-calibre, so there's nothing to identify it as British-supplied. Easy to load, 5-shot, highly effective at short range and, best of all, there's nothing to snag in a coat pocket if you need it in a hurry. Just squeeze the trigger...*bang*. That's the theory, anyway. I don't like guns myself."

"So what's changed?" said Thomas, with a rising sense of unease.

"One, the strategic importance of Norway. There's more at stake now. Two, we have intelligence that suggests we're not alone. Drøbak is the lynchpin in the defence of Oslo. We can't be surprised that the Germans also have an agent in the area. His mission — could be her, of course — is likely to be similar to yours, but more lethal if taking Norway is in their plans, which now appears more likely. You know their game: subversion, targeted assassinations, that sort of thing."

"So who is this German operative?" said Thomas, at once realising the stupidity of the question.

Pendleton rolled his eyes. "Find out. That's your job. Deal with the bastard if necessary."

"You're all the bloody same," said Thomas, unable to conceal his anger and fear, both mixed up in the knot in his stomach. "I've been here for just a month. I've come within inches of a bullet through my head at Kopås — no, you don't know about that. And now you expect me to start a shooting fight with a single revolver and no military training — bar a few hours target practice — against an unknown enemy."

"There's a war on, Galtung. Get it into your thick head. You need to defend yourself. As you say, you're no good dead, are you?"

"I frequently debate with myself that very topic," said Thomas, the knot in his stomach wrenching tighter. The seconds ticked by in silence. "One last thing."

"Ah-ha?"

He stood up and leaned on the table with both hands, fixing Pendleton with narrowed eyes. "Tell me," he said, slowly. "Truthfully, if that's possible. Did you have an agent here before me?"

"What do you mean?" said Pendleton, his frown lines tightening, his eyes seeming to wander. "No one tells me anything."

"*A gap to fill*...Does that mean anything to you?" I overheard Biggeloe and his boss, you see. "A gap to fill, that's what they wanted me for..."

"Means nothing to me, why should it..."

"Lying bastard. There was someone before me, wasn't there? What happened to him? What was his name?"

Pendleton drew a deep breath. "Nothing to do with me, but he could have moved on, I guess," he said, with a shrug of his shoulders. "If he existed."

"His name?" said Thomas, pushing his face closer. Disappeared around sixth, seventh maybe, October, just before the big snows came in...Ring a bell?"

Pendleton shrugged.

"Haugen, wasn't it?"

"No idea, old boy."

"Killed..."

"Oh no. If there was a Haugen, and I doubt there was, he'd have been moved on by the higher ups. They do that, you know."

"No, I don't know that's what they do." Thomas sighed. And, he thought in the silence that now filled the room, Biggeloe and probably the professor too: they both knew. "I was your only option for this mission, wasn't I? A Drøbak boy who could operate for the British. I filled the gap?" said Thomas, speaking more slowly and leaning deeper still into Pendleton's face. "I might be entirely unsuitable, but you need me to stay alive, don't you? I'm not easy to replace."

"It would help, yes, if you would stay alive." The man sounded almost optimistic, hopeful, as if he had just realised the possibility that Thomas could survive.

"And whoever did in my predecessor — Haugen, let's call him — is out there somewhere, waiting for the British replacement to turn up. Quite likely eyeing me up in the library or sitting behind me on the bus when I head off home."

"I wouldn't know," said Pendleton, planting a faux expression of exasperation across his face. "But there was no Haugen here, not one of ours, at least."

"Huh. And this German agent of yours...he's not just creeping around as eyes and ears, collecting information on Norway's wonderful fjords, is he?" said Thomas, a black bird writhing in his chest. "He's an assassin...who's killed once already...*and I'm his next bloody target.*"

PART TWO
THE COLDEST
WINTER

ELEVEN

Oslo. *2nd of January 1940.* Klara left early from the family home of her closest friend. Enormous snowflakes drifted through the darkness and settled as an unbroken blanket over Holtegata and its fine villas, only the yellow glow of the porch lights suggesting life inside. The previous evening they had met at Skansen, the popular jazz venue and café where, back in the summer, she had been introduced to the first man in her life she could accept as her equal. Confident, cultured and amusing, she had been instantly attracted. Now, approaching Palace Park, she pictured his face, his smile and tingled with desire, yearning for the moment she would see him again. But then the world intruded and the spell was broken.

"*Aftenposten,*" she said, taking hold of the folded newspaper.

"Not much to smile about today," said the kiosk-holder, a thin man with a bony face and two hats, one on top of the other. It was true: the war was all around, in the newspaper, on the billboards, on people's lips and in their minds. Everywhere, but not yet in Norway.

Crossing into Viktoria Terrasse, she glanced up at the police headquarters and turned down a narrow alley towards the back of the building. Later, she was shown by a secretary into the office of Kristian Welhaven, head of Oslo police. It was interesting to see him here, in his place of work. Balding, a clipped moustache, big hands, he was a powerful man. But she imagined him, at that moment, not as this figure of authority behind his vast desk, but relaxing and telling jokes with her father at the Castle. It was Welhaven who had identified Klara as the ideal agent for the Police Surveillance Centre, a specialist section dedicated to internal security and the identification of foreign spies. Having completed various assessments, Klara was ready for the greatest challenge of her life. Malicious foreign agents were already operating in her home area. All Welhaven wanted was someone to identify them.

Just one problem remained, and it bothered her. "What about people I know: friends, family? Employees? I can't suspect them all as foreign spies."

"You can't exclude them," said Welhaven. "It's exactly what spies would do: worm their way into the right places and secure a reputable job or friendships to gain legitimacy."

"Spy on my parents, for example?"

"Worst case, if needs be." He shrugged.

"Impossible."

"Sort it out with Johansen.

"Who?"

"You'll meet him," said Welhaven. "Alfred Johansen."

"One of your men?"

Welhaven nodded. "Your contact in the Surveillance Centre."

"Where would I meet him?"

"It's your patch..."

"We have a disused cabin on an island called Skarholmen."

———

Klara left the Castle at dawn as a watery sun rose to reveal a landscape of ice and snow. She steeled herself for the meeting with Johansen. To be accepted into Welhaven's world would be an opportunity to test herself, to free herself from her father's overprotective control. After buying a cinnamon roll at Gundersens, the baker and part-time gunner at Kopås, she arrived at the causeway to Skarholmen. The tide was low, the boulders covered in a layer of blown snow and thin, broken sea ice.

Crouching down to feel her way on the slippery rocks, she reached a track that ran along the edge of the island. Johansen waited, hidden behind the boatshed at the back of the harbour.

"See that" he said, his head immobile as she joined him. "Oscarsborg fortress."

The air was completely still, the fortress seeming to float on a thin film of mist over the fjord. It was so cold it hurt to breathe. "Hmm," she muttered suspiciously at Johansen's opening shot.

"Always been there, employs a few people, trains a few more, but never seen action." He turned to greet her, a broad beam fixed effortlessly onto his face.

Johansen was thirtyish and neatly groomed, the smooth skin of his plump face coloured bright pink from the cold. With an air of pompous self-assurance, he appeared anxious to project himself as a man in charge. "People can't imagine Norway being attacked," he said, theatrically, "so the fortress stands there. an historical oddity."

"That's not a police matter?" said Klara, trying to suppress a surge of impatience.

"Agreed. Our brief is foreign spies and what they might do in advance of an invasion, just as Germany did in overrunning Poland."

"Which was?"

"One example: the Germans placed one hundred and fifty men into the country, dressed them up in Polish army uniforms and then staged an attack on one of their own radio stations. Why would they do that?"

"To help justify Germany's attack, obviously."

"Exactly. We know that before and in the early stages of the invasion of Poland, the Nazis conducted many covert operations. Subterfuge, assassinations, diversions, sabotage, the lot. And how did they know what and who to target?"

"Spies."

"Precisely."

"And they operate here in Drøbak?" said Klara.

"Almost for sure," said Johansen, "and the best people to identify them are local people who know their patch."

"Hard to believe," said Klara, looking out over the fjord, feeling suddenly calmer about Johansen. Maybe he wasn't stupid. "But those local people don't live in a world of suspects, they live with family, friends and..."

"I know you raised this point with the chief and it's not an easy one. We'll deal with it if the problem arises. Yes?"

The matter unresolved, they left via a flight of steps cut into the rocks at the back of the quay, Klara leading the way through the trees to a small, timber cabin. She unlocked the door, lit the woodstove and set a battered black kettle on the hotplate, then sat observing Johansen: the fall of his hair over his high forehead and the unnecessary crossing and uncrossing of his legs.

"In the Great War — and few people know this — we were overrun with German spies," he said. "Norway was neutral then, as we are now. These spies operated out of their legations, as so-called diplomats or attachés for trade or shipping or some other made-up activity. They became friendly with our leaders, military men, top people in business. You can hardly imagine the scale of it."

"And now?" said Klara.

"Just wait. Please." He drew in a deep breath and puffed. "Their focus was the coast. And of course, the movement of iron ore, even then. They were everywhere. Oslo, naturally, here in Drøbak around the fortifications, Stavanger; many of them in Bergen. All the way up to Kirkenes."

"Coffee?" asked Klara, pushing herself up from her seat.

He nodded. "Now, what's the scale of espionage in Norway today? Much we don't know, of course, which is why we need more people in the field. What I can say is that foreign spies seem to have the same interest in the coast and maritime activity as they did before and during the Great War; watching our ports and harbours, monitoring trade movements, mapping and recording activity in the shipping lanes."

Klara poured the coffee. "I'm listening."

"They probably work in the same way now," continued Johansen, "out of seemingly legitimate set-ups: trade bodies, diplomatic offices, administrative positions in harbourmaster offices, that sort of thing. They may pose as journalists, set up trade newspapers and collect harmless stories to publish in Germany; but that's just cover. They might be traders, commodity dealers and middlemen, fish dealers, so they can move easily around the ports. Or reputable businessmen in any field you like. And there's another idea they've borrowed from last time."

"Which is?"

"Leading up to the war they posed as landscape artists, moving around and painting and drawing the fjords, the defences, towns."

"Not at minus fifteen they won't," said Klara.

"Very well, maybe not right now. But German activity of this sort has increased greatly since last summer, and we are struggling to keep an eye on it all. Another example: they used to employ German-born Norwegian citizens for many jobs in their legations. All perfectly proper. But over the autumn, they've nearly all been replaced, slowly and quietly, with people we know to be committed Nazis."

"Preparing the ground?" she mused.

"Quite possibly," he said, "although they didn't use all that espionage work to invade Norway in the Great War, did they?"

She studied him again. He was into his stride now. And she had learned something: that Norway was more at risk than she had imagined.

"I want to ask," said Johansen, "from what I have told you, and from what you have learned of the role in the last few days, are you willing to commit to a surveillance role for us? Here, in Drøbak."

"Yes," she said. "I do have some issues and concerns, but...I'll address them if they arise."

Klara rose to look out from the window. The fortress was just visible through the trees, framed by the flagpole outside and a large, russet-barked pine tree. "I'm not convinced you can keep me secure," she said. "I'd be on some list somewhere, a target for hostile forces as you people call them."

She looked at him, her head on one side, watching his jaw rippling as he held back his frustration. "So would you be," she added.

"What?"

"In the crosshairs."

"Maybe."

"It's not good for your dental health, you know."

"What isn't?"

"Grinding your teeth."

TWELVE

Far to the south, the fjord dissolved into the gloom of a mid-winter's day, the landscape devoid of colour: just shades of grey. A few snowflakes swept by, caught in the freezing updrafts and swirling aimlessly over the ridgeline. For an hour, Thomas had recorded shipping movements passing through the Narrows and had observed a couple of ferry crossings to and from the fortress from Sundbrygga, a small quay not far from Svensen's shop. Mostly, it felt safer up here on the high land, but the shiver of fear, of being hunted by Haugen's killer, was never far away; nor was the remorseless churning of his imagination. How had his predecessor met his end? If Thomas could escape Drøbak he would, but it was not that simple; it was hard to imagine literally running away from the responsibilities of his mission. No man on the *Glorious*, or any ship at sea, could do that.

It was soon time to leave the high land and he headed through town towards a boatshed at the back of Lehmanns quay. Leaning on a frosted door handle he pushed, emerging into a boat-building workshop with almost fifty men at work. A part-time job, as Pendleton had suggested, would bolster his cover story.

Part way along the far wall, he spotted the manager's office, a timber construction with windows giving out onto the working area. After wending his way between the boats and exchanging nods and smiles with the men as he passed, he knocked and entered. The manager, sat behind a dusty, untidy desk, lifted his eyes as Thomas appeared.

"I'm looking for work," Thomas said. "Marine engines, repairs, anything to do with wooden boats."

––––––

Late in the evening, a lone figure walked towards the Bell House. "You should keep your door locked," said Westervik, stepping inside and brushing snow off his jacket.

"Uh," Brann grunted, his massive hand grasping a glass of liquor.

"Kit safe?"

Brann eased himself up and pulled away a large, heavily worn rug to reveal a trapdoor. "Ready, plenty of ammo." He slid the rug back and dragged over a chair for his visitor. "What about our new tenant at Stensrud? he said, unable to disguise his curiosity.

"Thomas Galtung, that's who he is," said Westervik. "Stood out like a shining beacon in the passenger lists. Any Galtungs around these parts?"

"Galtung?" said Brann, frowning. "There was a Galtung used to live here, f'God's sake — in this place. Pa drowned, off Skarholmen. There was a kid, I remember a kid. Might have been him. Buggered off to Britain, he did, with his ma, once I'd bought the place. She was English y' know."

"I didn't," said Westervik, squeezing his lower lip with the fingers of his left hand... "Interesting...but it all fits: a Brit from Norway."

"Looks like it."

"Or a Norwegian from Britain." Westervik slowly paced the room, twice around the big table, stopping only to look at a cracked china plate hung on the end wall.

"She left it," said Brann. "Threw it in with the sale."

"Lucky," said Westervik.

"Best deal of my life — the house I mean. And the forest. But she was happy, just to get rid. Thought she was gonna kiss me, I did."

Vestervik laughed. "One other thing."

"Uh?"

"There was an incursion at Kopås, apparently, just before Christmas. Svensen, our shopkeeper friend, was rambling on about it. Incensed, he was; took a few pot-shots himself at the bastard, apparently."

"Galtung?"

"We don't know. He got away."

"Makes sense it was him," Brann rumbled.

"Right, so he's born here. Pa dies, you say, but he grows up in England. Recruited at some university or other, I guess; he's a student, shown as one on the passenger list, so it fits what Svensen says. As does the timing: a few weeks of panic whilst they figure out why Haugen went quiet, then time to identify and train his successor. British Intelligence then make up our student's cover story. Glaciers, according to Svensen. Glaciers here in Drøbak! They must think the whole of Norway is covered in bloody ice."

"No harm taking him out," said Brann, crackling like a lightbulb coming to life at the stupidity of the new English Spy.

"Not yet. He could be Haugen's replacement," pondered Westervik, "but we don't know for sure, do we? So, hold off, right?"

"Huh."

"Also...we don't know what he looks like, do we?"

The two men slipped into silence, taking occasional sips of the colourless alcohol brought up from the cellar. "D'ya know," said Brann. "Maybe I do know what he looks like. I met a tall, gangly bastard one day, damn near a month ago, up above town. Never seen 'im before, but he was wandrin' around like he owns the fuckin' place."

"Could have been anybody."

"Don't think so. Who the hell goes up there but a so-called ice age student skiin' up from Stensrud to look at snow. And, by the way, to cast an eye over the fortress, the ferries, shippin', all that stuff. Perfect bloody cover and no one but me to ever see 'im doin' it."

"Interesting."

"And yuh...I remember now...Thomas, he called himself." Breathing heavily, he poured them another glass each of his gin-clear moonshine, full to the brim.

"Right," concluded Westervik, "see what else you can uncover about Thomas Galtung."

88

THIRTEEN

Matthias stepped off the bus on Kirkegata and headed for the bank. More pronounced than normal in this cold winter his limp, far from being the disability it had been as a child, gave him, in the eyes of some, a hint of mystery and distinction enhanced by the confident flourishes and sharp taps of his black, silver-capped cane. In all other respects he would appear to passers-by the very model of probity and discrete prosperity, a man of affairs which, if we could peer into his mind, he would have been exceedingly ready to accept. Even his tailored wool coat, caught in the breeze and revealing a hint of its blue silk lining, could only reinforce the impression he conveyed, so close was it to the attire of the wealthiest and most powerful men in the city.

Climbing the six granite steps into the foyer of the bank, few could have imagined that here was a man harbouring the darkest of secrets. Once in the basement he greeted the guards as usual. "Good day, all well with you both, I hope?"

"Well indeed, Mr Holmbekk. Time for you to dress up again," said the taller of the two guards, smiling and handing over a pair of insulated overalls.

"I have to say they're life savers," said Matthias. "Sitting still all day, you get **so** cold."

After a cursory inspection, the guard handed back his sandwich pack and Thermos, and wished him a successful day. Matthias picked up his cane and limped off down the corridor towards the vaults, *tap...tap... tap* echoing off the bare walls. Once inside the vault, he resumed work on the Governor's plan and after several minutes set aside the register. Taking out his Thermos, he poured himself a coffee and placed the stopper on the table in front of him. He thought carefully about what had become a daily operation, his security assured only by the flawless execution of his finely conceived trick.

Glancing towards the vault door and listening for footsteps on the corridor outside, he satisfied himself he was alone. He picked up the stopper and checked it, as he always did, for any damage or flaws in his workmanship. It was perfect but the shiver of fear — the fear of being caught — was never far away.

With a squeeze and twist of his hands, he separated the two halves of the stopper and eased out a small coin, secreted there the previous evening. It dropped onto the table in front of him, spinning around several times and settling with a rattle. He then placed the coin in an open canvas bag sitting on a shelf on his left side.

Glancing again at the vault door and forcing himself to slow down to control the shaking in his hands, he leaned over and selected a seemingly identical coin from the top of another bag on the floor next to his chair. He slid the coin neatly into the stopper, which he twisted and then closed, pushing it back into the flask. Breathing out in relief, he picked up the cup and took his first sip of coffee for the day, pondering a career that early on had become stalled on the lower rungs of advancement. But, at last, his special knowledge had placed him on a pinnacle; no one else in the bank had even thought of the possibilities he had.

At the end of the day, Matthias submitted himself, his lunch bag and, especially, his cane to the customary search as he left the vaults, exchanging friendly banter with the two guards as they went through their routine, which always started with a violent shake of his empty Thermos flask, turning it upside down and peering in for good measure. His stomach churned as he watched them, as it had done since he had, after months of preparation, come up with his killer idea. In the early days it was a coin a month. Then, towards the end of the year, he began working every day in the vaults. Now, as they fiddled with his cane, always looking for a secret compartment to be revealed by a twist of one of the silver ferrules, a coin every day had become a real possibility.

"Shoes, please, Mr Holmbekk."

As usual, they performed a *faux* sniff of the finely-lined shoes in a joke that had long since ceased to be funny. It was a perfect diversion. He then removed his heavy overalls, which they hung on a peg behind their desk, and changed into his suit. Finally, donning his overcoat, gloves and hat, he tapped the floor with a single affirmative thrust of his cane and held out his hand for the return of his briefcase. With a smile, he wished the guards good day.

Making his way up the steep backstairs to the main lobby, Matthias nodded to the doorman and descended the granite steps into Bankplassen, feeling the tension leaving his body like a great wave, and set off ambling along Kirkegata until he reached *Domkirken*, the cathedral. Here, he selected a seat in a quiet corner beneath a large tree where, within the confines of his lunch bag, he removed the coin from the stopper of his Thermos flask and dropped it into his inside jacket pocket. Returning to Prinsens Gate he then headed towards Berkowitz Mynthandel, one of Oslo's premier coin dealers. It was already dark, but they worked long hours there.

"Good afternoon, Jakob," he said, addressing the proprietor.

"And what have we today, Mr Holmbekk? Another sovereign?"

"Indeed," he said. "A nice one."

"Come into the back room," said Jakob.

Matthias reached into his pocket and drew out the gold coin. "George V, 1928, Melbourne Mint," he said. "And what's more, very fine condition."

"Lovely," said Jakob, examining the coin and then weighing it. "A rare coin, very collectable."

The dealer pushed up his glasses to rest on his forehead, scribbled a few notes and figures onto a sheet of paper and, after a few seconds, made Matthias an offer.

"You have a small cash balance on account and, if you use that, I can offer you three ordinary sovereigns for this wonderful coin."

"I agree, thank you," said Matthias after a few seconds of mental arithmetic.

"Very good," said Jakob, smiling. He placed the three coins into a small envelope and slid it across the table.

"I have another," Matthias added, placing the envelope in his bag.

"You have a good eye, Mr Holmbekk. I have a growing group of customers I am confident will be interested."

"Jakob," he whispered, "it's a Victoria shield-back Young Head sovereign, 1843/2. A little worn but the exciting thing is it has a rare 3/2 overdate. It's a beauty."

"Very rare. Tomorrow?"

"All being well." Matthias smiled broadly and they shook hands. "And your wife, Jakob?"

"As well as can be expected, but she worries, as we all do."

Matthias headed back to the cathedral square. Here, on the same bench, he secreted one of Jakob's three sovereigns in the Thermos stopper ready for tomorrow's swap. He then headed back home for the night, where he placed the two remaining gold coins in his safe to add to his rapidly accumulating fortune.

———

A few days later Thomas started his part-time job at the boatworks on Lehmanns Quay. Working here was a step in finding a more balanced and secure life. It would give him the cover of normality, plus additional income, and it might also help yield useful intelligence, more so than being locked away at Stensrud. He looked out through a small, dusty window to the fjord, the mountains and the quay, then turned to watch and listen to the clatter of chisels, saws and drills and to the hubbub of voices of his fellow workers. Suddenly, he felt the stress drain out of him: here he was in Drøbak again...and there was no sign yet of Haugen's assassin.

Later in the day, he latched onto banter amongst the mechanics about the trade running through Lehmanns Quay to Germany.

"Who handles that trade?" he asked.

Many ships, it transpired, traded with Germany, but most sailed direct to and from Oslo, appearing only sporadically at Lehmanns. Just one company, Nordic Trading A/S, run by a Carl Westervik, stopped regularly in Drøbak to take produce from the local area.

———

Westervik slid a shot across the table and laughed as Brann caught it before it flew off the edge. He raised his glass. "Schnaps this time," he said, smiling. "Much as I like your moonshine, it's a bit heavy for me." Looking across at the big man he felt once again assured of Brann's loyalty. It was in his blood. Fearless, he was drawn by action, yet craved recognition and was motivated by gold; especially gold, much more than money. These were useful qualities. There was only really one problem, he thought: he never quite knew what Brann was thinking. There was a darkness to him, an absence of empathy, a morose and sometimes gleeful disregard for another person's plight and a singular focus on his own goals. Yet, strangely, his mind could flip and alight on a small detail or connection which he would twist into the funniest of insights. It was unsettling although, as he thought about it, it hardly mattered. There was a job to be done...and he knew Brann would stay the course.

"Anything new on the Brit?" he asked.

"I see him go by sometimes," said Brann, "when we're workin' those two blocks I bought off the ma — y'know, up above his cabin. Does an occasional walk. Goes skiin'. Svensens for food. That's it. Maybe he's not spyin' after all?"

"And...?" Westervik sat back and waited, confident more would come, and letting another swig of fine German schnaps warm his throat.

"Well, yeh...there is somethin' else I picked up in passing from my men. You won't believe this, but it's true. Galtung...he was friends once with the rich bastard Holmbekks, when he was a kid. The fuckin' Holmbekks," he shrieked in mock disbelief. "Used to go to that Castle place. Everyone knew. How'd he do that, huh? A penniless brat. And another thing...he used to play around with the eldest daughter, he did."

He sniggered, a wide grin glued to his face. "A real something, she is. Lara, Kara, Laila...whatever her name is."

"Who?" said Westervik.

"Kaila, Daila, Dallah... I don't know."

A shiver ran up his spine at Brann's leering reference to Klara. He took a deep breath, struggling to think straight at the revelation...if it were true. After a moment of silence, he said: "It's exactly why we need to be cautious; there's now a Holmbekk connection to our possible English Spy. If Galtung were to disappear, it would have consequences. The Holmbekks are tied into the police, top level, mates with all of them; military, too, business types, the mayor, politicians. If he disappears, we'd have half the police in Norway fishing around. So, we hold back. Got that?"

"Right," said Brann, frowning, his eyes slits of black jade.

"Right?" said Westervik, almost shouting the words. "Anyway, for all we know, he's just a mad professor."

"Yeh, yeh."

Westervik refilled his glass and pushed the bottle across the table. They were both silent for a while, then Brann shifted in his chair and said: "Okay, here's another one. My men picked this up, too. Easy it is; there are woodsmen all over Drøbak...and they gas, like old women. Got himself a job, he has, this Galtung, at the Holmbekk boatworks down at Lehmanns. Why would he do that, eh?"

"Hmm, why would he? It wouldn't yield much to British Intelligence, would it? Maybe he just needs the money. But why would he need money?"

"Maybe he's hopeless, like Haugen. Pay by results...an' he's got no results."

"We'll find out eventually," said Westervik. "And I'll tell you how. He would have to communicate, wouldn't he? Back to London or somewhere."

"Yuh. Radio."

"No, unreliable, not secure; dead drop most likely, and there are not many options, are there? Not in winter, what with footprints in the snow, drifts covering drop points...So, if we find the dead drop and if our student uses it, then..."

"Clever one, boss," said Brann.

Westervik still tingled at Brann's revelation. It was a fact from hell and it massively complicated the hunt for the English Spy, if that's what Galtung is. He stood up, a little unsteady, and wandered over to the window. His eyes followed the track leading downhill into the forest. An hour away were the Holmbekks...the Castle...Klara. He shuddered at the idea that she once enjoyed a friendship with Thomas Galtung. *Even worse, what if she still did?*

FOURTEEN

Klara loved one room above all others at the Castle. Ever since she could remember, the heavy door at the end of the dark stone corridor had held secrets. There were, in fact, two rooms beyond that door. The first held estate records and was of little interest for her as a child. Shelves were dedicated to different parts of the business: farming, forestry and timber processing, the port and the shipping operation, minerals and quarrying and, finally, property. What lay beyond, through an almost invisible door constructed to be part of the room's wood-panelled walls, was far more absorbing. This was the map room, where plans of the estate were held in large cabinets. It was the oldest map, dated 1875, which fascinated her most. Displayed on one of the walls, it showed the Castle as a new building. Each of the fields and ice lakes were named and each block of forest numbered.

What interested her now was the property portfolio. In the early days, the estate owned little property but, as the different enterprises grew, a need evolved to provide accommodation for managers and workers close to their place of work. By 1940 a total of twenty-five cabins and houses were scattered about the estate, some high up in the forests, others on the farming plain and still more in town by the port. Nowadays, with improved transport and more staff living in Drøbak close to the school and other facilities, some of these properties were rented to people not employed by the Holmbekks. A number of farmhouses connected to rented farmland completed the portfolio, but these were let on much longer leases.

Klara sat at a vast mahogany table in the centre of the room. She liked the atmosphere here, the sense of history, the view from the window over a sweep of snow-covered farmland stretching away to the forested horizon. But today she had a specific reason to be here. In front of her lay a file with the details of all tenancies dating from January 1930 to December 1939. The files were updated every month with information held in the Estate Office. Once a new tenant had signed the rental agreement and paid the deposit, the Estates Manager would enter the details in the records at the Castle.

She thought it most likely that any new tenant of interest would date from some time in 1939, but she decided to extend the search back a further year to be sure and selected the tabs for both years. It took her barely a minute to see that there were recorded two new farm tenancies, but these were significant commitments by people long known to the family, so were of no interest.

Of more potential were five new tenants who had taken detached cabins and smallholdings for various terms. She ran her finger down a column of names and dates. Two were tenancies taken out in '38. Both were family men who had worked as farm labourers on the estate for many years and had moved on to their own smallholdings. Again, no interest. That left three new tenancies in '39. One, dating from May, had been taken out by Vladas Shukis, a Lithuanian farmer with a large family, who had taken on a smallholding in a wooded area on the eastern side of the estate.

The next was Peter Haugen, who had taken a small flat on Storgaten near the port from the beginning of September. He gave his profession as 'boat hand' and had settled the deposit and three months' rent. However, there was no record that December's rent had been paid and a note in the right-hand column indicated that he may have 'disappeared.'

The most recent tenancy was Thomas's which, of course, she was aware of. He was listed as a 'research student', but no more details were given: they were yet to be transferred from the Estates Office.

Of the three new tenancies in 1939, Shukis seemed above board, simply because of the way he was recruited; he had been selected from several aspiring smallholders after a couple of years working as a labourer on land farmed in hand.

Haugen. He had signed up for a year, the minimum contract period, but had then disappeared — moved on, more likely, although she would see if the Estates Manger had anything to add.

This left Thomas. She slowly closed the tenancies book and looked out of the great window. Huge snowflakes drifted down in the still air. She thought back to her recruitment by Johansen; here was just the problem she had anticipated, and which had been left unresolved. Thomas as a spy was impossible to imagine but...could he have been recruited in Oxford by the Abwehr? It didn't seem likely; he had no connection to Germany as far as she was aware, but many years had passed since she knew him as a child. He could have been motivated by grievances or political beliefs she was unaware of. Equally, Thomas as a British agent was a possibility. The timing was right: a spy needing somewhere to live in the Drøbak area once Britain entered the war on 3rd September. But she could hardly treat her childhood friend — someone invited into her family by her father — as a suspected spy. *Could she?*

———

Thomas became fixated on Nordic Trading. The company handled Norwegian agricultural commodities and forestry products, much of which was sold in Sweden using a German freighter, *S/S Martina*, a frequent visitor to Lehmanns Quay. Nothing more was known, not least, apparently, because no Holmbekk produce had been sold through the company, so no more information was forthcoming from the men at the boatworks. This was progress, of sorts, but what he had learned rein-forced his appreciation of how poorly equipped he was to act as a spy. He was too isolated and had no contacts of value. His only option was to winkle some information on Nordic Trading out of Svensen who, at the shop today, would hopefully be in expansive form.

"Good man, Carl; respected member of the Drøbak Men's Club," said Svensen, clearly pleased to be able to talk about his enviable social network. "Very generous, too. But I'm not sure about jobs. A trading company hardly needs Ice Age experts." He laughed at the incongruity.

"No harm in asking?" said Thomas. "I need work for the summer."

"Lives out to the east, he does, a place called Bergholt. But you're wasting your time."

Thomas thanked him and headed for the door, where he stopped, looked back and was about to open his mouth.

"No," said Svensen, a look of incredulity on his face. "You were about to ask, weren't you? The club doesn't take students. Or boat mechanics."

————

The door closed on the backroom at Hans and Louisa Schmidt's café off the Palace Park. "Studie Nord," said von Elverfeldt, taking a sip of brandy. "A plan to take Norway."

Westervik lifted his eyes, expectantly. He tapped his R6 on the beer-stained table and lit up.

"Just completed and presented to the Führer by OKW. The outcome is that the plan will be upgraded. More resources, faster warships, probably led by Kriegsmarine."

"They'll still go for Oslo?"

"For sure, assuming it proceeds, though I'm just piecing together the bits I see at the legation."

Westervik took a deep draw on his cigarette, releasing twin jets of smoke through his nostrils. He was keenly aware this was where the last ten years of his life had been leading: to make good the wrongs of history following the Great War. But there was a niggling doubt, too, about what the Nazis were drawing Germany into. The annexation of Austria or military action against an aggressor was one thing; an inva-sion of Norway was another. These were difficult issues, but his mind was not allowed to drift for long.

"One other matter," said von Elverfeldt. "Any developments with the police Surveillance Centre? We're now sure they've installed someone in Drøbak."

"Nothing yet," said Westervik, "but I've set Brann to find out if anyone new has joined the Drøbak police in the last six months. It'll be a start."

Von Elverfeldt was silent for a while, and then said:

"We have an interesting situation developing; a potentially critical one given the strategic importance of Drøbak and the fortress to the approaches to Oslo: Germany's Abwehr, British Secret Intelligence and now Norway's police surveillance outfit...all circling around each other."

"It's becoming congested."

"Never mind that, Carl. Just make sure that we come out on top."

FIFTEEN

Thomas closed the hazel gate and headed uphill towards Torsrud, the farm where 'Mad' Severin Nordby and his sister, the rumoured *Silver Girl Ghost*, once lived, and he at least probably still did. He hoped the old man would remember him, confident that his madness was no more than eccentricity, a farmer's curmudgeonly outlook on the world.

Approaching Torsrud, barely visible through low cloud, memories were rekindled of just how high up Severin lived: on the limit of human life his father had once said, by which he meant that the barley and oats would fail one year in three, that the cow would be brought in two weeks earlier than lower down and that a good store of grass was a matter of survival for the animals. In one especially bad winter, Thomas recalled his nine-year-old self riding atop a cart full of tottering bales, his father leading the horses along a snowy forest track to deliver hay to Torsrud: a gift between farming friends who shared life on the edge. This, years ago, had been his first and only sight of 'Mr Nordby'. By then, the myth of Marta, the *Silver Girl Ghost*, had begun to fade although, recalling Severin's empty barn on that day more than a decade ago, the grown-up Thomas could still visualise the diaphanous form of a young girl he was convinced had passed through the shadows as he dragged the first hay bale across the earthen floor.

Torsrud now emerged from the mist. It was much as Thomas remembered it: a decaying redoubt perched on a rocky mound protruding like a long nose into the clearing below, now deep in snow. Around the farmhouse, scattered outbuildings provided for the animals and storage. The hay barn was still there: a little more battered, perhaps, but childhood memories were never reliable. A column of blue-grey smoke drifted upwards from a stone chimney, dispersing into the foggy air.

Maybe he had never looked up as a child but now, as Thomas approached the house and the smell of woodsmoke became more intense, he could see that the roof was a work of Herculean stonemasonry, with slabs so massive he wondered how anyone could have lifted them up there; their weight so great it was hardly a surprise that the great, blackened logs of the walls below had sunk and twisted over the years. It was as if the whole house was crumbling back into the earth.

The door opened slowly, its hinges creaking. An old man of average height peered out, his tousle of hair, once brown, now greying. Dressed in clothes from a bygone era, patched, with threads of wool hanging loose, Severin stood with his weight on one leg, the other swinging slowly back and forth.

"Galtung," said Thomas. "We lived at the Bell House."

"Gudmund's boy?"

"Yes, I'm Thomas. I visited you once with him."

"Hunted together at times, we did, your father and me; helped each other out. Your mother, too, came here a lot when my parents passed away. Very kind she was, your mother."

"We left after my father died," said Thomas. "You know that?"

Thomas looked at Severin's face as the old man tightened his lips in answer to the question. The deep folds of his face were reminiscent to Thomas of a contour map, except they were constantly on the move as he thought or talked, his lower lip pouting rhythmically, turning out and then receding as his jaw moved up and down. His eyebrows worked, too, but never in unison, and his fleshy ears seemed to follow guidewires from his hollow cheeks, responding to the flow of words as he spoke.

Severin stood stationary now, his leg having stopped moving as they talked and as he came to understand who his visitor was, but his protruding lower lip kept working, in and out, pondering the turn of events. "Come on in," he said with a jostle.

Thomas ducked his head and followed the old man into a darkened cave-like room, heavy with the tang of woodsmoke, and felt himself transported into a world of Norwegian fairy tales. It was as if he had entered a troll's house, where the chimney was a rockface and the low beams of the ceiling the roots of a massive tree. Tiny windows let in hints of a refulgent world outside and tree trunks, laid one upon another, formed the walls, bastions he knew could withstand the harshest of winter storms despite their crumbling air. As he looked around, he found little to ease the eye; there was no hint of decoration which might suggest that Severin valued the finer things of life. Maybe he didn't have time; more likely he didn't care. Just some framed photographs, lit for a moment by a haze of grey light cutting through the open door, gave any sense that connections to life beyond Torsrud had ever been formed.

Severin grunted, pointing his visitor to a battered pine chair next to the woodstove, a nod and a brief smile confirming his offer. Thomas looked around. Amongst the flotsam of farming life was a dust-covered, unpainted wood settle, in the corners of which were two ragged cushions of uncertain colour, their woven patterns worn away by years of use; they were testament, Thomas thought, to welcome slumber after hard days in the fields, perhaps by more than one generation of Nordbys. But parents, brothers, sisters? It was hard to imagine them, now or at any time in the past, so powerful was the sense that Severin and Torsrud were one, made of the same stuff, that no one else had ever lived here and that this had been true since the beginning of time.

"Coffee?" Severin asked.

Thomas looked through to a small kitchen. An old, black range occupied an alcove in the far wall and on the hotplate was a black kettle, in which Thomas guessed the coffee had been simmering for hours: it would be potent stuff. Severin poured some into a cup for his guest.

The two men, surprisingly, Thomas thought, kept talking, without effort or a break, covering many subjects of common interest. At least,

Severin talked and Thomas listened, nodding and proffering the occasional question, with much agreement and ah-ing on both sides. Perhaps the conversation was a one-sided affair, but Thomas found Severin to be engaging and intelligent, quite unlike the first impressions he offered or his reputation as a mad man and a fool.

"I've been wondering," said Thomas. "Who lives at my old home now?"

"The Bell House...Brann, he's a forester. Rough kind of character, you could say. Does a bit of fishing, too; boat down on the fjord."

"And the farm? Does he keep it going?"

"Can't see how he makes a go of it, what with no animals or nothing like the Galtungs had, like we all have. I guess he lives off his wood."

By now it was early in the afternoon, still misty and very cold. Severin had shown Thomas around the fields, explaining how the stone walls — each boulder dragged from the stony ground — had been formed over the years and how lush the grass would grow in summer, fed on pig muck, cow muck, every sort of muck, all loaded up onto the cart, stored for a while in a great muckheap, then dragged around by his horse and spread with a pitchfork. The small garden grew potatoes, carrots, lettuce and a few black currants, if the birds didn't get them first.

The greatest worry in Severin's life was what would happen after he died. Who would take on the farm and keep the traditions going? He spoke of his younger sister, but had lost touch with her years ago and had no idea where she lived now; even if she were still alive. A picture of the ghostly Marta flashed into Thomas's head once more, but his rational sense could no longer sustain the ideas of childhood. Marta — it must have been her that Severin was fretting about — had simply moved away. There could be no ghost. Severin went round and round, wrapped up in worry. Just take expert advice from a lawyer, Thomas suggested, an idea Severin instantly rejected.

It was now time to go. The light was fading. Thomas offered his thanks and goodbyes once, twice, several times, but Severin kept talking, reluctant to let his visitor go. Eventually, risking an abrupt farewell, Thomas pulled his hat and anorak over his head and set off down the hill for Stensrud.

He had not gone far before he stopped. Looking up, he decided another change of weather was coming, but his mind was made up. He would take a diversion to see his old home, the Bell House.

———

The forest and the paths he once knew so well had grown over in the years since his mother had sold up and left. But he had now arrived on a rocky area, well screened from view. He pulled back a juniper branch and cleared away the snow with his boot. Smoke rose from the two-storey farmhouse, the blue haze caught and dispersed in the rising wind. Snowflakes hurried by.

The Bell House, in many ways a typical Norwegian farmhouse, had a personality of its own. Its crowning glory was a small belltower which had inspired his mother to change its old name to bring something of England to her new home after she had married and moved to Norway. The belltower, in truth, was hardly a tower; it was more a tiny house for the bell perched at the top of the gable end of the main house. Beneath a steeply sloping roof, the bell was clearly visible through the open sides of the tower. Some decorative woodwork gave the whole structure a romantic flourish in the Swiss style, perhaps chosen to celebrate a few years of good harvests or to mark its owners, long before the Galtungs, as people who had risen a little above the ordinary in their taste and appreciation of modern trends.

One tradition was revered whilst Thomas had lived at the Bell House. Twice a year, a ladder would be placed against the house and his father would polish the bell so perfectly the brass would glitter in the sun. Then, on special days, it would be Thomas's role to stand in the narrow stone enclosure in the kitchen and ring the bell for the king, or for God, or for a family birthday. Looking at the house now, he saw with sadness there was little sign of Brann keeping the tradition alive; the bell tower was in a sorry state of disrepair.

It was now late in the afternoon and little light remained. The snow-fall was now unremitting, the sky darker, the forest canopy more agitated. It was time to go, except there ran through Thomas a compulsion to be taken back to the summer of 1928, the last before tragedy struck. Then, grassy meadows, full of wildflowers and alive with bees and butterflies, supported a small herd of milking cows. A couple of pigs occupied an enclosure by the side of the barn, separated from the fields by a wooden picket fence, which still existed; he remembered helping his father to build it. A dozen chickens had wandered free, scratching around the barns and beneath the kitchen window, in the fruit bushes and under the apple trees. It was an idyll, but it was also a hard life and the family was poor; he understood that now. He missed his parents: there was no one left with whom to share memories or make plans with for the future.

Everything that was wrong went back to that night on the fjord on the 10th of April 1929. If his father had not been caught up in the nets and dragged down by the heavy weights, then the family would still be at the Bell House. If he, Thomas, had been quicker — had jammed the ropes somehow, had grabbed his father's outstretched hand as he had toppled overboard, had been strong enough to pull the nets back in — everything would be different. His mother might still be alive, too, spared the hardship of trying to make a new life in her native Cornwall during the worst of the depression years.

As he turned to go, a figure emerged from the house, faint and blurred, leaning into the wind as he made his way towards the wood-store. This must be Brann, the man who had bought the Bell House. It had been terrible timing for his mother: a forced sale at the beginning of the depression. But at least it had sold and mother had been so relieved to put it all behind her; happy, she said, that it would go to a good man who would keep it all going. Whether her assessment of Brann was accurate he was unsure; the bell had not been polished for years.

———

Carl met her as she stepped out of the taxi into the gently falling snow. She wore a tightly-fitting jacket with a fur collar, which he especially liked. He helped her over the icy kerb, and they embraced. Tingling, he knew for sure he had fallen in love with Klara Holmbekk. It was both the most exciting development of his life and the most stupid lack of self-control he could imagine.

"I've missed you so much," she said, and they locked eyes, then kissed, oblivious to the crowds of people all around.

For several months they had met in secret in Oslo, for dinner and, often, a visit to a jazz club. It was a risk for her to be seen here, with no chaperone, and it was a risk for him, too, the more so now if Galtung was indeed the new English Spy; it had seemed almost certain at first, but now...he was far from sure.

These worries Carl would set aside for now: they had arrived at Kaba, one of Oslo's best jazz venues, to dine and to hear Svein Øvergaard's orchestra.

"Here's your ticket," he said, handing it to her and then, laughing, shoving it back in his jacket pocket. "I know Svein; we don't need tickets." She laughed, too, and Carl felt an uncontrollable urge to kiss her again, the most beautiful and beguiling woman he had ever known.

"We've seen him before," said Klara, her slender fingers combing through his hair to brush away the light coating of snow. "On the drums, wasn't he?"

"With the Funny Boys, yes. He's the best; but he's on the sax tonight." He looked at her, wondering how deep her warmth towards him really was, whether she was in love with him or whether she was simply a carefree girl enjoying the thrilling city life an older man could offer. It was impossible to know and, equally, impossible to let go.

Arm in arm, they stepped into the thrilling world of Kaba.

SIXTEEN

Following the usual search as he left the vaults, Matthias headed for Berkowitz Mynthandel, struggling through the blizzard which had subsumed the city since the morning. The Victoria Young Head with the interesting flaw should be worth at least two standard bullion coins. In two days, two gold coins would be turned into five. Two of these would go back into the vaults, leaving a profit of three. It was not theft, either legally or morally, Matthias was clear on that; not a single gram was missing from Norway's gold vaults.

Matthias had now accumulated twenty of the world's rarest and best condition gold sovereigns for his collection at home. These he would never sell. In addition, over the past few years, he had accumulated over two hundred standard sovereigns which, despite seeing their brethren every day in the vaults, gave him immense pleasure, simply because they were his, and they had a purpose. These coins had a value sufficient to buy back the top field from Christian, giving him the chance to rebuild the inheritance lost by his father; to put things right.

The fences defining the small fields around Monsbu were buried by snow, just a few scattered posts appearing where the wind had funnelled through the forest breaks to create sweeping valleys and hollows. Matthias looked out from his family home and today he was grateful. In winter, like everywhere around here, the tracks would be blocked in the worst of the weather, and it would be hard work for the horses and men to clear them. But the snow was even deeper higher up. Monsbu was not a bad spot...especially if the original land could be restored to him.

"You seem out of sorts, love; distracted," said Lisbeth, as Matthias returned inside. After fourteen years of marriage she still looked with admiration at her husband.

"No, no, not at all."

"You are. We women know when our men are not happy."

Matthias pursed his lips; it was true, he was unsettled.

"I wish I could help, darling," she said.

"There's something on my mind," he responded, almost in a whisper. Never would Matthias normally express his inner worries, not even to Lisbeth, but today he'd decided to share the truth. "You know I'm working in the vaults," he said, "checking the registers and so on?"

"Yes, how interesting."

"I want to talk about it."

"Very well, darling. Let me sit down."

Matthias clasped his wife's hands and looked at her longingly. "It's seeing Christian again before Christmas," he said, feeling more despair and frustration than he ever had before, "sitting there in his great, bloody castle. My own cousin. It always brings it back to me, the injustice of it all. And it'll be Klara who inherits it all from him. Our boys will get nothing. And so it will go on."

"I know, it's wrong, it's unfair. But we can't rewrite the story, love. It's how it will be."

"We were left with almost nothing. The farmland around Monsbu, our forest, the loveliest of all the ice lakes. All gone."

"Your father was young, it wasn't his fault. There were hard times then. Many lost everything."

"No, it was the alcohol and the gambling," said Matthias. "He ruined it all."

"But it's more than that, isn't it, my love?" said Lisbeth, quietly. "Something else?"

"It was Christian's father who bought it all from Pappa," shouted Matthias, shaking with anger. "So Christian's family is even richer now. Go back another generation and Christian's grandfather did exactly the same...with the port, the harbour buildings, the ice lakes and all that forest owned by Agnes's father when the ice business went bust."

"That was a long time ago and it was nobody's fault," said Lisbeth. "All the ice businesses closed down then. And at least we have Monsbu, the house, the garden; a little grass, too.

"No, they just sat there, waiting like vultures. The grandfather, then the father buying up the rest of the family, then Christian holding on to it all, just counting the money. My bloody cousin lording over everything whilst we sit here barely getting by."

"But they bought everything, Matthias; they didn't steal it."

"Yes, because no one else could possibly afford it. They bought it all, in both cases, for almost nothing. And look now what it's all worth. A fortune."

"But they saved Monsbu," said Lisbeth. "And that lovely villa, Furuly, by the fjord, for Agnes. The properties are all still in the family because of what they did. With their own money, they saved us."

"I know, I know, but it's still theft. One branch of the family sucking dry the others."

"What do you want, my love?" said Lisbeth, whispering. "What can we do?"

"I want to take us back to where Pappa started, to our family's true inheritance, to be able to buy it all back." Matthias stood up, snatching himself away from Lisbeth. He was looking for something to kick and she frustrated him beyond measure when she tried to be fair to Christian.

"Of course, but it's not possible. We could never afford it."

"That's not true," he said. "Through my hands there passes each day more wealth in gold than you could imagine."

"But it's not ours."

"If just a small part of it were to be..."

"But Matthias..." she said, grasping his shoulders.

"There is a way," he said. "And I've already begun."

"Matthias, you would never...."

"No, Lisbeth. Not theft."

"Matthias...?"

He smiled. "It's genius..."

———

It took barely five minutes for Klara to walk from the Castle to the Holmbekk Estates Office, comprising two ground-floor rooms in a red-painted timber building at the home farm. It was run by Henrik Birkrem, who had held the post of Estates Manager for as long as Klara could remember. He never needed much encouragement to talk about his domain to the pretty daughter of Christian Holmbekk.

"Twenty-five residential," said Birkrem, with no more than a few pleasantries needed to set him going on Klara's scheme. "Plus commercial, moorings, fishing rights, the quarry; lots to keep us busy. Gunnar, too, always busy." He glanced at his young, ruddy-faced clerk by way of introduction. "Brave warrior," he added with a smirk, "that's what Gunnar means."

Klara smiled, turning towards him. "You keep the records, Gunnar?"

"Yes, Miss." He flushed even redder.

"Residential, commercial?"

"All of them, Miss."

"Very good," she said, "and how many new tenancies do you set up in a year, Gunnar? Residential, for example."

"Three last year, Miss," said Gunnar, his head dropping back into the ledgers.

Klara knew from the bustle in the corner of her eye that the Estates Manager was about to intervene, unwilling to allow any more light to shine on his junior employee.

"Lots of other property work, mind you, with the existing tenants," Birkram said. "Always something to be done, there is. Repairs, building works..."

"And chasing payments, I guess?" said Klara.

"Top priority, getting the money in," the Estates Manager said. "We were worried for a while about Haugen, though. Evasive, he was; we never even resolved his last address. Took a flat by the harbour back in the autumn, then he just disappeared."

"Disappeared?" said Klara, with a little more shock than she had intended to convey.

"One day he was there, on the boats. The Harbourmaster saw him, down on the quay. Next day he was gone. Never seen again."

"What happened to him?"

"Probably did a runner," said Birkrem. "Saw our Gunnar here and... well, he scooted. But don't worry, Miss Klara. He's all paid up and we have a new tenant lined up for the flat, haven't we, Gunnar?"

"From next week, sir," said Gunnar.

"Excellent," said Klara, firmly. "On top of everything as ever. And the latest tenant on your list, who would that be?"

"Thomas Galtung, a student. He's taken Stensrud; it'd been empty for a while, so we're very pleased."

"Excellent. And who pays his rent?"

"Three months deposit and first month's rent were paid by Jesus College, Oxford, commencing 1st of December. Nice and safe...in the bank."

"That's odd, his rent paid from England," said Klara, aware she was again testing the boundaries she had set on her recruitment.

"We thought the same, Miss Klara," said Birkram, "but subsequent payments will all be made by the Geology Department of the University of Oslo. All tied up in the contract."

"Nothing out of place, then?"

"All shipshape, Miss Klara," said Birkram.

———

In front of Thomas lay a thick book: *Die Alpen im Eiszeitalter* by Penck and Brückner, written in 1909. No progress had been made since these two researchers had proposed four distinct glacial episodes based on evidence from river terraces on the Danube. "Thirty years ago," puffed Thomas, "and no progress since."

A letter in the morning's post changed everything. He ripped open the envelope and walked slowly across the room, the missive held tightly in both hands. It was from Milutin Milankovitch, a Serbian researcher who was developing ideas about how eccentricities in the earth's orbit could cause cycles in the amount of sunlight reaching Earth. This, he suggested, could induce fluctuations in climate.

"And therefore multiple ice ages," said Thomas, his mind drifting to his new study site — 'over the hill', as Biggeloe had put it. Two layers of permanently wet peat with well-preserved pollen were apparently sandwiched between deep layers of glacial clay from a cold climate. It was a research opportunity even more valuable than Edgington's river terraces on the Upper Thames and, most exciting of all, a deposit consistent with the theory proposed by Milankovitch.

He thought about the end of winter when, in an unlikely perfect world, he would start work in the field. For now, tucked away in his cabin below the wooded crag, the woodstove gently crackling, he had completed a good part of his mission for Biggeloe and felt no need to do too much more — just another dead drop and, perhaps, follow up on Nordic Trading if the opportunity arose. Be a student, act like one...and stay alive.

SEVENTEEN

A grey pall glowered over the lightless, frozen forest. Thomas trudged through wind-sculpted snow towards Torsrud. "I've brought you something," he said, removing his skis and leaning them against the wall inside the outer porch.

"And what would that be?" said Severin.

"Here," said Thomas. He opened up his rucksack to reveal several silver-barked birch logs. "It would have made a nice present for Christmas, but I didn't know you then."

"Ah," said Severin, nodding and slowly sweeping snow off the shovel with the back of his gloved hand: it was his way of acknowledging the gift.

It had been an afterthought. The idea of logs he had split himself came to Thomas just as he'd closed the door at Stensrud. Now, he saw on Severin's face what it meant. Perhaps the poor man had not received a gift of any sort for years. Perhaps logs, especially in this freezing winter, for a man who lived a simple life so high up, were the perfect way of expressing friendship.

Inside, Severin offered coffee, still intensely strong and bitter, from his black kettle. The roof creaked and a candle on the stone mantlepiece, set amid years of accumulated lava-flows of wax, sent a flickering light onto the old man's face.

"I've been thinking about your father," said Severin. "He used to sit there, where you are now."

Thomas ran his hand over the armrest, feeling the curve of wood smoothed by touch over many years. "He always spoke well of you, Severin." In the background the BBC's beeps sounded. "You follow the war?"

"Aha. Not that I can do much about it. Big fighting in Finland, sad to say." He was silent for a while, then added, "You won't know this, but it's true."

"What's that?"

"I was a King's Guard when I was your age. I was there the day King Haakon the seventh was crowned, at the Palace. June 1906 it was and I was just twenty. *Everything for the King*: that's what we sang."

Thomas realised at that moment that Severin was not as ancient as he had assumed. Born in 1886, so only fifty-four, he thought, as he watched him rather stiffly rise to take a photograph off the wall.

"This is me," said Severin, jabbing his finger at one of the guards. Tears wetted his eyes and Thomas looked away to save embarrassing him, standing to look at the other pictures: old, dust-covered images scattered over the wall, all in black frames. Most were a set of some sort: groups of people, carefully composed, placed against backdrops of buildings, fields and forest, in their places of work, in the town, in the countryside. He now realised why Severin's photographs had lurked in his mind since his first visit. They were a possible thread back to his own family, a connection through time and in the landscape.

He looked at the photographs again. They must have been taken locally. Nowhere, in the meagre possessions Thomas had inherited when his mother had died, were there any photographs, family trees or letters related to family history. Nothing, except for that one picture of his parents and the young Thomas from early 1929.

Maybe Severin could help reveal that world? Who were the people in his photographs? Where were they taken? And could his parents be there, somewhere?

"They came from *Amta*," said Severin from over Thomas's shoulder. "They were running a series about local scenes, people, events. One old photograph a week, after the births and deaths page, I think. '*Around Drøbak*' they called it. All sorts of family groups, staff in the big houses, some businesses, main street in town, the quay."

"So what started it, your interest?"

"Me sister. Here she is. They named all the people, see." He reached up and lifted a small photograph off a tack on the wall, revealing what looked like decades of accumulated cobwebs and dust.

"Marta Nordby, it says. Marta, what a lovely name," said Thomas, studying the photograph. "You mentioned her last time."

"This is the only picture I have of her," said Severin. "There she was, in the paper," he said, pointing at a neatly-dressed girl in a group of what looked like cooks, gardeners, a butler and maids. He turned the photograph over. "The date, look."

Thomas took the photograph from him and held it by the window. "1915, two years before I was born."

"That's it, 1915," said Severin. She was fifteen then. Recognise the building?"

"Of course. It's the Castle," said Thomas.

"That's it."

"She worked there, for the Holmbekks?"

"A maid she was. She left here when she was fourteen. Never saw her again."

"What do you mean?"

"Must have thought she was up in the world, working for the Holmbekks. We all would, I suppose, but she never came back. Just disappeared she did."

Severin seemed to drift away as he spoke of his sister. He was silent for a long time, looking at the photograph. The fire settled and a short burst of flame hissed out of a glowing pine log. "Thomas," he said.

"Severin?"

"My little sister, Marta," said Severin. "I'm older now. I think about her."

"You would, Severin. It's natural."

"I mean, I don't know where she is. She's all I have."

They stopped talking again. The building creaked and exhaled the sounds of time. Thomas could almost see Severin's mind drifting, allowing Torsrud to fill the silence, as if it were alive, like all these old farmsteads. It was as if their constituent parts were talking to each other, drawing on the toil of the past and on the landscape and the seasons, the storms and the rain and the sun. For sure, thought Thomas, the ghost story of Marta could be laid to rest: she had just gone away to work...at the Castle and, later, would probably have moved on again.

"I visited the Bell House after I left you last time," said Thomas, conscious he hadn't followed up on Marta.

"You didn't?" said Severin, a hint of alarm in his voice.

"Oh, no, not to knock on the door, I just looked from the forest. I saw Brann; it must have been him."

"Huh," said Severin. "Be careful, that's what I would say. Wouldn't trust him as far as I could throw him. Not that I could throw him; built like an ox, he is."

"Well, I'll remember not to cross him." Thomas thought for a moment. "Long, black curly hair?"

"That'll be him."

"A forester, you said?"

"Yuh."

"Well, it must have been him I met, a month ago, up on the ridge-line. Huge man."

"Be careful, that's what I would say, though in truth I don't really know him." Severin shrugged. "We shouldn't always believe rumours, should we?"

The day was short and light was beginning to fade; it was time for Thomas to leave. He said goodbye several times, taking a few steps towards the door each time, Severin always delaying his departure. Some while later Thomas managed to reach the little outer porch.

"Thomas," said Severin.

"Mmm?"

"You, you're clever. A student. You work things out."

"What do you mean?"

"I knew your father; he was a kind man. You're his lad. You're educated. I mean...you'd find her, Marta. Find out what happened. It's been near twenty-five years since she went. All I know is she left the Castle long before these pictures came out in Amta. She just...vanished."

Thomas thought back to the photograph: a group of people on the steps leading up to the main entrance of the Castle. Sitting, a little on her own, was Marta, neatly-dressed as a maid, her hair drawn up beneath a white bonnet. And, at the back of the group, standing at the top of the steps, was Christian, a younger man then, at ease, heir to the great house. And, close by, his parents, now both dead.

"I'm a geologist, Severin. I am not sure where I'd start."

"Maybe you could try?"

"Let me think about it."

Thomas turned to go again and Severin called out. "Thomas."

"Severin?"

"There's no company for you down there at Stensrud," he said, looking down, shuffling his feet.

"Never mind, you get used to it when you're on your own."

"Well, stay here at Torsrud a couple of days. We can keep each other company. I have some pork, plenty of potatoes...a few bottles of Mack. We can celebrate together, a late New Year party."

Thomas stopped for a moment. "Why not? Thank you. Actually, I do sometimes feel lonely. And I enjoy it here."

"Hereabouts; this is where you belong, that's why," said Severin, as if he was stating the most obvious fact in the world.

———

"What about the police?" The possibility of a new police agent dedicated to identifying foreign spies had gnawed at Westervik's peace of mind since the meeting with von Elverfeldt.

"You'll like this," said Brann. "I've got a cousin, of sorts; a bit distant, but I call her cousin. Cleans the station, she does. Been working there for years and knows 'em all."

"Anyone new?"

"No. All been there since the beginning of time. If they have an agent looking for us, he ain't based there."

There was still a niggle. A Norwegian police operation could use

Oslo or somewhere else as their base, or recruit from outside the police force. Westervik hated the feeling of uncertainty, another itch that would be hard to reach. He would certainly keep the local police agent on his agenda, but there were many pressures on his time, not least the main operation...and the constant fretting over his relationship with Klara.

"I've narrowed down Galtung's likely dead drop," he said. "There really aren't many options: it has to be somewhere he can legitimately visit on a regular basis, safely leave boot-prints in the snow and have cover where he can leave a package; it's no good if it's buried in last night's snowfall. In fact, I think there's only one option: the church and cemetery, where his father is buried. I'm having it watched."

EIGHTEEN

Matthias toiled on the Governor's plan. The government, whilst firmly maintaining Norway's stance of neutrality, had quietly authorised the Bank to make further increases in the gold reserves, mostly British sovereigns, yielding many opportunities for Matthias to find rare and unusual coins. He now brought in two flasks, each with the secret recess in the stopper. "So damn cold in here," he said to the guards, holding up the new Thermos. "Lisbeth heats one just for the milk."

It was now past the middle of January and Matthias calculated he would be able to buy back a nice block of forest, in addition to the top field. This still left many more fields and the lake, plus a lot of forest, so at the current rate he could not see how his plan to buy back the original inheritance would be possible unless the Governor's operation were to extend well into the summer, which seemed unlikely. But it was a start.

To generate usable wealth Matthias was keenly aware he would need to convert the gold bullion at home into cash. The whole venture would then be clean. This must be undertaken in small steps, to avoid suspicion. A clerk, even one with such an important position in the bank, suddenly becoming wealthy....it could risk wagging tongues. There was, however, a flaw in his plan. Such was his success that the number of gold coins was increasing much more rapidly than he could ever hope to convert into cash.

The top field, assuming Christian would sell it, would cost the equivalent of two hundred gold sovereigns. If he were to sell an average of two sovereigns a day, he would need one hundred working days, or five months. To make matters trickier, he would need several different gold dealers to swap his coins for cash without suspicion. But there were only a handful in Oslo.

Perhaps Jakob would take the lot, he thought, for a small discount and solve the problem in one day? But Jakob was an honest man, he was sure, and there may be limits to what the coin dealer could do or risk doing. He had no idea what the limits were to normal trading. Was it possible to sell fifty or even a hundred sovereigns in one trade? There was no reason why Jakob would not regard Matthias as a wealthy and respectable entrepreneur; I dress well, he thought, no different to the Governor, better on some days.

Matthias went home at the end of the week with the conundrum unresolved. He could offer to pay for the land in gold, of course, but that could raise even more questions than money in the bank. Having achieved so much, now was no time for mistakes.

———

Short days of calm, ferociously cold weather followed the heavy snowfalls of early winter, a glacial freeze penetrating every living thing. Thomas sat with his notes, distracted and restless. His professor in Oxford had slipped behind with the reading list or, more likely, had either given up altogether on his former student or had found it impossible to communicate with Norway in wartime conditions. The mysterious tutor in Oslo had faded away, too. Ingrid, on his most recent visit to Ås, had shaken her head and was unable to help; no new reading material had arrived at the library. If this carried on, Thomas would not see her again, an even deeper loss than the dwindling momentum of his doctorate research. But Ingrid was just a fantasy, he told himself: impossibly attractive, too far away...and probably, he concluded, soon to be engaged to a wealthy property owner.

The following day, spurred into action by his own lack of initiative and bravery since the Kopås incident, he decided to tie up some loose ends on his mission. He should better understand the role of the Husvik battery, a small artillery position on Storgaten and seemingly part of the line of defensive structures across the fjord. It would be safe enough; Husvik sat by the side of the road close to the fjord.

The final descent to Husvik was over a low, jagged cliff which dropped onto a track extending north from Storgaten. He removed his skis and climbed down. As he reached the track, he noticed a man walking towards him dressed in a long wolfskin coat. The wolf-man half raised his hand in greeting. "Olaf Backer," he said, as Thomas took in his weathered face, well-furnished in a dense white beard. Bright blue eyes, a broad nose, his body a little stooped and a gold ring in his right earlobe showing below his battered hat. He was every inch a Drøbak fisherman.

"Thomas Galtung."

"Join me, Thomas. I'm out to check me boat."

Following the water's edge, they passed by the Husvik battery, where two soldiers now stood, almost frozen to the spot. "Not a good place to be stationed," said Olaf. "You'd freeze to death before you ever fired off a gun. But it's Hallangspollen I'm headed for."

"I used to fish in the fjord, just there," said Thomas, offering a flick of his head as a guide.

"Good, we've something in common, then," said Olaf. "I'm always up for chatting, about fishing, that is."

Where the track ended, a narrow path ran on in deep snow. Before long they came to the two islands guarding the entrance to Hallangspollen, the secretive branch of the main fjord which seemed to have become important again in Thomas's life.

"Skarholmen," said Olaf, looking to the outer island. "The other one, that's Gyltenholmen. Like a brother and sister you could say." They stopped to take in the view.

"Yes," said Thomas, "this is where we fished: at the mouth of Hallangspollen and out on the main fjord."

"Well, see the harbour there, on the tip of Skarholmen?" said Olaf. Thomas followed his arm to the outer tip of the island. Facing the island fortress of Oscarsborg was a stone seawall, shaped like a shepherd's crook, and enclosing a small harbour. "There's no ice in that harbour," said Olaf, "even now, even when the waters nearby are icing up. D'you know why it doesn't freeze?"

"I've no idea."

"There's a current," said Olaf, his hand spiralling up. "It brings water from an undersea spring to the surface there. In my lifetime it's never frozen. The whole of Hallanspollen, that can freeze, but not that tip of Skarholmen, even though the water's not that deep just there."

There must be doubt as to how an underwater spring could keep the harbour from freezing, but Thomas stopped himself from challenging Olaf's theory. It was a nice story.

Soon they arrived at Olaf's boathouse. The fisherman dragged open the doors and pulled a canvas cover off his boat.

"I've been ill for a while," he said. "The roof leaks and I was afraid water might have got in and iced her up."

"She looks alright to me," said Thomas, checking inside the boat and underneath to make sure she wasn't sitting in water under the keel. "We had a similar one, a clinker-built fjord boat, not far from here."

"Galtung, you say your name was?" Olaf lifted his bearded chin. "You must be his son? Gudmund's boy?"

Thomas nodded.

"You grew up with boats, then," said Olaf, closing the boathouse doors.

"I suppose so, yes," said Thomas. "And I'm working with boats again at the Holmbekk boatworks; engines mostly."

"You've done well to find work," said Olaf, as they looked out over Hallangspollen, already frozen over like an expanse of the Arctic. For a while, they were both silent and still, as if held in a block of frozen air. Then Olaf said, quietly: "You were with him that day?"

"It's hard to talk about," said Thomas, his eyes suddenly wet. "I'm sorry, crying like a baby. It's coming here again that's doing it. You know, I never went back to his grave after it happened. I was scared he would reject me."

"Of course he wouldn't," said Olaf, kindly.

"I should have saved him."

"It was an accident, everyone said so."

"No. It was my fault," whispered Thomas. "I just froze when it happened."

"You were just a lad."

Thomas looked out across the ice to the dark water of the main fjord beyond. "It's like a film clip in my head," said Thomas, "played over and over, and each time I want it to have a different ending. I miss Father in my life. Mother, too. I've no family left, you see."

———

Klara reached the top of the hill, breathless. Removing her skis, she waited until Carl emerged from a nearby copse of birch trees. She took a couple of steps through the deep snow and stopped, falling towards him and wrapping her arms around his shoulders. She then lifted herself up and they met in a deep, lingering kiss. He ran his fingers through her hair and she trembled, as she always did. She knew she had fallen in love. She had tried restraint, to not care too much, to suppress the feelings coursing through her. Perhaps she had always known it would be useless to resist, ever since they first met. His ski poles fell and she felt his arms wrap around her, drawing her tight. His hand was inside her pullover, her blouse, his strong fingers against her skin, running up the knots of her spine. She could smell him against the pure frozen air, a trace from the last time they met in the forest.

"It's so difficult for me to be here, alone," she said.

He pulled away and looked her in the eyes. "Nothing is impossible, Klara," he said. "The world is changing."

"Not my world," she said.

"One day, then. Let me into your world. Let me meet your friends, your family."

"I don't know, Carl," she said. "But I do know I must go now. Father will already be pacing."

"He can't control your life like this."

"You don't understand. I'm here, in secret, without a chaperone.

Father's terribly wary if men take an interest in me." She kissed him again and turned to leave, following the route she had taken from home, skiing hard through a drift of trees until there, above her on its rocky hill, was the Castle. Alone on the balcony, her father was waiting.

NINETEEN

Klara had known Egil Alvestad, the harbourmaster, since she was a child. Standing on the quay, they scanned the still expanse of water, the colour of pewter, already succumbing to ice spreading out from the shallows. A coaster made its way slowly up the fjord, its engines beating a dull, throbbing rhythm. A solitary gull wheeled overhead. Later, the wash from the coaster splashed against the quay, breaking up the thin ice into glassy fragments tossed around in the waves. Towards the Narrows, the mist drifted, like a veil, cloaking the fortress so that only the wooded hilltop remained visible, its flagpole standing proud like the mast of a ship.

After walking the length of the quay, they arrived at a small shed, painted green. A year ago, Christian Holmbekk had commissioned the restoration of his 32' launch, *Terne*, and Klara was keen to view progress, her father having planned to gift the boat to her. She climbed the ladder and peered inside, running her hand alongside her newly painted beam. It was hard not to admire the skills required to restore a boat.

"Ready for the spring," said Egil, sounding strangely confident. It was his primary fault: wanting to please to the extent that it clouded his judgement.

"We can only hope there will be no war in Norway," said Klara. "But I hear tittle-tattle: spies, here on the fjord."

"There's rumours, yes," he said, dismissively. "Spies, working as fishermen, in shipping and so on, but I haven't seen 'em. There's even a story of troops holed up in ships, waiting for the order, moored here in Drøbak, ready to jump out and kill us all when the time comes. Ridiculous!"

"We have German ships here, don't we?" asked Klara.

"Fewer now, what with the war — but the regulars, they keep going, although...well, there's fewer of them too. Only *Martina*, really, though she's not here so often."

"Maybe we have to do more to generate new business," said Klara. "I've been talking to Father about the little harbour at Skarholmen. It's not used anymore. The harbour should have a purpose again, like it used to in the old days when we exported ice to England.

"What's on your mind?" said Egil, looking at her quizzically.

"What if we make a small start with *Terne*? When she's finished I'd like to base her at Skarholmen, clear out the shed and make it all ship-shape. I hope you'll be able to help?"

"It will be a privilege, Klara."

"Then," she said, "in time, if things work out well, I thought we might develop the harbour for other pleasure boats. You see it starting in Oslo, but a few people in Drøbak also now have boats, and I think it'll be a trend, more and more. It would be another source of income.'

"And Egil," she said as she was leaving, "it's interesting, seeing *Terne* being restored. I'd like to see how it's done, come down again and learn more about what goes on in the harbour."

———

Two days after meeting Olaf, Thomas returned to Husvik battery and made a few notes, which would be deposited in the dead drop in due course, though there was little to say. On his return trip he stopped to buy a few supplies from Svensen's, keen to enlighten the sceptical shopkeeper that the ice ages could be studied without Drøbak being buried beneath an ice cap and, hopefully, kill any stories of doubt that might be spreading about his own status as a student.

"So you really are a student?" Svensen said, seemingly surprised.

"Of course. My superviser's in Oslo and I use the geology library in Ås." He waved Ingrid's library card, as he liked to think of it.

"Superviser? You need a superviser?"

"All research students have a superviser," said Thomas. "I'll be seeing him soon, a professor in Oslo. Anything you want there, just let me know."

Heading back to Stensrud, he approached the ridgeline and, as he reached the top, he saw two figures silhouetted against the skyline: Klara and, with her, a man he had not seen before. She waved as he pushed up a steep bank of snow.

"This is Carl," said Klara, glancing at her companion and touching his arm. She looked at him with a glow and a smile on her face. Thomas knew instantly she was in love with him.

"Carl, Carl Westervik," the man said, introducing himself with a vigorous handshake. A fluent, confident voice; tall, formidable, at least ten years older than her or himself.

Klara pressed up against him and said: "This is Thomas Galtung, an old friend...and a very good skier!"

"No longer, sadly," said Thomas, feeling a warm glow at how Klara had chosen to introduce him. He almost wanted to thank her.

"Good to have met you," said Carl. "I hope we'll meet again."

Thomas watched them slip off a steep edge towards the fjord and disappear into the trees. "Carl Westervik," he whispered. So, this was him: the well-liked member of the Drøbak Men's Club according to Svensen; lived 'out east' at a place called Bergholt; boss of Nordic Trading. And...Klara's lover, he was sure, conscious of an unjustified flash of jealousy rippling through him.

———

The snow had returned, falling soundlessly through the darkness and burying Stensrud so the windows barely let in the morning light. The grey assassin still hung like a heavy cloud over every minute of Thomas's life, his only defence his identity as a student and the avoidance of any more adventures. He pondered again about using the gabby Svensen to spread, to anyone interested, gossip about the student's dedication to his eccentric research and, with some enthusiasm, he began to concoct the idea of decoy days in Oslo in the form of sham meetings with his supervisor and time spent in the library.

At the same time, the idea of an escape to Sweden began to settle in his mind, the best opportunity being an approach to Carl Westervik and his Swedish company, Nordic Trading. He would use the connection he had established to apply for a job.

TWENTY

Smoke drifted up from the chimney: Severin was at home. He mostly was, of course.

"Severin," said Thomas, as he settled into his chair, "I've been thinking about Marta."

"Ah?"

"She was born in 1900?"

"Yes, 1900. A good year."

"It was a good year. Do you have her birth certificate?"

Severin's brow furrowed and his hand shot to his chin, massaging it furiously.

"Would your mother have had it, perhaps?

Severin's eyes lit up. "Yuh, she had a drawer with things like that." He jumped out of his chair as if he had sat on a mouse and stomped up the stairs. A few minutes passed and he returned, brandishing a brown-coloured folder, which he passed to Thomas in a state of high excitement.

"Here we are," said Thomas. "Marta Lovisa Nordby. Born 21st of May 1900, registered in Frogn Church."

"That's where we went to church," said Severin, electrified.

"Good," said Thomas. "What I'll do is check in the church records to see she hasn't died, which I'm sure she won't have, but we need to be certain. Then, all we have to do is find her."

"How're you going do that? Find her?"

"I could start with the Holmbekks."

"You know 'em?"

"Yes."

"You do! How d'ya do that?"

"I have no idea, Severin, it just happened. When I was a boy — they used to invite me."

"Well, I'll be damned. The richest family for miles around, and you're in cahoots with 'em."

"Hardly cahoots," said Thomas with a short laugh, "but I'll try; speak to them about Marta I mean, when the time is right."

"But she was there! She was in that picture. At the Castle."

"She was. It'll be a start."

Severin sat, rolling his hands, looking at the glimmer of flames through the air vent in the stove. Thomas watched him, slumped lower in his old, worn chair, ankles crossed, in a state of fevered emotion. He could also see they were low on logs and he went to the door to collect some from the barn.

"I'll come with you," said Severin. "I need some air."

As they loaded up the log boxes, a thought came into Thomas's head. "Severin," he said, twisting to look the old man in the eyes.

"Yuh?"

"Can I ask something of you? A different subject."

"Of course."

"Say someone wanted to leave Norway now and go abroad, safely I mean, and find a job."

"Why would they do that?"

"Never mind why, just say they wanted to. They felt threatened, for example."

"And need to find somewhere safe? Where they could live?"

"Exactly."

"OK. But that's no one around here? Is it?" Severin said, turning to look at Thomas and, after a moment of silence, adding, "It's not you?"

"No, this is theoretical."

"Don't sound it t'me. Why would you ask if it wasn't you?"

"This is just an imaginary situation, Severin."

"Not in trouble are you?"

Thomas sighed. "I'm unsure, that's the problem. Best not ask."

"Right. Well, what was the question again?"

"Never mind the danger, the threats. If I had to go abroad, in secret, and not starve to death, where would I go? Sweden? What do you think?"

Severin stretched his back and kicked away a few of the wood fragments that covered the floor of the barn.

"Yes, Sweden's yer best bet. That's what it used to be; guess it still is. Train from Oslo. Or down the fjord on a boat. Or you ski to the border if you had no alternative. No problem getting there. I knew these things when I was young."

"The issue is what I do when I get there. I would need work, a place to live."

"You need a contact, don't you? Those Holmbekks of yours?"

"Maybe, but there's a company called Nordic Trading, run by Carl Westervik. It's Swedish I think but they have a Norwegian operation around here. Ever heard of them?"

Severin pursed his lips then, after gazing into the rafters, shook his head.

"Just wondered."

"But what the hell; who's after you?"

"I can't say, that's the trouble. Maybe it's all in my head; I'm imagining it all."

"Come on, we'll freeze to death out here."

They returned to the house and sank into silence again. A mouse scuttled along the end wall and a lump of snow slid off the roof and fell with a thump somewhere at the back of the house.

"Have you ever read *Hunger*?" said Thomas, leaning back into the chair, gazing into the fire, feeling its heat on his feet.

"Of course. Stays with you, that story," said Severin, his words drifting away. "*It gnawed without mercy in my chest.* That's what he said. Cold and hungry."

"Exactly."

"But I'll say this," said Severin. "If you ever need a friend, you've got one here. If you need to hide away or whatever you must do, stay here. I ask questions, I know, but I don't care really; not if there's nothing I can do about it."

Thomas stared at the stove as if it would give the answer. "You're kind," he said, eventually. "Let me go back to work something out."

"But you're in danger. What are friends for?" the old man said. "You're Gudmund's lad. We went fishing together, off Skarholmen, your father and me. You've never seen such catches. No, I'll help you. Stay here. They'll never find you here."

———

Thomas returned to Stensrud, Severin's offer lodged in his mind. It was now minus eighteen degrees, and a harsh easterly cut his face in the time it took him to check for mail from the little green mailbox. It was a surprise to receive anything at all so, after the thrill of Milankovitch's letter on cycles of sunlight, another hand-written note in a sealed envelope piqued his interest. He opened it as soon as he was back indoors.

>Dear Thomas,
>
>I spoke with the adjutant today. We need more help with the engines because of the cold. There is a job for you here, on the ferries to the fortress.
>
>Can you meet me at Sundbrygga, 0900 hours tomorrow?
>
>Your friend,
>
>Olaf Backer

Thomas fired up the stove and fell into his chair. Olaf had said nothing about a connection with the ferrymen. But finding a way into the fortress was Biggleoe's top priority. A job there could also give him greater legitimacy and that might help in reducing any lingering suspicions regarding his loyalty. Equally, as he thought it through, it might be seen suspiciously: a Brit in the heart of Norway's defences. "Who knows," he muttered.

Early the next day, Thomas made a decision, of sorts. He took the first bus into town and walked up Storgaten towards the quay at Sundbrygga. It was dark and bitterly cold. As he arrived, a ferry was waiting, engine running, with two men aboard, both armed soldiers. Another figure, an older man, stood on the quay under the light of a single lantern, waiting. It was Olaf, wearing a massive seal-skin coat, half-length boots and a thick woollen hat. He would never go cold.

Thomas looked into the blackness across the fjord, out of which a few pinpricks of light were visible on the fortress. He felt wracked by doubt, feeling himself being dragged inexorably into doing his duty and having to abandon the idea of Sweden.

"We're not military," said Olaf. We just do boats. Civilian, but subject to military orders, if that makes sense."

"Yes, I see," Thomas said. Perhaps a non-military position would excite less interest from the assassin...if he really did exist, which was beginning to feel more uncertain as time went on.

"I knew your father," said Olaf. "You've operated boats on these waters, as a young lad. You have good references from the boatworks. That swung it. We desperately need engine specialists. The pay's good. That's it."

"Olaf, it's a great opportunity, but I have a job already, and I have to study."

"The adjutant will sort out the boatworks," said Olaf. "And study, huh? There's a war on out there."

"For how long?" said Thomas. "I mean, how many weeks, or months?"

"As long as there's a threat of war."

Thomas took a few strides to look into the boat from the edge of the quay. He listened as Olaf spoke: "We need to move men and supplies from the town to the fortress, 24 hours a day. You'll be a ferryman, operating the launches, maintaining the engines, whatever's needed. But engines are number one, keeping 'em going in this devilish weather. That's what got you the job: engines."

"Between Sundbrygga and the fortress?"

"Just this route, out and back and back again, that's it."

"Very well," said Thomas. "I'll do it." A good decision or bad, he was not sure, but there was an element of adventure that took over when the moment arrived, and how could he say no to Olaf. That, and an opportunity too good to let slip.

They shook hands. Thomas looked out again towards the fortress and wondered what the future would bring. Descending the ladder he stepped into the launch and watched as Olaf cast off. As the boat powered away into the darkness, the old ferryman pulled him under the shelter of a small canvas awning.

"We start now," said Olaf.

Thomas nodded.

"One more thing. Are you a Brit or Norwegian? That's what he asked: Colonel Eriksen, the commander. One or two think you're a Brit. So they checked you out. You're one of us, they said. Norwegian. But I knew that."

They had arrived at a small quay on the northern tip of the fortress's southern island. The glow of the rising sun picked out the silhouette of the ridgeline above the town while, down to the south, a bank of mist hung over the fjord, faintly luminous in the morning light. Behind him he heard voices from a single storey wooden building, light spilling out through the windows onto the snow.

"Ferryman's hut," said Olaf. "They'll give you breakfast."

———

In the days ahead, Thomas took up his position as a mechanic and ferryman on the fortress, using his newly gained knowledge to feed two further dead drops. Working erratic hours, he shared the ferrying role with several retired fishermen from the town, but much of the specialist marine engine work fell to him. On occasions, he would spot Colonel Eriksen, the commander, often accompanied by an officer.

"Helberg, his adjutant," said Olaf. "Does the colonel's running around."

A variety of boats served the fortress. Some, the larger ones operated from Lehmanns Quay, the main harbour, and transported food, military supplies and most of the men. At Sundbrygga, the smaller quay from where he worked, there were just six launches used mostly for officers and NCOs, although at any one time only one or two boats were typically in use. On several occasions, Thomas ferried the colonel, always accompanied by two guards, often across and back again within the hour. Life became more normal, his worries more distant. "Every day I look over the fjord to where my father drowned," he said to Olaf as they stood outside the ferryman's hut. "It was an evening like tonight, very still, though not as cold."

"You're adapting, coming to terms with it," said Olaf.

"It's the opposite to what I expected," said Thomas. "But somehow...you're right, I feel closer to him. More and more, I remember the good times. Even his voice is coming back to me, the way he walked and savoured his morning coffee. I can even run a short film in my mind: us taking the path down through the forest from the Bell House to Hallangspollen."

Once again, he felt himself welling up. He turned away, pulled the glove from his hand and dragged the tears away.

"You're good for me, Olaf," he said to the old fisherman one day as they crossed the fjord. "I've forgiven myself. I even start to feel at home again."

TWENTY-ONE

A dry, lethal cold invaded Norway in the early days of February. Dragged off the frozen tundras of northern Russia and the ice-flows of the Arctic, it cut through Klara's clothes and numbed her face. The turned-up tip of her nose was coloured a bright pink. She knew the dangers of a day like this, with the temperature now below minus twenty, and falling. But she was at Lehmanns Quay for a reason. After reviewing the business in Egil's office, she checked progress on *Terne* and wandered along the quay towards a coaster, the *S/S Martina*. It was the only ship of any size now moored in the harbour. With no sign of life aboard, no loading or unloading, she headed back to the harbourmaster's office, glad to be inside again.

"Egil, that freighter?" she said, standing in front of the paraffin stove.

"*Martina*," said Egil, enthusiastically, "built 1924 by AG Weser, out of Bremen. A tramp freighter, that's what you would call her, about eight thousand deadweight tons; steams at barely 7 or 8 knots I would say."

"A plodder then?" she said. "That's such an elegant name for a battered working boat." She laughed.

"Yes, she's a plodder, as you call her. Local work, up and down the fjord, loading up, over to Germany, then back again."

"And where else would she stop?" she asked, picking up a copy of *Amta,* the local newspaper, and idly sifting through.

"Wherever there's cargo to move. Moss maybe, Frederikstad, then she's out of our jurisdiction. Sweden after that; Gothenburg probably. Then Germany." He let loose a laugh, part in humour, part a snort of disgust. "Sorry, Miss Klara, but her captain, though, he's a right one. Reckon he's got a woman hidden away somewhere in town, I do. You know what they say about sailors."

"A woman in every port?"

"Off he goes into town every few weeks when they moor up, at least, since the summer. Stays a day or two, then off again."

"The hidden goings on in sleepy Drøbak!" said Klara. "Is he really that handsome?"

Egil walked over to a filing cabinet and drew out a small file.

"Here he is. We keep records for everyone moored here."

Klara looked at the grainy passport photograph of a youngish, fair-haired man in a merchant navy roll-neck sweater. "Never seen him before!" she smiled. "If I do I'll have to watch out. What's his name?"

"Hartman," said Egil. "Günther Hartman."

Klara thanked him, telling him not to worry about the lack of business at the port ("we'll get through this somehow,") and headed towards her father's Mercedes, her mind on Hartman. As she reached the car she noticed Thomas walking towards the harbour.

"We must be mad," she said, "outside in cold like this."

"I'm wrapping up my job at your father's boatworks," he replied. "Making sure I'm paid." He laughed at his aside and waved as he headed off, shoulders hunched against the freezing air.

Klara had spotted Thomas when she visited the boatworks to see *Terne* a couple of weeks earlier, but had chosen not to speak to him. Now he was moving on after only a month, which struck her as unusual, although she quickly discovered where he was off to.

As she fired up the car, her thoughts returned to Hartman. She had seen the ship's captain, she was sure, walking away from the port towards the church when she'd arrived. That was nearly an hour ago. She decided to drive along Storgaten to the northern limit of the town. From there she proceeded on foot. There was no sign of Hartman but fresh boot-prints showed someone had walked this way, continuing along the eastern side of Hallangspollen.

Later, she stood on the beach opposite Skarholmen: her island, its stunted, twisted pine trees coated white. Beyond, as far as she could see, Hallangspollen was frozen over, a sea of ice. A light fall of snow drifted down. The boot-prints had faded away and, after a while, she gave up looking. It was too cold to be out, but she would look into Hartman and his ship if the opportunity emerged.

As she started to return, a shiver passed through her. Beyond Skarholmen's little harbour, out into the main fjord, was deep water: dark in colour now, indigo, almost black. It was there that Thomas's father had drowned. She had only met Gudmund Galtung once, when she was nine or ten-years old; he had brought Thomas to the Castle one day. It was a faint memory, of a strong, solid man, barrel-chested, a dark stubble. He had appeared at the door, greeting her as she stood by her father. A quick nod, a wordless stare of embarrassment, or maybe curiosity, then he was gone.

She thought back to her whiff of suspicion concerning Thomas. He had appeared only weeks after Britain had entered the war and shortly after another man, Peter Haugen, also half-British, had disappeared from his flat at Lehmanns. And now, he would be working at Norway's most important fortress, the key to the defence of Oslo.

———

"We are both lucky, you know that. The Holmbekk estate, stretching as far as the eye can see," said Christian. "And you, at Furuly; such a lovely house by the fjord."

"And no money. You are the only one with money, remember that," said Agnes, regretting the words as soon as they slipped out of her mouth. They had met at her insistence, at the Lookout, the octagonal folly situated at the end of a curved promenade, which was one of the joys of the Castle's garden. This was the first time they had set eyes on each other since Thomas's visit nearly two months ago. The sun, low in the sky, glowed white through a thin veil of cloud. Everywhere there was snow, a deep blanket hiding the texture of the landscape.

From the top of the Lookout, she broke the silence that had already set in.

"It's deeper up here," she said.

"What is?"

"The snow, it's deeper than by the fjord."

"It would be."

"Yes, and the snow covers secrets. Conceals history. Maybe that's it?"

"You've lost me, Agnes. Conceals what?"

"Some people and events are suppressed, even forgotten," said Agnes, already feeling nervous about her planned approach to the meeting with Christian. "Life is like the landscape in winter."

"What do you mean?"

"Can I ask, Christian?"

"What?"

"A sensitive question."

"What question?"

She sensed the tightening in Christian's voice. It always happened the moment he knew he would have to defend himself and, by softening her approach, she had let herself slide into speaking riddles.

"There are not many who know what happened," she said, sensing he now understood where she was headed. "Your parents have gone. Now it's just you and me."

"But I'm still young!" said Christian.

"Well, I'm not. If I drop dead, it'll just be you. And how will you handle it? If you wait for ever, and you go, it'll just be the letter, read out with the will."

"I suppose so."

"Can you imagine? It'll be revealed, Christian, to everyone, the family: a shot from nowhere. It'll have catastrophic consequences for the estate and, in all probability, inheritance."

"Maybe you're right," said Christian, his voice dropping to a whisper.

"Well, you need to sort it out," she said. "And I can help you, if you ask."

"But think of the upset." He held out his hands, his eyes alive and searching.

"It'll be even worse in the future...if you are not here to explain it all."

"I'll think about it," Christian replied. "I really will."

No, you won't, she thought. *No, you won't.*

———

"Met Galtung the other day," said Westervik. "Out skiing he was, up on the ridgeline."

"Gangly git, doesn't even shave yet," said Brann.

"Anything new?"

"You'll like this. He's got a new job...on the ferries to the damned fortress."

"What!" said Westervik, grasping the edge of the table with both hands and lifting himself up. "Come on..."

"Yea, out of Sundbrygga."

"That nails it; that and what I have to tell you. You're sure, though?"

"Ya. Just started."

Westervik held back his response, giving himself time to think. He was now sure that Galtung was a British agent; a replacement for Haugen. Eliminating him would ensure the British operation would be stopped in its tracks. But...but...issues remained: the Holmbekk connection and, especially, the ramifications of Galtung's childhood friendship with Klara. "We've tracked down his dead drop," he said. "It was right where I said it would be, in the church, and the signal is a turn of a finial on the Hansen enclosure."

"Good one, boss. What's he say, then, in the dead drop?"

"Nothing of value, as I guessed. He's not been here long, he barely leaves his cabin and he has no associations with anyone, except he sees Mad Nordby, who can't possibly know a thing. But now...now he's at the fortress, it changes things."

"Bloody well does..."

"But...I'm still not sure. Remember, we can't risk anything which might knock off course the main operation. We can't have police crawling all over the place: questions, investigations. Also, if we leave him be, we can monitor his dead drop...send back disinformation to the Brits."

"Leave 'im free? Doesn't look right to me."

"If we do eliminate him, it has to be out of area, not around here, and I've got a useful lead on that, courtesy of our friend Blabbermouth Svensen."

Brann smiled at Westervik's reference to the shopkeeper, and said: "If you need me to...?"

"I know. You're my man." Westervik felt his shoulders tightening. "But just wait for now," he said. "In the meantime...a glass of your strong stuff, please...and what about the Police operation?"

"We checked around," said Brann, "and I picked up an interesting sniff."

"Aha?"

"There may be someone. We assumed it could be a man, right. Logical. But what if it wasn't. What if it were a pretty, sweet-lookin' girl?"

"How'd you work that out?"

"Sources. Wandering around town she was, down on the quay at Lehmanns, pokin' around the shipping empire, asking questions. A girl like that isn't out in this weather." A grin slowly spread across his face. "And she's not any sweet girl, either..."

Westervik was sure he could hear the man's bristles rustling. "Spit it out," he muttered.

"It's the fuckin' Holmbekk girl," Brann whooped. "That Klara thing. Yea, Klara she's called. I'm bloody sure. Well, I'm not sure, but it could be. An' wouldn't it be great if it were. One over the fuckin' Holmbekks at last. Rich bastards. All stolen it was. Stolen off ordinary working people; you don't get that rich any other way."

Westervik's body stiffened. He looked at Brann. The man just smiled, his face lined with anticipation.

"No, Brann, that's not possible. Women, even rich ones, go outside sometimes, you know. And her father owns Lehmanns, so why shouldn't she be there?" He shrugged. "But if it is her the surveillance police have recruited, which I doubt, leave it to me. Got that? I'll deal with it."

Brann's grin faded.

"And remember, the same applies to Galtung. Hands off until I say."

Twenty-Two

Thomas looked forward to seeing Severin again, already a trusted friend and his best connection to the old life. After a long slog up through the forest towards Torsrud, he leaned his skis against the wall and, responding to a loud grunt from Severin, stomped inside.

"You're shivering," Thomas said. "And the place feels damp."

"Never known it so ruddy cold," said Severin. "This freezing fog: it creeps in everywhere. Comes in off the fjord and there's no sun to burn it off. Not much hay left either. And we're going through wood like never before."

"I've brought a few candles," said Thomas, reaching into his rucksack. "At least we can make light. Some bread, too, and cheese from Svenson's. And I brought you a new wool blanket, made in Lillehammer."

"You're a kind lad, like yer father."

"We'll take the horse and sled back to Stensrud tomorrow and bring a load of wood back. I'm not using it there if I'm here, am I?" He dragged the chair closer to the woodstove. "I have a new job," he said, "with the ferries out to Oscarsborg. I stay overnight on the fortress, in the ferryman's huts near the boats, for several days on each shift. It pays

149

the same as I was earning at the boatworks, so I can keep saving a bit, although it wouldn't last long if I ever make it to Sweden."

He picked up a log. Severin nodded, and he added it to the fire. They looked at each other and smiled, and were silent for a while.

"I've also done one or two things regarding Marta," said Thomas, eventually. "I checked in the church records and with Frogn Commune. There's no record of a Marta Nordby dying. She could have married of course and changed her name, but there's no Marta of any sort on the marriage register."

"Good God, that's a relief, to finally know," said Severin. "It's been hanging over me for years."

"So, she's out there somewhere," said Thomas. "I just have to find the right moment to speak to the Holmbekks."

"We'll find her," said Severin, an enthusiasm in his voice which seemed to strip away the years. "Well, you will. You'll find her."

Severin brought in two more mugs of coffee which he laid on the floor in front of the stove. Torsrud was like the Bell House used to be when Thomas was a child: the wood smoke, the candlelight in winter, sometimes the sound of a storm outside, the short days and long evenings of winter spent talking, telling stories and passing time. He felt a tingle of optimism, a sense that here, at Torsrud, he would no longer be alone, shivering in fear at every creak in the roof timbers, tensing at every rustle of branches and whistle of the wind in the forest.

"I've been thinking about what you said, about coming here to stay," he said, looking at Severin, watching for his reaction. "Do you mean it, that I could hold out here sometimes?"

"Of course."

"People know where I am at Stensrud, that's the trouble."

"They'll never find you here, up in the forest."

"Hopefully not," said Thomas, "not for a while, at least. And remember, I have to work on the ferries and I may be away for my studies...in Oslo, so anything you want, let me know." A sigh of relief escaped, and he almost apologised.

———

Too cold to venture out much, except on duty, Thomas spent long hours passing time at Torsrud in the days that followed. Severin had loaned him some Norwegian classics and he began to reread the novels of Knut Hamsun. He thought about his research, but the ambition was fading. A few snowflakes drifted down in the still air. He picked one out and followed its path until it disappeared around the corner of the house. Minutes passed. He picked up his notepad and climbed the stairs to place his research material into a cardboard box in the corner of what was once Severin's mother's room. That was it. None of the papers he had ordered had arrived at Ås and there had been no contact from either of the two professors. This really did feel like the end of his research life.

———

Westervik paced Bergholt's polished floorboards, unable to resolve the crisis which had kept him awake all night. Befriending Klara had been a great move for his mission, a step in his plan for infiltrating the highest echelons of local decision-makers. But it had all gone to hell. To let himself become close to his target was contrary to every facet of his training. To fall in love with her was potentially catastrophic.

He pulled open the thick pinewood door and looked out over snow-covered fields towards the Castle, hidden behind the forested horizon. It was one of those still, cold days with crystal clear air that usually lifted his spirits and pulled him out for a long, testing ski trip. He flicked at the snow with the toe of his boot. Maybe he didn't really love her: that would be easier. How could he separate love from infatuation, or lust? How could he know whether Brann was right in identifying her? Maybe it was no more than the big man's damned fantasy, fuelled by the prospect of taking down the Holmbekks. He could only hope Brann was wrong.

And then there was Galtung. Not only, for sure, the English Spy, but once Klara's close friend; maybe still. Hell and damnation. How messy could it get...

As he walked aimlessly back into the lobby, the telephone rang. He picked up the receiver and listened in shock at the friendly but wavering and excessively familiar voice. It was Galtung, for God's sake, seeking a job in Sweden with Nordic Trading. Both Klara and her father would provide references, he was sure. There were no jobs on offer, of course — an easy response, and that should have been the end of it, should have shut him up. But the creep was insistent. Maybe Herr Westervik had contacts who could help? Could they meet to talk further?

Westervik put the phone down with an unsteady hand, already balancing the risks. Clearly Galtung had no idea of the fire he was playing with. At least, that's how it looked: the English Spy, untrained, installed in a panic; a naïve, hopeless kid out of his depth, and probably looking to escape to a safer country. But something in Westervik's gut felt there could be other possibilities. His training had taught him to look for the less obvious: subterfuge, deceit, hidden realities. It was impossible to know, but the Brit could be closer to the main operation than it appeared, the whole hopeless spy routine no more than a charade. The risks were now too great. Galtung was too close. He clambered down the cellar steps and carefully lifted his prized Mannlicher-Schönauer rifle from a hidden recess at the back of a rather beautiful armoire; the ornate cupboard had been left by the previous owner. Too large to fit through the trap door, it must have been there since the place was built; brought from France and placed on the end wall before the floor of the main house was constructed.

TWENTY-THREE

A pall of low cloud the colour of pewter weighed heavily on Oslo. Arctic air, filled with snow, clawed at people brave or needy enough to risk showing themselves to blizzards cascading off the mountains. A dozen passengers left the bus at Kontraskjæret. Thomas, the last to step down, faltered on the lower step, looked back to the driver, nodded and then scanned the bleak city ahead. He crossed the street and slunk into the shelter of a kiosk, its roof smothered in snow.

"*Aftenposten*," he said. "Any good news?"

"Depends," said the kiosk-holder, a heavy woman, enlarged beyond parody by many layers of clothing, her sad face coloured a deep red by the cold.

"Depends on what?"

"The Altmark Incident; haven't you heard?" She jabbed her finger at the headline.

GERMAN NAVAL AUXILIARY SHIP, ALTMARK, TAKEN BY BOARDING PARTY FROM BRITISH DESTROYER.

Thomas took the paper and read on, the pages flapping angrily in the wind.

Three hundred British prisoners rescued.

"It happened in Norwegian waters," the kiosk lady said. "A fight. Brits and the Nazis."

Thomas looked out over the harbour, the islands beyond lost in the gloom. A British warship in Norwegian waters... Had the British handed to Germany the justification they sought for an invasion? Hitler could take Norway posing as her protector, to save the country from the imperial instincts of the British and to avenge the German sailors lost. A shiver ran up his spine. He glanced over his shoulder, scanning the figures hunched and heavily clad, and wondered how many of them felt as he did — that a dark peril was stalking Norway; that war was ever closer.

A half-empty tram rattled by. A young girl, her features shrouded by the iced window — just her eyes bright and clear — looked out through a melted peephole. Moments later she was gone — the girl with no name — and the rattle faded, merging into the whistling storm careering through the city. She would mention to her mother the man she had seen, his newspaper shredded in the wind as she watched, his eyes picking her out through her secret spyhole, and she might wonder, when she was older, if their paths would ever cross again and, if they did, how they would ever know they had actually met before, on the 24th of February 1940?

Turning up Tordenskiolds, his hands shielding his eyes from the stinging bullets of snow, Thomas soon arrived on Karl Johans gate, where he dodged between two black Volvos into the shelter of the high buildings. Huge banks of snow lined the street, smudged grey by dirt from the road. Nearby, he found a café and he pushed on the door. It was warm inside and opulently attired, far too grand for a student, but he was here now and a waiter was already taking his coat. Selecting a finely upholstered chair by the window, he ordered a black coffee and a cinnamon roll, and was soon drawn to the drama of Norway's finest street, framed by the great curved glass window with its ornate gold lettering: *Café Marianne est.1896*. An old woman walked by in a long brown coat, trimmed in fur, speckled white with snow on the shoulders, her handbag flailing in the wind. Then a younger couple appeared, arm in arm, staggering from side to side. A gust caught the man's hat and threw it into the window with a thud. The woman, her hair loose beneath a beret, laughed, gathered the hat for her man — he with his clipped moustache — and shoved it hard back on this head before they disappeared from the frame, his arm over her shoulders, pulling her to him, as lovers do. He could hear their shrieks against the storm as they disappeared up Karl Johans.

Taking a sip of his coffee from a black, wide-rimmed cup, glazed gold on the inside, he thought ahead to rehearsing his carefully constructed diversion into the academic world of Oslo: to the university, its corridors and libraries; to his mythical tutor in his ancient study and to the crowds of students he would mingle with, before catching the late afternoon bus back to Drøbak. He would visit them all, or at least a version of them, Svensen would lap it up: Galtung really was a student, spending days in the capital studying senseless icy worlds and drawing mad ideas from eccentric white-haired professors.

It was time to pay for his coffee. He looked to the waitress and lifted his eyebrows, pulling his wallet from the inside pocket of his jacket. He would leave a nice tip. Pushing back his chair as he rose, he felt a flash of embarrassment at the noise it made on the polished parquet floor.

"Uh," he mouthed, shrugging at a man with neatly parted grey hair and expensively finished clothes sitting alone in a booth a few steps away, working through a crossword and tapping his table with the butt of a blue-coloured pencil. The man looked up, his skin somehow younger than his hair, his lapels broader than Thomas had ever seen in Drøbak, his eyes glimmering and his ample lips quivering as he pondered the clues.

"No need to apologise," the man said, after filling in a short word on the top row. "All the chairs do that. Been like it for years." He then dropped his eyes to confront the next clue.

Thomas turned and smiled at the waitress — middle-aged, elegant, beautiful; he had only ever seen a waitress like this in films, at the cinema. She moved towards him, gracefully, like a ballet dancer and, as she handed him the bill, several coins slipped from Thomas's purse and fell to the floor with a clatter.

"Sorry," he whispered, with a flash of embarrassment, and he bent down to search in the shade of the table.

At that moment, the great window shattered with a terrible crash, fragments of glass falling over the table like a fusillade as he sunk to the floor. From the corner of his eye he saw the waitress reel back in terror, the bill floating in the air, hanging. Screams sounded from across the café. Then, a deadly stillness. He looked up. He could see the waitress sat on the floor, her eyes wide open, her face frozen with fear. Kneeling, he scanned the café. It was then he saw the crossword man. He had toppled back in his chair and was lying sprawled on the floor, a large, bloody hole in his forehead, his face broken and distorted, his grey hair streaked red.

Thomas let out a long moan, glass shards grating as he squirmed on the fine parquet floor. Snowflakes blew in from the street and floated, spinning around the tables and chairs, in front of his eyes. They dropped into the stream of blood slowly creeping towards him, and vanished.

PART THREE
OUT OF THE MIST

TWENTY-FOUR

Crawling through the chaos that Café Marianne had become, Thomas made his way to the back of the building, stopping briefly in the abandoned kitchens to wash blood from his face and hands. He found his coat, unmarked, on a toppled coat-stand which enabled him to be attired with few outward signs of the violence he had experienced and, a short time later, to climb into the Drøbak bus without the driver or anyone else being troubled.

Late that evening, he fell into a chair by the woodstove at Torsrud and shared with Severin the story of how his life would have ended, but for the broken zip through which a few coins had slipped and rolled so embarrassingly under the table. The police may conclude that the cross-word man was, for a motive never likely to be discovered, the intended target of the shooting, although there was little doubt in Thomas's mind that it was he who had come into focus in the crosshairs of the German assassin. Yet, despite weeks of intensive investigation by Oslo Police, the man who ducked under the table to recover his coins was, like the shooter, never identified.

In the days that followed, Severin cared for Thomas as if he were his own, shocked and accepting in the same breath. But, for Thomas, a deep quandary still lingered: whether it was possible to both continue with his mission and stay alive.

"Stay at the fortress," said Severin, "surrounded by the best moat in the whole of Norway."

This, he concluded — once the scars on Thomas's face had healed — would be 'a right healthy plan'. In the meantime, he pressed Thomas to stay on at Torsrud. The deadly cold easterlies, held there on the compass point as if commandeered by a great malevolent force, would become their ally. No one would be out in the forest, lying in wait with their rifle, in conditions like this.

And so the days passed, February slipping into March with the tundra, far away in Russia, providing a seemingly endless supply of icy wind which, as Severin had counselled, kept the enemy at bay.

When the day came to leave Torsrud, Thomas and Severin embraced. They stood by the window looking out onto a landscape still as frozen and white as it had been for many weeks. A row of icicles lined up like glistening daggers under the eaves as Thomas set off for the fortress after, as he would report to Olaf, a really quite nasty bout of the flu.

———

At the Castle, the staff laboured to keep the cavernous Great Hall warm. Klara sensed a grinding malaise in her father, a despair he did his best to hide, but she was gradually earning his trust and today had manoeuvred him into revealing the truth about the estate's business. "Norway might be neutral," said Christian, "but half the rest of Europe is at war, or soon will be, and the seas are no longer safe. Our export markets have crashed. You've seen it yourself, Klara, at the port. We have finished timber and seasonal farm products that we can't move on. We have bad debts from abroad and longer settlement times. Cash is drying up; the downturn's running through everything. It affects tenants, too, so I worry they won't keep up with rental payments."

"And we have staff with no productive work," said Klara.

"Many of whom have been with us for generations. You know how loyal they are..."

Klara sensed a picture which felt terminal and that her father had run out of both ideas and energy. It frightened her and it sat uneasily with her lifelong belief that any adversity could be overcome by the will to succeed. "Can we try again to clear unsold stock?" she said. "What can I do?"

He shrugged. "Why not try that friend you mentioned the other day? The potato merchant?"

"Carl?"

"Invite him to the party. We often complete a few deals as the evening wears on...but I can't see it happening this year."

———

The Holmbekk's winter cocktail party was fixed into the social calendar. Thomas had, for reasons he could not deduce, been invited and despite his misgivings, he decided to accept. There was talk at the Castle that the war might dampen gatherings of this sort and, if not that, then an untimely snowstorm or the dangerously cold weather. But they were lucky and, on the day, guests made their way up the spiralling drive amongst the trees, couple by couple, in fine limousines, and were greeted in the spectacular setting of the Castle by Christian and Sigrid Holmbekk. The flickering light from hundreds of candles, the roar and crackle of log fires, ample food and drink and smartly-attired staff all conveyed a message that, despite the war, all was well with the Holmbekk family.

As the evening progressed, Thomas wandered nervously from room to room, finding himself unable to join any of the tightly-knit groups which had formed, all in animated discussions with no gaps that invited anyone new. He spotted Klara and Carl in discussion with Christian and watched the arrival of Colonel Eriksen with his wife, son and two daughters. Soon after, Chief Constable Paul Sandvik strode in and was immediately sucked into a high-spirited group gathered under the head of a huge elk high on the end wall of the Great Hall. Everyone except the family was unknown and all were expensively dressed. It was like a reunion of an exclusive club, of which he was not a member.

There was relief, of sorts, when Christian took his arm. "Thomas, let me introduce you to Jon Sundby. He's a farmer from near here, at

Vestby; a former government minister and still," he added with a glance at Matthias, "a board member of Norges Bank."

Sundby, it transpired, was the first person outside academia keen to hear about Thomas's research, and he had his own theories about the impacts of volcanic activity, water disturbance by shipping and the burning of fossil fuels on the climate. "All very exotic, I'll give you that," he said, "but look into them and let me know what you find."

On several occasions, Thomas had spotted Klara, working her way through the guests with Carl in close proximity. Now she picked him out and said: "Thomas, you remember Carl?"

"Of course. We met at Steinborg," said Thomas, greeting Carl with a firm handshake. "My apologies," he said, "for bothering you about a job. It was rather out of the blue, but maybe we could meet up some time?"

"I'm sure he would help," said Klara, as she took Carl's arm and steered him towards Jon Sundby. "Politically, he's the best-connected farmer in Norway," she whispered.

Late in the evening, Thomas found Christian sat by the fire in the Great Hall with his youngest daughter, Katrine. "Time for bed," Christian said to her. "It's terribly late."

Thomas for a moment studied Christian, sat comfortably into a high-backed chair facing the huge open fireplace. He wondered again why he had been selected to be a friend of such a great and wealthy family. Perhaps it was guilt that Christian felt: that the Holmbekks had inherited such wealth when so many lived in near poverty, scraping a living from a few scraps of grass up in the forest. Or, perhaps it was that Thomas, a good sportsman as a child, had been chosen as a skiing companion for Klara and had become embedded for a while in the family, like Toni, their maid. Who knows? Yet Christian was, as always, kind and hospitable, and here he was taking time to speak with a penniless student.

"Thomas, I've got you to myself at last. Find yourself a brandy." Christian nodded to a walnut side-table where a large array of bottles were carefully arranged. Thomas's hand hovered over them. "To the right, yes, that one," said Christian. "And have a cigarette."

"I don't smoke, thank you, just the odd pipe. But I've never seen anything like this."

"I'll bet it was just as happy at the Bell House?"

"It was, yes, in its own way."

"I'm very glad," said Christian.

It was now late. Most guests had left and the house was silent, just the crunching of burned-out logs settling in the fireplace. Thomas glanced again around the Great Hall, its walls rising like a cathedral into the massive timbers of the roof. Alone with Christian, it seemed a good moment to ask:

"Could you help me with a puzzle?" he said.

"Happy to," said Christian, shuffling in his chair and leaning forward to look directly at him.

"It's on behalf of a friend, Severin Nordby, a neighbour; you may have heard of him."

"Hmmm?" murmured Christian.

"He asked for my help."

"Aha?"

"He had a younger sister, Marta."

"Did he now?"

"She worked here, at the Castle, many years ago."

"A long time ago...maybe..."

"She left somewhere around 1917," said Thomas.

"Please, just wait a moment," said Christian, rising from his chair.

"Severin wants to find her," said Thomas. "I was hoping you could help."

Christian put his hand on Thomas's shoulder, squeezed it, and hurried towards a door at the far end of the room, wrenching it open and slamming it behind him without a word or a backwards glance.

———

"Agnes, I'm sorry to wake you," said Christian, after falling into his great aunt's bedroom with the briefest of taps on the door. "It's dark; I can't see you, but I may have to take back everything I said. Thomas has just spoken to me. He's trying to trace the mad dog's long-lost sister."

"I did warn you," said Agnes, grappling to find the switch on the bedside light. "And it's your problem, remember, from start to finish."

"Yes, yes, but he obviously had no idea what he was asking me for," said Christian, his voice close to panic.

"Of course he didn't. What did you expect?"

"I don't know. I must think this through," he said, taking a deep breath. He helped Agnes find the light switch and turned away while she slipped out of the bed and pulled on her dressing gown.

"As I said to you at the Lookout, it's time to open up," said Agnes, sitting in a chair next to him. "You must delay no longer."

"No, no, it's not necessary, they won't find her. Surely?"

"Maybe not..."

"Not if we keep *shtum*."

"It's your decision."

"But what the hell am I going to tell Thomas? He's down there, now."

"If you must have your way, say nothing," she said. "Pretend the question never existed and resume your chat with quite a different subject. Just sound convincing for a change..."

"You think?"

"Yes, although one day you'll regret running away from it all."

———

At Norges Bank, icicles hung from the flag balcony and a top hat of icy snow perched on the heads of the granite lions guarding the entrance. The doorman had retreated inside. In the basement, a kerosene heater warmed a small radius in the vaults, but the cold crept through the thick walls and, day by day, Matthias's chilblains caused him increasing discomfort. But, by the middle of March, he had prepared 818 large crates, each nearly forty kilograms in weight, and 685 small crates, each twenty-five kilograms. "A monumental achievement," said the Governor.

"That just leaves the coins," said Matthias. "The existing stock has been counted, weighed and bagged, and is ready for final loading: thirty-five kegs in total. Most will hold British sovereigns: ten bags of one thousand coins per bag, so each keg will weigh 80 kilograms."

"Very good," said the Governor.

"That will then be that, apart from the new 1940 stock, which needs sorting, counting, bagging and clearing by Audit. Small amounts are expected in the next few days, and some may drag on into early April. All sovereigns."

"Excellent work, Mr Holmbekk," enthused the Governor.

"Lorry 27, it'll be," said Matthias. "An additional lorry, just for the 1940 coin-stock. Six or seven kegs by my calculations; just under a half lorry-load."

"Keep up the good work," said the Governor, as he left the vault.

TWENTY-FIVE

Thomas held tight his cup of steaming tea. Whilst the recurring vision of the poor crossword man's death was hard to expunge, and his own skirmish with the Grim Reaper kept him awake at night, he was beginning to find some sort of equilibrium out here at the fortress where it was, without doubt, safer. Certainly, his experiment with meeting his mythical professor in Oslo would not be repeated and it also crossed his mind that using Svensen to spread the right sort of gossip might have less to commend it than he had thought. More positively, he was developing a deep comfort from being with Olaf. The fisherman had lived his whole life in Drøbak and was part of the place, living a sort of symbiosis, and it helped to reconnect Thomas with his old life. Then the telephone rang from its perch on top of the make-shift kitchen table.

"It's a job," said Olaf. "Come on."

They walked down to the quay, the air so cold it felt as if it could shatter into countless invisible pieces.

"Who this time, Olaf?" said Thomas, once they were underway.

"Guess."

"The King."

"Nearly. Just as good."

"No idea."

"Old Anderssen."

"Who?"

"Andreas Anderssen. He was once captain commander of the torpedo battery," said Olaf. "Retired thirteen years ago."

"Torpedo battery?" asked Thomas.

"You haven't seen it?"

"No, show me."

"It's top secret. Well, it was until I told you." Olaf laughed.

As they approached Sundbrygga, an old man in full uniform from a bygone era stepped towards the edge of the quay. "Thank you, gentlemen. I never thought I'd see this day," said Anderssen.

"Back again, Andreas!" said Olaf, clearly happy at the turn of events.

"The new and youthful captain commander is sick," said Anderssen, "so they dragged me back to take his place. Good job I'm still alive," he shouted over the roar of the engine. "No one else can work the bloody things, they're so ancient."

———

Klara sat on a wooden bench along the back wall of the estate office. Carl had never attempted to seek any business with the estate but that was just typical of him: not wanting to use his relationship with her for his own benefit. As he walked in and greeted her and her father, only one thing mattered.

"I have a buyer for your potatoes," said Carl.

"Not in Norway?" said Christian.

"No. I have a contract in Sweden but many of my growers have had a bad season and are struggling to deliver," said Carl. "The contract price to me is fixed and is a good one; I can pass that on to you if you can deliver quickly. It gets my growers off the hook: I fulfil my contract and you get a good price. We all win."

"Who's the buyer?"

"I can't reveal that. But as soon as the ship leaves Drøbak, and I get to the bank, I'll hand-deliver a draft to you for the full amount."

"How can you do that?" said Christian. "No one can offer those terms."

"I only deal with people I know, which means there is trust all round. My credit is good and the bank will advance me funds against bills of lading, so I can pay you. I will need to check your potatoes, of course — they are perishable, and my reputation stands on always supplying faultless products. All being well, we'll be ready to go within three days. I'll use *Martina*; you may have seen her here before."

Klara watched her father study the offer Carl had placed in front of him: the transport arrangements, Nordic Trading's modest cut, the final totals. As she held her breath, Christian took a pen from his jacket pocket, unscrewed the cap and signed the contract.

Carl rose to shake Christian's hand. Klara raised her coffee cup and smiled, deeply happy. "*Skål*," she said, 'cheers'. She had helped secure her first deal on behalf of the estate. It felt good.

"There's something else, if you're interested," said Carl. "I can take your sawn timber, which a bird has told me you're having problems selling."

"The whole lot?" said Christian, unable to disguise a look of incredulity and hope.

"Yes," said Carl. "I'll need a larger ship, so it'll be a week before I can move it. Same terms. Good prices."

He drew a new set of papers from his case and placed them in front of Christian, making handwritten additions to the delivery date and price. Klara felt the stress drain away. The estate was secure, at least for a while.

———

"Right, Olaf," said Thomas," where's this ruddy torpedo affair?"

"It's secret. I don't know, and neither should you."

"Come on," said Thomas, laughing. "A boat ride. She needs testing anyway, after that problem we had with the fuel pump."

The two men set off into the fjord and turned north, rounding a rocky cliff on the fortress's north island.

"See that, up there?" said Olaf, jerking his head towards the wooded clifftop where two concrete bunkers were just visible amongst the rocks and vegetation. "Command positions."

They continued along the shore of the north island and a small bay came into view, within which was a quay, two small huts and an access track. Above, almost hidden by rocks and trees, was another bunker on a low cliff.

"That's it," said Olaf. "See the steel doors at the back of the quay? It's all in there. They release them under the water. Clever, eh?"

As he laid down in bed that evening, the question of the torpedoes played continuously in Thomas's head. He found it hard to sleep. Olaf had several times implored him to keep the discovery to himself; none of the other ferrymen were aware and Olaf should have kept his mouth shut. Thomas thought again about the unknown German agent. He too might be unaware of the torpedo base and it was critical to Norway's security to keep it that way. By the morning, Thomas had come to a firm decision. He would ensure no one ever discovered Andreas Anderssen's underwater base; the information released by Olaf would go no further, and that would include Biggeloe and the British.

Thomas had now resolved the old question: where do my loyalties lie? It's a complex answer, but that's how it is.

———

"All done, Klara," said Egil. "We can close up the shed until spring. She'll be safe enough here."

"*Terne* restored at last," said Klara, looking around. "How many islands are there? In the whole of Oslo fjord?"

"Enough for a lifetime, I'd say," he replied, with a broad smile.

As they left the island to walk back to town, Klara watched a figure approaching along the shore.

"Good day, Captain Hartman," said Egil as they met.

"We've had recurring problem with the boilers," said Hartman. "I'll call in tomorrow to see you about extending our mooring times."

"Well, I'm glad you fulfilled our deliveries first," said Egil. "There'll be no problem with mooring space."

Klara watched as the sea captain disappeared behind a wooded bluff.

"And where would he be going?" she pondered, half to herself and half hoping Egil would enlighten her.

"Oh, his woman probably," said Egil, with a straight face. "Up there in the woods."

It was hard to know if Egil was serious or not. Perhaps, she thought, he had a dry sense of humour no one had seen before?

———

Carl Westervik wandered past the stables, the smell of horses dominating that part of town. Piles of hay were stacked on the snow, but none of the stableboys were outdoors; it was too cold. Ahead was the church, and he stopped by the gate to the cemetery. A little early, he watched the minutes tick by. At one minute to two he set off walking up Seimbakken. Towards the top of the hill, where the road bends, he entered the garden of Colonel Eriksen's family home, was searched by one of the guards, and then knocked on the door.

"I don't have long," said the colonel, showing Carl into his office, where a second guard was stationed.

"Thank you for meeting me," said Carl. "Christian Holmbekk suggested I might be able to help you. We met at his party; you might remember."

"Yes, yes," said the colonel, with a hint of impatience in his voice.

"You have more men to feed, I gather. New recruits."

The colonel shrugged.

"I deal in commodities, especially agricultural, but food generally," said Carl.

"Very well."

"I have sources, in Sweden, and shipping connections which are still running and have capacity. Grain, potatoes, even pork, beer, all the staples."

"And where does this food come from?"

"Sweden."

"I mean before that? Everyone's short, so how are you able to source it? Not Germany is it?"

"No, my source is Swedish, as I said. Gothenberg."

The colonel sat back in his chair, his arms folded. "I'll give it some thought," he murmured.

An hour later, the colonel picked up the phone to his adjutant, Helberg.

"I've been speaking to a food trader, Westervik, Nordic Trading. Says he can make up any shortages. Done business with the Holmbekk estate."

"Our supplies are sufficient for now, sir."

"Good, don't deal with him. He was fishing, eyes wandering."

TWENTY-SIX

The *31st of March 1940*. Westervik returned to the Bell House. He kicked his boots against the step, pushed open the door and felt with relief a wave of warm air. Brann rose from his chair and offered his visitor a glass of aquavit.

Sitting at the table with Brann was Günther Hartman. "Alexander looking after you I hope?" said Westervik, nodding to the sea captain.

"A foresters' breakfast, that's what he got," said Brann, intervening.

Hartman smiled. "Better than I get from Hofmann onboard. You wouldn't give it to the dogs."

They all laughed, but this time, thought Westervik, it was nervous laughter; it didn't last, and there was no banter. They both sensed what was coming.

"Gentlemen," said Westervik. "Operation Weserübung, the invasion of Norway, is go. It's close, maybe a week. Everything in place, the kit, the huts? My team?"

Brann and Hartman both nodded.

"Good. We'll run through the details again later. First, our other operation, the local one," said Westervik. "Galtung has more lives than a bloody cat..."

"What?" Brann stiffened.

"Never mind. Something's not right," said Westervik. "He's been on the ferries for almost two months. Lives most of the time out there, on the fortress. Comes back now an' then. But all we've seen are two worthless message drops in February...and nothing since. All of it low value, no more than the local hairdresser knows. So, what's going on? Why isn't he supplying a stream of high value information — he's on the fortress, for God's sake."

"Yeh, every night sharing a beer with Colonel Bloody Eriksen," said Brann.

"That's a fantasy. I doubt he's even set eyes on Eriksen," said Westervik, grimly. "But...he must be picking up intelligence of more value than the rest of us can get hold of, so why don't we see it? Maybe he really is an idiot, untrained, shoe-horned in by British Intelligence when there were no other options. Or does he send high value stuff by dead-drop, or meet someone and pass it on?"

"He's useless, that's what he is," muttered Brann.

"Maybe, but...I've thought for a while...maybe he's playing us. Yes, he's a British agent alright, who knows he's under suspicion, but he's far more dangerous than we thought. The rubbish dead drops, the witless student, the dream of running off to Sweden: it's all a diversion."

"Sweden?" exclaimed Hartman. "He wants to leave?"

"Yes. I picked this up through Nordic Trading. He rang me, some time ago, all very friendly, says he wanted a job in Sweden. Well, I tickled him along, tried to find out why he wanted to work in Sweden, what skills he had, experience with commodities, grain, timber...But the bastard was evasive. And then I thought. Hell, maybe he's inside the operation, knows everything, is the biggest danger of the lot. Then he nails me again at a party at the Castle, couple of weeks ago, all bloody chatty and 'how's your grandma'. I sent him packing, but he can't take no for an answer. He contacts me again, a few days ago; 'could he meet me, please', he says — in my own bloody home — still pressing for a job with Nordic Trading, or with someone else I might know in Sweden. If I'd agreed, which I didn't, and I let him into my home, he'd no doubt be sitting there with a gun in his pocket, aimed right between my eyes, waiting to extract the details of the operation. You, too, Brann; he'll want you too."

174

"Seems pretty clear to me," said Hartman. "Doesn't matter who he is, what he is, we take him out. There's too much at stake."

Westervik nodded. "Now's the time. Brann, dispose of him. Quietly. He just disappears, right. But don't under-estimate him."

"When?" said Brann.

"Soon, but I need a day or two to plan. The timing must be perfect."

All three men were silent for a while. The wind moaned in the eaves and the stove released a sharp crack. Westervik flinched, then glanced out of the window. It had started to snow again. He took in a deep breath. "Brann, don't fail me. Eliminate him. And at the same time I'll give the Brits some far more interesting intelligence through Galtung's dead drop than he ever managed to do."

TWENTY-SEVEN

Thomas leaned over the tiller. It was now the 2nd of April and there was no hint that spring would ever return. A relentless easterly battered the final ferry run of the day and the last batch of new artillery recruits huddled together on the bottom boards, heads down.

"Not even out of school," hissed Olaf.

Once the recruits were marched off to the barracks, the two ferrymen headed back across the Narrows towards Sundbrygga. Thomas shivered and tightened the flaps of his hat over his ears. He thought momentarily of life on the *Glorious*, whether she were sailing in freezing conditions like these, then lifted his eyes towards the shore and the small battery off Storgaten.

"See that, that fortification," he shouted over the noise of the engine, "down by the fjord?"

"Husvik?" said Olaf, tucked in under the awning.

"Yeh."

"It defends the underwater barrier across the Narrows, you know that? Well, it would do if there was one. A barrier, I mean. But there isn't."

"Why's that?"

177

"They haven't got 'round to it. It'll be a training exercise apparently. They'll be mining the Narrows, too. But not yet. Everything is not yet."

Minutes later, they landed at Sundbrygga. Thomas waved to Olaf, who was already reversing the ferry for the return trip. As he walked towards Storgaten in the dim evening light, he directed his torch at a garden entrance in a wall nearby; a sheltered niche, kept clear of snow by a high stone arch. Standing beneath the arch his torch picked up a small blue chalk mark at head height. Pendleton wanted to meet. He rubbed out the chalk and headed south along Storgaten, hurrying to catch the bus out of town and preparing himself to face Pendleton's tired cynicism and his insulting and careless banter. It was hard to accept he, Thomas, was risking so much for such a dislikeable envoy of his own country. But there was also a hint of acceptance, that Pendleton must be risking something too, was also a pawn in the game. Maybe they were in it together.

He pushed open the door at Stensrud. A candle flickered on the mantlepiece, casting a yellow light onto Pendleton's face and the green-covered chair he had selected.

"You ruddy Norwegians. How do you survive this?"

"I just have," said Thomas.

"Minus twenty-two your thermometer says," said Pendleton. "It's a miracle the mercury hasn't frozen, shattered the whole thing; ended it all."

"It's hardy. It's Norwegian," said Thomas, setting some wood-shavings alight. "More to the point. I worry about meeting here."

"Quicker than Ås, and I wanted a change. Never stick around in one place too long."

"I've moved," said Thomas. "Best you don't know where."

"Quite. Why's that?"

"A bit exposed here. And events, you could say...in Oslo."

"Ah, that was you, was it? And it's why you've gone quiet on me...?"

"Unfortunately, yes."

"It was all over the papers," said Pendleton. *The Man Who Disappeared.*"

"I don't see the Oslo papers."

"Well, let's try to keep you safe — although now is the time when we need to make the most of your position on the fortress, all the more so with what I have to tell you."

"Which is...?"

"A naval force is assembling in Kiel, northern Germany. Ships, troops, supplies, ammunition. A new heavy cruiser, *Blücher*, is being fitted out and stuffed full of shells, torpedoes, the works. What does that look like to you?"

"The invasion of Norway."

"We don't know for sure, but think about it. They can take Denmark across the land border. And Hitler doesn't need to conquer Sweden: he gets his iron ore without fighting for it."

"Could it be a breakout into the Atlantic," mused Thomas, "...and it's really the convoys they're after. It could even be Narvik, don't you think, just to secure the iron ore? Not Oslo, not us."

"How would I know? Maybe they give me false intelligence, they think I'm a double agent. Disinformation, you know. Confuse the enemy. Confuse everyone. Stalin came up with that, you know: disinformation." He smirked. "Anyway, if Jerry plans to take Norway, he has to take Oslo, not just Narvik."

"You're probably right," said Thomas.

"Oh, I'm rarely right, so don't count on anything I say. Anyway, what's new?" Pendleton looked at Thomas, eyebrows raised as usual when he awaited an answer to a question.

"Several hundred new recruits arrived at the fortress yesterday, and a few more today. They plan to deploy naval mines as a barrier to close off the Narrows, starting on the 9th, I think."

"They'd better get on with it," muttered Pendleton, "though it's not my job to tell 'em. Anyway, what about personnel? I mean artillery men, officers, NCOs?"

"They don't have sufficient trained men on the fortress. That's what the recruits are all about." Thomas shrugged. "Any idea on the timing?" he asked. "This *Blücher* operation, I mean?"

"Who knows? Week, ten days, maybe less — I really don't know; it may never happen. Keep us in touch, anyway. You'll have to check the archway every day. I'll leave a time and date for meetings, coded — I'll take you through it before I go."

"I have a couple of days off now," said Thomas, "then I'll be on duty the whole week from 0800 hours on Saturday the 6th, but I can arrange a break to meet you."

"Here again? The 7th?" said Pendleton. "1000 hours."

Thomas nodded. "Okay, Sunday. And Pendleton..."

"Uh?"

"When I was recruited into this business, my other option was to join the navy and serve on the *Glorious,* an aircraft carrier, I think. I sometimes wonder what it would have been like if I'd taken a different path: where she is now, how she's doing. You don't know, do you?"

"No idea. Never heard of her. And they wouldn't tell us anyway," said Pendleton. "And before I go, what about this place?"

"It could still be useful," said Thomas. "Easy to get to, a telephone, another option if things turn bad."

"Agreed. But make it looked lived in, as if you're still here. Stay here sometimes, light the stove."

A mouse sprinted along the floor in the shadows at the end of the room and they exchanged a shrug of the shoulders.

———

"Minus forty up in the mountains," said Elverfeldt, breathing fog from his R6.

He looked tense, thought Westervik. His eye then caught the door, which had come ajar. He rose and walked over to close it, looked into the bar, raised his chin towards Schmidt and then leaned on the handle until he heard the latch click firmly shut.

"News?" he asked.

"Your team will arrive at the Bell House on the 6th of April, 1800 hours," said von Elverfeldt. "Four men in total, headed by Herman Wesner."

"I don't know him, do I?"

"Major, so he's your superior. Tough, very capable. We need you to brief his team. Your strategy is approved in broad terms, but once the operation is live, he'll be in charge."

"I thought I was in charge?"

Von Elverfeldt shrugged. "Berlin."

Westervik sat back and looked up to the ceiling, trying to hide his emotions. "Why?"

"You failed in Oslo, Carl. Decision made, not by me. Move on."

"But I'm involved in the operation?"

"You'll take Eriksen. Without him they're leaderless."

"A date?"

"Imminent, that's all I can say."

The door opened and Schmidt appeared with two brandies and a bowl of sweets on a round black tray. He nodded to von Elverfeldt and silently left the room, Westervik listening for the click of the latch before resuming.

"Other matters?" asked von Elverfeldt. "Galtung?"

"I may have missed the bastard once, but next time we won't. We'll take him out before the operation commences. I need a date."

Von Elverfeldt rose and stood at the window, looking out onto Norway's capital city. The snow had started falling again. "A quick takeover of Oslo would be best for everyone," he said. "It's a fine city. I would hate to see it damaged. And you'll get your date as soon as I do, later today."

———

Westervik returned to the Bell House as daylight faded. He drew Brann over to the table, drawing a slip of paper from his pocket. "Galtung's rota. This is when you take him," he said, circling the date and marking the time.

TWENTY-EIGHT

The 4th of April 1940. "There's a German coaster, the *Martina*; captained by Günter Hartman," said Klara, pinning down Johansen with her eyes. "She moors up in Drøbak every now and then. Sometimes it's a short stop; sometimes she unloads or takes on some cargo, all normal. But twice since I've been watching she seems to stop for no good reason; and she's empty as far I can see from her waterline."

"Ships often do this," said Johansen. "They stay in port waiting for the next load to tie into another shipment — from down the fjord, or in Oslo — before heading off again."

"I know that."

"She may have repairs, take on fuel, chandlery; all sorts of reasons."

"Maybe, but it doesn't feel right. Shipping is now much reduced because of the war but *Martina* has docked at Lehmanns more than any other ship. She's taken nothing from us until recently and we are the largest exporter from Lehmanns, so what's she been doing there? And I've seen Hartman out at Hallangspollen. Why would anyone go there, an isolated branch of the fjord...anyone who's not local?"

"A walk, some bracing fresh air? You would, cooped up on a ship for days. A bird watcher, maybe — some people are."

"I'm not sure. The harbourmaster thinks Hartman may have a girl-friend in town. He gets excited by the idea. But even if he's right...up in the forest? In Hallangspollen? There are no girlfriends there, just a few cabins and smallholdings."

Johansen sighed. "We can't go arresting German sea captains because they have a woman up in the woods somewhere," he said, "or because they count Arctic terns."

"Alright, but can't you take this on? Remember, I'm just a pair of eyes, the local girl. I'm telling you what I see and what I feel."

"Feelings are no good. I need evidence. Just keep watching and I'll see what I can turn up on *Martina*."

Klara looked at Johansen. She already wanted to give him a thorough kicking. "Alright, there's one other lead," she said. "You might consider this even more speculative."

Johansen crossed his arms and leaned back in his chair. It saved him the effort of speaking. She still wanted to kick him. Hard.

"Almost everywhere to rent around here is owned by my family," she said. "I checked the records. There were two new tenancies during 1939, both taken by lone men claiming to be Norwegian, but I can't reliably check that. Even a spy needs somewhere to live."

"Aha..."

"One, a boat hand, took up a flat by the harbour in September." She looked for some sort of encouragement.

"And...?"

"Well, he just disappeared, at some point in early October. Peter Haugen was his name, but we know little about him. Now, let's say he was a spy...Then assume he was given instructions to relocate or something and had to be replaced. Or was 'taken-out' as you might say, killed for some reason. What would the Germans do? Or the British? Whoever ran him."

"Replace him."

"Exactly. A few weeks later," said Klara, "early December, let's say. Yes? And when do you think the next tenancy was taken up?"

"Go on. Early December?"

"The seventh."

"And who would that be?" said Johansen, leaning forward, urgency in his eyes at last.

"That's where my theory becomes less convincing," said Klara, "at least, to me."

"Try me."

"It's hard: he fits into my no-go area," said Klara. "He's a friend of the family. And he's not German. So it's probably a wild goose chase. But it's all I have so far."

"The cleverest infiltrators are often the most charming, the best of friends."

"He's Norwegian, grew up locally, but has lived in England for nearly ten years. Then he just...reappears; when I said: December. With good reason I must say, but the timing..."

"His name?"

"It's not easy. I know him."

"It doesn't matter."

"I have no evidence. He's done nothing wrong as far as I can see. It just seems, well, coincidental that he appeared when he did. And...one more thing. I know one person who saw him up on the ridgeline, above Kopås, looking out over Oscarsborg. Mind you, lots of people go up there, but...in this weather? And he's on the boats now, the ferries."

"You mean, to the fortress?"

"Yes, ferrying officers and so on from Sundbrygga."

"Good God. Right in the heart of our defences. Come on, Klara, I need to know."

"I've been agonising what to do."

"Your loyalties are to Norway."

She took a deep breath.

"He's Norwegian, but his mother was British."

"Yes, yes, but he could have been recruited by the Germans. That's where the risk lies."

"In Britain?"

"Could have been," said Johansen. "I'll need time to look into this. Got a lot on. Who is he? His name?"

"He's not military. Not a Nazi, for sure."

"You can't tell. He's infiltrated the fortress for God's sake. His name?"

"Galtung. Thomas Galtung."

———

Klara's meeting with Johansen had not ended as planned. He showed little interest in Hartman or *Martina*. Instead, she had been pressured into releasing Thomas's name, about whom she felt ambiguous as a risk to Norway. In fact, it was hard to believe he could be a spy for anyone. She shivered at the thought she might have placed Thomas in danger, potentially for no good reason.

Returning to Lehmanns Quay, she met up with the harbourmaster again. "*Amta* is always interested in local stories, Egil," she said. "I am thinking about an interview with Captain Hartman: the friendly relations between Germany and Norway, trade and how our forestry and farming products end up in Germany."

"Well, he's there, on board, sorting out his boilers I think."

Martina: the only ship moored at the harbour, the gangplank tied up; it was difficult to see how she could find a way onto the deck. She shouted, with no effect. There was no sign of life on the ship, but she waited and shouted again.

A while later a figure appeared on the weather deck.

"Captain Hartman," she shouted. "I'm a friend of Carl Westervik and we met briefly a couple of weeks ago, at Skarholmen; I was with the harbourmaster."

"Aha..."

"I'm writing an article for *Amta*, our local newspaper."

"Why would that be?" he shouted back.

"It's about trade around the fjord, the harbour here. Germany takes our agricultural products. We import your machinery. A good news story."

"I don't do interviews," he shouted. "Sorry."

"*Martina*, it's a great story..."

"We have an engine to sort out."

"I can come back."

"Maybe later, in the spring?"

Hartman disappeared back into the ship. He was in no mood to talk and Johansen gave little encouragement to pursue him either. But, but...

Klara returned to the Castle and found an estate map showing forest parcels, field names and the buildings and smallholdings which were rented out, together with buildings and farms in other ownerships. With the map spread out in front of her, she traced her route along the edge of Hallangspollen to locate herself. Fixing the point where she had met Hartman on the shore by Skarholmen, she then worked out his possible route up into the woods. Most of the area at the head of the fjord was dense forest, much of which was on steep ground, but there was one track she had never herself walked. It followed a shallow valley and appeared to link the fisherman's huts along the east side of Hallangspollen with a scatter of smallholdings and cabins up in the forest.

She followed the track with her finger. It split into two at one point, and each branch then split again a number of times, ending in named smallholdings or forestry cabins. They were all isolated places within the great sweep of forest which continued down to merge with the farmland to the east. Continuing to study the map, she counted six smallholdings and a couple of cabins with clear links to Hallangspollen. She took a sheet of paper and began to write:

Valheim
Lauvberg
Engdal — later called the Bell House
Bjerkekollen
Torsrud
Sandbekk
Solåsen
Gaupåsen

Beyond them, on lower land to the south and east, were other farms, smallholdings and houses, one of which was Stensrud — the cabin which Thomas had rented off the estate, but they were all closer to the main Drøbak road and it would make no sense to walk to them from Hallangspollen.

So, there were eight possible destinations Hartman could have been heading for.

"Günther Hartman..." she whispered, tapping the map with her pencil. "Maybe you really do have a secret woman? One in every port? But if not..."

She looked again at the list.

The Bell House: Thomas's old home. Could Hartman be meeting him there? Could her two lines of inquiry be linked in some way — Thomas and Hartman? But who lives there now? And were there national ties she didn't know about? Could Thomas really have been recruited by Germany, as Johansen had mooted?

———

Oslo. Later that day, Carl Westervik met Hanna Gjertsen, an accounts clerk and one of two German agents working undercover in the Police headquarters at Victoria Terrasse. She stood on the bridge in Frogner Park, leaning on the parapet and looking over the iced-up lake. Westervik ambled up close to gaze at one of Vigeland's snow-covered statues, a powerful male figure with a child in each arm.

"I need to know," he whispered, "if the name Klara Holmbekk appears anywhere in the records. An expenses claim, an employment contract, anything. And I need to know today."

"Impossible. It's too late. Those records are kept in another department."

"When?"

She was silent for a while, gazing over the frozen park. "Meet me 1700 hours on Sunday, the Palace Park. There's a bench fifty metres south of the King's Guards' hut." She threw a few more breadcrumbs to the ducks slithering on the ice, and disappeared.

TWENTY-NINE

The 5th of April 1940. Late in the day, Pendleton received an intelligence report from a well-placed agent in northern Germany:

Blücher set sail from Kiel in preparation for a major battle training exercise. Passed Laboe at 1800 hours. Strander Bay, Battle Group Leader, Konteradmiral Kummetz reported to have come aboard. Blücher joined by heavy cruiser Lützow, light cruiser Emden and other ships including torpedo boats, mine sweepers and auxiliaries.

———

The 6th of April, 0345 hours. Stensrud. Brann eased a red-painted crowbar into the window frame. The latch broke with a sharp crack and he waited, listening intently. A faint light showed through from the next room, casting a glow onto the kitchen floor and picking out a pair of boots neatly aligned by the woodstove in the room beyond. A cup and plate lay unwashed on the kitchen worktop. He pulled open the window and peered in; the house was warm, but silent. No one down-stairs, no thumps or squeaks from the floorboards upstairs.

He squeezed with difficulty through the small window opening, catching his hat on a splinter in the frame, and fell onto the hard wooden floor. "Damn," he whispered. He waited, not moving. But still the place was quiet. Slowly standing, he reached up to retrieve his hat. Shaking off the snow from his trousers and boots, he crept through the open doorway into the living room. The light issued from a small lamp on a table by the window opposite. The woodstove was still hot. Stopping again and listening, he then eased his boot onto the first step of the narrow stairs which spiralled up above him. There was a loud creak as the step bore his weight. He stopped again, not daring to breath. It was quite silent and the stairs above horribly dark. Feeling his way along the handrail, he moved up, step by step, listening for any sound that would confirm that Galtung was where he should be: asleep.

Brann shuddered on the threshold of the room at the top of the stairs. It was utterly black, which he hated: it gave him the creeps. He waited. Slowly, the shape of two windows emerged as a ghostly glow: moonlight seeping through the flimsy curtains. He felt another ripple of anxiety mixed with the thrill of his victim being so close. Gradually, his eyes adjusted. The faint glow of light escaping up the stairs from below, combined with the barest luminescence from the windows was sufficient to show the outline of a bed. He crept towards it, rolling his feet and holding his breath, then slipped off his left glove. Holding out his hand in front of him, he searched for his target: Thomas Galtung's throat. Quick, clean. And personal.

He stood over the bed, then lunged, growling, both hands forced onto the dark shadow, an indescribable thrill coursing through him. Tearing at the blankets, he threw them across the room, pummelled at the bed and swept aside the wool pelts. Roaring in frustration, he then staggered over to the wall, groping for a switch. The ceiling light flickered on.

He looked in disbelief at the chaos.

The bed was empty. The room was empty. The house was empty.

Galtung had escaped.

———

Half an hour before Brann's abortive raid, Thomas had left Stensrud to start his next five-day shift. He had stayed the night, at Pendleton's suggestion, to maintain some indication that the place was still his home, but one of the ferrymen had been taken ill the previous day and the rotas had been adjusted. It meant a horribly early start, but it was in truth a relief as he couldn't sleep in the place and it felt better to be on the move.

Walking into town, he had time to kill before meeting Olaf. Turning into a side street, he walked past the stables and followed a path over an embankment, lit by a lamp hung off one of the houses nearby. On the other side of the embankment, a dark lane ran alongside the cemetery. When he reached the lane, he turned right towards Drøbak church, its doorway lit by the golden light of a large lantern and a nearby streetlight. The whole scene was framed by the shadowy outlines of an avenue of ancient lime trees.

As he approached the church he noticed the silhouette of a figure, a man in a long coat, leaving the porch and walking towards the cemetery. He froze. He had stopped instinctively, and it took him a few seconds to realise why. The man's height, his gait, the general form of his outline: he knew who it was.

Moving closer, he concealed himself behind one of the great lime trees and watched as the figure walked into the cemetery, the gate squeaking in the still air, and move slowly towards the grave of Gudmund Galtung. There, the man stopped and knelt down for a few seconds, then stood, looked around and moved a few steps towards the Hansen enclosure. Thomas clearly heard a faint grating noise as the finial turned. A few seconds later, the man walked back towards the gate. Outside the cemetery, the profile of his face was clearly lit by the streetlight until he turned and hurried away past the stables. There was no doubt: *it was Carl Westervik.*

Thomas waited, his heart pounding, before he walked warily up the lane, trying to control his shock. As he let himself into the cemetery, he could see immediately the footsteps in the fresh snow marking the route Westervik had taken from the gate to the grave, and then to the Hansen enclosure and back again. The finial had been turned. The operation was blown. There could be no doubt. And it was Carl Westervik who had blown it. Thomas hurried into the church and up the stairs to the dead drop. As suspected he found a message: a false message. It advised repositioning the British fleet to the west of Norway, far away from Skagerrak and the Oslo fjord...*leaving a clear run for an invasion fleet from Germany.*

Immediately, the implications became clear, and they hit him like a succession of hammer blows. First, he now knew that Carl Westervik was Pendleton's German spy. He could also have been Haugen's killer and the assassin who had nearly split his own head in two at Café Marianne. Second, an invasion must be imminent. Westervik must be intimately involved and there were probably others around him. Finally, it was now certain the whole of his own operation had been blown: the dead drop, everything.

Before leaving the cemetery, there was a decision to take. If he were to turn back the finial and remove the message at the dead drop, that would signal that Westervik's actions had been discovered...with unknown implications. Instead, he decided to leave Westervik's planned deception untouched. He would close off the disaster in another way.

Returning to his father's resting place, he looked to his left. All was as it should be. No one, Pendleton had said, ever tended the adjoining grave, a memorial to a young girl, Sarah Dahl, who died in 1923. Looking around, he cleared away the snow at the base of the girl's gravestone, revealing a small stone memorial cross. He listened intently for any sounds, but the cemetery remained completely still. He then turned the stone cross so that it faced the main gravestone, a simple act which would signal to Pendleton's local agents that the dead drop was compromised and their services were no longer required. It might save their lives.

Finally, he walked to another grave nearby and kicked out a few of his own footprints around his father's grave. Westervik's tracks remained, largely undisturbed.

He now needed time. He walked as fast as he could towards Sundbrygga, hoping he could arrange to take a few hours out to sort out the mess he was in. Olaf was waiting and in good spirits. It transpired there was a light workload that morning, so there was no difficulty in Thomas taking some time to resolve a water leak back at Stensrud.

———

0600 hours and no sign of the morning sunrise. Thomas returned to Stensrud and checked the place was empty. Unlocking the door, he crept to the telephone. Still connected. He knelt down and, in the light of his torch, eased out a section of timber beam at the base of the wall, behind which was a scrap of paper with several numbers written on it. In the silence of the room all he could hear was the thumping of his heart.

Picking up the receiver, he asked for an Oslo number, deducting one digit from each of the numbers in front of him except for the last.

"Hello, Frank," he said.

"Who?"

"Is that Frank Nilsen?"

"Wrong number."

The line went dead.

He replaced the receiver, locked and wedged the front door, and slumped into the old green chair. The conversation which had just taken place was a coded exchange to communicate a blown operation. Within minutes Pendleton would know that any message in the dead drop should be assumed false and that the extraction plan for his agent should be triggered.

Thomas breathed heavily, his body shaking. His mind was on Pendleton's extraction plan, but Westervik's unmasking felt so shocking it was hard to think clearly...and someone else was confusing the picture. Klara.

He doubted she would be in any immediate danger, but she couldn't be aware of who her Carl Westervik really was. Unless she were part of his spying operation? The thought of it was too terrible to contemplate. There was no way to tell at the moment and he couldn't see a way to warn her without endangering himself if the worst were true. But if she really was in danger, and not part of Westervik's plan at all, he could never abandon her. He needed to see Severin, too. Maybe Christian. He wanted a credible story to tell them. And if an invasion really was imminent, as the false dead drop seemed to suggest, he would need to advise Pendleton as soon as possible.

For now, working the ferries and living for a few more days on the fortress was the safest place to be. Westervik, or one of his men, would hunt him down if he remained on the mainland. Before leaving he should check the place remained secure.

In the kitchen, a wet mark on the floor caught his eye. He knelt down and felt it, certain he had not carried snow in when he first arrived. His eyes drifted up, to the window...an icy shiver ran through him. The window had been forced, the frame split, then pushed shut again. Someone had broken into Stensrud in the time he had been away.

Slowly, he crept up the stairs. There was no sound from the room above. What he found confirmed the raid. Pillows had been thrown across the room. The moth-eaten, dusty blankets were scattered on the floor, the table turned over. He now knew for sure that he had been the target. It was the killing attempt he had been so worried about. But who had been the raider that night?

It could not have been Westervik. It was physically not possible: he'd been at the cemetery. He returned to the kitchen and, with his torch, cast a light over the window frame to examine a fragment of fabric that he had not noticed earlier on. Rolling it in his hands under the torch-light, it told him little: dense, green wool; it could be anyone's. He then kneeled down and scanned the floor with his torch, systematically looking for another clue. Just as he reached the conclusion there was nothing to be found, he spotted a long strand of wavy black hair lying in the dust under the window. He picked it up and examined it under the torchlight. Then, he knew...

Brann. The thought of it hit him like a runaway train. He opened the window and looked out at the footprints in the snow. They were at least two sizes above his own boots. It must have been Brann. But it made no sense. Why would a Norwegian want him dead? He searched again and found another long black strand of hair. He knew no one else who would fit. Yes, it was Brann. Severin's instincts were correct.

If this were true, he thought, what was the connection between Brann and Westervik? They had to be linked. His own planned killing and the false message in the dead drop must also be related; they were minutes apart. Thoughts rushed around his head. Brann, Westervik, possibly Klara. Could they all be Pendleton's German agents? Westervik

the leader and spy, Brann the assassin and the raider on Stensrud? But...
Klara? He shuddered at the thought. It was still too much to contemplate that she could be a Nazi sympathiser and a traitor, but it was a terrifying possibility. After all, how well did he really know her? His mind returned to what had taken place at Stensrud. He had escaped death by an hour, probably less. The black bird inside his chest writhed.

A short while later, he closed up Stensrud and arrived at Sundbrygga in time to meet Olaf. Trying to hide his fear and uncertainty, he welcomed the two waiting gunnery sergeants, both loaded with enormous kitbags and shivering despite their heavy wool coats. The three men stepped into the boat and Olaf immediately set course for the return journey to the fortress.

———

As dusk fell, Captain Günther Hartman walked into the harbourmaster's office on Lehmanns Quay.

"Sorry to say it, but we'll be staying a few more days," he said.

"What's up?" said Egil.

"One of the boilers is struggling. We need time for repairs."

"How long can this go on for? I mean, Germany at war, and you just carry on."

"Why not? Germany needs Norwegian goods, war or no war. And you need ours."

"So you'll carry on?"

"That's my job, it's what I do."

———

Darkness fell and obliterated the flat grey sky over Oslo. A scatter of shop staff and late leavers from the offices trudged the city streets or queued for the trams and buses. Snowflakes drifted into pools of light, then disappeared into the shadows.

Carl waited in a small café tucked away in the old city. The lights were dim and the custom slim, the waitress glancing at the clock and counting the minutes to the end of the working day. Tapping the table with his forefinger, he checked his watch again, as he had done by the minute since his arrival. But now, the door opened and she was there.

"I am sorry, my love," she said. "So much is happening: father needs me, the estate, so many problems."

He drew breath at her embrace, her slim body lost within a great bear of a coat. "I'm glad you could come," he said. "I need to see you." He shivered at the sight of her; her silvery fair hair, her smile, the wonderful upturn at the end of her nose, her intensity, the way her eyes held him. He knew it should not be, but it was impossible to feel any other...except his feelings for the girl he loved were tempered with agonising uncertainty. Had Brann been right? *"It's the Holmbekk girl."* Had Klara, who he had trapped into love as part of his mission, become the hunter, a Norwegian police agent? It was all quite possible, and he would soon know. So, did Klara really love him? And could he still love her?

At first no words came, just their fingers entwined, their bodies leaning into each other, their calves touching beneath the table, their boots moving against the other's, their eyes locked. Carl shook with uncertainty and fear. Nothing in his military training had prepared him for this. How he wished the war would fade away and he could spend his life with Klara...but of course it was not possible.

"It's been too long again," he whispered. "A month, nearly a month. But I had to see you." He sensed her questioning mind, felt uncertainty at his own insistence that she be here.

"Carl, my love, you're tense. I can see it."

The waitress appeared, hovering. "Closing in five."

He had practiced the words, rehearsed them several times in his mind, but was no better prepared. "I need to know..." he said.

She gripped his hand. His eyes searched hers. But there were no words that would unlock the dilemma.

"Do you really love me?" he whispered, throwing a quick glance at the girl behind the counter and then at the only other customer in the corner to his left: an old, bearded man seeking the comfort of the café.

"You know the answer to that, my love."

"Say you love me," he said. There was no other way, no other words.

"Carl, I love you. Why do you question me? You know I love you."

Carl shifted his hands, grabbed her arms, drew her closer still. "Thank you," he said.

"Why do you thank me?" She looked puzzled.

"I worry for you," he said.

She raised her eyebrows. "For me, why?"

"These are dangerous times, my love."

"Of course, for us all."

"For us all, yes. The war, I mean. Can't you go away, somewhere safe. Your cabin, up by the border...?"

"Carl, why...? What do you know?"

"Nothing, of course not, no more than you. But maybe you could go away for some time, a week, for me, to be safe."

He felt her eyes, boring into him now. Her questioning. "Why now?" she said.

"I pick things up. From Sweden, my contacts." He held her hands, tighter, beneath her bear-like coat.

"I know you care so much for me," she said, softly. One day, we can go there, to the cabin. It's so beautiful, high up and wild. But not now, I simply cannot."

"Please, my love, go away for a few days. Find somewhere safe."

"Carl, I cannot."

THIRTY

The *6th of April 1940*. The Bell House. Westervik arrived shortly before 2200 hours. He pushed open the door, escaping a steady fall of snow that had blown in that evening, and nodded a greeting to Brann, who took his jacket and hung it on the only spare peg left on the wall behind the door.

Striding over to the table, he greeted five other men: Captain Hartman, of course, he knew; then Major Herman Wesner and, one by one, Wesner's team. It felt as if they had been here for some time. A chair had been left empty for him, facing Wesner; he pulled it aside and looked around, nervous at whether his plan had survived.

Brann poured him a black coffee. Several candles cast a flickering light and pine logs crackled and spat inside the ancient log stove. The door rattled in the wind and outside the storm moaned through the forest and whistled around the eaves.

Wesner sat in a rustic wooden chair at the head of the table. Westervik studied him: early thirties, lean, smaller than average in height; a lined, angular face with a long, chiselled jaw; clipped dark hair, greying above small, neatly-shaped ears; his voice quiet, his demeanour intense. His arms were laid out in perfect symmetry in front of him, his hands loosely clasped together by the fingers, and quite still.

"I will start by extending my gratitude to Hauptmann Westervik," said Wesner. "A German officer with a fine military and intelligence record, on whom this operation has been built. He has spent over a year familiarising himself with this area, the most critical point in the coastal defences of Norway. He has supplied intelligence of the highest quality which will underpin the success of this operation. He will continue to play a particular but vital role, but will otherwise be visible and will be acting as normal in the local area; this is to ensure he remains unconnected with the actions to come..." Wesner paused. "...thus protecting his identity."

This was new and Westervik felt himself twitch at what it could mean. Wesner continued: "He will then remain in Drøbak after the operation is complete and will play his part in the occupation and neutralisation of Norway, with particular emphasis on continued intelligence operations."

It was now clear to Westervik that Wesner, as von Elverfeldt had said, had replaced him as leader of the operation. In normal circumstances, he would have regarded being passed over as a disaster for his career: a humiliation. But his own plan had one unavoidable and terrible consequence: after the completion of the mission, he would have no choice but return to Germany with the team and would be reassigned elsewhere. He would never see Klara again. He dared, for a moment, to imagine the future differently.

"Brann, thank you also," said Wesner. "You've been a great support for this operation. To your men, too, our gratitude in helping to contain the scope for British nuisance-making."

Brann sat next to Westervik wearing an ancient, off-white cotton vest, with three buttons undone to reveal a small area of the hair that no doubt covered his whole upper body. His vast bulk spread over the edge of the chair, which creaked when he moved. Westervik's eye caught Brann about to intervene; he touched his arm, but was unable to prevent the big man opening his mouth...

"I've got one thing to say," said Brann, half standing. "Galtung..."

"Just wait," said Wesner, motioning him to sit down.

Westervik sighed, thankful that Brann had obeyed the order; he was out of place in a military setting.

They all waited for Wesner to speak, who looked at them, one by one. Time went by before he spoke.

"Gentlemen, we have our orders. Operation Weserübung has been committed. Our own operation will save hundreds of German lives, maybe more. It is critical to the Reich's strategy to secure Norway and thus thwart British plans to control the Atlantic coast and their desire to prevent Swedish iron ore reaching Germany."

From the corner of his eye, Westervik noticed as Brann nodded, clenching his huge fists. Wesner continued:

"We know from our surveillance operations that a few days ago a large number of raw recruits were shipped to the fortress for training as gunners. Our job is to ensure these men will be neutered on the day that matters, that the defences around the Narrows will fail, and that the big guns will stand idle. Finally, the planned naval mine barrier will never be laid, never even be started; we can thank the Norwegian government for that and an element of luck in our timing."

"We have tonight and tomorrow until sundown for final preparations. Tomorrow evening, we will focus on targets who live out of town. The operation will continue through Monday when we will be back on *Martina* at 2000 hours."

"We'll have PO8's for close quarter work," Wesner continued, "specially adapted."

Leaning over, he took a small but weighty-looking oilcloth parcel from the canvas bag that Brann had placed by his side, cut the string binding and extracted a PO8 Luger pistol.

"It looks standard, and you will be familiar with it, but the silencer is a new special adaption," said Wesner, scanning his team. "It may differ from the one you trained with."

He put the muzzle between his thumb and forefinger and twisted and unscrewed the foresight, revealing a threaded end to the barrel. Reaching again into the parcel he took out a silencer, which he then screwed onto the end of the muzzle. "These pistols have all been thoroughly tested," he said. "Each of your packages will contain five loaded magazines, each with eight rounds, which should be sufficient for all eventualities. We will use subsonic rounds that will cut down on the muzzle report. If the muzzle is pressed into your target, a shot will be no louder than a small cough."

He stood and, pushing the magazine through the butt of the pistol until it clicked into place, looked around the room. Eyeing a sack of potatoes, he racked the action and picked up a rag which was lying nearby. He stuffed the rag into the sack and pressed the gun vertically downwards into it.

There was a dull thud as the pistol fired.

"Almost silent if pressed against the target," he said. "No flash and the pistol has not ejected the fired case. But remember this: these rounds will not cycle the action, so you'll need to rack the pistol again before taking a second shot, which, of course, we must assume will not be necessary until your next target."

Wesner returned to his seat and reviewed the men around the table. Another minute passed until he spoke again.

"We work at close range, in darkness where possible," he said. "The objective is to avoid alerting the police or military in the early hours of the operation, and to leave them confused when reports start to emerge. So, drag your targets into a quiet corner somewhere. Hide them well. Outdoors, in the forest, cover them with snow, away from the paths. This is especially important early in the operation: tomorrow evening. A fresh fall of snow would help, but we can't rely on that, even in this winter. We will focus on officers and NCO's at the main batteries on Oscarsborg fortress and the guns at the Kopås battery. My understanding is that the small Husvik battery will not be manned."

He looked at Westervik, who nodded.

"In addition," he continued, "we will eliminate the ferrymen and the ferries at both Lehmanns and Sundbrygga, which will prevent reinforcements reaching the fortress."

"Sir..." Westervik intervened.

"Hauptmann, your plan has been modified," said Wesner. "Just wait; I will finish."

"Sir, forgive me. The ferrymen are not military; they are all civilians. We can achieve everything by sabotaging the ferries, everything, and then, in time, we can arrest the ferrymen if required...after the operation is complete."

"Hauptmann, Germany is at war," said Wesner. "Thousands of German lives are at stake in this operation, never mind the strategic importance of Norway. We need certainty." He looked at Westervik with a steady glare, then around the table. "I trust we are all clear."

Wesner then drew several maps from his pocket and spread one on the table.

"You will all stay here tonight, at the Bell House. Brann will feed us. You will each be given a map, like this one. You will have individual targets. Each target has been carefully researched. We know from the Hauptmann's work where they live, their routes on the changeovers, the rotas. Each target has a key role in operating the artillery or the ferries. But we cannot guarantee anything on the day. You will have to adapt if necessary."

Wesner cleared his throat and continued. "I'll now run through your targets, individually, with the Hauptmann's help. Mostly you will work alone, but we need the whole team for the final operation at Sundbrygga; there may be up to ten men there, and they will be armed. You must commit your instructions to memory, but you will have use of the maps. None of you will know what the others' instructions are. None of you have heard of the Bell House, of Hauptman Westervik, me, or Brann or each other. We don't exist...When the job is done, leave everything connected with the operation here, at the Bell House. Brann will be waiting. Change into shipping gear, the woodsman's coat over the top. Make sure you retain your Norwegian identity papers. Avoid any shooting unless there is no option. You must reach Lehmanns harbour for departure by 2000 hours on Monday — the 8th. The timescale is very tight. Shortly before you approach the town, dump the woodsman's coat and destroy your Norwegian identities. From that point on you will be German sailors making your way back to *Martina*. The ship will be moored at the same location as when you arrived. Move slowly, naturally. Don't attract attention. Once you are aboard the ship, get below deck."

Wesner then looked towards Hartman.

"We'll slip down the fjord and hold up off Gothenburg," said the captain. "We'll then join a convoy returning from the initial phase of Operation Weserübung, with light cruiser *Emden*, torpedo-boat *Möwe* and two motor minesweepers R17 and R18 as escort, back to Germany. We'll be well protected."

Wesner then added, "Brann, as I said, will remain here. He's local, known in the area. His role is the one you see: armourer, a central point to support the operation. This is your safe house if you need it, but only in an emergency. You stay out, as planned, tomorrow night. You all have keys for the huts. The following day, make use of morning and evening darkness, but work more slowly during daylight. This plan gives you one hour to reach *Martina*."

"Now," said Wesner, standing and leaning forward on his fists. "The commander, Colonel Eriksen. Given the political ambivalence in Oslo, it is possible that even strategic decisions at the fortress will fall to Eriksen and him alone. As commander, he will give the orders whether to fire on the invasion force or not. Hauptmann Westervik, we will talk separately..."

"Very good, sir," said Westervik, keen to resume some authority. "But can we now deal with the English Spy...?" Wesner nodded and Brann half stood.

"Yes, a problem," said Brann.

"What's that?" said Westervik, a jolt running through his body.

"He wasn't there."

"What do you mean?"

"The place was empty."

"So he's still alive?"

"Yuh."

Westervik thumped his fist hard onto the table. "He should have been there, in the night, sleeping like a bloody baby," he said, holding out and shaking a slip of paper with the ferry rotas.

"Sorry, boss."

Westervik looked again at the ferry rota and groaned. For Galtung to escape was bad enough, but all of this in front of bloody Wesner and his men...he should have checked with Brann before it all came out...but there was no time. "Galtung must be back at Oscarsborg by now, on the ferries," he said. "We'll have to leave him for now. But...it's normally him who ferries Eriksen. We'll get him Monday, for sure."

"It's unfortunate," said Wesner. "We hardly want a British agent running loose, do we? Hauptmann, double-check the schedules to ensure we take him this time."

As they broke up for further briefings, Westervik's mind drifted back to Klara, his worries as to where she would be when the invasion started, and whether she would be safe. If only he could have persuaded her to leave the area. But, beyond that, there was now the possibility that he could stay in Norway, untainted by the violence to come. He might see Klara again...but nothing was simple.

THIRTY-ONE

The 7th of April 1940, 1000 hours. Stensrud. Pendleton arrived as arranged, looking even more miserable than usual and accompanied by a blast of cold air as the door blew open. He removed the snow from his coat in rapid sweeps of both hands, a routine gesture of disapproval which Thomas now understood was a denunciation of life in general, not just of the Norwegian winter. He had begun to feel sorry for the man. Every joy in life seemed to have passed him by.

"*Blücher's* been out on battle training, bloody Admiral aboard, lots of activity," said Pendleton, wandering around the room, his head slumped into his chest. "Expected any time now at Swinemünde. Waiting to load up are — now, hear this — Gestapo, administrators, supplies, army troops, the works. Later today, Generalmajor Engelbrecht and elements of Staff of Army Group XXI and the 163rd Infantry Division will be embarked. Army, right. And then, to put on a show as they march through Oslo, Staff and Music Corps of the 307th Infantry Regiment 2nd Battalion. Postal staff, wireless technicians and war correspondents, the works. You don't need to be secret bloody intelligence to figure out what that lot means."

"So this is it," said Thomas, flatly.

"I'd say so. Could be the last time we meet, old boy," Pendleton murmured.

Thomas shrugged. "What do you make of Westervik's message, then?"

"How would I know?" Pendleton's expression adopted a look of despair. "But we can assume Jerry wants the Brits to accept the fake intelligence and send her fleet up to the North Pole, or somewhere. So... we should do the opposite of what they want. Seems obvious to me. We should close off Skagerrak, block the fjord and stop the invasion in its tracks at sea...though what the higher-ups in the Admiralty will make of it, who knows. We have only so many fighting ships and there may be other priorities. They may worry about air attack, too, this close to Germany. I don't know. We can only do our bit."

"Which we have done," said Thomas. "Now I need out. I've done my job."

Pendleton shrugged, averting Thomas's glare.

"The extraction plan?" said Thomas, his voice rising. "You received my message?"

"Obviously. I'm doing what I can...but it's not easy."

"What do you mean, not easy?"

"The embassy doesn't have the resources."

"Resources?" Thomas snapped. "There's a whole bloody building full of resources."

"Diplomats, paper-pushers...You know how it is."

"No, I don't know how it is. So you'll have me stay here, with my cover blown? A couple of assassins after me?"

"There's nothing I can do."

"This was not the deal."

"Sorry, not my call."

"You bastard."

Both men looked down at their feet, neither speaking. Thomas shook with anger. Let down again by his own supposed side. *We're all disposable.*

"There's a bus to Oslo in twenty minutes," said Pendleton, glancing at his watch and leaning against the door. "I'll be on it. Take it; then a train to Sweden."

"Just like that — the only bus of the day. And live off thin air when I get over the border. I have no money; haven't been paid for more than a month, damned near two. Do you know that? Not by you lot, anyway."

"Sorry, but not my department."

"Nothing's your department."

"Get out, as I said; it'll be best for you." Pendleton reached into his pocket. "Here, some cash for the train."

"I can't. I have responsibilities. There are people who have helped me...I...I'm not sure I want to leave."

"Your choice, old man. The game is playing out...and there's nothing more we can do by staying."

———

Klara worked through her plan hunched over the great table in the map room. Using a lined page torn out of her notebook she prepared a pencil copy of the farms and smallholdings she would visit on the way to stay with her aunt Agnes.

Leaving the car on the Ås road she entered the tract of ancient forest that cradled the sweeping arable lands of the Holmbekk estate. After skiing uphill for nearly an hour, a clearing came into view and then a small group of buildings. She pulled her map from an inside pocket. The track she had followed was direct from the main road and, aligning the map, she could see it ended at the Bell House, continuing as a path winding through the forest towards the head of Hallangspollen. If Hartman had come here from the fjord, that would have been his route.

As Klara pondered what to do next, a huge man with long black hair and dressed in a thick green jacket stepped out of the house and plodded with a rolling gait towards her.

"Private land," he said, stopping a short distance in front of her, feet apart, a shotgun hanging from a thick finger on his right hand.

"I'm on a ski trip to Hallangspollen," she said.

"Off," he growled, lifting the end of the barrel.

Klara raised her hand, apologised and started back down the track. Looking back a minute later, he was still there: a sentinel, the shotgun over his shoulder, so she kept walking until he was out of sight. After a short distance, she stopped, leaned her skis against a well-hidden rock and entered the forest. Skirting the clearing around the Bell House, she completed a wide circuit until she joined the path down to Hallangspollen. The last snowfall had filled the footprints, but a deep single-track path in the snow was still visible and she followed it all the way to Hallangspollen. People had passed this way and all must have used the beach near Skarholmen, where she had seen Hartman, and the track to the northern end of Storgaten.

She now repeated the walk in the reverse direction, using her estate map as a guide. Carefully estimating distances and, by studying the landforms, she found each of the paths which split off towards one or more of the eight properties she had identified. None had any sign of use, except for one: the route she had walked down to Hallangspollen. For sure, Hartman had been heading for the Bell House. The hair on the nape of her neck tingled.

Later on, she returned to the car. Sat in the driver's seat, she gripped the steering wheel. Who was this giant of a man who now lived in Thomas Galtung's former home? And what were the connections between them all? The giant, Thomas and Hartman?

————

The fiery disc of the sun balanced for a moment on the far mountains as Klara arrived at Furuly, Agnes's villa by the fjord. Sunlight infused the clouds with colours of extraordinary intensity: great masses of bright pink combined with streaks of grey and light indigo touched with yellow and even green, spreading across the pastel blue sky. It was a scene so unreal — in one way heavenly, in another frightening — it rooted her to the spot as she watched the orb finally sink behind the mountain ridges and, as it did, the clouds turned a pure, even more intense pink.

Klara prized the time she spent with her aunt. Most people talked about things, or today's events, or they liked to gossip, but she and Agnes talked ideas, meanings, the unexplained. There was a connection between the two of them. They stood together on the balcony, taking in the view over the fjord.

"I've been skiing up in the forest, near Thomas Galtung's old home," said Klara. "What happened to the Bell House?"

"It was sold, maybe ten years ago," said Agnes. "It went for a song apparently."

"Who bought it?"

"A local man, Alexander Brann. A bit of a loner, apparently, and a thug if you believe the rumours."

So, the giant was Brann. They were all connected: Hartman, the ship's captain; *Martina,* his ship; and the Bell House, which Hartman had visited and where Brann now lived. All of them must be suspects in Johansen's mission to find Nazi infiltration.

But was Thomas linked with them? Or was his former life at the Bell House misleading her? The house was sold when he was a child, so why would he have a connection now?

———

Later that day, Westervik wandered the snowy paths of the Palace Park in Oslo, stopping and retracing his steps at random. When he was confident he was not being followed or observed, he sat at a bench with a view of the King's Guards' hut and the paths leading up from Karl Johans gate. Before long, he was joined by Hanna Gjertsen, who cleared away a fresh fall of snow on the opposite end of the bench and proceeded to pour herself a coffee from her Thermos flask. Pulling out a copy of *Aftenposten,* she read the headlines, finished off her drink, looked around and then departed in the direction of Kristian IV's gate, leaving the newspaper on the bench. Wrapped inside it was a short note.

Westervik now had the exact details he needed. No claims for expenses or other payments had been made to Klara Holmbekk. But an account had been set up in her name on the 9th of January and any expenses were to be paid from the operational budget of the Police Surveillance Centre. The record was held on a single sheet of paper.

Leaving the bench, he ambled towards a secluded path that ran along the north side of the park. Coming the other way was Hanna

Gjertsen. As they passed, she slowed, just long enough for him to whisper: "Remove her from the records. She never existed as a police surveillance agent."

As he walked on through the park in a blur, his heart pounded as if his chest would explode.

THIRTY-TWO

T*he 8ᵗʰ of April 1940.* Oscarsborg fortress. The orange glow of early morning spread over the treetops and lit up the snow covering the ferryman's hut. Patches of fog drifted over the fjord, their pearly, ragged tops caught in the first rays of sun. Thomas stood with his head back, catching the sun on his face, but there was no warmth and soon his skin was numb with the cold. It was worth a try, as if it would bring spring a little closer.

It was hard to accept his discovery that Westervik could be both a German spy and Klara's lover. He relived the events at the cemetery, questioning whether his memory was playing tricks, whether he had dreamt it all or had been mistaken. No, it happened, but how would he resolve whether Klara was part of Westervik's operation or was caught up with him quite innocently? Should he confront her, or stay schtum? And, if the German invasion fleet was even now approaching the fortress, was it too late to worry either way? It was impossible to know.

Half an hour later he set to clearing ice around the boats and running the engines, but there was no sign of any unscheduled work that morning so, after breakfast, he joined three of his colleagues and they passed time playing backgammon. Later, he ambled outside to await the arrival of the ferry with officers and NCOs due to start their new shift on the fortress, but there was no activity on the fjord or on the quay at Sundbrygga. He felt a twinge of unease.

Looking south, the fog still covered the fjord off Horten. In the stillness and silence he drew his hands from his pocket and held them out in front of him. They were shaking. Shivers ran up his spine. He was sure: a disaster was unfolding, unseen, all around him. Scared and beset by uncertainty, he faced too many dilemmas. Was it rational to risk his life by remaining here, on the fortress, out of loyalty to his mission, when there was nothing he could do to help either Britain or Norway? Was it his responsibility to unravel Klara's role in Westervik's terrible enterprise? Was she now the enemy, or should he save her? And should he reverse his decision made when eye to eye with Pendleton? Take his offer of money and join him on the bus? Then, the train to Sweden...and live out the coming storm in safety? There was still time and his ferryboat was just a few steps away.

Something deep inside told him that the cards had already been dealt and chance would determine what would happen next. He waited, watching. Still the mist hung low over the fjord.

———

Climbing the steep, snow-covered steps from Storgaten, Klara and Agnes eventually reached Steinborg and took in the long, misty view down the fjord and across to the far mountains. To complete their walk, they would follow the ridgeline and drop back down the fjord-side towards the northern extremity of Storgaten, where it faded into a narrow, snowy path. It was icy cold and completely still; nothing moved, not a bird or a twig at the top of the trees. Pushing her hands deep into her pockets, Klara marvelled at a landscape of endless space and frozen beauty.

As they made their way down the steep slope towards a scatter of houses at the northern end of town, a disturbed area of snow amongst a drift of scrubby aspen trees caught her eye: an elk, perhaps, had been feeding. But something drew her to look closer. A strange frozen object stood out. She took a few more steps and then, realising what it was, she recoiled, grabbing Agnes' arm in horror. A human hand, covered in a thin and crusted layer of ice, protruded from the snow. A boot, signs of clothing, strands of hair. Rooted to the spot, she was transfixed by the sight of what was clearly a dead body.

"You know who it is?" cried Agnes. "Oddvar Halvorsen. I recognise the jacket. It was a present from his mother. And his hair..."

"Are you sure?" said Klara, shaking.

"Quite sure. He lives at Nesbu," she said, looking towards a small red house visible through the trees just below them.

Klara crouched to look more closely. It was clear Oddvar had been there for some time, long enough to freeze solid. She cleared a little more snow from his face, torn between the fear of what she might find and a desire to reveal what lay beneath. As she swept with her gloved hands, the snow started to colour pink, then bright red as his head was exposed.

She immediately stopped and stepped back, clinging to Agnes. In a frenzy, she threw away one of her gloves which had brushed against the dead man's face; it had picked up small fragments of bone, frozen flesh and blood. The whole of one side of his head had been broken away. His ear hung from a strand of skin. His brain had been exposed. She groaned in disbelief.

"Oddvar," said Agnes. "I can't believe it. What could have happened?"

"We can't stay here," said Klara, dragging Agnes back to the path and down the hillside. Clinging to a frosted metal handrail, they slithered down a flight of snow-covered steps, past Nesbu, until they reached Storgaten.

"It could have been a hunting accident," Agnes said, blowing hard as they hurried back towards Furuly. "A bullet can travel a long way, especially from an elk rifle. Maybe a wolf got him?"

But Klara knew: this was no accident. Oddvar had been killed, dragged there and hidden; there were clear tracks in the snow from Nesbu. The realisation that this was a murder, unheard of in Drøbak, heightened the sense of dread she felt. Something — the playing out of something bigger — was happening, and they had stumbled upon it.

———

Arriving at Furuly, they slammed shut the front door and only then did they both begin to shiver uncontrollably.

"We have to report this," said Klara.

"Oddvar, such a nice man," Agnes said, over and over, wringing her hands.

A short while later Klara entered Drøbak police station, a green-painted wooden building further along Storgaten towards town. On duty were Police Constable O.L. Mørk, on the desk, and the 'piket', Police Constable Arnt Jørgensen. Townsfolk were crowded into the small reception area off the main door at the back of the building, sitting and standing, all appearing shocked and anguished.

Constable Mørk raised his chin, enquiring.

"I've found a body, further up Storgaten," said Klara. "Oddvar Halvorsen."

The two policemen looked at each other.

"I need a statement, right away," said Mørk.

"That's the fourth military," said Station Sergeant Rolf Hansen, emerging from a door behind the two constables. "And I've just received a report: two ferrymen have been found, dead."

———

The 8th of April 1940, 1400 hours. Four ferrymen settled down for a late lunch. Olaf scooped herrings onto the plates Thomas had set on the table. Still they waited.

Thomas looked again through the window towards Sundbrygga. It should have been a busy day; change-over for the NCOs on the main guns. The knot squeezed tighter in his gut. For certain, something wasn't right.

Later, as the light was fading, a young messenger, short, fair-haired and with his jacket undone, crashed through the door.

"Orders," he said, breathlessly. "None of today's shift turned up at Sundbrygga, so the ferry hasn't come back to collect the officers waiting to return. Take them back, but use two boats."

"Just as we were brewing our afternoon coffee," scowled Olaf. "Anyway, why two boats?"

"I haven't finished yet," said the messenger. He looked down to his slip of paper. "You are to return with another load of NCO's and Major Jenson who were off duty but have been recalled and will be waiting for you by the time you arrive. There will be a few ferrymen, too. Don't know how many, but that's why you have to take both boats across, apparently, though there will be boats there, too. I guess they think they might need them all. It seems there's a bit of a mess with the schedules."

"Ruddy chaos," said Olaf. "All the boats will now end up at Sundbrygga."

"And I have to collect the colonel, as usual," said Thomas, trying to sound positive. "I'll need one of the boats for that." He shoved his hands into his pockets to hide their shaking.

———

The 8th of April 1940, 1700 hours. Klara returned to Furuly. The two women huddled together around the fire, fearful and uncertain. Several other bodies had been found, all shot, all men. 'There may be others', she had overheard the police say, 'but they were to be confirmed'. She had heard the name 'Svensen' spoken. Svensen, the shopkeeper. And Gundersen's wife had rushed into the station with a neighbour, both in tears. Gundersen, the baker, another artilleryman: *could he, too, be one of the victims?*

"War has started," said Klara, nibbling her fingernails.

"Impossible," said Agnes.

"It has," whispered Klara. Brann. Hartman, *Martina*. They're connected, she thought. She slumped into a chair, her head in her hands. And the killings — Halvorsen, Svensen, Gunderson — they were all artillerymen on the fortress and at Kopås. Ferrymen had been killed, too, the police had said. She thought of Thomas, and shivered. Agnes had also joined the dots; she knew them all and their connections to the fjord's defences. The police must know that, too, and would surely alert the military. Or maybe they hadn't and were just collecting evidence until they were sure?

"I need the telephone," said Klara, running out to the hall. With no emergency number for Johansen she failed after several attempts to reach him via the police headquarters in Oslo. The station in Drøbak had never heard of him.

Next, she phoned the colonel, but there was no reply from his home. She tried the fortress.

"I need to speak to the colonel," she said.

"I am sorry, he doesn't take civilian calls."

Now certain of a bigger disaster looming, Klara raced up the stairs and pulled open the door onto the balcony, stepping out into the cold night. She scanned the darkness for a few pinpricks of light on the fortress — they always showed, but none were visible this evening. She clasped her hands together, her fingers twisting and untwisting. The fortress is preparing, she thought, going dark for what is to come. She listened for any sign of activity on the fjord. Silence prevailed, aside from the hammering of her own heart. A wisp of fog drifted past the boathouse's lantern. Far away, a wolf howled.

Transfixed by events and the darkness of the fjord, Klara jumped as a hinge creaked from behind her. It was just Agnes hanging onto the door, fear painted onto her face. "You frightened me," she whispered. She took Agnes's hand and dragged her across the landing into a room on the other side of the house, overlooking the garden towards Storgaten. A few outdoor lights sparkled in the cold, still air. Nothing moved and everything outside seemed deathly still and heavy with malice. She was unable to contain a raw fear, an overwhelming and terrible sense of dread. War had started, she was sure. Its tendrils were here, in Drøbak.

"We should lock the doors," she said.

Only then did Klara's mind slip back to just two days ago, to the little café in Oslo, to Carl and his worries for her, his pleadings that she go away to stay safe. Was this what he warned of?

And if so...how did he know?

THIRTY-THREE

T*he 8ᵗʰ of April, 1900 hours.* Sundbrygga: dark, still and very
cold. The sun had long since crept away and still a blanket of
mist lay over the water. Approaching the quay, Thomas
studied the town as he guided the ferry through a thin layer of ice on the
edge of the fjord. Ahead was Olaf with two other ferrymen. A few lights
in nearby houses glowed through the mist. There was no movement; no
traffic, just a dog barking far away. The air was completely still, as if it no
longer existed, except for the cold. Climbing the ladder onto the quay,
he moored up and spotted Olaf in conversation with the newly arrived
NCO's and a senior officer. Several ferrymen, who must have volun-
teered to fill the gaps in the schedules, were huddled together in their
shelter. He stopped to look around, nervous, wracked by the feeling that
something was wrong.

"You'll need to hang on," Thomas heard the officer say to Olaf and
the two other ferrymen who had come over from the fortress. Turning
to the NCO's dragging their kit up from the ferry, there were more
unwelcome words from the officer: "You'll have to wait, too. You might
have to return to the fortress; we're having difficulty in finding anyone."

Leaving the disgruntled men on the quay, Thomas threw a quick
smile at Olaf, then headed towards Seimbakken. A few minutes later,

after greeting a short, fresh-faced guard, he knocked on the door of the colonel's home, relieved to see it opened by a taller, more mature soldier. All seemed normal. Perhaps the scheduling chaos today was just coincidence, a series of administrative blunders, a few people with a bug of some sort? Perhaps Pendleton's intelligence was incorrect, or disinformation? The warship's military band could have been a decoy, the real Nazi objective a breakout to the Atlantic? He tried to relax — after all, some of the gaps in the schedule had already been filled by new men arriving at the quay and there was no sign of panic amongst the officers.

Ambling into a small drawing room, where he always waited, he looked out onto Seimbakken. The road was sparsely lit by several streetlights and the glow of a pair of lanterns on the entrance pillars of one of the villas. He settled into a chair by the window and watched the guard pacing the path outside, slapping his arms around his body trying to keep warm. "Poor bugger," he whispered. He stared out, still unable to let go of the worries that had gripped him most of the day. Then a booming voice from behind made him jump up from his chair.

"Ready to go, Galtung?" said the colonel, stepping heavily off the last stair.

As he stood to take the colonel's bag, Thomas noticed a figure walking steadily up Seimbakken. Approaching the villa, the figure, a man in a dark coat, waved at the guard and stopped, one hand resting on the gate, as if to exchange a few words. But something made Thomas stop to watch; he knew who it was. He heard the colonel come into the room and sensed his presence just behind his shoulder. Shivers ran through his body.

"Wake up, Galtung; time to go," said the colonel, impatiently. "Guard, open the door."

As Thomas turned to warn the colonel, he heard a faint thud from outside and glimpsed, out of the corner of his eye, the guard at the gate reel backwards and fall with a sharp cry, his legs quivering and then still. Thomas gripped the back of the chair unable, for a moment, to speak, his chest suddenly gripped by a crushing vice. Stepping back from the window he caught the colonel's eyes.

"What's up?" said the colonel.

"Secure the door," shouted Thomas to the guard. "A gunman. A handgun. And... yes, a rifle, hidden under his coat."

At that moment he heard another thud and the indoor guard fell backwards with a grunt, his rifle clattering noisily onto the hall floor, his hand visible through the doorway, twitching for a moment and then lifeless. A waft of cold air entered the house. "Close the door," he urged.

The warning hit home. The colonel pulled a revolver from his holster. He leaned out of the drawing room and released two shots through the half-open door. Calmly kicking it shut, he slid the bottom bolt closed and dipped in behind a bookcase in the hall. "Silenced handgun," he said, dragging Thomas back along the hall towards the rear of the house, where they stopped.

Thomas leaned towards the colonel. "It's Carl Westervik," he whispered, urgently. "He's a Nazi spy."

"Who? What, the potato merchant? How do you know this?"

It was impossible to explain. Thomas stuttered, shaking his head. "It's an assassination attempt...on you, sir. The invasion is coming."

"For God's sake, and you're part of it for all I know?" said the colonel, switching off the hall lights. The house was now in darkness, just a faint light seeping down from the upper floor, but Thomas felt the colonel's revolver pointing into his midriff. He looked towards the back of the house, into the darkness of the garden.

"We must both stay alive if we are to get you back to the fortress," said Thomas, "And of course you can bloody trust me," he hissed, glancing towards the back door.

They looked at each other in the faint light, then at the back door and the darkness beyond.

"Go," breathed the colonel. "Now."

His ears ringing from the revolver shots and surging adrenalin, Thomas sprinted towards the rear doorway, pulled it open and ran almost blind into the night, falling over and breaking a white-painted picket fence. Moments later the colonel appeared and Thomas followed him across an open snow-covered area. They then entered a small copse, giving good cover in the darkness.

"My God, you were right," said the colonel. "It's the potato merchant. I saw him."

He crouched down and listened. There was no sign of Westervik. The colonel, gasping with the sudden exertion, set off again and they weaved a path through an orchard towards a yellow-painted outbuilding, lit by a single light in a nearby house. A door slammed heavily somewhere close. The colonel was heading for Sundbryyga. Olaf would have left but there would be boats and at least one other ferryman.

"Westervik," the colonel said, panting. "I met him. Three weeks or something ago. Tried to flog me some Swedish foodstuffs, he did."

At that moment, a stone wall behind them exploded with a loud crash.

"A rifle, for God's sake: you were right, the bastard has a rifle," the colonel whispered. "Galtung, get to the quay. Get the boat ready. I'll just have to trust you. Go."

Thomas nodded and, looking around, selected a route with good cover provided by another barn and several houses. Bent double, he weaved between the trees and around rocky outcrops in the gardens, falling once into a pocket of deep snow. From behind, another shot sounded — the rifle again — and the sound of breaking glass. Dodging into a gap between two houses, he reached Storgaten without further incident. Was the colonel still alive? Several revolver shots then sounded out of the darkness. A woman leaned out of a window nearby, shouting at him with incomprehensible words. He stopped for a short rest, his heart thumping.

Racing up Storgaten he turned onto the quay, panting heavily, but when he arrived he was met with a scene so shocking his legs almost gave way. In front of him, sprawled in the snow, lay eight or ten bodies, most in Norwegian military uniform, a few ferrymen... Blood stained the snow. They all appeared to be dead.

"Olaf," he shouted, moving towards the boats, but there was no reply.

Standing on the edge of the quay, he looked down into the shadows. The boats were not floating as they should be. As he leaned forward to look closer, he realised with horror that every one of them was half-submerged, that a faint light caught the water inside them and that the engine covers had been dragged off and were floating freely. The whole lot had been sabotaged: every ferry.

"Olaf," he shouted again.

It was only then that he glimpsed the body floating face-down in the broken ice and water between the quay and one of the ferryboats. He knew instantly it was Olaf. As he struggled to take in what he was seeing, he heard the sound of running and the colonel appeared, barely able to speak with exertion. Thomas ran up to meet him. A door opened in a house nearby and people started to appear.

"I delayed the bastard, pinned him down," said the colonel. "But he has a rifle, so he can pick us off at distance...if he can see us. Stay out of the light."

Only then did the colonel see the disaster on the quay. "Good Lord," he whispered, walking slowly between the bodies. "Sverre Lindeman, poor man." His head was shaking. "Osvald Sørsdahl; Parr, Ringal. Christ, all gunners." He seemed to be frozen to the spot. "And...the Lord above, Major Jensen, too."

"Sir, the ferries have all been sabotaged," Thomas said.

"Good God. So we can't stay here."

"I have an idea," said Thomas. Looking at the colonel for confirmation, Thomas pushed open the gate in the chalk-marked archway. It led into a garden of snow-covered lawns, rocky outcrops and trees next to the fjord. Beyond was the profile of a large villa: Furuly.

"Agnes Holmbekk, you can get there through here," Thomas shouted, panting as he ran. "She has a boat." Arriving at Furuly, two lights showed in upstairs rooms. After a shouted exchange, the door opened and Agnes stood there, rigid, her eyes drawn with anxiety.

"Thomas...?"

"We need your boat" he said.

"There is no boat," she said, as the colonel appeared, "not here." She looked up, following Thomas's eyes to the boathouse, its outline visible against the fjord. "She's in store at Lehmanns."

At that moment, Klara appeared at the door.

"You need a boat?" she said, looking at the colonel.

"Yes," shouted Thomas, "I need to get the colonel back. War has begun."

"There," said Klara, looking at Agnes, "I said so."

"There must be a ruddy boat somewhere," said the colonel, the first hint of panic sounding in his voice.

"I have a boat at Skarholmen," said Klara, her eyes switching between Thomas and the colonel. "And a car to get us there."

"You, girl. You knew too?" said the colonel, jabbing Klara with his finger. "You knew war has begun. And so did he," he said, turning to confront Thomas. "How did you know?"

"Your gunners are being killed," she said, struggling to pull her boots on. "There's a big flap at the police station. They are finding men all over town, dead, shot. Ferrymen, too."

Thomas looked at the colonel. He clearly didn't know anything of any events at the police station. But his worries about Klara returned; her association with the assassin, who could have them all in his sights even now. Was she part of the Nazi operation? Was she leading the commander of Norway's defences into a trap? Or was she unaware of Westervik's true identity?

He stepped up to her and looked into her eyes. He saw her as a child, laughing, those same eyes projecting her intense and funny view of the world, her pretty upturned nose defining her optimism and determination. They had kissed once, held hands, skied together. They had shared ideas and thoughts. He had been taken into her home.

"Let's go," he said and they ran, into the darkness, towards her car.

With Klara at the wheel, the next few minutes passed in a flash, Thomas being buffeted and sliding across the rear seat as they careered along Storgaten, the colonel issuing a flow of instructions from the front.

Stopping abruptly in a bank of snow, they abandoned the car and crept into the night towards Skarholmen, feeling their way in silence above the treacherous drop into the icy fjord. Arriving at the island, Klara went ahead and Thomas stayed with the colonel to guide him over the slippery causeway and along the track under the pine trees towards the quay. It felt unreal, as if he were outside of himself, looking down at some sort of game, or in a film. But he knew that Westervik was out there somewhere, hunting them down.

"I'll cover the crossing," the colonel whispered, dipping behind some rocks, "although I can't see a damned thing."

Thomas reached the boathouse. The mist had eased, and the outline of the shepherd's crook harbour was just visible. It was a relief, of sorts. He could now see a way to escape the madness, to help the colonel back to the fortress. After this, war really might come to Norway; it seemed quite likely.

A shout from Klara guided him to the boatshed, and he helped her drag open the big doors, then watched her go back inside and switch on a single bench-light, enough to illuminate the winch.

"You know who he is, the assassin?" said Thomas, still panting heavily as she released the winch, leaning on the brake as *Terne* slid towards the harbour. "Tell me you're not part of it?" he urged.

She stared at him, her face appearing blank and scared in equal measures. "Thomas, I don't know what you mean." She pulled a hat out of her pocket and buttoned up her thick sheep's wool coat.

"All of this," he said. "Are you part of it?"

"The boat's in the water," she said, again looking blankly at him. "She's all yours."

He looked into her eyes. He nodded, kissed her hard on the lips and set off, running down the beach towards *Terne*. Splashing through the freezing water, his feet and legs, already bruised and frozen, felt as if they were being sliced by sharp knives. He had never before understood how painful freezing water could be. Reaching up to the transom, he dragged himself aboard, started the engine and waited anxiously for the colonel to appear.

Soon, he could hear him struggling down the beach, slipping and falling, and he helped drag him into *Terne*. There was still no sign of Westervik.

"Go," the colonel ordered, aiming his pistol back into the darkness. "He's out there, probably still on the mainland, probably with a damned scope on his rifle. "We're alright here, below the harbour walls — it's darker and he'll struggle to pick us out — but that stupid girl..."

"Klara," shouted Thomas, looking back. She was the faintest of shapes, standing beside a heap of crab pots and timber baulks, washed by an ill-defined light from a window in the boatshed.

"Klara," he shouted, "come with us." Holding his breath his mind went to Westervik. Was he yet on the island? How much time did they have? He willed her to move. "Klara," he whispered, his hands holding his face, frighteningly aware of the danger she was now in. Unless....unless she was part of Westervik's plan? A lingering doubt remained. Uncertainty held him tight. Surely, he should leave her: the risks to himself, to the colonel, to Norway were too great.

Cold metal suddenly pressed into Thomas's neck. "Get moving, Galtung," shrieked the colonel. "Now."

He looked again for Klara. She stood on the quay, just visible in the faint patch of light. He shouted for her to find cover or run for the boat. Still, she stood. As he watched, a rifle shot sounded. His heart jolted. He heard a crash and wood splintering. Then, a faint sigh and he watched as Klara crumpled and slowly fell.

Sweeping the colonel's hand away Thomas thrust his face at him. "I'll come back."

Jumping from the boat he ran back up the icy, snow-covered beach. Slithering and falling, his legs barely functioning, his feet screaming pain from icy water in his boots, he kept running and reached the top of the quay. He bent over to pick her up and, as he did so, there was another shot and a bullet cracked the air.

Placing his hands under her, he felt her warm body lying against the snow, then threw her over his shoulder and set off towards Terne. The freezing water was again like knives on his legs.

"Take care of her," he shouted to the colonel as he fell into the cockpit. Blood poured from Klara's face, covering his hands and clothes.

"You fool, Galtung, I'll have you for this."

Thomas fell against the controls and rammed open the throttle. The engine roared into life and, at that moment, he felt they might escape; it was now so dark he could barely see the harbour walls. Another two shots sounded but they were wild and soon the boat was safely out into the fjord, heading for the fortress.

"Sir, I can't see. How is she?" shouted Thomas over the noise of the engine, his feet and legs now numb, his trousers already stiff with ice.

"You were bloody lucky I didn't shoot you," the colonel responded.

Thomas, breathing hard, felt barely able to take in what had happened. He sought out the island in the blackness of the night. As they entered the main fjord a patch of mist slipped by, the air eerie and damp. A further shot sounded, but he ignored it; they could not be seen. He shuddered at all that had happened and eased back on the throttle as the ferryman's harbour appeared, two tiny points of light marking the edge of the quay.

"Klara?" he said, leaning down to touch her still figure laid out on the bloodied bottom boards. He looked up.

"Alive," said the colonel.

———

Alone in the darkness, Westervik shook with anguish. His mission had failed. He knew it was the end. The shots he had taken on Skarholmen... it was all a blur. There had been no time to settle, to brace. The light was terrible, the crosshairs barely visible. It had been impossible to gauge the distance; the darkness and mist could play tricks. And the damned misting on the scope...everything had been against him. Worst of all, as he replayed that shot in his mind, he was far from sure it was Eriksen he had hit, even whether he had hit him cleanly. Why would the man just stand there? Maybe it was not Eriksen; maybe there were other guards on the run? But the more he pondered, the more he convinced himself the target he had hit was too small to be Eriksen. The uncertainties were crippling his mind and it was impossible to think straight.

But it was too late to worry. His only hope — with just twenty minutes left — was to reach *Martina* before she departed Drøbak. It would be impossible to stay in Drøbak, his identity now revealed.

With his mind in a turmoil, Westervik threw his treasured rifle into the fjord and, struggling through the deep snow, he reached Storgaten still with some hope. But at Sundbrygga the road was blocked by a police cordon. Worse, the whole damned town had come alive. He looked at his watch. With only six minutes left, in despair, he knew he would miss the departure of *Martina*. He had no option but to mingle with the crowd, to slowly ease his way through and amble the remainder of the distance.

Arriving on the quay fifteen minutes later, he slumped, exhausted, against the upturned hull of a small boat. *Martina had disappeared into the night.*

His final hope of sanctuary was Walter von Elverfeldt; he could still catch the last bus to Oslo. But as he walked back along Storgaten, the despair brought on by *Martina's* departure eased, and only one thought was on his mind. The shot he had taken...the height and build of his target...and the moment it had crumpled into the snow. If only he could go back and make that decision again, to assuage the terrible doubt and panic he now felt.

THIRTY-FOUR

In the early minutes of the 9th of April 1940, led by the heavy cruiser Blücher, Warship Group 5 passed the mouth of Oslo fjord, unopposed by the British fleet.

At Oscarsborg fortress Col. Eriksen, now aware of an approaching armada, awaited orders from Oslo regarding what action to take to confront the invasion. A severely depleted force of mostly inexperienced artillery men stood by.

———

0015 hours, 9th of April 1940. Oscarsborg fortress. Locked into the ferryman's hut, Thomas slumped to the floor, shivering and in shock. The ferryboats had all been sabotaged, Olaf and the others were dead, Klara had been shot and it seemed likely that, at some point, an invasion force would appear, head-to-head with the very island on which he was now held. He dragged off his boots, freezing water splashing over the floor, and prized the tops of his socks from his iced trousers. Crawling across to the stove he looked down in fear at his numb, deathly white feet, his hand shaking as he held a match to the dry birch bark.

Somewhere in the darkness outside, two guards were posted. Despite saving the colonel, Thomas had been arrested as a suspected spy for his knowledge of a German invasion force and for disobeying orders. He tapped on the window, hoping to attract the guards' attention, but there was no response: just the distant hoot of an owl. Later a match flared, silhouetting the outline of a soldier, his head dipping as he edged the cigarette into the flame. The haze of his companion's breath hung in the air, then faded away.

Thomas stared out of the window into the night. A few lights in the town twinkled in sharp, clear air above tongues of mist drifting over the fjord. Then, as he watched, the lights disappeared, one by one. Just a single glittering pinprick stood defiant high on the fjord-side; perhaps a family preparing supper, children being readied for bed. Then it, too, disappeared.

Drøbak had been blacked out.

He tensed and pressed his nose to the glass. From the far distance, away to the south, the faint shaft of a searchlight escaped the fog. Then came a flash of light and a deep rumble of heavy guns, the vibration passing through the hut like the tremors of an earthquake. From the ferryman's clock, the one they had always used to regulate their working days, came a despairing thud from its broken chime as the thin floorboards of the hut trembled. Then, there was silence again and the shiver of fear in his gut.

Events then moved fast: more rumbling from down the fjord, louder now. He tapped on the window, trying to attract the guards. From buildings nearby alarms sounded: shouted commands, running boots, the clatter of men called to arms.

"It's started," he whispered.

An air-raid siren in the town sliced through the night air, then faded away. Silence again: a dense, freezing stillness. Away to the south, darkness. Then, a heavy knock on the door, a key rattling. Two guards entered.

"The colonel wants you."

Thomas pulled on his wet, steaming boots, grabbed his coat, hat and rucksack and was led over the quay towards the fortress's main defences.

"Guards. Stay with that boat," shouted one of the new arrivals as they left. "And extinguish that candle in the hut. Enemy ships are approaching up the fjord."

"This is it," Thomas said. "I hope they got you lot trained in time." But he doubted it.

"Just shut up," hissed the guard.

Following the guards in the darkness along a broad track Thomas entered the main fortress and, a short time later, the inner slopes of the huge, curved embankment came into view, at the base of which were dimmed ground-level lights. As he reached the embankment, the outline of one of the massive Krupp cannons loomed out of the darkness. Clustered around it, a small group of officers stood being addressed by Colonel Eriksen. Waiting on the margins of this group, he sensed their tension and strained to take in the colonel's briefing... "severely reduced artillery crews"..."killings of gunners in town"..."new recruits..."not yet trained"..."Krupp guns...each needing a trained crew of eleven men....sufficient trained men for just one gun."

Little of the briefing surprised him. But to hear it spoken was frightening. It seemed the defence of Norway hung on just one of the large Krupp cannons...and the time taken to reload would mean only one round could be fired if a warship were to appear. He felt his heart deflate. Thousands of men on the fortress, all this activity, these great ramparts...and it could all come down to one round.

But Eriksen hadn't finished. Thomas managed a step or two closer.

"I shall split the crew," the colonel said. "This will enable us to service two guns, Moses and Aaron. We will find men to work under your command to make up the numbers. They will be arriving soon from the barracks, and you must brief them as best you can."

The wheels of an ammunition trolley rattled, appearing out of the darkness, transporting a massive shell along a cleared path in the snow towards the cannon. Ahead of him, men were working to ready the guns. Orders were issued, stark with tension. Another lantern was brought forward, lighting up the base of the cannon.

Instructed to wait by a flight of steps leading up to a platform on the embankment, Thomas watched Eriksen moving between groups of men. A short time later he came down the steps and approached Thomas.

"Galtung," he said. "The earlier events will be put aside, for now. There are urgent matters I need you for. You are the only ferryman on the island, probably the only one alive. But we have no ferries, only that boat belonging to the Holmbekk girl."

"*Terne*, sir. She's moored where we arrived," said Thomas. "She will need her engine turning over to keep it warm."

"This is the situation," said the colonel. "Norway is under attack. A flotilla of warships is approaching up the fjord. They have ignored searchlights and warning shots from the outer batteries at Bolaerne and Rauöy. There have been actions over the past hour. The naval base at Horten is being attacked. We do not yet know the exact intent of the enemy or whether they are German or British."

He broke off to supervise the lifting of a shell into the breach of the cannon.

"The invaders are German," said Thomas, as the colonel returned. "The killings were all part of an operation to disable the guns here on the fortress by taking out you and your officers and NCO's. By killing the ferrymen and sabotaging the ferries they hoped to ensure no reinforcements would be possible. The fortress would be disabled. That was their plan."

"How can you possibly know the ships are German? You're a student for God's sake, a ferryman."

Thomas spoke, quietly: "Sir, I can't tell you, but please don't doubt my loyalty to Norway. Westervik shot at me too, remember. You don't need to guard me."

"All this will be dealt with in the future. *Terne* is the only craft operational until and unless we can get other boats across. I need you, Galtung, to ensure that boat is prepared for action. It will be used only if there are express orders from me or my Adjutant, Helberg."

A small, slimly-built man with round, wire-rimmed glasses, fair-haired, around thirty years old, stepped forward and responded to the order with a sharp nod of his head.

"Galtung, she must be ready, fuelled, operational," said the colonel, and then, turning to his adjutant, "Helberg, double the guard on the boat. And Galtung, too. Keep him under continuous watch."

Another quick nod.

"Galtung..."

"Colonel...?"

"The Holmbekk girl is alive, not badly hurt. You can see her. Two minutes only. Then back to your boat. And no ruddy adventures."

"Thank you, sir."

"And Galtung,"

"Sir."

"You don't tell me whether I need to keep you under guard."

———

Thomas entered the military hospital and was shown into a small room where Klara lay in a cream-coloured, metal-framed bed. He laid his hand on hers.

"He missed," she said, her voice a faltering whisper. "Pure luck."

"But your face."

"The bullet hit a pile of wood. I caught a splinter."

"A splinter caused all that the blood?"

"It just missed my eye, apparently. Then I must have fainted."

"Klara..."

"There's no damage to my eye, the doctor said, but I'll have a small scar. It's nothing. I'll be out tomorrow."

She slumped back in the bed and looked up at him, her forehead furrowed as if asking why it could all have happened.

"I'm so sorry," he whispered. "I should never have asked you for help."

"How on earth did you get mixed up in this?" she said, shaking her head.

He shrugged. "The invasion has started, you know that?"

"I guessed that much."

"There's no way back to the mainland, but you should be safe here."

"They have shelters in this building," she said. "But if it's an inva-

233

sion...? Are you helping it or opposing it? I don't know. You're involved, I know it."

"Later I'll explain," said Thomas. "There's no time now, but please forgive me."

"I can't work you out, Thomas. When all this is over we must talk. You appear one day, just after Britain enters the war on Germany. You don't seem to have an income, or at least, you didn't until the boat and ferry jobs came up."

"Klara...."

"You wander about looking at the defences. You know some suspect you for the Kopås incident, don't you? You poke around the harbour. You ingratiate yourself into my family. You seem to know all about the invasion. Someone wants to kill you. What's going on?"

He had run out of words. He dropped his head in a wave of guilt and despair.

"Are you really who you say you are?" she whispered.

"And are you?" he replied as he left the room, dragged out by the guard. "You knew, too."

THIRTY-FIVE

Terne gently rocked in a freezing soup of water and ice by the quay. Lying on the frost-covered boards by the engine, Thomas tensed at the scraping and cracking of ice against the hull. It was a familiar sound but, amplified inside the wooden boat, it carried a tingle of menace, adding to his sense of dread about the prospect of invasion. Above, he heard the whispering voices of the guards. After several turns of the starting handle, the engine coughed into life. Relieved, he was ready to return to the ferryman's hut.

At that moment, far away to the south, a flash of light lit up the sky. A rumbling noise echoed off the mountains. Then, a deathly silence. "What...?" exclaimed Moen, one of the guards, a new recruit for whom Thomas had come to feel genuine sympathy; the poor boy seemed constantly close to death by freezing.

"Lightning," said the second guard, Grambo, emphatically. "There's a storm coming."

"Never seen lightning in winter," said Moen, dubiously, slipping a square of chocolate to Thomas. "Not when it's like this."

They all waited for what was to come and Thomas eventually returned to the ferryman's hut. Inside, the minutes ticked by on the tired old clock, each hour marked by the anguished thuds of the chime hammer on the cracked metal bell. The ferrymen, of course, had known their timepiece was unreliable and far past its best; but it had been a fixture in their hut for many years, like a resident cat, and they resisted any move to change it.

Slowly, the faint light of the pre-dawn softened the blackness of the night and, through the window, an outline of the ridgeline above Drøbak emerged. Mist drifted over the quay. Thomas walked to the bookshelf and straightened up the untidy pile of tattered books that made up the ferryman's library. After several circuits of the hut, he returned to the table and rearranged the scatter of boating magazines in perfect date order, then stacked them neatly on the shelf. It made no sense, but it was the only gesture he was capable of constructing for Olaf and the other ferrymen. All, it seemed, had shared the fate of the gunnery officers and NCOs.

It was only then that it struck him: he, too, must have been a target as one of the ferrymen, but had escaped because he had seen Westervik's approach and had warned the colonel, giving them both a few vital seconds to mount a defence. Westervik: at the centre of it all. He shook at the thought of his own stupidity, his naivety, in trying to seek a job with the man who had twice tried to kill him and could still be a danger to Klara, his oldest friend.

Another hour passed, his whole body dulled by the intense emptiness of the senseless killings. And then, two gentle knocks sounded at the door: another session on *Terne*. Moen, the guard, appeared and slipped him a small paper package. "More chocolate?" Hopefully the kind boy would survive whatever was to come.

All was well with *Terne* and Thomas resumed his vigil at the window in the ferryman's hut. Clouds over the ridgeline coloured, a faint glow of yellows and reds. The clock struck a single fraught thump: 0430 hours. He stood, waiting, fearful, trapped. A few minutes later another bright flash of light escaped the fog and lit up the sky, then faded, then flashed again. A faint rumble resonated through the hut, then nothing. His hands shook, his fingertips rattling against the glass as he peered out.

Fear kept him awake. The clock thumped five times and there was another tapping from Moen at the door. Thomas dragged himself up and resumed his duties, breaking up with the boathook the film of ice that had formed again at the base of the harbour wall, starting up the engine, checking the fuel and engaging the guards to extract the latest news, of which there was none.

"Where are you from, Moen?" asked Thomas as they stood on the quay. "I recognise your accent, but can't quite place it."

"Nord Trøndelag, sir. Ytterøya, an island in the fjord."

"And what brings you here? Another island..."

"No idea, sir, but stay out a bit if you want. Watch the sunrise."

"I shall," said Thomas, peering into the gloaming. Far away lay Germany. He had nothing against Germany or the German people. The Kaiser had led the country to calamity in the Great War and that had triggered economic ruin. Hitler could do the same.

Who knows what the future would bring? Thomas shuddered, locking this moment of calm into his memory: the misty half-light, the dawn in sight, pink clouds turning bright red over the ridgeline, spreading and intensifying; the town in darkness. He absorbed the eerie, portentous stillness; a spectral mist, diaphanous over the ice and flat, blackened water; silence across the fortress, a thousand men marking time; a clink from a rifle against the buckles on a soldier's belt; the crunch of snow under Moen's boots as he paced the quay nearby, the stamping of his feet, the muffled sound of his whispered exchanges with Grambo.

He glanced at his watch — 0515 hours — then tensed. Away down the fjord, he picked up a faint, continuous rumble. Straining to hear more clearly, he knew the sound well enough: a ship's engine, not heavily loaded, barely ticking over. Another minute passed. The sound became clearer. Steam turbines, a heavy ship. Now, the wash of bow waves carrying through the still, cold air. A ship, shrouded by mist, somewhere off the town. His skin prickled; he held his breath, sensing, yet not knowing what was to come.

He looked again at his watch...0518 hours.

Suddenly, a bank of mist off the town was flooded with dazzling light, illuminated by searchlights from either side of the fjord. He peered out, straining to see. The deep, powerful rumbling of the engines: harsher, threatening, growing louder as the seconds passed; the ship still invisible. The wash of bow waves was now quite distinct. A big ship, closing in.

Then, emerging from the shining mist, he watched as the bows of a dark grey warship appeared, pushing for the Narrows between the fortress and the town. More of the ship appeared: a long forward deck... a huge gun turret...more guns and a high foremast all lit up in the searchlights. A massive warship, less than half a mile away, her guns strangely silent, passive, forward-pointing; her engines throbbing, her own searchlights now directed back onto the land.

He heard Moen stutter, "Good God in heaven."

"This is it," whispered Thomas, staring, fixed, as if tied to where he stood.

Images flashed through his mind. Pendleton's briefings, the assassinations in town, Westervik's attack, Oscarsborg's huge cannons, their 28-cm shells. Yes, this is it. And now, this would be Pendleton's *Blücher*, Germany's advanced new heavy cruiser. He had never seen a ship so immense, so powerful. This was the invasion of Norway. The game, as Pendleton saw the war, was playing out.

He glanced at his watch and held his breath, his gloved hand to his mouth: 0519 hours.

The full length of the warship had now emerged from the mist, barely 600 yards away, her profile clear in the light of the advancing pre-dawn. Still her main guns were aligned dead ahead, her speed barely twelve knots. All this Thomas took in as he watched, spellbound. His mind then shifted to the fortress, the cannons, the great embankments. The colonel...

At that moment, the island was shaken by a deafening, crashing boom which passed like a wave through his body, a shock wave like a heavy punch. A flash of light lit up the island and smoke emerged over the trees. One of the Krupp guns had fired on *Blücher* at almost point-blank range.

At the same moment, a huge explosion ripped through the upper section of the ship's foremast. Jagged metal fragments were thrown into the air. Thomas crouched down, shaken and incredulous, in a flash remembering Svensen's exclamation...'*bloody great guns, pointing down the fjord*' and the thump as the shopkeeper hit the counter with his fist.

Within seconds, guns from all over the warship opened fire on Drøbak and the surrounding shorelines. Arcs of tracer bullets, the clatter of machine guns and bursts of flak emerged from the stricken ship. Still she powered forward heading up the Narrows; magnificent, beautiful...wounded.

Then, muzzle flashes and the sound of artillery emerged from above the town: *Kopås was joining the fight.* The warship, just seconds ago so majestic, was being hit, time after time, like a powerful boxer overwhelmed by a mob, a bull elk ravaged by a pack of wolves. Explosions, fire, black smoke, the muffled sound of voices shouting. Her engines grew louder, more urgent; she picked up speed. She was returning fire. All around was the chaos of battle, a deafening din. He held his breath... *Blücher* would escape and, treacherously, he willed her on.

His eyes then picked out a smaller drama above the town. Lights moving, a car racing up a steep road, its progress marked by headlights lighting up trees on the fjord side: someone, a family, trying to escape the battle. He willed them on, too, tracing their progress through a bank of mist, then out into the open, between trees, a bend, doubling back, then higher and higher. As the car accelerated, now high above the town, almost safe, two shells hit just above and ahead of it. Flashes of red and yellow light, dark puffs of smoke, rocks thrown into the air. But the gunners had missed and the car raced ahead, through the dust of the explosions, disappearing into the trees and over a hilltop, to safety. Who were they? Then, another explosion, further away in the town. A house had been hit and was on fire. Someone's home.

Dozens of guns were now in action, from the land, from the ship, in a maelstrom of violence and shattering noise. *Blücher* powered ahead through the Narrows, her engines an angry roar, her bow-wave sharp in the faint morning light. Yes, she would escape. He held his breath: the magnificent ship — too beautiful to be harmed any more.

But it was not to be.

A second thunderous explosion sounded from the fortress's main battery, followed immediately by a heavy shockwave: a ground-shaking earthquake rippling through the island and the freezing air. At the same moment, another flash of light and fire appeared on the stricken ship. She visibly shuddered. An aircraft in the centre of the ship was engulfed in flames. More explosions followed, one after the other, *Blücher* quickly becoming a terrifying inferno.

"Wooh," shouted Grambo, the guard, an incredulous grin plastered to his face, as if it were a game they had suddenly won.

At that moment, it struck Thomas that not a single bullet or shell from *Blücher* had hit the harbour or anywhere else on the fortress. The warship had just attacked the town, which made no sense. He stood, transfixed and perplexed. The mist and the faint light of the dawn seemed to have saved them. But how could the ship's commanders be so unaware of the largest fortress in Norway? With all their spies? Why weren't the ship's main guns being used? Could the control centre have been knocked out? One by one these thoughts ran through his mind. He stepped back, as if a few yards would make him safer.

Thomas now stood side by side with his guards and other soldiers drawn by the spectacle, their faces flickering and coloured by the light of the inferno as *Blücher* slid by, the screams of men on the ship clear in the still air: men running, working firehoses, manning guns, all framed against the fires, then engulfed in smoke, the horror frighteningly human. He looked at Grambo: young men just like you, he thought. But mostly less stupid.

The firing from Kopås slowed, then stopped. *Blücher*, now level with the ferryman's harbour and no distance away, powered north up the Narrows, still gathering speed. She would escape...if they could bring the monstrous fires under control. But then, without warning, two massive explosions in quick succession hit her at water-level. Once again, the great ship shuddered.

"Torpedos," breathed Thomas.

"What?" Grambo looked at him.

"Andreas Anderssen."

Grambo shrugged.

Within minutes the ship disappeared behind a wooded promontory on the island and the terrible cacophony began to wane. Yet smoke poured into the sky: black, white and grey suffused with angry reds, orange and yellows. Even the forests on Hallangstangen and the little island of Skarholmen, with its tall white flagpole, were lit by the inferno.

Gradually the victory — or was it a tragedy — faded away, out of sight. Thomas stood, unable to move, his emotions shattered. Nothing in his mission, and in everything he had learned, could possibly have prepared him for what he had witnessed. Around him, in silence, stood his guards and groups of soldiers. They were all in shock. The terrible events had happened in a just a few minutes.

"Was that it?" said Moen, appearing utterly bewildered. "Is that the end?"

"There were other ships," replied another young soldier who had just arrived, "further down the fjord, turning back now. A long line of them they said."

"You can hear them," said Thomas.

As if to confirm the soldier's statement, Kopås opened up again, chasing the retreating flotilla back down the fjord, flashes of fire showing high above the town. A cheer went up from the guards. Several flashes of light appeared through the mist over the fjord; the crumps of more hits on the invaders.

"We've seen them off," said a young and enthusiastic voice. "Hoorah for Norway."

No, thought Thomas, *this is just the beginning.*

Part Four
THE GAME
PLAYS OUT

THIRTY-SIX

A group of officials gathered at Norges Bank early on the 9th of April. Straight-backed, the Governor slowly replaced the telephone receiver at precisely the moment his Senior Clerk (Gold Reserves) appeared, a sheet of paper floating off the pile of documents he carried as he rushed through the door. Matthias was the last to arrive, tightening his tie with his spare hand and feeling the effects of a broken night and an overdose of fear.

"My apologies, sir," he muttered, collecting the paper from the floor and finding a place towards the back of the informal array of chairs gathered around the Governor's desk.

The Governor nodded to him and began.

"Gentlemen, Norway is under attack from foreign forces. You may have listened to bulletins on the BBC. You will have heard the air-raid sirens and experienced the black-out. This is no trial run. We are now at war."

Matthias took in the news in silence, suppressing a deep sense of shock and awaiting what was to follow. This was the moment he had prepared for, yet hoped would never come. He watched, knowing he was witnessing a great historical event play out in front of him.

The Governor continued: "Yesterday, the British navy mined Vestfjord to prevent the movement of iron ore from Narvik to Germany. It has been a long time coming. Our government has protested. Worse, there are reports of German warships early this morning attacking several coastal cities, including the fjord here in Oslo. There was an action in the Narrows at Drøbak. The invasion force was repulsed by the fortress and other batteries, but there have been landings at Son just to the south. There are rumours of Wehrmacht troops already in Oslo, some emerging from merchant ships in the harbour. Various installations have been bombed. Germany says they are defending us from the British and come in peace. This is bunkum."

"Norway, I am sad to say, is unprepared. Our armed forces have been called to action...by letter. It is unbelievable. However, Finance Minister Oscar Torp has instructed emergency action to evacuate the remaining gold reserves. Meanwhile, he has joined the rest of the cabinet and, I am pleased to say, arrangements have been made to ensure that they and the King and the Crown Prince and his family will be taken to safety."

Several staff briefly clapped. The Governor stood up and walked to the front of his desk. Matthias knew what was to come.

"We at Norges Bank are not as prepared as I would have liked," said the Governor, "especially with regard to labour and transport. However, we have reason for some optimism. Our gold reserves have been packed such that they can be rapidly moved in an emergency. The first lorries are already on their way from Christiana Coal & Firewood Company. Our goal, gentlemen, is to transport Norway's gold to safety...to the vaults at Lillehammer."

A murmur of approval and excited chatter arose from the staff. The Governor then looked to Matthias.

"Mr Holmbekk..."

"Sir, I have secured twenty lorries so far and a colleague expects to hire several more shortly. In round terms, we have fifty tons of gold to move, all crated up and numbered, just under two tons per lorry. We will need twenty-six lorries. To this we must add recent coin purchases, which will require one more lorry, Lorry 27, a part load."

"It's essential," said the Governor to the room, "that the drivers are not informed of the nature of their cargo. There will be no military presence in the area, in order not to draw attention to this operation. The guards will be our own, two per truck. Mr Holmbekk, pl..."

As Matthias drew breath to speak the air-raid siren started up again and dull thumps and the clatter of machine guns shook the building. A secretary knocked and ran to the Governor.

"Fornebu is under attack," she said, visibly trembling.

"Time is against us," said the Governor. "If the airport is taken..." He shook his head, his lips tightly drawn. "Mr Holmbekk, continue please."

"The registers are updated and there are around fifteen hundred crates of gold bars and 39 kegs filled with gold coins of various denominations, all packed in batches ready to move. The recently purchased gold sovereigns will require final auditing and packing, and I will commence this immediately."

"Gold, as you know, is heavy," said the Governor. "We require many hands."

From the office's large window came shouting and the revving of car engines. The Governor looked out into the dawn.

"The panic has begun," he said, shaking his head.

Matthias gripped the arms of his chair. He looked around the room and cast his eyes over the top officials and board members. Catching his eye, board member Jon Sundby, who he remembered from the party at the Castle, left his chair and leaned over to shake his hand.

"Well done, Matthias, good to see you involved," he said. "I must leave now for the station. I will be pleased to report to the cabinet the effective operation we have here at the bank. Good luck." With those words, he picked up his coat and slipped away.

Matthias looked around the room: the Governor stood by the window, his silhouette showing against the grey morning sky. A searchlight, somewhere up in the hills, lit up the sky as it swept the clouds. The low drone of an aeroplane rattled the glasses on the Governor's desk. Within the room, the whispered voices of the staff expressed the fear and anticipation which everyone must be feeling.

"This is a moment of great importance for Norges Bank, for Norway," the Governor said, walking back from the window, his voice raised. "The plan is as follows. I will be on Kirkegata by the side exit. I will personally log every load and check the contents of each lorry against our central register. We start with Lorry 1 and finish with Lorry 27."

"And our role, sir?" asked one of the officials, a teller who worked in the main banking hall.

"I was coming to that," said the Governor, sharply. "You will all become labourers, moving the gold from the vaults to the lorries. Then, many of you will join the convoy to Lillehammer for the unloading. Detailed responsibilities are being prepared."

Walking over to Matthias, the Governor continued: "Our Senior Clerk, Mr Holmbekk, has special responsibility for managing the registers for the gold reserves. He will station himself in the vaults and will instruct you on the contents of each lorry-load and check each one against the copy-register which he holds."

"Gentlemen, we have very little time. Can I thank you all for being here and for your loyalty. I would expect no other."

———

A volley of thuds from the clock in the ferryman's hut marked 0600 hours. There was a crash on the door and the colonel's adjutant barged in.

"Galtung, you're needed," said Helberg, breathlessly. "We've lost communications with the government. You are to take me to Oslo. I am to brief Defence Minister Ljungberg on the situation here. I must catch him before he leaves with the rest of the cabinet." He stepped outside: "You, too Private Grambo."

Minutes later, Thomas ran *Terne* out into the Narrows and turned north, towards Oslo, and into the oil-covered water left by *Blücher*. As they rounded the rocky headland on the island, a shocking sight came into view. The stricken warship was listing heavily and lying stationary in the channel close to the low, rocky islands of Askholmene. Smoke poured from the middle section of the ship and was blown by a fresh breeze across the forward deck.

"Keep clear," said Helberg, "they could fire on us."

Thomas looked at him sceptically. It seemed barely credible that men fighting for their lives would fire on a slow-moving leisure craft.

But Helberg was right...though for the wrong reason. *Blücher* was suddenly engulfed by an ear-splitting and massive explosion, a column of fire rising up to the masthead. Flames and a cloud of steam poured from the funnel. A shockwave passed through *Terne,* and Thomas felt his legs buckle beneath him. Landing a short distance away, a jagged fragment of steel, almost the size of a car, fell into the fjord, covering the boat with freezing spray and oil.

"One of the magazines must have gone up," shouted Helberg, crouching, his face lined in shock.

Grambo sunk beneath the gunwale, his face white with fear.

It was impossible not to be transfixed by the drama. As Thomas watched, shaking, *Blücher* began to roll. Men, small black shapes against the vast ship, crawled onto her exposed flanks. Individual figures were silhouetted by the conflagration. The noise of the fires, escaping air and the groans of collapsing steelwork combined into a terrifying cacophony.

"Can't you make this thing go any faster?" shouted Helberg.

"We're flat out," Thomas shouted back.

Another drama now came into view. An overloaded launch full of men emerged from the smoke, heading away from the sinking ship. As it approached the rocky island, it hit a rock and heeled over, throwing dozens of men into the water.

"God," said Grambo, his hand to his mouth. "The water's freezing."

Thomas was clear: no one on the burning hulk was capable of firing on *Terne.* Men were jumping and falling into the fjord, clinging to floats and small dinghies, and sliding off the hull. Others were swimming, heading for the islands and the shoreline. Many seemed trapped, struggling in the oil. Some were close enough for Thomas to hear their screams. As *Terne* closed in, he could see terror on the men's faces. One by one doomed figures disappeared below the surface, dying in the freezing water or becoming consumed by the flames in patches of burning oil. He looked across to the shore. It was too far away for those men swimming in the freezing fjord. More groans and grinding noises sounded from the ship as it broke up and was torn apart by exploding ammunition; her port guardrail was now touching the water. More men jumped, their arms flailing. It was hard to watch.

"Nearly 1900 hours," shouted Helberg. "We need to press on."

Thomas had let *Terne's* speed slacken, so they were barely making three knots. He was watching a figure in the water, a fair-haired young man little more than a boy, swimming towards them, struggling with the drag of his heavy clothing. Now only yards away, his oiled face hardly showed above the surface of the water, his blue eyes pleading as he struggled closer.

"Galtung," shouted Helberg. "What the hell..."

"I'm picking him up," Thomas shouted. Throttling back, he crashed into reverse then, leaning forward, grabbed the boathook as another volley of explosions sounded from the sinking ship and a cloud of hot, stinking smoke drifted over *Terne*. Thomas grabbed a cloth and held it to his face, then leaned over the port-side gunwale. But the boy had disappeared. In panic, Thomas leaned over further, trying to see beneath Terne's hull, then behind and along the starboard side. But he had gone.

For a moment, the fight which had consumed Thomas as he had watched the young man's plight drained away in a wave of grief; when the moment had come, and a life hung in the balance, he had again failed. He looked across the fjord, almost frozen in shock. *Terne* was now drifting, surrounded by acrid smoke. The fjord was thick with dark, bobbing figures, struggling to survive, some waving and shouting, others quite still. Then, a deafening roar came from the great ship as she began to capsize. Dozens of men clung to the upturned hull and, one by one, they slid and jumped.

Blücher was now almost vertical, the stern towering above them. Then, with a deafening roar and a hissing of fire and steam and escaping air, she began to sink. Within a minute she was gone. Just a mass of debris, foam, a maelstrom of churning water and oil fires remained.

Helberg and Grambo crouched in the well of the boat, coughing as the smoke thickened and drifted over *Terne*. Their wheezing and fear acted like a trigger. Thomas shouted at Helberg.

"I'm going to rescue them."

"No," screamed Helberg, standing unsteadily. "These are enemy combatants."

Thomas pushed the throttle forward and *Terne* gained speed.

"They are Nazis," spat Helberg, taking out his sidearm.

"We are going to help," said Thomas quietly, leaning in to Helberg's face.

"You will not. That's an order," hissed Helberg, pointing his revolver at Thomas's forehead. "This is a betrayal of our mission."

"You have no authority over me," said Thomas, looking the adjutant in the eye. "This is a civilian boat. And I am a civilian."

Suddenly, the cold steel of the guard's rifle pressed into his neck. "Galtung, don't be stupid," said Grambo. "We need to get away from here."

Slowly, Thomas turned and took hold of the barrel, moving it aside. He then looked at both men. "We're picking up those people, as many as we can. The more we help, the quicker it will be done and the sooner we will arrive in Oslo."

"I warn you," said Helberg, calmly, "I shall shoot."

"No, you won't," said Thomas.

The adjutant glared at him, his revolver hand shaking. The guard's rifle again pressed hard into his neck.

"Nor will you, Grambo," he said.

———

In Oslo, a biting northerly whipped off the mountains and cut through the grey city streets, the sun low in the east and diffused by scudding, snow-laden clouds. Westervik trudged up Hegdehaugsveien, head-down into the wind, exhausted and fearful. Entering the café, he nodded at Schmidt and squeezed behind the counter into the darkened back room. For half an hour he paced the lino, numb, hungry, unshaven. Eventually, as he slumped into one of the hard wooden chairs, von Elverfeldt arrived, hurried and distracted.

"*Blücher* went down an hour ago," said von Elverfeldt, without preamble. "The finest ship of the invasion force."

Westervik felt the last vestiges of hope drain away. A bomb blast, quite close, shook the room; his coffee cup, half drunk and now cold, rattled violently on its saucer. He steadied it, trying to suppress a rising wave of panic, but the rattling carried on until he removed his hand and dropped it to his lap. Von Elverfeldt had watched, a mixture of pity and anger etched onto his face.

"The rest of the warship group turned back and is landing further south," continued von Elverfeldt, speaking rapidly and pacing, three or four steps each way, his voice steely and tight with stress. "The whole invasion has been delayed. The King and government have had time to escape. You know what that means, Carl...Norway will fight on. Their bloody gold may get away, too. It's a catastrophe. Hitler's apoplectic." He glared down at Westervik, clenching his fists and shaking like an injured animal. "And don't look away when I'm speaking to you."

Westervik knew that no words, no excuses, no apology would save him. It was the end, a terrible humiliation, and every sinew in his body shook.

"I don't have much time, so I'll be blunt, said von Elverfeldt. "Two of the Krupp guns scored direct hits on *Blücher*; they were not disabled. Krupp, for God's sake, pride of the German economy. On top of that, *Blücher* was hit by two torpedoes from a bunker you failed to identify. Hundreds dead: key military personnel, top brass, young soldiers, civilian administrators, Gestapo; many killed trying to save the ship, others drowned in the freezing water. Worst of all, Eriksen — your prime target — survived to direct the whole bloody show."

He leaned on the table; his knuckles white. Pushing aside the coffee tray left by Schmidt, he looked at Westervik through tightly-drawn slits.

"The mission failed, Carl. You're finished."

He turned and moved towards the door. "You will not be safe in Norway. Neither can you contemplate a return to Germany; you will be arrested." He replaced his hat and, with his hand on the doorhandle, looked over his shoulder. "There's nothing I can do. We've probably all had it."

A short while later, Westervik stepped out onto Hegdehaugsveien. He lifted the collar of his coat against the biting wind and flurries of snow and hurried through the Palace Park towards the station, hoping that the trains to Sweden might still be running. All around were the sounds of war: the drone of German bombers, deep crumps from explosions across the fjord, the alarm cries and fear of people fleeing the city. In just a few hours, his life had been dismantled.

As he hurried past the National Theatre, the figure on the quay at Skarholmen again crept into his mind. So, it wasn't Eriksen; von Elverfeldt had confirmed that. The commander had survived and had ordered the salvo that had sunk *Blücher*. As he replayed those moments when he had taken his shot, he pictured again the person's stature, the profile, the movement. His suspicions, so misty up to now, quickly hardened into certainty. It *was* a woman...it had to be a woman. And, on Skarholmen, it could mean only one thing. He pictured again the faint, misty figure wavering in the scope. He could see her crumple and fall. He had shot Klara, the girl he had stupidly, traitorously fallen in love with. There was no other possibility.

Little more than an hour later he joined the massed throng queuing for the last train to Stockholm, heavy with sadness and in despair.

THIRTY-SEVEN

"The first lorry's away," said Matthias, stretching his back and addressing a small group of bank staff gathered outside the vaults. He looked at his watch. A quarter past eight. To be moved: fifty tons. Two tons so far. It had taken time to secure the lorries, drivers and guards at such an early hour and to cart the first batch of gold to the service entrance on Kirkegata. With Lorry 1 heading for Lillehammer the operation was now underway, but...

"It took twenty minutes to load. Too long," he said. "At that rate it'll be well into the afternoon before we're done. We need to achieve ten minutes per batch."

"There are hold-ups," said a teller from the main banking hall, his voice tense. "People are panicking, running to get out of the city; it's difficult to keep them away." He shook his head, a look of despair on his face.

"We've posted guards on Myntgata and Kirkegata," said another man, someone co-opted from the Finance Ministry. "That should help."

"There's something else," said an actuary from the audit team, half raising his hand. "Every time a plane goes overhead, the loaders all head for cover. We have to work hard to keep the drivers here too; they're in a right state."

255

"Reassure them," said Matthias, his tone more resolute and his voice firmer than he felt inside. "The Germans wouldn't bomb the gold reserves, would they?" As he spoke a shell detonated somewhere in the city — a deep crump. The vault vibrated. Then one of the senior bankers returned, struggling to push a small-wheeled cart through the door into the vault, ready for loading.

"Parachutists taking Fornebu," he said, "And Kjeller's under attack."

"The sooner we shift this, the sooner we're out of here," said Matthias. He thought back to the Governor's words after his meeting with the Prime Minister. *The Nazis will come straight for this bank.*

"How long do we have?" he whispered to himself.

How long do I have?

————

Thomas hid the shaking of his hands by gripping *Terne's* wheel as they approached Vippetangen, following a narrow channel, a freezing gruel of ice and slush. All around, the fjord was covered with thick ice. Columns of black smoke rose from the city and from across the fjord out to the west, where the sounds of battle raged. The airport had been bombed, or so Helberg had said to Grambo, and the sounds of a ground battle indicated German troops had already landed.

As they moored up, Helberg turned to Thomas, a look of distain on his face. "You are the luckiest man alive, Galtung. And the most stupid." Then, gathering his papers, he turned to the guard and said, firmly, "Galtung stays here. Keep your eye on him, Grambo."

The adjutant then spun around and disappeared along the quayside towards the station, dodging groups of people and carts piled high with domestic belongings. Thomas was glad to see him go; the man might still make the station in time. Shivering in the sharp wind, and despite the rattle and rumble of war all around, he felt an overwhelming sense of relief. By taking control of events during the drama of *Blücher's* sinking, he had saved dozens of German sailors, troops and civilians from the cold waters of the fjord. Young men, just like him, although he equally understood they were invaders, aggressors, ready to kill young Norwegian men, maybe innocent women and children. In that sense,

Helberg was right. The truth was complex — beyond resolution, with *Blücher* sinking as he watched — but, for himself, his actions somehow assuaged months of indecision and lack of resolution in his mission and, more than that, the weaknesses and moral ambivalence he saw in himself. With a gun to his head, he had confronted danger, taken a stand for what seemed right at the time and he'd seen it through, acting on instinct and principle. He could not have lived with himself if he'd shut his eyes as men died all around, the enemy or no. The leaders were the enemy, not these young men.

"When will the adjutant be back?" asked Grambo, interrupting Thomas's thoughts and looking around nervously.

Thomas shrugged. He felt some sympathy for the boy; he was scared and had obviously lost any interest in guarding a fellow Norwegian. But he was first to hear a low drone from the south. Picking up Grambo's fear, Thomas watched as three twin-engine planes appeared, low over the water and heading directly towards Vippetangen. Too late he realised the danger. Akershus fortress lay immediately behind them: the main base for the Norwegian defence forces in the city.

Within seconds the first of the bombers careered overhead, shaking the ground, so low Thomas was almost eye to eye with the bomb-aimer looking down from his glass nosecone. A second plane followed without incident. It was the third that released a stick of bombs onto the quay, the first landing in the fjord close to *Terne* and sending up a column of water and ice. Running from the open quay, Thomas dived behind a nearby wall. Two more bombs hit nearby in huge, fiery explosions, enveloping a group of civilians as they ran for shelter, shaking the ground and sending debris into the air. Bricks and large blocks of stone crashed down on the quay.

Thomas dragged himself up, his clothes and hair covered in cold water, dust and stony fragments. He looked around and could see that those few seconds of terror had wrought terrible damage. *Terne's* cabin had been smashed, and all the glass broken. Grambo was struggling to stand up, blood pouring from a nasty gash in his head. "You're on yer own, sorry," he said, as he ran towards the railway tracks and disappeared behind a line of lorries.

Thomas, his ears ringing and unsteady on his feet, felt his mind taken back in an instant to his arrival on the *Black Prince*, at this very spot, all those weeks ago. Looking over the shattered quay and dead figures lying in the dust, he pictured his meeting with Pendleton. Once again, he felt alone and drained of the spirit that had carried him this far. The reckless bravery — if that was what it was — that had driven him to accept orders and race up the fjord to Oslo, to face down Helberg and rescue the German sailors: all of that was now gone, punched out of him by the tragedy that lay all around. He slumped back onto the quay, his body shaking uncontrollably.

———

By one 'o'clock, twenty-five lorries had been loaded with gold and were on their way to Lillehammer. Matthias jumped as the Governor ran into the vault, his nerves frayed.

"Mr Holmbekk, we have two lorries left to load. They're parked outside: twenty-six and twenty-seven. German troops are marching down Carl Johan's, so they must be at the palace by now, and they seem to have taken Akershus Fortress too. Hell, they're almost on our doorstep."

"The King, the Crown Prince?"

"They're safe. They left a while ago with the government, although the trains are in a mess and they were delayed. Sundby is with them and will reassure them on operations here. So now it's just us to tidy up and get out."

"We're nearly finished," said Matthias, his shattered emotions alternating between relief and desperation, so his voice quivered as he spoke. "Twenty-six has just left the vaults: twenty kegs sealed and numbered. That leaves just twenty-seven." He walked over to the final seven kegs collected together next to his table. "Batch twenty-seven, all sovereigns," he said. "I've checked; it's correct and audit are happy. Six full kegs, each with ten bags of one thousand sovereigns per bag. Plus the seventh keg which is a little over half full. So, sixty-six thousand, five hundred and eighty coins in total."

"So they just need sealing, numbering and signing off?" said the Governor, fiddling with the metal bands and tags.

"Yes, said Matthias. "It won't take long."

"I don't have time," said the Governor. "I'll sign off twenty-seven now and leave it to you. Just..." A series of heavy explosions and a dull rattle of machine guns interrupted the Governor. An assistant ran into the corridor outside the vaults, flanked by two guards, and called to the Governor.

"Twenty-six is loaded and ready, sir," the assistant said. "There's bad news from the city. We need to go."

The Governor left the vault and Matthias sensed the urgency of the assistant's report. The Governor then reappeared.

"It sounds as if the only routes out of Oslo will soon be closed," he said. "I have to leave now to give me a chance of reaching Lillehammer. I'll travel in the cab with twenty-six. A driver and two civilian volunteers are waiting in the corridor to help you load twenty-seven. But we have a problem with guards; you'll have to manage without them."

"As you say, sir," said Matthias.

The Governor was now moving out of the vault door, and shouted, "Make sure you secure the copy registers. Leave the vault door open. If you move fast, you'll get away, but it's finely cut."

"Very well," shouted Matthias as the Governor disappeared down the corridor. "And good luck, sir."

Matthias heard the Governor's footsteps fade away but, after a few seconds, he came running back and stood in the vault door. Thinking for a moment he said, "My Mercedes is parked in the usual place. Here are the keys. It's a nice car and I would hate to lose it. Take it, but make sure you stay close to the lorry."

"Very well," said Matthias, pocketing the keys, but a little unsure as to what he was agreeing.

"You've been a rock, Mr Holmbekk," said the Governor, vigorously shaking Matthias's hand. "A credit to the Bank. I could not have wished for a braver and more reliable clerk to handle this operation."

"A pleasure, sir. Of sorts." Matthias smiled at his own irony as the Governor's footsteps again faded away down the long corridor. This time the top man was running. The Governor never ran!

Thomas's ears whistled and buzzed following the aerial attack on the quay. The sounds of the battle for Oslo had faded, muffled by his deadened ears. Skirting the bodies of workmen and families lying broken and bloodied in the rubble, and with no clear plan, he wandered along Langkaia towards the central railway station. He should move faster, he knew, but he was shaking and couldn't.

There were only two ways off the quay, and this was one. As he walked he struggled to think clearly. There was no chance of a return to the fortress or Drøbak via the fjord. A train to Ås? Unlikely. Yet he needed to escape the city.

Looking along Langkaia, dotted with running figures, he retraced in his mind the route he had walked with Pendleton on the day he had arrived in Norway. Turn left, away from the water then, on the right, Norges Bank. He pictured the building as it was then, a massive square block looming out of the falling snow. Matthias's bank. Would he be there, the only person he knew in Oslo?

———

After sealing the final keg, Matthias walked, as fast as he could, tap... tap...tap, out to Kirkegata to check on the loading of batch twenty-seven.

"Six kegs loaded, sir," said a portly, middle-aged man threading the ropes securing the canvas cover. Judging by his attire, he probably worked as a greengrocer and would be the driver. Behind him, two other men were adjusting the kegs already loaded on the flatbed of the lorry. They were almost there.

"One more keg to go, part-full," said Matthias, turning back into the service entrance. "It's ready," he said to the loaders over his shoulder, "but not yet sealed. It'll take me two or three minutes."

Matthias returned to the vaults and quickly hammered home the black-coated nails which secured the metal band and top of the last keg. Looking around the vault, all that remained were a few spare metal bands and a couple of wooden boxes. Satisfied, he grabbed the register and, in frustration that the loaders had not yet arrived, hurried back to the service drive, where he was greeted by a shocking sight: there was no sign of the two loaders. The trolley, empty, had been left on the service drive.

"They ran," shouted the driver stepping down from his cab, anxiety etched onto his face. "There are German troops on Kongens Gate and a bloody machine gun just took chunks out of the wall there."

Matthias made his way to the corner of the bank as quickly as his legs would allow and looked up Myntgata. A group of German soldiers stood by the fort, almost within shouting distance. Turning back to the lorry, he saw with rising horror the driver sliding back along the side of the lorry and shout: "Head east, then north; the Governor's final instructions. Avoid Karl Johans gate, he said, and keep clear of central station, too."

"What are you doing?" yelled Matthias, struggling through the snow back to the lorry, a wave of panic coursing through his body. "At least, help me load the final keg."

"I can't do this," said the driver, his voice shaking. "A bullet just came through the cab door. I'm retired, I delivered vegetables once. My family..." He backed away.

"For God's sake..."

"Sorry, sir, I'm sorry. The loaders have gone. A few coins from the tills, it's not worth it."

The driver shuffled backwards, his face pleading to be understood. He then turned and fled, his brown apron flapping, his short legs wobbling and sliding through the snow.

Matthias stood alone, trying to suppress his panic. The lorry driver's door hung open, the engine running. A two-engine bomber flew low over Akerhus fortress, a terrifying noise which shook the ground. Walking back to the service drive he eyed the trolley, lying askew in the snow, but he knew that even a half-loaded keg was too heavy for him to manoeuvre up the steps from the vault and into the lorry. Yet, so close to completing what he had worked for weeks to achieve, it was unthinkable that the last keg would be left in the vault.

"Cowards," he screamed in despair and frustration, thumping his fists on the lorry's bonnet.

Then, from the corner of his eye he saw a single figure approaching through Grev Wedels Plass. He recognised the gait, the profile.

THIRTY-EIGHT

Thomas turned into Grev Wedels Plass and then Myntgata, his body shaking, his head pounding, his ears ringing. Norges Bank appeared as he remembered. On the otherwise empty street was parked a single lorry and, by its side stood a figure. As he approached, it was Matthias Holmbekk who ran towards him. In normal circumstances a flood of questions would emerge, but now he felt no more than a dull wave of relief washing through his body.

"You're injured," said Matthias, a look of disbelief and horror fixed on his face. "Your hair: it's full of dust, bits of stone. And blood, you're bleeding."

Thomas ran a hand over his mouth and looked at the smudge of blood. "Nothing serious, just a bit shaken."

Matthias stood blankly for a few seconds, his face tense with worry. "It's too heavy," he said. "My leg, I can't. The trolley..."

Thomas followed Matthias's gaze at the abandoned trolley. A lorry stood nearby, its engine rattling. The clatter of machine guns still echoed from across the fjord. "What's going on?"

"Never mind," said Matthias, "we have to get out of here. Please. No time to explain. Take this key. The Governor's Mercedes is parked just around the corner, in Bankplassen." He pointed down the road. "He asked me to save it. Start it up and come back here."

Thomas struggled to make sense of the situation that now confronted him. But he sensed a plan of some sort into which he had barged, and it included the prospect of a car. He accepted the key, muttering as he walked away, "I'm not much of a driver, you know."

Several minutes later he nervously nosed the Mercedes out of Bankplassen, turned towards the parked lorry and drew slowly to a stop.

"Follow me," called Matthias, disappearing into the bank. "And bring that trolly with you."

Several minutes later, breathing heavily, they stood together with a wooden barrel dragged up to the street on the trolly. "Now what?" said Thomas.

"Last lot of loose change from the tills," Matthias said in response to Thomas's puzzlement.

"Can you help me out of the city?" Thomas asked.

"Yes, if you'll help me," said Matthias, dragging away two planks laid against the lorry and repositioning them against the Mercedes. "It'll be easier to load than the lorry. The keg's very heavy."

Seeing no alternative to following Matthias's instructions, Thomas helped roll the keg off the trolly and, together, they pushed it up the ramp and guided it with a heavy crunch into the boot of the Mercedes.

"We're getting out of the city," said Matthias, waving his cane in the air to indicate some sort of direction. "Now. Take the Merc and follow me; north along Kirkegata."

Bewildered by events, there nevertheless seemed to Thomas every prospect that Matthias could engineer an exit from the city. Diving into the car, and barely more enlightened, he gunned the engine and, clutch squealing, followed close behind the lorry, picking up speed as they went and crunching through the gears. Over Rådhusgata and Prinsens Gate they raced before, suddenly, the lorry stopped. Matthias slid out of the cab and approached the Mercedes.

"Roadblocks ahead," he whispered, panic in his voice as he leaned through the car's window. "The driver said Karl Johan's been taken, so I had to try this way; there are not many options to Lillehammer."

"What do you mean? The driver, what driver? And where's Lille-hammer, anyway?"

"That's where the other lorries have gone. Mine was the last load, Lorry 27."

Matthias turned away, staring into the sky. He appeared lost, in anguish. Kicking a lamppost, he looked to Thomas.

"I did my best, didn't I?" he said. "To get to Lillehammer? You saw I tried. But...the roadblocks..."

"I suppose you did," said Thomas. "We're not going straight ahead, or left, that's for sure. And there's no point going back..."

"So we go right, through Old Oslo," said Matthias. "Then we'll head for National Highway 1 and try to go north."

Thomas shrugged. What else could he do but follow and hope? Further on, roads became increasingly jammed with people, handcarts, vans and cars fleeing the city, but Thomas could feel only a rush of opti-mism. By an extraordinary stroke of luck, he had found a way out of the city. His head was clearing. The injury had stopped bleeding. They moved forward again, away from the noise of battle from across the fjord. Eventually, as the junction with National Highway 1 came into view, the lorry slowed and Thomas pulled the Mercedes onto the verge behind it.

"Another bloody roadblock; you can see German troops, trucks across the road," said Matthias, pulling open the car's door. "The route north is closed." He looked at Thomas with a grimace. "Lillehammer is impossible. We have no option; we head south."

It was true. South was the only option unless they were to carry on eastwards to some place Thomas had never heard of and which seemed of no interest to Matthias. It was only at that point, as Thomas took in the road signs, that he begun to understand the geography of their flight from Oslo. South was Svinesund...And Svinesund was Sweden, just over the border! He drew breath. Sweden. Of course: this must be Matthias's new plan. But for his exhaustion and aching body he would have shouted with joy.

National Highway 1 south was lightly trafficked, and they made good progress, the Mercedes purring along behind Matthias's lorry. Thomas felt he should sing the national anthem: amid the chaos and the shock, he had found what looked like a route to safety with one of the best-connected people he knew. And in a Mercedes, a car more luxurious than anything he had ever seen.

After a while a column of vehicles approached, heading north: buses, trucks, a few cars...all full of German troops and, thankfully, showing no interest in a greengrocer's lorry or even a fine Mercedes heading in the opposite direction. He recalled the chatter at the fortress: *landings, further down the fjord.*

"Come on, go, go," he shouted at the lorry ahead, pounding on the steering wheel in a confused mix of frustration and jubilation. But instead of speeding up, the lorry's brake lights glowed and Matthias pulled into a layby, skidding to a halt on the hard-packed snow.

"Good God in heaven, we're going to make it," said Thomas as Matthias stepped out of the lorry. "I can't believe it: two sets of wheels, some loose change from your ruddy tills and Sweden here we come."

"You're joking," said Matthias. His face could not have appeared more agitated; his eyes blinking constantly and his hands dragging over his face as if trying to wash away the panic. "The invasion fleet landed at Son, down the coast from Drøbak. That's why the Wehrmacht are passing us, coming the other way in commandeered transport, heading for Oslo."

"The opposite way to us, so that's fine by me."

"They'll close the border to Sweden. Probably done it already."

"How do you know that?"

"Briefings at the bank."

Thomas stepped out of the car, looked down the road and kicked the lorry's rear wheel. "There must be back roads, other routes?"

Matthias ignored the question and wandered a short distance down the road, tapping his cane furiously. After a while spent gazing into the forest, he returned and said, "Thomas, can I trust you?"

"What do you mean?"

"I can't do this on my own."

"Do what?"

"The lorry has a consignment of coins, the last to come out of the bank," said Matthias. "I should have taken them to Lillehammer with the rest of our coinage, to the bank vaults there to escape the invasion;

you know that; I said so. And you saw I tried, didn't you? I tried." He was panicking again. "But the roads were blocked, you saw?"

"Hell, yes," shouted Thomas, "the roads were blocked, but who wants to go to Lillehammer with a few coins. We can get to Sweden instead. If there are more roadblocks we'll work around them, take a back-route. Something," he said.

"It's not that simple. The kegs are too heavy."

"Kegs? What, more than one?"

"There are six more, full ones," said Matthias, pulling back a corner of the lorry's canvas cover. "They're even heavier, eighty kilograms each, more than I can possibly lift. We need to stay together and I need someone to drive the car." Walking one way then the other, he thumped the air in frustration. "It was easier to dump the final keg in the Merc, a quick decision; good or bad, I don't know, maybe a bad idea. But that's what we did, didn't we? The Governor wanted to save the Merc. Hell, I don't know...."

"I really don't understand," said Thomas. It was hard, with Matthias as he was, to stay calm, and his guts were trembling. "But we can still reach Sweden, surely?"

"It's too dangerous. If we are caught with this lot..."

"Well, dump it."

"Thomas..."

"So what now?" Thomas flung his arms into the air.

"We should head for home."

"Home?"

"Drøbak."

"Drøbak? I thought you wanted Lillehammer. Or Sweden? Why Drøbak?"

"We need to get rid of the lorry," said Matthias. "Then we must hide the kegs. It's Bank property, we have a duty. I need it to be somewhere I know. Hell, almost all the coins got away to Lillehammer, but these six... seven...time ran out."

Another convoy of vehicles loaded with German troops passed by, heading north. A few isolated snowflakes fell lazily from the heavy, grey sky. The bank clerk's plan made no sense and Thomas slowly shook his head.

"Let me put it this way," said Matthias, stepping forward, close enough for Thomas to feel the warmth of his breath. "Help me with the kegs and you can have a share of the coins."

"You said they belonged to the bank."

"Thomas, they're gold coins. Gold. You can have enough to live safely in Sweden for the rest of your life. You can get there, like you said. Back roads."

"Gold?"

Matthias groaned. "Hell, I don't know, yes, gold coins, bullion," he shouted. "The ruddy war has started. We have a lorry, a car; we have a fortune in gold. And we can't take it to Lillehammer, you know that. We tried, for God's sake. Help me secure the kegs, then take a bag and disappear. A whole bloody keg if you want. I'll take a bag too. We'll have one each and bury the rest until they can be returned."

"What are you talking about? You said they were coins from the tills. Now you say they're gold bullion and we can take some." Thomas stared at Matthias. "I'm not taking anything. And what would I do with a bag of stolen gold coins, if they really are gold?"

"Nobody will ever know. The Governor is long gone, halfway to Lillehammer. The loaders and the driver ran away before you arrived. It's true. I was there on my own. The Germans took the last keg, didn't they, the one left in the vaults; I couldn't move it on my own, could I? German soldiers, coming down the street from the fort. They took the Merc, too. I just got away in time, didn't I? In Lorry 27. I had six kegs in the lorry but they took that, too, didn't they. At the roadblock. They took Lorry 27 and all the gold. It wasn't my fault. I tried."

"You've lost me..." Thomas shrugged, bewildered, his arms outstretched.

"We can share it, can't we," cried Matthias, "don't you see? We can share the gold when the time is right. But now, all I know is we must get this lot hidden somewhere. Thomas, get it into your head. These kegs... they're full of a fortune in gold bloody sovereigns...which...have...been... taken...by German troops. Yes?"

"Matthias...who do you think I am?" Thomas shook his head.

"Oh...forget what I said then, forget it, forget everything," screamed Matthias, stomping up and down, waving his cane around and hitting at the bare branches of a scrubby willow by the roadside. "If we don't get these kegs to somewhere safe, all this gold will end up in the Reich Bank in Berlin, financing the Nazi's war. Is that what you want?"

Thomas looked up the road, to Oslo, south to Sweden, to the lorry, to Matthias. He kicked the lorry's tyre again. He had no map, it was unknown country and German troops seemed to be everywhere. "Oh hell," he said, ripping open the driver's door and slumping back into the Mercedes. "I'll follow you. Do what the hell you want. And here's the deal: as soon as we're done, all I want is a map, the car — this car — and your help on how I can get to Sweden. I want nothing to do with your ruddy kegs. Although..."

"Yes?"

"A couple of coins would help me buy supper tonight. Or some normal cash. I have nothing, no money, spare clothes, nothing."

Matthias nodded, his lips tight, his eyes closed. "Thank you, thank you, Thomas. Agreed. Yes, you can have your coins, as many as you want...as soon as we've hidden the kegs. It's for Norway, Thomas, it's all above board."

Thomas watched as the lorry set off again. He waited, confused and still unsure, then thumped the steering wheel and stamped the accelerator to the floor in frustration. The wheels spun and the Mercedes slithered away to resume the journey southwards down Highway 1.

Minutes later, the lorry signalled right, leaving Highway 1 across what had now become an almost continuous flow of Wehrmacht troops in purloined Norwegian vehicles. It was a good decision and, for the first time, Thomas began to grasp where they were: travelling westwards towards the Nesodden peninsular, home territory.

Passing through the small settlement of Nesset, they drove along the edge of a frozen inlet and then turned right, a brief but intense flurry of snow falling as they climbed a steep, twisting road through dense forest. Eventually, Thomas recognised a road name: Holtbråtveien, another snaking forest road which he knew ended at Drøbak.

Ahead, the lorry slowed and they pulled into an overgrown forestry track. Matthias slid out of the cab, his face lined with stress. Sounding morose and edgy, he clearly had no plan other than a vague intention to bury the gold somewhere in his home area.

"Remember," said Thomas, "I need to be in Sweden by tonight. God knows what I'll do there, but it can't be worse than what's happening here."

"Fine by me," said Matthias. "Once the gold is safe. It's then my problem and you can forget the whole thing." Thomas could see Matthias staring at him through the corner of his eye.

"So where do you want to hide it? asked Thomas. "You'll have a cellar at Monsrud..."

"Too dangerous to have this stuff at home. And we're on a road with other farms nearby," said Matthias. "I can't afford for the lorry to be seen anywhere near home. What I really want is to get off this road and find somewhere isolated to bury the kegs, somewhere where no one would bother to look or associate with me," he said, studying the Governor's road atlas.

"Plenty of isolated places around here," said Thomas.

"There's a snow spade in the boot," said Matthias, with a hint of hope in his voice.

"But everywhere's frozen solid. Or it's rock. Or ice. What's the good of a spade? In fact, how can you bury anything?"

Matthias stared at Thomas, wide-eyed. "Yes, yes, you're right. I can't think straight. So where the hell..."

"In a barn, with animals. You have a barn? It might not be frozen."

"We don't have animals. And again, too close to home."

Then, suddenly, Matthias's face lit up: "I know somewhere, the one place with a farmer so stupid, no one would ever suspect anything. And it's away from everywhere, up in a wilderness."

"So, who's that?" said Thomas. "Not...?"

"Yes," said Matthias, triumphantly. "The mad dog."

"It would put him in danger."

"Nonsense, he won't know."

"Severin's a friend, a neighbour..."

"Where else, then?" Matthias was starting to shake again, his voice quivering.

"I don't know. It's your problem."

"It may be my problem, but it's Norway's gold," said Matthias, his arms flailing.

"Some of which you were quite happy to steal and give to me."

"Stop being so ruddy clever," Matthias screamed, his voice cracking, his eyes bulging. "There are no alternatives," he said, more slowly. "We — have — to — save — the gold. And it's far too dangerous for my family to take it home, for us to be found with it."

"But what about Severin's safety? said Thomas, despairingly, although it was becoming clear the options were narrowing and Torsrud was a possibility...isolated, up in the forest. "It will only work if we can find a quiet part of his land, well away from the farmhouse, although God's knows where you'll hide it; as I said, everything's frozen solid."

"All you do is come up with problems," said Matthias.

"Matthias, this is your show. I'll help you dump the stuff, hide it at Severin's if we can find a safe location, but then we split, as agreed. I'd like this bag, too; the Governor's I guess," he said, glancing at the rear seat. "For food and spare clothes..."

"Of course, take it," muttered Matthias.

"And the road atlas. And you'll have to walk back to Monsrud on your own. Yes?"

"Yes," said Matthias. "And I'll dump the lorry in the forest somewhere, not on Severin's land, once we're done."

"And you must agree this never happened and had nothing to do with me."

"Agreed. You were never at the bank, never saw me, never saw any gold, never saw or drove the Mercedes."

"We must move fast, but we still need to overcome the problem of the frozen ground," said Thomas, picturing Severin's land.

"A lake?" suggested Matthias, his eyes lighting up. "Just break the ice and dump the kegs.

Thomas thought for a while and said: "No drill or saw to get through the ice. And we'd have no idea how deep the water would be or where the kegs would end up."

"Think, man..." urged Matthias. "You're the bloody geologist."

Thomas fell silent for a while, looking out into the snow, working an idea through in his mind. "There's one place at Torsrud which is never frozen..." he said.

"Where, show me," said Matthias, his voice quivering.

"I will only allow this and help you if you move the kegs away from Torsrud as soon as the ground elsewhere thaws," said Thomas. "To your farm, wherever."

"Agreed."

"And we move fast?" said Thomas, jabbing Matthias in the chest with a clenched fist. "I have to be in Sweden before the back roads are closed."

THIRTY-NINE

By the early hours, the job was done: the gold buried, the excavated material covered as best they could with snow pulled out from the forest and an unobtrusive marker stick carefully placed to help locate the kegs in the future. Another light snow shower further covered their endeavours; they had been lucky and Thomas knew it.

"I'll say again," said Matthias. "You can take a bag of coins, a thousand sovereigns from the part load. One bag won't be missed and I couldn't have done it without you. I've taken a bag myself, see..." he held up a canvas bag with both hands.

"Not a chance," said Thomas.

"You fool," replied Matthias, harshly. "You'll have more wealth than you will ever acquire as an unknown geologist. And there's no risk. Look around, there's no one here. It's dark, it's snowing."

"It's not just the morality of it," said Thomas, "I don't want the risk. I've no idea what I'd do with so much gold. But I do need cash, for food."

"You've no idea how much gold is worth, do you?"

"Why should I? Tell me, if you must."

"A thousand coins: that alone is enough to buy Monsrud, for example; our house and the land around it. All in one canvas bag."

"That's unbelievable," said Thomas.

"Exactly," said Matthias. "It equates to everything I inherited — well, what was left of it after my father drank and gambled it away. Second thoughts?"

"No. It's mad, and I can't deal with it; my head is exploding with everything that has happened today."

"Very well, here you are," said Matthias, walking over to the Mercedes. "Car and map. All yours. And some cash. Take the road to Ås, continue through the town and then keep going to Elvestad. It's a quiet crossing into Sweden, provided it's not yet taken by the Germans. If it is, double back and try the next crossing to the south.'

'And Thomas...' Matthias said. "Remember, we never met, not at the bank, not afterwards. Sort out your story. If you get stopped, just hand over the keys. You must have no association with this car. Don't keep it. Just walk away from it when you're over the border. No one knows how it could have ended up in Sweden."

"Okay, thanks. And good luck to you, I suppose."

Thomas eased on the accelerator and the Mercedes started to move forward, its tyres crunching through the fresh snow and slithering on the uneven ground. The headlights picked out a steady fall of snow and he engaged the wipers. He still shook from the events of the day and perspired from the effort of the digging, but he knew that, if ever he was to reach Sweden, and safety, this would be his best chance. Then, as he lifted a hand to wave to Matthias, invisible somewhere in the dark, he heard the rear passenger door open.

"Thomas, take it," said Matthias, his voice firmer now, "You deserve it." There was a heavy thump on the floor, a chink of coins and the door was slammed shut. Thomas glanced over his shoulder but could see nothing in the darkness. For a moment he thought he should stop. But he was moving now and, with the weather closing in, time was short.

Pressing his foot to the floor, he thought only of Sweden. The Mercedes accelerated down the narrow track towards the Ås road and weaved through the forest. Turning left where Severin's track met the main road, he then headed east, full of hope and fear in equal measure. But it was not long until conditions worsened.

Snow raced out of a point in the night, picked up by the Mercedes' powerful headlights. The wipers swept an ever-decreasing area as the snow built up. The wind howled and, hunched over the wheel, Thomas struggled to suppress the panic rising inside him. He had driven very little in his life and never in such conditions. Time was slipping by, the route unclear. He knew, in weather like this, he could miss a turning or simply drive off the road into a ditch. On foot he would be secure, but this scared him: the car sliding fearfully on the road, the shrieking wind, the charge of the snow in the headlights and glimpses of trees swaying wildly in the storm. Alone, battered by the day and heading for a new country, he now felt far from sure whether his plan was the right one.

"Hell," he shouted, thumping the wheel with his fists. The road had vanished in a wall of snow, but a barrier, just visible, marked the entrance to a forest track and he pulled in, safe. He would wait, but keep the engine running. Leaning into the back of the car he tried to lift the bag of coins. It was awkward from where he sat, so he stepped outside and opened the passenger door, the wind threatening to tear it away. Grabbing hold of the Governor's bag, he dumped the bag of coins inside along with a few items of emergency winter clothing which had come out of the boot of the car.

After a while, it seemed the wind had reduced, the snow lighter. Minutes passed and it continued to clear. He then started to worry about petrol and searched for the gauge. Somewhere less than half...but what did that mean? Would it take him to the border? He had no idea.

"Come on Sweden," he whispered, slipping into first gear and pulling onto the road again.

Studying the map as he drove, he knew the junction with National Highway 1 lay ahead. Up a short hill, over the crest, then a long left-hand bend and back into forest. The junction came into view shortly after. Two trucks and a car were parked across the road. He stopped and peered ahead. There was no sign of German troops and he set off again, hoping for good luck.

But it was not to be.

As he approached the junction, a soldier jumped down from

another truck sitting askew on the verge, his torch flashing left and right: a short man, rather over-weight, his gun pointing at Thomas through the windscreen. This was the end. He wound down the window. Another soldier appeared and dragged open the driver's door. "Out," he wheezed, with his boy-like face and unconvincing voice.

"A Merc," said the dumpy soldier at the windscreen.

"Nice," replied the boy, settling into the driver's seat and running his hands over the steering wheel. It was the car they wanted. "*Gehen!*" he shouted, pointing back along the road towards Drøbak.

Thomas walked slowly around to the other side of the car, opened the passenger door and calmly withdrew some of the Governor's emergency winter clothes in full view of the watching soldiers, and put them on. He picked up the Governor's bag and started walking back down the road. Snow was slowly falling again and the night quickly turned black as the roadblock was left behind.

It was a long way back and the night was cold, but Thomas decided to close off one possible risk: he would stop at Monsrud and let Matthias know what had befallen the Governor's Mercedes. They needed consistent stories.

FORTY

orsrud, timeless on its little rise in the land, had been carefully selected by Severin's ancestors as a perfect spot to build. Today, the 10th of April 1940, could have been late in the winter a century ago. If a visitor had walked by then, as now, he would have lifted his nose to the sweet smell of woodsmoke, spread out as a thin haze below the treetops, as if an invisible hand had pressed it down and swept it all into the clearing, as a sheepdog rounds up its flock. It was, for now at least, an island of tranquillity, as Norway began to fall under the thumb of Nazi control.

Exhausted, yet unable to sleep, Thomas talked with Severin through the night. "I thought it was artillery practice at first, one hell of a din," Severin had said. "So I got onto the BBC. They were bombing the ruddy fortress, they said. Worried sick for you, I was."

For a long while neither man spoke. Thomas, absorbed by the faltering flame of a candle, watched it slowly disappear into a caldera of wax on the ancient stone mantlepiece. Everything comes to an end. After a while, he pushed himself out of the chair and walked over to an ancient pine coffer on the back wall. Selecting a new candle from the small wooden box inside, he melted the base of the new candle over the final gasps of the old and lit a new flame for the days to come. He sat down and looked up in satisfaction. Perfectly upright, he thought, as it should be.

On the morning of the second day back at Torsrud, the outer door crashed open and a thud of rubber boots sounded against the doorpost, as it did when Severin came in after tramping around in the snow. He stumbled in from the porch carrying a bucket of milk and a small wicker basket of eggs.

"Someone's been wandering around the bottom field," he said, as he disappeared down the trapdoor into the cellar, his voice gruff from the cold air. "Chewing up the snow."

"Elk maybe?" said Thomas.

"No doubt," mused Severin.

That was the end of it, thought Thomas, relieved. But there was much else to occupy his mind. "You know I've felt unsafe," he said after breakfast. "A sort of shadow after me."

"Aha..."

"Well, a few days before the invasion, Stensrud was broken into."

"But you were here then, with me."

"I'd moved here, yes, but I was on the ferries for several days, remember...staying overnight on the fortress. I took a short break to go back to Stensrud to make a phone call and discovered the break-in then. That raid was intended to kill me. It was pure luck I wasn't there."

"The Lord God, who would want to do that? At least, you'll be safe here. No one ever comes here."

"I'm not so sure and the point is you're now in danger, because of me."

"Oh, I doubt that. But who the hell is it?" said Severin.

"Brann," said Thomas, "...and he'll find me. I need to move again. And soon."

———

Matthias sat at his usual place in the clerk's office on the day the bank reopened after the German takeover. It had not been an easy decision, but he was anxious to keep an eye on events. A young Wehrmacht soldier stood guard at the door, constantly adjusting the grip of his rifle, his eyes nervously flickering; other guards had been placed at the main entrance and at intervals along the corridors.

An official in the audit team, Henrik Dahl, had also responded to the call to reopen the bank and was temporarily in charge of the clerk's office, the audit team and various administrative functions. Dahl had been the most senior manager given responsibility for the gold audit in the weeks leading up to the German invasion and had helped with the evacuation of the gold to Lillehammer, after which he returned to Oslo. Such was the gossip surrounding the final minutes before the bank was taken, he had asked Matthias to meet him in a café on Prinsens gate during the lunch break on the 12th of April.

For Matthias, information was hard to come by. There had been no news on the radio about the flight of the gold to Lillehammer, so the meeting was a welcome opportunity to catch up on events and also measure whether any suspicions lurked regarding his own role. As it turned out, Dahl gave little away but said enough for Matthias to know the primary objective — to keep the gold reserves in Norwegian hands — had been achieved. It was a great relief. He also discovered that the King and the Crown Prince, the government and some of Norges Bank's senior staff were on the run, heading north with the gold. Dahl quickly turned to the question on his and everyone else's lips at the bank: what had happened to Lorry 27?

"I nearly made it," said Matthias, picking up the steaming black coffee. "I was a couple of blocks down Kirkegata but was stopped by a Wehrmacht unit. They were all over the city by then; at Akershus, on Karl Johans gate, everywhere. There was no way out. But it was the lorry they wanted. They couldn't have known about the bank, where I'd come from or what was under the canvas."

"We knew you'd had problems once twenty-seven didn't turn up," replied Dahl.

"You know what happened?" said Matthias. "My two loaders and the ruddy driver just took off when the bullets started flying. I was left on my own. I had to load the last keg myself, the half load, shove it up the ruddy planks; it was hellish heavy." He shook his head. "Then I was held up. I tried to stop them taking the lorry, but they almost shot my feet off."

"Twenty-seven was on a knife-edge," said Dahl. "The Governor knew that; he was worrying about it when we met at Lillehammer."

Matthias felt a wave of joy pass over him at Dahl's words. No one could know what had really happened.

"Anyway," said Dahl, breaking his thoughts, "regarding twenty-seven, I've looked into it from all available sources, including speaking to the driver who did the runner. I'm pleased — if that's the word — to verify your account."

"Who knows where those kegs are now?" said Matthias, trying to disguise a long, deep sigh with another sip of coffee. "Maybe one day we'll get them back?"

"Huh, I doubt it," said Dahl. "It'll be melted down and recast as Nazi gold, then converted to currency and used to buy iron ore or oil or something."

"As you say, a good job it was such a small load."

"I'll complete my final report later today," said Dahl, "and that will be the end of the matter.

———

Nicolai Rygg, the Governor, returned to the bank on the 15th of April, the same day that the Administrative Council took over after Quisling's failed coup. Deeply affected by Norway's failure to maintain its sovereignty, a terrible foreboding hung over the Governor's head. Fear and uncertainty cast an eerie atmosphere over Oslo; the Germans had enforced lightning control over the city and the levers of power.

Yet, the Governor also felt satisfaction at having prepared the gold so well for the emergency evacuation. After days of interrogation, only when he knew the gold had again been moved north, did he reveal Lillehammer as the initial destination. He had done everything possible to secure Norway's gold reserves; no one could say any other. But it was only after his return that he began to piece together the events which followed his own departure in Lorry 26.

Early in the afternoon on the day of the invasion, Norges Bank had been surrounded in force by German troops, although it was the following day before the bank was fully secured and placed under guard. Once it became clear that the vaults were empty, the Germans had arranged a meeting with the Governor's deputy, Sverre Olaf Thorkildsen, and a few remaining bank officials, to discuss the fate of the gold. Little of substance, the Governor was satisfied to hear, had been revealed. On the 11th of April, Major Fr. W. Neef of the German Wirtschaftstab — an economic exploitation group — began harsher and more extensive interrogations of bank staff, but once again the Governor discovered, with great pride, that no useful information had been extracted.

One matter remained: what had been the fate of Lorry 27 and his clerk, Matthias Holmbekk? He read Henrik Dahl's report to find out. Later, he passed through the clerk's office and offered to Matthias a barely discernible lift of the eyebrows as he walked by.

Several days then passed before the Governor called Matthias into his office to thank him for the many weeks of hard work which had underpinned the successful flight of the gold. There was one more matter, a small one in the scheme of things, and Matthias suspected the worst.

"My Mercedes?" the Governor asked, with a wry smile.

"I'm sorry, sir: it's not good news. As I think you know, I was left with no driver, no one to help me. So, of course, I had to drive the lorry and leave the Mercedes. Once the lorry was lost, er...you know what happened to it?"

The Governor nodded.

"Well, I ran back for the Mercedes, started her up and returned down Kirkegata, but only for a couple of blocks because of the roadblock on Karl Johans gate, so I headed down Prinsens gate. There was a lot of civilian traffic, but I kept going, through the Old Town, heading for National Highway 1. My plan was to turn north for Lillehammer. But when I arrived at the junction, the Germans were setting up a roadblock there. Two trucks, a barrier, lots of soldiers. They forced me to stop, dragged me out and dumped me on the road. Gave me a right ruddy kicking they did when I tried to fight them off. They just took the car and set me off to walk home in the snow."

"You are not the only one who's had a vehicle taken, Mr Holmbekk."

"I am sorry, sir. I did my best," said Matthias, relieved beyond words that Thomas had dropped in at Monsrud that freezing night to tell him the true story. The student deserved a thousand gold coins for that alone.

FORTY-ONE

The *22ⁿᵈ of April 1940*. Thomas continued to hide at Torsrud, despite knowing that every day he stayed brought increasing danger to both him and Severin. The month had turned grey, damp and cold with misty air, the sort that creeps into people's bones and freezes as rime on the trees. He eventually decided to walk into town for supplies. A collective trauma had crept like a plague through Drøbak since the events of the ninth; there was barely a person who did not know one or more of the ferrymen or the gunners who had lost their lives. Two women had been killed in the house Thomas had seen hit by fire from *Blücher* and there was damage throughout the town. Many shops which had been part of daily life for decades had closed, either because supplies had dried up or because their owners were dead: Gunderson, Svensen and several others. Svensen, with his funny ways: it was shocking and hard to believe.

With several days of supplies secured, Thomas knew he must now move on from Torsrud. Most of his belongings, such as they were, would be hidden in the barn and he would take just one case of essentials with him, plus his rucksack.

An escape to Sweden, he decided, would be impossible at the moment with troops everywhere, nervous and liable to shoot at any suspicious activity. The same applied to a train journey north, to hide away in the mountains in Rondane, where the problem would be lack of food and shelter, or Trøndelag, where Severin had a distant cousin, but where there was still fighting according to BBC reports today. "Hear that: British soldiers killed yesterday at Krogs Gård," Severin had said. "I know the place from when I was a kid. Near Steinkjer, it is. Furthest away I'd ever been. Still is."

There was only one option: he would stay locally and well hidden. "I'm not saying where I shall go," he said to Severin. "For your safety and mine. But I've had a nod; someone I know."

"I'll miss you," said Severin. He was close to tears and Thomas felt just the same. Here at Torsrud was where he felt most at home.

"One more thing," said Thomas. "Keep an eye out for Brann. If he discovers you've been helping me..."

"See this?" said Severin, walking over to a cupboard by the front porch and grabbing hold of a shotgun. "He'll be tasting lead shot if he tries any tricks on me."

As Thomas left Torsrud with a heavy weight of sadness in the pit of his stomach, it was in the knowledge that Severin had become the best and most unlikely friend. As he walked down through the forest, he wondered once again what he would do with the thousand gold sovereigns weighing down his grey canvas rucksack. It felt like a bad idea to have it in his possession, but you never know when it could be a life-saver.

———

The stove was well-charged, the room warm; the Bell House was amply supplied with wood. Three men sat at the table: Brann and his two foresters. Anskar Helgeland and Petter Berg had been active all winter in ferreting out information amongst the local forestry community, particularly on the question of the English Spy.

Brann handed them each a glass of aquavit.

"You know a man by his principles," he said, a hint of a grin on his face. His men looked at him, silent.

"Make sure you're on the winning side," he said, smiling and lifting his glass. "That's my principle." His voice rumbled theatrically as he stood.

"Not National Samling?" said Helgeland.

"Na, dead, they are."

"Hitler," said Berg.

"Exactly, my friend," said Brann. "And we're happy with that," he said, raising his glass. "Aren't we...?"

His men followed his lead, cackling and growling. Brann then dug into the pocket of his trousers and withdrew six coins, which he placed on the table in front of him, slowly building two piles of three each on an imaginary line between his two men and his own huge hands.

"Know what these are?"

The two men looked at each other. "Not gold are they?" said Helgeland, hesitantly.

"Exactly. Gold."

"Good God," said Berg, stretching forward his wiry neck for a better view

"And they are yours, three each," said Brann. "Twenty Mark German gold coins." He pushed the coins to both men, who took them, holding them and studying the fine detail, weighing them in the cups of their hands.

"A thank you," he said, "for loyal service, for helping to get Haugen and to celebrate good times to come. But there's more to do. Forget the King, the old Government; they've run away. Germany's in charge now." His voice fell away to a gravelly whisper. "I'll pay 'em a visit, those Wehrmacht. They'll need help, you wait and see. They'll need to know who's who, who's a traitor, a royalist, an old-style political type. They'll need to get hold of supplies, food, horses, workers, the lot. People to print stuff, make stuff. They'll need to know who they can trust. And they'll want someone to find the English Spy..."

FORTY-TWO

Dark brown, almost black cladding, small white painted
windows and a shallow roof formed of great slabs of slate:
Myrstua stood empty. The migrant forestry workers had
stopped early this year and moved on. At the back of the cabin, a rough
lean-to sheltered the woodstore and, to the front, the hooks and shelves
in a substantial porch seemed forlorn without the boots, jackets,
helmets and other paraphernalia of outdoor work.

Around the hut was an open area, rather wet much of the year, so
Christian said, with a single pine tree standing on a rocky hillock next to
the entrance track, now deep in snow and, beyond this, birchwoods and
mossy mires.

Thomas's new home was hidden deep within the dank southern
forests of the Holmbekk estate and would, he hoped, be safe for a while.

———

Formless clouds glowered down on Torsrud. The woodstove worked
hard fighting the remorseless cold, and the final stack of split birch had
almost gone. On the mantlepiece, a new candle flickered, slowly

contributing another layer of wax. Mice scuttled along the back wall more freely than ever. Severin yearned for spring.

A knock at the door interrupted his slumber. He jumped up. "Thomas," he said in an excited whisper. He dragged open the door, joyous at the prospect of his young friend returning to see him.

But it was not Thomas, with his handsome smile, standing back as if with no expectation of being invited in, although of course he always was. It was Brann, his huge mass cutting out the light from the doorway.

Severin reacted quickly. He leaned over, flinging open the door to his cupboard, his hand closing on his shotgun.

"I wouldn't," said Brann, lifting his rifle, pressing the barrel into Severin's chest and pushing him back into his fireside chair.

Heavy boots on the wooden floor: Severin could hear Brann's two men striding noisily into the room. Brann leaned over him, his face inches away, the warmth of his breath laced with alcohol, his eyes black and angry.

"Where is Galtung?" he snarled, smashing his fist into Severin's face.

———

Norges Bank attracted much interest as the population of Oslo began to return. People walked up Kirkegata, past the service exit from where the gold had been loaded into lorries, along Myntgata to see where the German soldiers had gathered by the fort, back along Kongens gate and then, to complete the circuit, through the tree-studded square at the front of the bank to eye the detachment of troops positioned by the main entrance. Bit by bit, people pieced together an account of the flight of Norway's gold, a story full of errors, of course, but untruths became fact and it lifted their spirits to know that the staff of Norges Bank had outwitted the Nazi invaders.

Matthias shivered at his desk in the clerk's room, suffering from gripping stomach pains and palpitations. He knew the gold hidden on Nordby's farm should be moved in the next few weeks, that there had been no fresh snow and that any new excavations would be immediately visible. What if the mad dog started digging, which he would, and exposed the kegs? Furthermore, he had been unable to work out to where the gold should be moved, and how. With the ground still frozen, it would be impossible and too dangerous to relocate it in one operation at home. He could not use his own small tractor for the job for fear of being recognised, even if he could work out how to lift and manoeuvre the impossibly heavy kegs.

The only option was that the gold be shifted a few bags at a time. He worked it through in his head. Two bags, two thousand coins: sixteen kilograms. That seemed manageable, leaving space to hide the bags beneath a few spare outdoor clothes in his rucksack. The total haul was 66,850 coins minus, of course, one thousand held by Thomas — a neat move, that, he thought. But his optimism quickly dissolved. Two bags per visit meant over thirty visits, which felt neither safe nor practical. Even if a purpose-made underground store could be constructed in the slither of forest he owned, how on earth could so many trips be made without suspicion and completed before the mad dog discovered a fortune in gold was buried beneath his prized muckheap?

Beyond these practical challenges, one more quandary had been circulating in his mind. Everyone knew, or thought they knew, that Matthias Holmbekk was successful, comfortably off. But, at a time of national crisis, to one day simply buy back large areas of land from his cousin, even if Christian were to sell — and that was not a given — would instigate further unwarranted peril. It wouldn't require anything like sixty thousand gold sovereigns to buy back the land — that would probably buy the whole Holmbekk estate — but any sign of instant wealth would be suspicious, especially so under German occupation. And if the gold was never spent, if his legacy were never to be restored, what was the point of his new-found fortune and the terrible risks entailed? And, above all of this was the old conundrum: before anything could be bought, at least some of the gold must be turned into cash and made legitimate: not one or two coins at a time, but in large numbers and without raising suspicion.

As he walked along Kirkegata towards Berkowitz Mynthandel, his coin dealer, he found himself wondering why, why, hadn't he thought through his report to Dahl? It had seemed a triumph at the time. Now, though, his story was cast in iron and, in consequence, hanging over everything was the fact that he had, without question, become the perpetrator of theft on a grand scale, even if he had not intended to or actually taken any of the gold for himself; put it in his own pocket, so to speak. He could not now go back on the story and say he'd saved the gold from the Nazis, tell the Governor where it was hidden, and be feted as a hero of Norway. It was this impossible dilemma that was the cause of his terrible pains and aching, throbbing heart. At times, he worried he would die of stress.

So, all he could do now was to make a start and turn at least some of the gold into cash. And he must separate in his mind the plan to buy back the land his father had lost, from the question of what to do with the bulk of Lorry 27's hoard. To buy back the land, he would aim to turn four bags of gold into cash: four thousand coins, two trips to Torsrud. He would sell the gold over a few years if necessary, quicker if he could. This would enable him to restore to his family, as quietly as possible, a large area of forest, the beautiful top field, a block of fine arable land and hopefully the lovely ice lake, too. The seemingly impossible issue of moving the rest of the gold would be left to another day.

Approaching Berkowitz Mynthandel, he rehearsed his conversation with Jakob, trying to think through the consequences:

A lifetime's collecting, Jakob, can you imagine? At some point we must sell up. The wife, she wants improvements. I'd like to expand the farm, buy a little more land. A thousand coins, Jakob, what can you offer me?

Swinging his cane with a careless sense of optimism and kicking snow from the steps, he pushed on the door of Berkowitz Mynthandel. It was only then that he saw the sign:

CLOSED

FOR THE FORESEEABLE FUTURE
Jakob Berkowitz

His heart started up again, racing and thumping, and his hands shook. After a minute spent trying to calm himself, he stepped across to the adjoining door, a small shop where he usually bought his Lucky Strikes.

"Good day, Georg," he said, slowing his breathing. "Twenty of the usual please."

"It's nice to see you in these troubled times, Mr. Holmbekk," he said.

"Next door, closed down...?"

"Jewish," said Georg. "He closed the shop on the ninth and I gather he was in Sweden with his family a day later. They're probably on a ship to America right now."

Matthias returned to the bank. He was, his own problems aside, pleased for Jakob and his family, to know they were safe. But his conundrum now felt impossible to solve and the knot in his stomach wrenched yet another turn tighter.

———

Matthias's demeanour would have been even more fraught if he had known anything of another series of ominous events, many set off by his own decisions.

The first arose late on the 9th of April, the day of the invasion, at the roadblock where Thomas had been held up at the junction on National Highway 1. The fine Mercedes-Benz 540K, which Thomas had been forced to surrender, had caused some interest amongst the German troops. Such was the quality of the car it was not, like most vehicles commandeered by the Wehrmacht in the early days of the occupation, pressed into immediate service, but was respectfully driven next day to Drøbak, where Oberst Baumann of the 307th Infantry Regiment, having survived the sinking of *Blücher*, was in the process of establishing a new command base. The car was duly garaged and placed under guard until the situation in the town settled down.

Sometime later, the new Wehrmacht administrative team, now ensconced in the Fjord Hotel on Storgaten, with its well-stocked cellar and views across the fjord, was given the task of tracking down the ownership of such a special car. Not that the owner would be paid for it, of course — not more than a few kroner at best — but it would mean the records could be completed and the legal niceties tied up.

It was not long before a hand-written entry was made by a young clerk, Hans Schiller, in the register of assets: 'Mercedes-Benz 540K: Norges Bank'. To this was added a note giving details of where and when the car was taken. These facts came to the commander's attention as he cast an eye over the schedule of vehicles now forming part of the occupiers' fleet. Why would such a vehicle, the property of the central bank in Oslo and quite likely the car of a top bank official, have been driving **away** from Drøbak, little more than twelve hours after the invasion? Many people in his position would have let it pass by, but Oberst Baumann possessed a particularly analytical and methodical mind, one unsettled by loose ends.

He was by now aware that Norway's gold reserves had been spirited away by the Norwegians on the day of the invasion and that, at this moment, Mölde was being bombed in an effort to disrupt attempts to complete the escape. He had also picked up, in a briefing from troops who had helped to secure Akerhus fortress on the day of the invasion, that a lorry had been parked outside the central bank minutes before the Wehrmacht had entered the area. Indeed, one of the men had described both a lorry and a car — probably a Mercedes — turning on Myntgata and racing off together down Kirkegata.

These facts posed to Baumann a compelling scenario as he accumulated more evidence. Could it be that the rumour circulating in Oslo was true: a final consignment of gold — the last lorryload — had failed to escape north to Lillehammer and had disappeared, or had been commandeered and not recorded as such? The evidence supported this: at the time the lorry was seen leaving the bank, routes north were effectively closed. He was also aware from Schiller's schedules that a small greengrocer's lorry had been found dumped in the forest to the east of Drøbak. Interestingly, the lorry was not dissimilar to vehicles thought to have been used by the bank to transport the gold to Lillehammer, and it appeared to have been abandoned just a few miles away from the junction on Highway 1 where the Mercedes had been requisitioned. Taken together with the events at Norges Bank, a scenario formed quickly in

Baumann's mind. Could it be that the final lorryload of gold might have found its way into his area of control?

There were many other matters which occupied Baumann's mind, including intelligence that a British spy was operating in the area. A local man, Alexander Brann, whose name had been listed on a secret schedule of potential sympathisers prepared by a local Abwehr agent, had offered his services in the early days of the occupation. Intelligence from trusted sources, already vetted, was to be greatly prized and the costs were modest. A few days later, Brann was called in and Oberst Baumann set out his requirements and the prospect of a secure position and regular payment for him and his men within the occupying forces.

"To start with, find the British spy," said Baumann.

FORTY-THREE

The final days of April 1940 saw little sign of the spring weather Thomas yearned for. No new snow appeared either, but what had been dumped earlier on the frozen marshland around Myrstua was now slowly melting into a quagmire and turning icy overnight; it was typical of the fleeting transition between the harshness of winter and the kindly airs of spring.

A maid from the Castle brought a cache of food every day. Thomas watched her from the window as she trudged across the clearing, her squat frame lurching every now and then as she slipped on the uneven and sometimes icy snow path, coming to a halt with arms waving as she attempted to avoid falling into the slushy mire. It was a miracle the food she brought survived the ordeal.

Several wallops sounded as she kicked each of her boots against the porch and a resounding crash marked the moment when she knocked with gusto on the door.

"Good day, Mr Galtung," Maria would say. "A fine basket we have this time. Cook's best."

She gabbled away about this and that, ran through her delivery and asked what Thomas would like for next time, invariably forgetting his reply at some point between him speaking and her point of arrival back at the Castle. In fact, he thought, she never actually listened to what he said —so she never knew, so therefore never forgot.

The visit from Maria was the high point of life so far at Myrstua but, after the fifth day, Thomas's mind began to drift when she talked, simply mumbling agreement to whatever she said. Agreement, disagreement, it made no difference until, suddenly, he wondered why he had not thought of the question before:

"You've been at the Castle a long time, Maria, in service to the Holmbekk family?"

"Indeed, Mr Galtung, since 1916. Longest serving, I am, sir. Apart from Antonia, that is; she's been there forever. Toni, the family calls her, but she's Antonia to us. Oh, and Turid, the cook. She's been here all her life I reckon, like her mother before. Ah, and of course Mr Gustavsson, the head gardener. Swedish he is you know, talks funny, but you get used to it: half Swedish and the rest a west coast dialect, all mixed up. He's been here a long time, too."

"Do you remember Marta?" said Thomas, patiently. "She was a maid, like you, around the same time. A young girl, then."

"Of course. Nice she was, worked hard; lovely hair. Yes, I remember her."

"You do?" The nape of his neck tingled. "Where did she go?"

"Oh, away, sir, away. I don't know where. One day she was here, the next she wasn't."

"You've no idea where she is now?"

"Why, you looking for her? I can ask around."

"Oh, no, Maria. Not at all."

"Just disappeared she did. Nice girl. And Mr Galtung..."

"Yes, Maria?"

"It's damp in here, and cold. You should light the fire."

————

After Maria left, and the thrill of having a lead on Marta, Thomas returned to the more vital question of his own future. He was grateful to Christian for helping, but there was no work available in the forests, so there was little to relieve his feelings of uselessness and frustration at not making good an escape to Sweden whilst the opportunity had been there. He had lost critical time on the day of the invasion. Driving to Torsrud, waiting for dusk, trying to hide the gold: it had cost him his freedom, all helping to solve someone else's problem. "Bloody Matthias," he muttered as he paced the earthen floor. He felt anger at his own weakness and unsettled by the bag of gold hidden behind a panel in the bedroom, the more so now that he had worked out just why Matthias had thrown it into the back of the Mercedes when he did.

He was now even more complicit than the bank clerk.

———

Brann successfully concluded negotiations to work within both the Frogn and Drøbak commune offices, in addition to his liaison role with the German army of occupation. Within days, he was helping to interview and advise on those who could be trusted in local authority and other administrative roles. Above all, he was enthusiastic at the prospect of rooting out those in positions of power whose tenure should, quite properly, be short-lived. Chief of Police Paul Sandvik was one name for Brann to consider; it was essential for Baumann that the local force could be called on to support the occupation, including the Nazi secret police, the Gestapo. That support must start at the top and Sandvik was suspect: it had been him who had prepared and helped implement an evacuation plan for Drøbak in the event of war and he had shown little support for Germany's claim to have come to Norway in a spirit of friendship.

It was in this position within the new administration that Brann began to work with and assist Hans Schiller, the German army clerk. It was natural they would exchange information and it was in one such moment that Schiller, who had an ear for interesting developments, shared with Brann not only the story of the Governor's Mercedes-Benz but also, on a separate occasion, the rumour of a hoard of Norges Bank gold which had ended up, he believed, somewhere around Drøbak, although he did not know where or how. His certainty was based on no more than an ambiguous note he was instructed to file and a half-overheard telephone conversation whilst waiting outside his superior's office.

Brann returned to the Bell House that night in a state of high excitement. It was not hard to conclude, as Schiller had, that a large consignment of gold was hidden somewhere in the home area, brought there on the lorry abandoned, sometime on the ninth, in the forest off the Ås road. But Brann knew one more fact than the Germans, and he had no intention of sharing it with them.

"No senior bank people around here," he had said to Schiller when the question had arisen.

But there was, of course, an employee of Norges Bank in this area, a man who had boasted for years of his role as the senior manager of Norway's gold reserves, but was in fact a lowly clerk who could not possibly be connected with either a hoard of gold or the Governor's Mercedes: that was Brann's defence if ever he were to be questioned on why this information was never released to his new employers.

It took a day or so for Brann to develop a plan. The story of the Governor's Mercedes: this was probably of no significance, although he was short of facts, so would keep an open mind. Many cars, stolen in the panic to escape the city on the day of the invasion, were dumped and subsequently picked up by the Germans, or were maybe taken by force by fleeing locals. But if the gold story was true, which appeared likely, then for sure Holmbekk was behind it...the man responsible for the gold reserves taking a share and bringing it back to his home area. A simple telephone inquiry confirmed Norges Bank had now reopened and that Mr Holmbekk was back in his post. The clerk often stayed in Oslo during the week but always returned on a Friday evening.

Brann smiled, squeezing his fists in anticipation.

FORTY-FOUR

Three weeks had passed since the invasion. As the occupiers tightened their grip, the threats to Thomas's life gnawed at his health every day. It was hard to sleep and impossible to move around normally, and he was unsure as to who might now be his likely assassin. Maybe no one now the invasion was done? Equally, it could be a whole platoon of marksmen or the German secret police, plus Brann, of course. To escape to Sweden was the only viable plan, but that was flawed; he'd be lucky to make it a mile up the road: roadblocks and identity checks were everywhere. There were no good options and he could do no more than assume the worst if he were to remain alive. In the meantime, there was much to resolve with Klara following the drama at the fortress.

The next day, they met in the Great Hall and he inquired about her recovery from the shooting, a question she ignored.

"Why," she said, fixing him with a penetrating glare, "why would a geology student become mixed up in the war; especially in a plot to kill Colonel Eriksen? That night I was shot," she added, cutting out any chance of a response, "I never got an answer. Why were you there, in the middle of a gunfight? And then the invasion...there you were again, on the fortress, in the thick of it, taking *Terne* up the fjord to Oslo. She's still at Vippetangen, apparently, half wrecked. But back to the shooting...the colonel came to see me — do you know that? — after I was shot; he wanted an explanation of why you knew, before even he did, that a German invasion force was sailing up the fjord. So how **did** you, a student, a lowly ferryman, know that? And there's more I find suspicious: the timing of when you arrived here...ever heard of a Peter Haugen? Hmm?" She waited a few seconds, staring, watching intently for his reaction. "Oh, you **have**. My God. I knew it. And what about the Kopås incident? That was you...?" Another short pause. "Yes, it was. I suspected so. Thomas, who are you?"

He took a deep breath. "Let me start at the beginning," he said. "I was there that night — I'm a ferryman, remember — to take Colonel Eriksen back to the fortress, as I've done many times before. I got caught up in the attack on him. They probably wanted to kill me too; they killed all the other ferrymen."

"Huh, but there's more. You're on the run. Why? You're now hidden away at Myrstua, never coming out. This doesn't happen to normal people."

"Klara, just take time to listen, please," he said, trying to remain calm.

"What I couldn't work out," she continued, "is whether you were working for the British or the Germans. I assumed at first it must be the British, because of where you had come from in December last year. Then you started working in the heart of Norway's defences, at the fortress, just before the killings and the invasion, so I began to connect you to the Germans. Now I don't know what you are, who you're working for."

"That's ridiculous," said Thomas, a shudder racing up his spine.

"So what are you?" she said, looking him in the eye. "You're no student; there's no geology here in winter, not this winter anyway. It's all covered in snow."

"We go back a long way," said Thomas. "You were my first and best friend in Norway. I cannot bear the thought of mistrust between us. But I have my own worries and you must hear them." He coughed and took a while to find his voice.

"Go on," she said, staring at him, her voice tense and controlled.

"Out with the truth. There's a link to the assassinations, isn't there? I found one of the bodies, you know."

"Listen to me. Your association with Carl Westervik...I chose to believe in you, that night we rescued the colonel, and I hope I was right to do so."

She opened her mouth to speak, but Thomas put his hand up.

"Your Carl?" he said, looking back at her. "Where is he now?"

"I don't know. Bergholt is closed up and I haven't seen him. I worry every day for him."

"Of course it's closed up. He's disappeared."

She sat back and half smiled.

"The man who shot you," said Thomas. "Do you know who it was?"

"I've no idea. Whoever wanted the colonel dead. A German agent I guess. Some friend of yours perhaps. You haven't answered my questions and you're changing the subject."

"A German agent, yes, but the shooter was no friend of mine. He tried to kill me too, at the colonel's house."

"What's this got to do with Carl?"

"Everything." Thomas spoke slowly, letting the words sink in. "Carl was a German spy and it was he, Carl, who shot you."

"That's ridiculous," said Klara, sharply.

"Is it? The assassinations were a German operation with Carl at the centre of it all. It was Carl who tried to assassinate the colonel. And was behind the killing of the artillerymen. And the ferrymen...my lovely friend, Olaf Backer. Think of the timing: immediately before the invasion. And then...Carl disappears. He was identified by the colonel and would have had no choice but to leave the area."

"It was dark when we were on Skarholmen. You couldn't have seen the gunman."

"I didn't need to. I saw him earlier, on Seimbakken, walking up the path to the colonel's house to kill him and me too, probably, a ferryman. I saw him shoot the two guards, right in front of my eyes. The colonel saw him, too, and knew who he was. He said: it's the potato merchant."

"Carl would never kill anyone." For the first time, Klara framed her reaction as much a question as a statement in his defence, a hint of doubt creeping in as she slowly slumped back in her chair.

"It was Carl who shot you, I'm a hundred percent certain," said Thomas. "His only defence is that he couldn't have known at the time that it was you. Not for sure. You were just a figure, a silhouette in a murky night. You were unlucky. It was the colonel he was after."

Still Klara maintained the last vestiges of her mocking challenge, but the attack had faded, the case against Thomas lost. She sat back, folding her arms high on her chest in a show of incredulity at Thomas's accusations. But the arms were slack, no more than a wrapper to hold in her doubt and fear. Thomas could see her certainties fade as he waited. Maybe she already harboured confusion and ambiguity about Carl which her love for him had hidden? It was painful to watch.

"But the assassination didn't succeed," he said, quietly. "Carl failed. The colonel wasn't killed: he escaped. And there were consequences. The colonel ordered the firing of the big cannons. He defended Norway. There were torpedoes, I saw the explosions. *Blücher* sank. Hundreds of Germans died in the fjord. The whole invasion was delayed; despite all the killings. Why?...because the colonel survived."

Klara's lower lip started to drop and quiver, just as it did when she was little, on those rare occasions when she was thwarted by her parents.

"Carl could have stayed here, cementing his innocence," said Thomas, sensing, for the first time, her rising sense of despair as her convictions crumbled. "Probably that was his plan. But two people saw him and survived — the colonel and me. The colonel has now been arrested and taken away, but no one knows how many people he told about the events of that night. The only certainty is me; I am the only person still free who can identify Carl as the assassin."

A single tear ran down her cheek. She sat, quite still.

"Carl's mission failed," said Thomas. "And failure doesn't sit well with Nazi high command, especially in this case given the number of lives lost and the delay, meaning the King and the government escaped. So who knows: he may have been arrested or he's on the run or hiding somewhere. But he won't be coming back. And now, my dear friend Klara, you know why."

She didn't reply and her eyes dropped as she slumped into the chair, staring at the fire, her hands cradling her face. Neither spoke until she looked up and said, almost as if speaking to herself, whispering:

"Damn."

"You knew, didn't you?" said Thomas, kneeling in front of her and gently holding her hands. "A niggling doubt?"

She didn't move.

"You loved him. But he was clever; he wouldn't reveal to you who he really was, of course. And you were blind to it all."

He had never seen her like this: silent, deflated.

"There were other signs, indications," she said, her voice weak and uneven, her head shaking. "It seems impossible to believe."

"He used you," said Thomas. "That's what an agent like him would do: he wheedled his way into relationships — people with power, connections, knowledge. Your family, the Holmbekks. What better way to garner information, to make connections into politics, the military? He may never have loved you, I don't know."

"No, you don't know; but I do. He loved me. Maybe, he knew the invasion was coming, I can see that now. He tried to make sure I wouldn't become caught up in it, just a few days ago. He wanted me to hide away, up in the mountains, to get away from here. I couldn't understand why he would do that. He was so insistent."

Tears slipped down Klara's face. "I see it now," she said, sobbing, "the small signs. He just appeared late in 1938. He said he had worked and lived in Norway before that, and had Norwegian ancestry, but never talked more about it. And just before and during the invasion he disappeared. He must have known what was coming."

"He was at the centre of it all."

"And the agricultural goods he sold when no one else could..." she sobbed.

"Don't tell me," said Thomas. "He magically came up with a solution, at a good price, didn't he, to whatever was your dilemma, your influential father's problem? With the help of Berlin, no doubt."

"Oh God..."

"I'm sorry, Klara," said Thomas. "I really am. Carl was intimately involved with the 9th of April. That's what he was here for: to prepare the ground by disabling Norway's defences...not by sabotaging the guns, but by taking out the men who operated them and by preventing reinforcements reaching the island by killing the ferrymen. He... and the team he must have had around him. And he almost succeeded."

"I can't believe it," she said, "but all the pieces of the puzzle come together now; everything makes sense. I'm so angry with myself. And now he's gone...Please believe this: he did love me. He must have been terribly torn."

"There's someone who still wants me dead," said Thomas, quietly. "He's a thug called Brann, and I'm sure he's connected in some way to Carl. He thinks, like you did, that I'm a British agent. But I'm not. Why on earth would the British spy on or act against Norway? At this moment the British are still in the north — at Narvik — fighting the Nazis. Our men are being killed to help save Norway. And anyway, I am Norwegian; I was born here and grew up here. This is my home."

"I need a break," she said. "Can we have some air?"

"Yes, of course. But let me say again. Carl knows I am possibly the only person not under arrest who witnessed, from just yards away, his attempt to kill Colonel Eriksen. If Carl and Brann are connected, as I suspect they are..." His hands suddenly shook, for just a second. "You can see why Brann is so dangerous for me."

Slowly, they walked through the snow along the long terrace towards the Lookout. It was a calm, sunless day. They clattered up the bare wooden stairs to the room at the top. Frost coated the windows. Klara collected some sticks from a basket and lit a tiny stove on the back wall. The fire crackled into life.

"Just like old times," he said, as they both sat down. "Even the chairs are still here."

She smiled.

"This is very difficult to adjust to, Thomas. You'll need to give me time, but listen."

She drew in a deep breath.

"I knew something was going on around Drøbak," she said. "Something that was not right in the weeks leading up to the invasion. But I could never put the pieces together. I got close, but never cracked it. There was a boat, *Martina*. She was moored at Lehmanns Quay, just before the invasion. I followed her captain, Hartman. I had suspicions because of what the harbourmaster said. Hartman ended up in the forest, above Hallangspollen. I saw him from Skarholmen. I tried to work out where he might have gone, and there weren't many options."

"And...?" There was more to come and Thomas felt a strange mix of relief and anticipation.

"There's a small farm there. Your old family home. That's where Captain Hartman went."

"The Bell House?"

"Yes. It was yet another connection to you — a German connection."

"The Bell House was sold after my father died. With Brann there now, it's hardly still home for me."

"Alright, but I met Brann there, briefly, when I became suspicious of Hartman and where he might have gone. I called in at the Bell House to see what would happen. Brann shouted me away."

"A huge man. Long black hair?"

"That's him," she said.

Thomas thought for a while, trying to piece together the story that was unfolding. "It's what you say about Hartman," he said, "that's what's important. I've never met him, but you're saying Hartman is connected to Brann," said Thomas. "The Bell House is where they would meet."

"I believe so, yes," said Klara. "So, you know this Brann?"

"Unfortunately, yes. I can tell you this now. He broke in at Stensrud planning to kill me, a few days before the invasion. The timing can hardly be coincidence. It's more evidence that Carl and Brann were connected. Brann must have been part of Carl's plot to clear the field of anyone in their way — including me, a so-called British spy — and disable the defences prior to the invasion. But my work rota had changed and I was on my way to the ferries when Brann raided Stensrud."

"Good God, it gets worse," she said, shaking her head. "If you are right, that Carl is connected to Brann, and Brann is linked to Hartman, the ship's captain, and therefore to the *Martina*, the escape ship...which I know from the harbourmaster departed immediately after the assassinations...then...they were all in it together."

"Yes," said Thomas. "They were all central to the Nazi plan to invade Norway. Carl was no bit player."

And so they carried on, once again conspirators dissecting a mystery, as they had as children. Somehow, fate had placed them both in the middle of it all. But this was no childhood game.

"We're lucky to be alive," she said. "You know that."

He drew in a deep breath. They looked at each other, their eyes connecting.

"I'm glad I believed in you," he said. "I had to decide when we drove the colonel to Skarholmen — when you offered us *Terne*. It seemed perfectly possible you were part of Carl's operation, and therefore I was leading the colonel into even greater danger."

"And I'm sorry I came to the wrong conclusion about you," she said, taking his hand. "Everything told me you were a British spy; if not, a German spy."

"It's all dynamite," he said, "everything we've discovered." Thomas held her hands tight. "It's a story that must die with us both. No one must know or our lives may always be in danger."

"I agree," she said. "But one part of the story is not yet complete."

Thomas knew what she was about to say.

"Brann is still out there."

"Yes, an assassin," he said, "and quite probably still looking for me."

FORTY-FIVE

The Oslo bus pulled into the stop at Uppegårdstjerne at the top of the long hill into Drøbak and two figures alighted into the cold, utterly still and moonless night. From a disused barn across the road, Brann watched them through a small, dust-covered window as they walked towards him.

"Damn you, Holmbekk," he whispered. The scrawny banker should have been alone. But Brann was in luck and he watched with relief as the second passenger waved to Matthias and headed across a snow-covered field towards a lone house, its lights just visible beyond a drift of birch trees. Brann now moved fast. He pulled the blackout across the window and felt his way in the darkness across the barn towards a rear door, the hinges of which he had oiled in preparation and which now opened noiselessly. He crept outside to the corner of the barn and scanned the area. Silhouetted against the light at the bus stop, Matthias was now alone, swinging his case and tapping his cane as he ambled down the road, weaving his way to avoid the last patches of icy snow. The other passenger had now disappeared into the darkness. Overhead, the first stars had emerged. Venus lay low in the western sky: it was the only planet Brann knew, and it gave him the perfect light.

Rhythmically stretching the rope between his hands, Brann shifted his weight from side to side as he waited. Matthias approached; he could hear him — the padding of his footsteps on the gravelly road, the creak of the handle on his case, a clearing of the throat and then a faint humming, perhaps a song of satisfaction after a week filling in his ledgers. Far away, an owl hooted, its plaintive call carrying across the snow-covered fields. Brann held his breath, tense and tingling in anticipation.

Seconds later, in his long dark coat, Matthias came into view just yards away, limping and swaying around his hips, his cane swinging with a flourish of little apparent utility. Brann waited a moment more, then lumbered onto the road. He ran to catch up just as the clerk stopped and started to turn towards him. Brann hissed in triumph as he looped the rope over Matthias's head, pulling it back into his chest. His victim squealed in surprise, dropping his case and throwing his cane into the air, his legs flailing as Brann dragged him off the road towards the shadow of the barn.

"Not a sound, you bastard," he whispered in Matthias's ear.

Crashing through the half-open doorway at the back of the barn, he pulled Matthias inside, writhing and kicking, and slammed the door shut with a flick of his hip and a thumping backward kick of his boot.

"Cut that stupid bloody noise," he breathed into Matthias's ear, fumbling for the light switch.

A single bulb flickered into life and cast a faint light onto a dusty workbench covered with rusty implements and tools, little used for years. A couple of outdated tractors, a cultivator, a stack of tyres and a large pile of hay were variously scattered about the barn. Slapping him hard to keep him quiet, Brann tied Matthias's arms behind a thick wooden column and shoved him down onto the earthen floor, a broad grin stretching across his face as a rat scuttled under the hay behind his hapless victim, who was clearly unsure whether his captor or the rat was the most frightening.

Brann adjusted his stance and swung a vicious kick at Matthias's legs, then hurried outside, picked up the case and cane, and returned. He could now relax and paced the floor in front of the bank clerk, humming tunelessly. He had already positioned a rusty metal pail on the barn floor and shifted it in full view of Matthias, who groaned in pain, his right eye half closed from the vicious slap.

Brann waited a full minute, then picked up the pail with a sweep of his arm. "Wake the hell up and stop fuckin' moaning or you'll get a face full of this," he growled. "In fact, you'll get it anyway." With that Brann heaved the pail of icy water into Matthias's face. Yelping and kicking, as a doomed rabbit flails around in a trap, it woke up the pathetic clerk as Brann had intended, and even prompted him to start talking: "There must be a mistake...?" he said, wheezing and already shivering.

"We can make this easy," said Brann, leaning towards him, "or we can make it hard. Here are the rules. Tell me what I need to know and you walk out of here intact."

He grabbed hold of Matthias's chin and shook it.

"Or you play stupid...and your head will change shape."

He watched the fear on Matthias's anguished, dripping face and gazed at his scuffling feet with fascination. He then poked at the banker's wet and bedraggled moustache which seemed to be fashioned, however unlikely it would seem, on the Führer himself.

"What do you want to know?" said Matthias.

"Gold."

"What gold?"

Brann swiped his hand across Matthias's face, instantly drawing blood from his nose and cracking his lip.

"You know what gold."

"At the bank?"

"Yes...but where did it go?"

"Lillehammer."

Brann hit him again, with a fist this time, knocking Matthias's head sideways.

"Some of it didn't make it, did it? It ended up here, with you."

He watched Matthias — the man's eyes blinking faster than he thought possible — brace himself for another hit, waiting for fear to do its work.

"I don't know what you..."

"A lorry-load of the stuff."

"What do you mean?"

"Don't remember?" Brann stood up and started to walk away, but turned to take a massive, swinging kick at Matthias's body, hitting him in the side of his ribs with a terrible crack.

Squirming in pain, Matthias began to speak in a frenzy, the words tumbling out. "I had nothing to do with any gold. You've broken my ribs, I can feel it. The gold...the gold all got away, to the north; the Governor went in the cab with the last load."

Brann picked up the fine, black cane and took hold of it with both hands. Nonchalantly, standing in front of Matthias, he then broke it in two across his thigh with a sharp crack. "Sorry about that." He leaned forward again, placing his ear next to Matthias's mouth.

"Think very carefully what you say next," he said.

"I had nothing to do with the last load of gold. It was Thomas Galtung, he took it."

"Come on, Mr Holmbekk," said Brann, "what's a so-called glacier student, a ferryboat man, a British spy, whatever he is; yes, a fuckin' British spy — but never mind that — doing driving gold away from Norges Bank? Galtung has nothing to do with Oslo, yet alone the central bank and the gold vaults."

"It was him, I tell you. Galtung."

"Mr Galtung will have his just outcome, but he ain't no bank clerk; he's not the clerk to the gold reserves, is he? But who is, Mr Holmbekk? You are." He leaned closer and whispered, "Come on. Where is it? The last load of gold? The gold you took and brought back here."

It came naturally to Brann, the rhythm of torture. He let his anger subside and wandered back to the workbench. Tidying a few rusty chisels, he selected one for sharpening on a whetstone, making sure Matthias could see and hear every sweep of his hand and absorb the harsh scraping of metal against stone. He then put the chisel down, very slowly and picked up a bowsaw, returning to Matthias. Standing in front of him, the implement swinging on his crooked finger, he let time pass.

"Well?" he mouthed, eventually, his head on one side.

Matthias shook his head. "All the gold got away to Lillehammer." His voice was quivering, barely audible. "Except the last lorryload. And it was Galtung who took it when the driver and guards ran away. I tried to stop him, but couldn't. That's the truth."

Brann laughed, a guttural grunt of a laugh. He knew that if anyone said, 'that's the truth,' then for sure it was not. This was the way in Brann's world. Calmly, he dropped the saw and it fell to the floor with a harsh clatter. Matthias's face twitched and he fidgeted violently as if one of the rats had got inside his trousers. Brann, stepping forward, knelt down and leaned again into his captive's face, their eyes connecting for a moment.

"I — don't — believe — you," he whispered. He waited for a reaction, anything. The clerk must know. Then, slowly, he placed his hands around Matthias's head, drawing it forward towards him.

Still there was silence; just the weedy banker's breathing and the patter of another rat at the back of the barn. Matthias looked up in terror, pressing himself back. Brann stared into his victim's flickering eyes, fascinated that such fast blinking was possible.

"Please," whispered Matthias. "My family."

Brann smiled and then, without warning, he shoved Matthias's head back with both hands, smashing it against the column. "Come on," said Brann, lifting Matthias's head to look into his eyes. "This will all stop when you tell me what I need to know."

Matthias breathed out with a short, faltering sigh. His eyes rolled and his head slumped forward.

"I said, tell me," said Brann, louder this time, pulling up Matthias's head by his chin.

He looked again at his captive's eyes. They were now closed. A gurgling sound escaped from the throat. Brann stared at him, fear rising. He grabbed Matthias by the shoulders, shaking the limp body.

"Tell me," he screamed. "Tell me."

But Matthias lay slumped, quite still. Brann kicked him again and slapped his face. And at that moment he understood. He had gone too far, further than he had ever intended. "You stupid bastard," he screamed, grabbing Matthias by his coat and shaking him. "You were not meant to bleedin' die on me."

He kicked the corpse again, then paced the barn in frustration. For once in his life he'd had in his power the prospect of a fortune. But now that chance was gone.

He roared again, seething in anger at the stupidity of the gawky, pathetic bank clerk.

———

A cold drizzle fell at an isolated, red farmhouse north of Oslo, the clouds pressing down to cover the tops of the trees. Waiting under an open porch by the door was a middle-aged woman, tall and slim, and at first seeming rather severe in her appearance. But she smiled as Klara approached.

"I remember: you showed me into Herr Welhaven's office," said Klara. "You were his secretary..."

"Yes, Reidun is my name, and I invited you here for a specific reason," she said. "I hope you can help."

Reidun led Klara to the back of a large barn where a lean-to was used for the storage of old farm equipment, logs and some children's playthings. In the centre of the area, on the earthen floor, was a blackened steel fire basket. "All the Surveillance Centre records since 1937 went into here," said Reidun. "I burned them myself, so I know for sure that everything at Victoria Terrasse was destroyed: details of all our agents, internal notes, reports to government, everything." She smiled. "We had to forget our own families on that terrible day, but I am proud of what we achieved."

"Everything went," she repeated, "except one hand-written note."

She led Klara to a stone-built pigsty nearby. With some difficulty she eased out one of the stones, revealing a small metal box which she removed. She prized off the top and took out a single sheet of paper.

"This was amongst a pile of papers left in a drawer by your controller," said Reidun.

"Johansen?"

"Yes. In his desk at Victoria Terrasse."

"He never said where he worked from. But he wouldn't, I suppose."

"The note concerns a suspected British agent, Thomas Galtung. It states you as his source," she added. "It was never followed up as far as we can see and never reported up the line."

"I said to Johansen that Galtung had British connections and there were some timings that could be looked at," said Klara. "But I never found anything to suggest he was actually a British spy. Or German for that matter. I simply gave Johansen a few facts."

"When was this? His note says the 4th of April."

"That's correct, a few days before the invasion."

"Did Johansen come back to Victoria Terrasse again?" said Klara. "After the 4th, I mean?"

"No, and it's a bit of a worry. He didn't turn up on the 9th and he's not back with his family. Neither has he returned to normal police duties. We wonder if he fled to Sweden on the day of the invasion, but there's been no contact. The residual worry — and this is what the chief asked me to speak with you about — is his suspicion Johansen was a German double-agent. We suspected a few found their way into the police service, but we were never able to identify them. We had no hard evidence to suspect Johansen, but his behaviour was strange, in small ways, in the weeks before the invasion. Nothing you could put your finger on. We simply don't know, and might never know, though the Chief was concerned, I could tell. You worked with Johansen: did you have any suspicions?"

"No, but he was my controller, not my target."

"And we have no reason for any concern regarding Galtung?"

"None at all. So we get rid of it? Johansen's note...?"

"Yes," said Reidun. She looked at Klara, who nodded, and she then placed the note at the bottom of the fire basket. Taking a box of matches from her coat pocket, she set light to it and they watched it flare and quickly turn to ash.

"You will be safe now, Klara. There's no record of you anywhere in the Surveillance Centre records. And none either of Galtung, though he's not our concern, of course. He's probably back in Britain by now, like others who fled."

"Most likely," said Klara, with a dismissive flick of her hand.

As she returned through the forest to the bus stop far away in the valley below, Klara shook at the event which had just taken place. The last of the Surveillance Centre records had been destroyed and her guilt in revealing Thomas as a possible enemy agent could be put behind her. He was now safe, and so was she...

...unless...

...unless Johansen really had been working for Germany inside the Surveillance Centre. He would not need that slip of paper to remember that she had been hunting Nazi infiltrators or that Thomas was a suspected British agent.

Only then, with a shiver, did Klara understand that she could never feel safe, and nor could Thomas. Not until the Nazis were finally driven out of Norway.

Or until she could be sure that Johansen was no longer alive.

FORTY-SIX

The disappearance of Matthias Holmbekk — cousin of the richest man in the area, an important employee of Norges Bank and, some locals said, the man credited with saving Norway's gold reserves — was the subject of intense gossip in Drøbak and the surrounding countryside. He had come home as usual on the bus on the evening of the 3rd of May and had walked a short distance with Jon Gabrielsen, the last person to see him. Gabrielsen had looked across the field a minute or two later as he'd lifted the latch on his garden gate and had seen a dimly lit figure — it must have been Matthias — swinging his case, as he always did, walking on alone towards Monsrud in the last of the silvery light. The weather was cold, but nothing like the intense freeze of winter, and the banker had been warmly dressed in his long black coat.

A search of every possible route and turning from the bus-stop to Monsrud had revealed nothing. There had been no communication between Matthias and the bank or its employees after he had left as usual on that Friday. He had simply vanished. In great distress, Lisbeth Holmbekk had reported her husband's disappearance to the Drøbak Police late that evening. However, the police service, although operational again after the closure of the station on the day of the invasion, had been severely constrained in their powers by the occupation force under Oberst Baumann. To ensure a good working relationship was established, a series of liaison meetings were set up between the Drøbak police and the German administration, who would be represented, in due course, by a new Gestapo unit to be established in the town. Many of those initially expected to set up the new base had perished in the sinking of *Blücher*.

At the first liaison meeting, brought forward because of the disappearance of the Norges Bank employee, it was made clear by Baumann, in the most direct terms, that the deaths occurring between the 7th and the 8th of April would be investigated by the Gestapo alone. Gentle probing by Sandvik, the head of the local police, suggested the Holmbekk case was unlikely to be connected to the earlier murders, a term not employed by Baumann, of course, and now banned, but it was nevertheless made clear that the case would be led by the occupying forces. A new Gestapo leader had just been appointed and a meeting had been arranged to deal with the case.

———

Squeezed into the interview room at Drøbak Police station on the afternoon of the 5th of May — two days after the disappearance of Matthias Holmbekk — were Chief Constable Sandvik; Superintendent Carl Henrik Gerhard Klouman, his deputy; Constable Arnt Jørgensen, who had conducted the initial investigation of the Holmbekk disappearance; Kriminalkommissar Frank Huber of the Gestapo (Department D, Norway, who had arrived in Drøbak that morning) and Alexander Brann, liaison officer and adviser to the German administration. Christian and Lisbeth Holmbekk, cousin and wife of Matthias, had been interviewed by Jørgensen and had been asked to wait outside.

Brann alone was not sat at the table: he occupied a corner seat, an observer. From there he waited to see who would speak first, but his attention was focussed on Huber, the newly-established Gestapo officer. It would be him, as well as Baumann, whom he would need to work with and impress; Huber would be calling the shots on the Holmbekk case.

"Good day to you all," said Huber. "I have spoken to Constable Jørgensen on the matter of Herr Holmbekk's disappearance, and to the family. They are still extremely upset, which of course we can all understand. There is no sign of a struggle anywhere after Herr Holmbekk left the company of, let me see...Jon Gabrielsen, a neighbour, and we found no blood or items belonging to Herr Holmbekk on any possible route he could have taken to his home. Fru Holmbekk confirmed he had no known enemies who would have wished him harm. This leaves another possibility to explain his disappearance; that is, one connected to his role as a clerk at your central bank, which I became aware of through my interview with his wife."

Brann studied Huber as the Kriminalkommissar took a sip of water from the glass placed in front of him. He wanted to know the man, see how he operated. Already, Holmbekk's role at Norges Bank was known to the new administration, including his connection to the gold reserves, which was interesting. Both Baumann and Huber would be all over that story, but events took an unexpected tack...

"To continue," said Huber, "Herr Holmbekk was a clerk responsible for keeping records for the gold reserves at the bank. This was further confirmed in advice I received this morning from Norges Bank. Most of Norway's bank staff appear, most unfortunately, to be on the run with the gold reserves somewhere in the north of Norway, on a fishing boat quite likely, creeping up the fjords; so Herr Holmbekk's job has effectively ceased. There is no gold and therefore no records to maintain. I have concluded that the disappearance of Herr Holmbekk is connected to the loss of his job at the bank."

"I am not sure we are in a position to assert this," said the Chief Constable.

"Thank you for this observation, Chief Constable, but the matter is concluded," said Huber, firmly.

"This can't be right," said the Chief Constable, his voice rising. "This is a Norwegian citizen, and the investigation has hardly begun."

Brann was unable to suppress a thin but prolonged smile. But the German was not finished yet.

"Put bluntly," said Huber, "the new administration does not want stories of invented and untrue murders to spread amongst the local community. And we certainly do not wish your German brothers to be associated with, or even blamed for, fake wrongdoings when all we desire is the truth and the best for the Norwegian people."

Brann again failed to suppress another lift at the corners of his mouth. However, his smile went undetected, such was the intensity of Huber's presentation, which he now drew to a close:

"Mr Holmbekk left the bank at the end of the week as usual, but because his job no longer exists — a disaster for the poor man — he decided not to return home. I have concluded, taking in all available evidence, that Mr Holmbekk therefore absconded, we believe to Sweden. I would add that there is no reason to suspect Mr Gabrielsen, with whom he simply shared a bus ride, of any involvement in Mr Holmbekk's flight. That is the end of the matter. The investigation is concluded."

The Chief Constable drew breath and opened his mouth to speak.

"Concluded, Chief Constable" repeated Huber, drawing his papers together. "There are more important matters for you to investigate. The period following the establishment of the new administration has so far, and will remain, one of stability and calm. Mr Holmbekk ran away because of the reckless removal of the Norwegian state gold by your cowardly King and government."

"And that," his black leather glove hovering over the doorhandle as he made his way out, "is your conclusion to this investigation. Which you will, of course, ensure is accurately reported in the local newspaper. Won't he, Herr Brann?" he said, in sustained eye contact with the Chief Constable.

———

Christian and Klara continued to fret about the collapse in business activity. After a sleepless night, weighed down also by Matthias's disappearance and angered by the plainly fake investigation by the Gestapo, they decided to conduct a tour of each of the estate's businesses. They began with Egil Alvestad in the harbourmaster's office on Lehmanns Quay.

"Nothing, sir. Not a ship in a month," said Egil. "The last to leave was *Martina* on, when was it, the evening of the 8th of April, a month ago. She took on nothing of ours — must have been damn near empty. She was here for a few days with engine trouble and didn't even use our people to help sort it out. That was it. We'd normally be flat out now, preparing boats for the spring. We could even be setting up that marina of yours at Skarholmen, Miss Klara..."

"Who would be leisure-boating now?" said Klara.

"All we see is German merchant ships," said Egil. "Into Oslo and straight out again."

"They'll be after our commodities before long," said Klara, breaking the despondent atmosphere. "This summer's potatoes, grain, timber, minerals, the lot: you wait."

"You could be right, my love," said Christian. "But we have to survive until then. Cashflow's in a perilous state and I worry whether we'll survive to the summer. The banks are barely functioning — I've tried them all — so they can't help."

"There are thousands of troops here in Norway," she said. "They have to be fed. Germany's at war; they need materials of every sort, not just iron ore. We can't wait for them to come to us. We have to go to them, sell our produce..."

"So we trade with the devil?" said Egil, "I'm sorry, miss — Herr Holmbekk, sir, forgive me — but where's the morality in that?"

"There isn't any," said Klara. She shrugged. "But what else can we do?" She looked at her father. "They will force us anyway, to produce food, timber and so on for them, at gunpoint if we object. They could just take over the harbour, couldn't they? Better we manage it on our terms and stay in control."

"There are not many comfortable choices," agreed Christian. "Let's hope we don't have to make them."

"I'm sorry, Father, but we will and we can't just wait and hope," said Klara. "It's a new regime now and we have to get used to it. We should trade basic commodities with them, take their money, bring in revenue and keep our people employed. Too many depend on us. When it's all over, we'll still be here, in business."

"Perhaps, but show me the dividing line between that and collaboration. Do we want our family to be seen by people as supporters of the Nazi regime?"

"We won't collaborate. We will fleece the Nazis for every krone we can, cheat every way possible, cook the books whenever we can, supply the resistance when it starts, help all our staff with food...find new sources of income. Do anything, anything to keep our people employed and to prevent them going hungry. Anything to save the Holmbekk estate." She looked across to her father. Christian was slumped, his head resting on his chest, his breath short.

"I don't have the energy," he whispered.

———

Thomas, trapped at Myrstua, felt as insecure as ever, his nerves on edge. He couldn't imagine Brann giving up. Every night the trees creaked in the wind, snow would slump down from the canopy, a wolf would howl; the forest gave him the shivers and he was unable to sleep. During the day, he spent hours lamenting the dangers and hardships of the occupation; there was no paid work available in Norway and his cash funds were perilously low. It was hopeless: waiting and holding out here in Norway, in this rotten cabin in a bog, in the creepiest forest he had ever known. Action was needed. He would make another approach to Christian and ask to spend a few days at the Castle, and then, at last, find a way to Sweden.

———

Christian, of course, agreed and offered Thomas a small, comfortable room in a tower overlooking the gardens. From here, Thomas pondered an unanswered question: whether there was a link between Matthias's disappearance and the gold hidden at Torsrud. Had Matthias simply run off to Sweden as the *Amta* story had reported? Or had he been forced to reveal the gold's location, and then perhaps killed, or even killed without revealing the gold's location? At some point the niggling uncertainty must be resolved.

———

A thin line of smoke drifted up from the Bell House. Brann sat by the stove, brooding on the death of Matthias Holmbekk. The banker had been disposed of, joining Peter Haugen in the fjord, but it gave him no pleasure. To the contrary, it was the biggest mistake of his life. Holmbekk dead was worthless. The worst of it was the uncertainty: maybe Holmbekk really didn't know anything? Maybe there was no gold in the forests around Drøbak? And could it be a coincidence: the lorry and the bank employee all together in this area? Maybe the story about the final consignment of gold was not correct and that idiot Schiller misheard or even invented it all?

Brann could see no way of answering these questions. The dilemma sat there like a terrible skin condition, itching, day after day, never healing. His anger and frustration would be endless. He smashed his fists onto the table for the hundredth time and wailed like a trapped bear.

Fortunately for Brann, there was a knock at the door: his men, Anskar Helgeland and Petter Berg walked in.

"Good news," said Helgeland.

"I need music in my ears, right now," said Brann, gloomily. "Sit," he said, pointing to the table.

"We were having a drink with some mates," said Helgeland. "Foresters on the Holmbekk estate, though there's not much forestry going on."

"That maid; you know, the one who's rather free with her charms," said Berg, smirking. "Gave a little more than usual, she did."

"Yuh, hear this," said Helgeland. "Galtung..."

"Come on," shouted Brann. "Don't piss about."

"We know where he is."

"Yea?"

"He's been on the Holmbekk estate, living in a cabin called Myrstua, pretending to be a forester. But he ain't working. There's no work for anyone; just us."

"So, we've got the pig in hell bastard," said Brann, clenching his fists.

"Except...wait," said Helgeland. "He's moved."

"Where to?"

"The Castle," said Helgeland. "He's holed up at the fuckin' Castle."

It took little time for Brann to alert Huber, and for an operation to be planned that night. There was little that could have given the big man a better chance to demonstrate his value, and nothing that would have given him a greater thrill than to be part of an assault on the Castle: *Galtung and the Holmbekks in a single raid.*

———

The great Gothic citadel appeared larger at night, a forbidding shadow looming above the raiding party, sharp-edged against the sweep of the Milky Way. Silvery birch trees, caught in the nightlight either side of the winding drive, emerged from deep shadows and cliffs that fell away to the rolling farmland below. Brann's mind drifted back to previous failures to capture and kill the English Spy, but it was not all bad. The best moments in life are rarely easily won. He even sensed Westervik had had a go with his expensive rifle, somewhere 'out of area,' but had never talked of it.

Looking low through the trees, Brann picked out a two-day-old crescent moon, so slender you could crack it like a porcelain cup. Like Galtung's skull, he thought. Tonight was the perfect, lethal night for the raid. Galtung would be reeled in and would suffer the best the Gestapo could give him and he, Brann, and his men, would be well rewarded in gold and new, more trusted positions in the administration.

"Tonight, we capture the bastard pig in hell Brit," Brann whispered to his men, his Mauser 96 hunting rifle strapped across his shoulder. He watched as dark shapes — a detachment of Baumann's men — moved out until they disappeared behind walls, trees and a small tower-like building off to the right of his view. They would be guarding every possible escape route.

Brann looked up to the Castle. Though never built as a true bastion, it would be no easy place to take if Galtung barricaded himself in although, as he imagined the scenario, he thrilled at the prospect. He pictured the English Spy cowering behind windows modelled for medieval defence, up on the roof hidden behind battlements; they would serve well even in the modern era...and prolong the fight.

Immediately behind him were Helgeland and Berg and, on a parallel course following the outer wall of the drive, was Huber with his team of Gestapo. A small unit of local police brought up the rear, reluctantly fulfilling their obligation to arrest the foreign spy.

Slipping the rifle off his shoulder, Brann ran his left hand along the barrel. His heart pounded in the stillness of the night. Never before had he experienced a raid of such intensity. And, hell, on the bloody Holmbekks.

"Go," commanded Huber.

Following the Gestapo chief, Brann crossed an open area and crouched by the side of a wall opposite the main entrance. He watched the Gestapo men creep up two curving flights of steps leading to the huge main doors, lit by an oversized lantern hanging off the stone wall. One of the men pulled on a metal ring and a bell sounded faintly from the depths of the building; hitting the door with his pistol, he shouted to be let in. Brann held his breath, then crept forward, anxious to join the action.

After a second strike on the door, a light appeared and a small window above opened.

"Christian fuckin' Holmbekk," muttered Brann, every muscle tense with anticipation.

"Police. Open up," shouted Huber.

A short while later, two bolts slid open and a key turned. Still Brann shivered with suspense and anticipation. Now, they would get the devil.

Seconds later, the door slowly opened. The Gestapo rushed in and, within minutes, were holding the family and staff captive in the Great Hall. They then fanned out across the house in search of their prime suspect, Brann joining the vanguard as they made their way upwards, floor by floor, searching, wrecking, shouting.

"I know the bastard, what he looks like," he said to Huber, as they burst into one of the bedrooms. "I'd recognise him dressed as Father Fuckin' Christmas." He laughed at his own wit.

Before long they reached the top floor, discovering a hidden doorway in a panelled wall, and then wound their way up a narrow spiral stone staircase into a high tower.

"He's here, I know it," shouted Brann, panting. "It's exactly where they'd hide him."

Moments later, Huber and two plain-clothed Gestapo officers stood outside a solid oak door leading to the tower room. Brann, one step down, twitched and waited. For sure, this is where the bastard Holmbekks would secrete that devil Galtung. They, too, the Holmbekks, must be implicated.

Huber, having forced a spare key from one of the maids, quietly unlocked the door. He eased down the handle, put his shoulder to the oak and barged in.

FORTY-SEVEN

B ut Huber would be disappointed.
Earlier that evening, Thomas had trudged uphill towards Torsrud and now stood at the edge of the forest next to Severin's muckheap. He was well aware that a large muckheap would rarely freeze in winter, as it generates heat as the organic material breaks down. So, when the gold was hidden on the night of the 9th of April, the digging was soft beneath a thin crust of frozen manure. It was the only place not frozen solid, the only place where they could dig...and bury the gold.

Shielding his torch, he found Matthias's marker-stick, untouched, and there were no signs of new excavations. But he needed to be sure.

The digging was still easy and, a few minutes later, the spade hit something hard: the metal band on one of the kegs. He dug around, revealing the half-load. It was an easy matter to remove the lid and, shielding his torch, he peered inside. All the bags were there, every one of them untouched, their lead tags intact. More excavation revealed the other six kegs: all sealed and unsullied. He stared at them, *a fortune in gold, buried beneath a muckheap.*

He could now be certain: Matthias had not been here since that night on the 9th of April. Equally, he could not believe in the story that

Matthias had fled to Sweden: it made no sense; neither did Christian believe it, nor anyone else it seemed, not even Maria, the maid. In any event, Thomas thought, if Matthias had fled as they said, he surely would have taken as much of the gold as possible; he would also have withdrawn some money from his bank account that day. But he had taken no assets, no cash, clothes or anything else he would have needed. There was only one possibility: *Matthias was dead.* And, whether or not he was killed because of the gold, he almost certainly never revealed its location to anyone.

Thomas stood back and looked at the excavation, then at his watch. Nearly midnight. There was still time.

To steal a single coin is to cross the line from an honest man to a thief. To take a thousand coins...the same line is crossed. There is no moral difference. Where that placed Matthias was ambiguous: he had tried to reach Lillehammer; Thomas had seen that with his own eyes. But he had been stopped by roadblocks. He had then hidden the gold and had taken none for himself, neither at the time, nor subsequently it would seem, although he had shown clear intent and had offered to steal a bag of gold to give to Thomas, and had done so in the end. Where it left Thomas, who never accepted or asked for the bag of a thousand gold coins, and had spent none, was also ambiguous: he had had no intent to steal anything, yet he was the one person who now held one thousand gold sovereigns, a fortune, and he had not dismissed the thought of spending some of it if it could save his life if ever he escaped to Sweden. Did that mean neither he nor Matthias were thieves? Or were they both? And then, he thought, whose gold is it now? The bank must now know the last load was lost, probably used to finance the Nazi's war. If the gold was no longer Norwegian gold...it was orphan gold. And to take it was therefore a victimless crime. It would never be missed.

In front of him, if Matthias was right, in these seven kegs was enough gold to buy the whole of the Holmbekk estate: its lands, the Castle, the many properties, sweeps of forest, the ice lakes and the whole shipping business and port. Just his own bag of coins was enough to live off for years, to escape to Sweden, to support himself whilst he studied or developed a career. One day he could come back to Norway, to see Klara and Severin, even Ingrid. All of these things, and more.

Kicking at the snow, he made a quick decision. In all probability, he alone in the world knew what was hidden here. But now was not the time for intemperate action. Tensing his muscles, he took hold of his spade and thrust it forward. He threw a spadeful of material over the exposed kegs. Then another. And more, until the excavation was filled and the muckheap restored. He then dragged from the forest a few spadefuls of snow and scattered it over the disturbed area. Finally, he covered his boot-prints with a further dusting of fresh snow and replaced the marker stick, just in case.

Walking up the hill towards Torsrud, there was one final act he must see through. The pinprick of light he had seen earlier at Torsrud no longer showed: Severin had retired to bed. A short while later he knocked on the door and soon heard the clatter of a heavy bolt being pulled and a call to demand who would visit at this time of night.

"Well, I'll be damned," said Severin, dragging open the door.

Thomas was overjoyed at seeing Severin again until he saw the wounds on his face and the ugly gap in his teeth.

"Brann," said Severin, shaking his head. "I was too slow."

"I'm sorry," said Thomas, grasping Severin's hand.

"Don't worry," said Severin, smiling, rather painfully. "He got nothing from me."

As Severin calmly told his story, Thomas felt unable to contain his anger. "The swine," he kept repeating.

"Here, some coffee," said Severin when it was over, the whole story.

"Like nectar," said Thomas with a wry smile.

"You can come back if you want to, you know that."

"I will," said Thomas. "I'll be back, of course, when it's safe. But now I must tell you something."

"Aha."

"The place you noticed the disturbance in the snow...down on the muckheap. I said it was probably an elk."

"Yuh..."

"I was not being quite honest, and I think you knew." Thomas drew himself up, took a deep breath and said: "I'm now going to tell you the true story. We are the only people in the world who will know."

———

Having spent time with Severin, Thomas hurried through a landscape of shadows and silvery light to be back before dawn. Approaching the Castle, the perfection of the night took his breath away: its ghostly, limpid beauty, the complete stillness and purity of the air, the immensity of the universe singing from a million stars. Feeling the bite of the air on his skin, he approached a rear door through an area of shrubbery at the back of the Castle, surprised to see so many lights and windows lit up. He slipped inside and made his way, as quickly as possible, towards one of the back stairways leading to his room in the East Tower. As he passed the door at the back of the Great Hall, he looked through a small window, recessed into the stone wall, to see the Holmbekk girls and several staff standing under the light of the high chandeliers. The girls were in tears, being comforted by Toni and their mother.

He rushed up the stairs and was shocked to find his room pulled apart. Furniture had been toppled and drawers pulled out. His case lay open, its contents spread over the floor. He rushed over to the wooden panel Christian had shown him, a secure place to leave his documents and money, and sunk back in relief. They, his revolver and the bag of gold sovereigns were still there. In shock, he ran down the stairs and walked into the Great Hall. Everyone immediately stopped talking and looked at him.

He sat in horror as the story unfolded. There had been a raid, the objective being the arrest of a British spy, Thomas Galtung. They had left barely half an hour ago. A huge Norwegian man had been here with the German police, kicking over furniture, angry, swearing. The local police had been here, too, waiting in the hall. They had apologised as they left for the damage occurred, but shrugged: there was nothing they could do.

Worse was to come.

"Mother and Father have been arrested," said Klara. "It's because of you, Thomas. They were after you. Father tried to protect you, to stop them going up to the tower. He pushed them back, shouting, hoping you would hear. Then they hit him."

"I'm sorry, Klara," said Thomas, weakly. "I wasn't there."

"We know that, so where were you? Father said you were never here, but they didn't believe him. It was obvious the room was occupied. Father said it was a business contact who stayed sometimes. They looked out of the window, thinking you'd escaped, though goodness knows how; it's such a long way down."

She stopped as the door opened and Agnes walked in. Klara rushed over and embraced her.

"Oh, thank you for coming Aunt Agnes. Thank God."

"I telephoned Paul, the Chief Constable," said Agnes. "He said your parents are in the gaol at Råkeløkka. They are fine, he said, except your father has a few bruises."

"When will they be released?" asked Klara.

"He wouldn't say. It's up to the Gestapo, but he didn't sound optimistic."

"Let me make us a drink," said Agnes. "After that I need to talk to you. You, Klara, and Thomas."

The first rays of the rising sun crept through the windows in the Great Hall. Thomas watched as Agnes and Klara, arms around each other, sat in front of the fire and was invited to sit with them.

"I'm cold," said Klara, shivering.

"It's the shock, my sweet," said Agnes.

"Arrested," said Klara, and she started to cry again. "I can't believe it. And you, Thomas, in the middle of it again. But this time, well...I suppose we should have expected it." Her words trailed away.

Thomas could offer no explanation. He had brought danger to the family and was the cause of this terrible event. He wished he had been braver, more decisive, had tried for Sweden when it was possible weeks ago.

"I want to talk to you both," said Agnes, "while I can."

Thomas's thoughts were stopped by the tone of her voice. He leaned forward and took a sip of the tea Agnes had prepared, staring down at the floor, unable to look Klara in the eyes.

"These are dangerous times," said Agnes, "for Norway and especially for the Holmbekk family. The Gestapo will come back for you, Thomas, and would arrest us too if they find you here. So, we must agree where you should go."

"Of course," said Thomas. "I can't stay here."

"We must do this together, as a family, said Agnes."

Klara looked at her. "I..." she began, but was stopped by a lift of Agnes's hand.

"Your parents, Klara, are gaoled," she said. "We must hope for the best, that they will come back."

Klara nodded, weakly, and brushed away the wetness below her eyes.

"Because of the situation,' Agnes continued, "I have something I must tell you. Both of you."

Thomas looked at her.

"Yes, you too, Thomas."

"At a time like this? Surely it can wait." said Thomas.

"No. Listen," said Agnes. "Your father would not approve, Klara, because he wants to protect your mother, although I suspect she has an inkling that something once happened. But I am the only one, apart from your father, who really knows. If, God forbid, he were not to return, and they decided to arrest me too and take me away, the truth would never be known."

"What truth? said Klara.

"The truth you both need to know," said Agnes.

A ray of the first sunlight caught the glass in a chandelier above Agnes, and it sparkled pink. A huge log on the fire spat a glowing ember onto the stone hearth. From the corner of his eye, Thomas watched Klara, sat like a statue, tense, her lips pressed tight. He saw Agnes take a deep breath; then she started to speak.

"There was a maid who worked here in the years between 1914 and 1917. She was young, and pretty. She turned your father's head, Klara. Your parents were not at that time married, of course, but they were courting and were betrothed soon after."

Thomas held his breath, a shiver running up through his gut.

"In 1916, she fell pregnant," Agnes continued, her voice dropping to a whisper. "And in 1917..."

Klara's hand rose to cover her mouth, her eyes wide open.

"It was impossible for her to stay here or keep the baby. It would have been a terrible scandal. So, your grandparents, Klara, arranged for the girl to move away and for the baby to be given to a childless couple up in the forest. Good people. The girl was given some money — a generous sum. She was only seventeen."

At that moment, Thomas felt as if his heart had stopped. His skin tingled all over his body. He gripped the arm of the chair, suspecting something of what was to come.

"Her name?" he breathed. "What was her name?"

Agnes was silent for a moment, as if remembering, and said, very slowly: "Marta." She stopped again. "Marta...Lovisa...."

"Nordby..." Thomas whispered. "...And the people who took the baby?"

"Gudmund and Josefine..." she said, slowly and firmly, "Galtung."

Thomas moaned, his head falling into his hands, his eyes closing.

Agnes rose and held him.

Klara gasped, "No."

"It means," Agnes said, holding Thomas's hand, "Christian is your true father. You are a Holmbekk, his eldest and only son."

Thomas's eyes opened and met Klara's intense, anguished stare.

"And Thomas...Marta is your true birth mother," said Agnes.

"Marta..." whispered Thomas. "Marta..."

"...and you are half-brother," added Agnes, "...to Klara."

Thomas looked at the two women, his mouth gaping as if to speak, but no words emerged.

———

The golden orb of the sun hovered low in a cloudless sky as Thomas, arm in arm with Klara, looked to the road ahead, long shadows and rays of morning sunlight dividing up the landscape. The longest winter for a hundred years was almost done and the sounds of new life could be heard amidst the dying breaths of winter. But it all passed him by. There had been too much to absorb, the night too long.

"I have no idea how to react, how to feel," he said. "You and me: we are closer than we ever imagined...but the circumstances...they are too complicated to take in. Where does it leave the people I have always taken as my parents? My relationship to Christian: should I reject him for his behaviour or celebrate being part of the Holmbekk family?

Maybe just a half part, I don't know. And me, as a person? Born to a woman out of wedlock who was forced to reject me and not allowed to bring me up."

"It will take a long time to resolve," said Klara, "but you have friends around you. For now, though, you have Brann trying to kill you and the police wanting to arrest you. Come on, full attention!" She slapped him lightly across the back of the head.

"It's a mystery, isn't it?" said Thomas after a short while. "Brann must still believe I'm a British spy. Maybe he has orders to fulfil? Westervik controls him from abroad or in hiding? Or is something else going on..." He took a sharp intake of air and a shiver ran up inside him.

Klara squeezed his hand and said after a while: "I'd never noticed it before, but you have Father's hands; just the same." He smiled and they walked on in silence, his long legs shuffling every now and then to match her assertive, bobbing gait.

"Myra," she said, stopping and walking over to a field adjoining the road. They sat on a fallen tree trunk together. "It's one of the oldest fields, reclaimed from the marshland by great great grandfather Nils. All the rocks in these walls — he pulled them out to make the field. Like it or not, it's part of your heritage now."

"Do you realise," said Thomas, "I'm directly related to Severin? He's my uncle. And his lost little sister turns out to be my mother. I've come to know her in my searches for Severin... know what she looks like, where and when she was born, went to church... all sorts. It's wonderful and mad. Both." It was impossible for his new discoveries not to fill his mind, and equally it was futile to try to understand what it all meant for his life. He walked in a dream until Klara brought him back again to reality.

"A plan," she said. "First, we must keep you alive."

"I must disappear," he said. "Sweden. If I stay whilst Brann is here, you and the girls will be in danger. Agnes, your parents, too, the whole estate. Worse, we now know Brann's tied in with the Gestapo. There's probably a bounty on my head."

Klara nodded. "I hate to see you go, but I know you're right. We'll do this together and no telling me otherwise. The safest route will be down the fjord; I have a plan forming. You can take *Terne*. I rescued her from Vippetangen — just walked in and sailed off and no one stopped me — and Egil has already patched her up. She's moored in the harbour at Skarholmen. And don't apologise for what happened. Not your fault. War wounds..." she said with a shrug. "It'll give *Terne* another layer of history.'

"I'll see you tomorrow evening, at Skarholmen," she continued with her plan. "I need more time to have documents prepared for you. You will find some charts on the table covering the fjord all the way to the Swedish border. Find a long inlet running up towards Svinesund. Part way up, on the Swedish side you will see marked a small bay. It's called Stenviken and we own it. It was part of a forestry operation once, but the quay's now derelict. Work out how to get there in *Terne*. I think you should use the hours of darkness as much as possible; the Germans have taken Horten and will have a good view of the fjord, so pass by in darkness if you can. And be very careful — there are countless hidden rocks."

She kissed him on his cheek and they set off, running back to the Castle.

After several days looking at the broken fragments of Galtung Senior's coffee cup scattered over the floor, Brann swept them up and dumped them in the bin. The cup had paid the price for his foul mood. A niggling doubt had kept him awake at night. He couldn't care less anymore if Galtung was a spy. British, Norwegian, Russian: it didn't matter. And nor was the failure of the raid on the Castle. Rather, it was the thought that Holmbekk, the weedy, pathetic clerk, might have been talking straight when he named Galtung as the gold thief. What if Galtung **was** involved? What if he had been the driver of the Mercedes that Schiller had been so excited about? The Governor's Mercedes, no less.

Brann thumped the table. The student, the spy, whatever he was, couldn't have stolen the gold alone, but he could have been the clerk's accomplice. After all, they knew each other. Pounding the floorboards, a story emerged in Brann's mind: Holmbekk, who couldn't even lift a bloody spade, needing help for his heist, goes to his mate Galtung, an old friend of the family. The dirt-poor kid, turned by the prospect of wealth beyond his wildest fuckin' dreams, takes the bus to Oslo and joins the weedy clerk. They steal the last load of gold, take the lorry, and maybe they nick the Governor's bloody Merc whilst they're about it.

There was a cast-iron way for Brann to find out if his hunch was true. The following day, he presented to the excitable Hans Schiller a bottle of Norway's best aquavit: "no other drink is matured like this," he said, "sloshed around in a barrel in a ship across the equator." It helped cement the unlikely partnership built on gossip and intrigue, and it was not long before Brann guided their conversation to Schiller's favourite subject: the Governor of Norges Bank's prized Mercedes-Benz 540K. From there, it was just one step to a discovery which set Brann's heart hammering: the car had been confiscated at a junction on National Highway 1 on the evening of the 9th of April, approaching not from Oslo, but along the Drøbak road heading for Ås, the same road where the lorry was discovered off a track in the adjoining forest... perfectly fitting his scenario for the theft and burial of the gold. Even better, the records taken by the Wehrmacht soldiers referred to the driver in a description which perfectly matched the gangly bastard, Galtung.

Brann was now sure.

With Holmbekk done for...

...only Galtung knows where the gold is hidden.

FORTY-EIGHT

Agnes and Klara were offered by Kriminalkommissar Huber a few desperate minutes to visit Christian and Sigrid at the town gaol. They then walked the short distance to the police station, where they met Paul Sandvik, the Chief Constable. Klara gripped Agnes's arm trying to suppress a rising mix of anger and panic for her parents.

"There's little I can do," said Sandvik. "The Gestapo show no sign of releasing them. And my own job...well, I doubt I will be here for long."

"They are innocent, Paul," said Agnes. "You know that."

"Perhaps, but I'm powerless."

"I'm not," said Klara, emphatically. "I'll speak with Huber."

"That's not possible," said the police chief, a doleful expression descending over his weary face.

———

Later that day, Klara strode towards the main entrance of the Fjord Hotel, the shared headquarters of the local Wehrmacht and, until a new building was found, the military police, the Gestapo. She was stopped at the door.

"I wish to see Kriminalkommissar Huber."

"Not possible," said the guard, looking down at her, expressionless.

"I have information he will want to hear."

The guard flicked his head towards the road.

"I am Klara Holmbekk."

Huber appeared from the adjoining room. "Let her in," he said.

"Kriminalkommissar Huber," said Klara, "I am grateful to you for seeing me."

"How can I help, Miss Holmbekk?" Huber settled into his chair, his legs on the desk, crossed at the ankles.

"You are holding my parents. They are innocent."

"We have a reliable source."

"Brann," she said, trying to contain her anger. "He's not reliable. He simply has a grudge against my family."

Huber's attention seemed to be captured by a speck of dried mud that had fallen onto the table from his leather boots. He flicked it away with his hand. "And why is that?" he asked, studying the spot on the floor where the mud had settled.

"Envy. Who knows."

"We think he's a valuable resource."

"My parents, please release them."

"Oh, your parents..." he said with an air of despondency and a tone suggesting he was now not quite sure who they were.

Klara stood up and slammed her fist onto the table. "You say Germany came here to save Norway."

"You are taking a dangerous course, Miss Holmbekk," said Huber, with well-practised menace.

"There is no evidence against my parents."

"They were caught harbouring a dangerous criminal, a British spy. So where is he? This Galtung, if he wasn't at the Castle? Hmm? If you tell us it might be to your parents' advantage."

"How would we know? If he's a spy, he would hardly walk around with a sign on his back, would he?"

Huber slowly eased himself from his chair and walked over to the window.

"You are right," he said. "We have no evidence in relation to Galtung. Just the word of one local man. That's all we normally need. And I also know how these situations can be used to settle scores."

"This is Norway," she said, calmly, "as you said, a friend of Germany, and we are an important local family. We run the port. We supply farm produce and timber to Germany. My parents are more useful to you keeping the economy going, providing food, than locked up in some gaol or sent away. You have thousands of troops here; you cannot feed them all from Germany."

"Maybe, maybe." Something else had caught his eye. "See that man out there, loading up his cart? And those women, passing the time of day? Everything is returning to normal. We want it to be normal, don't you think? Let me review the matter."

"Kriminalkommissar Huber, you have the power to make the decision now. I suggest you have no need to review it. We have a little grain left we can sell you; a few potatoes, at good prices; timber, gravel and stone. Spring is coming and we need to get the potatoes planted for next year, the wheat and the barley drilled. We cannot do this with my parents in gaol."

Huber looked back from the window.

"Your castle. I would like to see the flag of the German Reich flying from the flagpole. I plan to take the ground floor as our headquarters. We are already short of space here. We could just take it of course, but it would help to have your cooperation in various matters. It would demonstrate to local people the trust you have in the occupying forces. Your staff will stay on, to serve us. Your farm produce will be available at reasonable prices. Especially reasonable prices, Miss Holmbekk. Do you understand me?"

"That can be arranged."

"Good. You are lucky: you've caught me on a good day," said Huber. He then paced the room, silent.

For effect, thought Klara, her whole body trembling.

"I can arrange for your parents to be released," he said, quietly, his eyes staring hard into her face.

"Thank you."

"And you will cooperate as I suggest." He raised his eyebrows, holding them there until Klara responded...with the slightest of nods and an almost imperceptible twitch in the corners of her mouth.

———

"Find the fuckin' Satan in hell," screamed Brann.

"He moved to the Castle," said Helgeland.

"You thick bastard. He wasn't there when we needed him to be, was he? Find where he is now!"

Brann disappeared down the steps into the cellar and returned seconds later with a huge hunting knife and two coils of rope, which he set on the table with his Mauser 96. He then downed a large glass of aquavit.

"This time," he whispered, "I will take the bastard. I'll give him the death he deserves."

And, he thought, *I'll strip him clean of every gram of gold he stole.*

FORTY-NINE

By the end of May, the whole of southern Norway was deep in a short transition to summer but many places, out of reach of the sun, remained frozen, still shaped by the pitiless grip of the long winter. Thomas arrived at Skarholmen in the middle of the afternoon and, before settling into the cabin, ventured through the woods to a rocky promontory at the northern tip of the island. From here, he gazed over the frozen wilderness of Hallangspollen, hemmed in as it was by steep forested slopes and rocky crags, its surface sculpted into wind-blown dunes of snow and hard ice. A requiem to the death of winter filled the air: water trickling down gullies and splashing over rocks onto the icy surface and, from far away, the grinding, mournful death-throes of ice echoing as it heaved and broke along the shores on the flood tide. Spring had arrived, but the melt brought with it deceit: the wind had veered and swirls of high cirrus were blowing in from the north. Winter would return, he was sure, for a final bout.

Returning to the cabin, he locked the door and drew the curtains, then unpacked and checked his rucksack, heavy with the weight of a thousand gold sovereigns. He removed and sharpened the whittling knife strapped in its elk-leather sheath to his lower leg and fiddled with the Belgian .32-calibre revolver in his jacket pocket. Only then could he put his mind to planning his journey to Stenviken and Sweden, to evading patrols out of Horten and the searchlights and guns of the outer batteries at Rauer and Bolærne; to plotting a route around the hundreds of underwater rocks and to deciding how he would best use the limited hours of deep darkness.

As he leaned over the charts, instead of the fear he had experienced earlier in the day, and many days before, a wave of optimism passed through him. Never in his life had he felt such clarity and trust in himself but, equally, he knew it was Klara who had planned it all and put herself at such risk.

As the afternoon faded, the clouds darkened and lowered as the sun settled into the west and then disappeared. He opened the door and looked out. The treetops swayed as the northerly gained strength, and the first flurries of snow hurried past. He pulled his collar tight. Still he felt no fear. He picked up the shotgun which Klara had thrust into his hand as he left the Castle, stuffed the box of heavy buckshot into his left-side pocket and set off for the quay. Here he completed a check of *Terne*, her fuel reserves and the mooring ropes, before heading along the harbour wall to the boatshed.

At the seaward end of the shed a mezzanine floor had been constructed, once housing bunks for use by the ice workers, the cabin being reserved for the manager and his family in those days. Although dusty and untidy, the high platform was the perfect place for Thomas to wait, giving a view down to the main floor and entrance door and, from a balcony on the seaward side, to the harbour, where *Terne* was gently rocking. He thought again of Olaf, and his solution to the mystery of the ice-free water, and felt his loss with a wave of sadness and anger.

And there he stayed all night. As the sun rose, there was no sign of Brann. It was, for Thomas, both an anti-climax and a relief. He had spent the night watching the door, imagining the assassin slip into the boatshed and, only then, after calling him out, would he have pulled the trigger. There would have been no mercy. And no one, not even Brann, would survive a slug from a shotgun at twenty yards.

Through the morning Thomas waited, ticking off the hours until Klara would arrive at around three 'o' clock. Every now and then, he would stretch his legs and peer out over the harbour. He checked *Terne*, several more times, her fuel and engine, and the mooring ropes for quick release, each time returning to the boatshed. Snow was falling steadily, the wind rising, an incipient storm rattling the tiles on the roof. The walls vibrated and shook in the wind. He looked over his shoulder, across the balcony; a wall of dark cloud had rolled down the Narrows, shutting out the fortress. The storm was closing in on Skarholmen and the light was falling. He thought of the journey to come, about navigating the fjord in conditions like this: with poor visibility, then night, in a storm. It was beginning to feel horribly reckless. Worse, Klara was late and he feared for her and all she was risking for him.

Still he waited. Then, amid the din of the storm, he heard the scrape of the door on the barn's earthen floor. He tensed, kneeling behind the railings at the top of the wooden ladder, hoping to see Klara at last, yet fearing Brann's final strike. Thumbing the safety, he lifted the barrel of the shotgun and slipped his forefinger onto the trigger guard. His heart pounding, he waited. There was a kick and the sound of a shoulder on the door. The dark and indistinct shape of a figure squeezed through the gap into the murky light of the boatshed, moving slowly. He lifted the shotgun to his shoulder, following the figure as it moved, hesitantly, across the barn. It stopped and turned towards him, no more than a dark shadow in the blackness of the barn.

Then...a forced whisper: "Thomas".

He breathed out, a long sigh. "Klara."

He dropped the shotgun and almost slid down the ladder in his haste. They embraced tightly and Klara said, "I'm late, sorry; my contact had problems with the papers. They can't be rushed. Here's what you need." She laid several documents under the workbench light.

"You are Magnus Solbakken, a farm worker collecting, on behalf of your employer, the Holmbekk estate, some specialist machine parts for the grain drier from our supplier in Svinesund. The drier is essential for the coming year's harvest, half of which we are selling to the Wehrmacht. You have been given this signed consent from the head of the Gestapo in Drøbak, Kriminalkommisar Frank Huber, giving the estate authority to use a small craft for transport of essential economic goods. I forged Huber's signature from my parents' prison release papers." She drew in a deep breath. "You are taking the boat because all our lorries have been confiscated. Almost true: the old Ford has been hidden in the forest."

Thomas looked at her. She was so calm.

"Here is the purchase order, a duplicate of mine. It will only be used if you are stopped on the fjord," she said, handing him another forged document. "I will meet you at the quay at Stenviken. I will have already loaded up the Ford with the order from our supplier in Svinesund. You must help me transfer the goods to *Terne*, then you must destroy all your paperwork. I will change the number plates on the Ford to a Swedish number for you. You drive the lorry away and it's yours: the rest is up to you. I motor in *Terne* with the goods up the fjord to Drøbak, all legitimate. Here is some Swedish currency; thanks to Father for that." She looked him in the eye as if to say, 'what could be simpler,' but a tear slipped down her cheek, her eyes betraying the stress of the operation she had planned.

She took hold of him and said, "You need to go. Good luck." Then, stopping as she reached the door she looked back and held her hand up, a wave. "If anyone can navigate that fjord, it'll be you."

She seemed reluctant to leave, looking down at her feet, silent and breathing deeply. "I'll wait at the top of Storgaten," she said. "Only when I see you leave the harbour...only when I know you are safely on the way, will I head back for the lorry."

"Klara," he shouted as she disappeared through the door. "One last thing, in brief."

"What?" she said, impatiently. "I have much to sort out before I leave."

"I need to tell you. In case..." He hadn't planned this. "You know the story about the last lorry-load of gold to leave Norges Bank..."

———

Thomas picked up his rucksack and the shotgun, checked once again the Belgian .32 in his pocket and buttoned up his jacket. Reaching the door, he looked outside into the snow, only too aware of the dangers he now faced: guiding a small craft down a fjord strewn with hidden rocks in a snowstorm, with night just an hour or two away. It seemed madness to even try, he knew that. But he had no doubts.

Slithering down the rocky steps, he leapt onto the quay and climbed down into *Terne's* cockpit. The snow had already eased, the clouds had lifted, the wind less violent. There was sufficient light remaining to cover the first leg of the route out into safe, open water. Sweeping a thick coating of snow off the engine cover and thwarts, he primed the fuel pump and checked again the level of diesel in the tank. He glanced up, picked up the shotgun and took a few steps up the ladder to check the quay, dreading the prospect of Brann appearing out of the late afternoon gloom.

The whole harbour was deserted. At last, he had a fighting chance of reaching Sweden.

FIFTY

Starting up the engine, Thomas reflected for a moment on the unplanned direction his life had taken since that fine autumn day in Oxford. It had had one unexpected outcome: he now knew, for sure, that his future lay in the place of his birth. This is where he belonged, where he would return to and one day settle even as, now, he was fleeing to a country he had never visited and knew nothing of. He took a last look along the quay and stepped back into *Terne*, his stomach tingling, his breath tight. Opening the cabin door to throw in his rucksack and collect the lifejacket Klara had insisted he wore, it just remained to cast off.

It was then, from the darkness of the cabin, that Brann struck.

Thomas reacted too late. Already Brann was on him, his immense hands looping a rope over his head and tightening it around his neck. But he had prepared for this moment. In a single, twisting movement he threw a powerful left hook, hitting Brann square on the side of his jaw. The rope fell away, giving Thomas freedom to move. He threw two sharp jabs to the face and then a perfect right hook which caught Brann on the chin. Grunting with the impacts, Brann shuffled forward on the slippery bottom boards, throwing a wild left and a right in quick succession. Thomas stepped back and ducked, Brann's huge fists slipping harmlessly, once, twice, across his shoulders.

As he struggled to drag the Belgian .32 from his pocket, and in the half light, he failed to see Brann's next assault or appreciate how fast the lumbering giant could move. Brann's fist caught him with the weight of a steel bar, pain exploding across the side of his cheek. He felt his body crumble and he fell heavily, his head catching the engine cover with a glancing but harsh blow.

Half turning, he glanced up as Brann loomed over him, smiling. The rope pulled tight, trapping his arms. "Why..." he gasped, but the crushing weight and sharp studs of a heavy boot took the air from his chest.

As his hand burrowed deeper into his pocket, Brann had become a blur, snow drifting around his great torso. Shaking and barely conscious, Thomas's hand closed around the Belgian .32. Finding the trigger, he raised his head and drew in a deep breath. A ball of flame and gun-smoke exploded from his jacket at the same moment as Brann's heavy boot slammed into the side of his head.

———

As consciousness returned, Thomas felt his face scraping across a cold, broken surface, his body sliding freely down a steep slope, feet first, and crashing over rocks. Shooting pains ran up his legs. His ankles felt raw and numb. His face pounded, as if his skull was being punched from inside. His arms were pinned. Slowly, he opened his eyes; the light was fading and snow was falling, driven flat by a harsh wind which cut through his wet clothes. Gradually, he realised where he was. Then fear hit: the terror and the anger that Brann had finally taken him.

Lifting his head, he could see his legs were bound by a tight noose. From there a rope extended onto the icy surface of the fjord. Hallangspollen. His hands were numb and snow swept across his face, stinging his skin and eyes. Behind him he heard someone working, scrabbling in the snow and then, in the corner of his eye, a blurry image of a figure appeared: Brann, limping, breathing noisily and swearing. He was dragging a heavy anchor, clanking and scraping across the ice. As

Thomas's eyes cleared, he picked up the colour of blood on Brann's right leg.

"Bastard," shouted Brann. "My knee, you shot my knee." He groaned in pain, waving the Belgian .32 wildly in the air. "You'll suffer for this." He breathed in, struggling to find the words. "But you'll have to wait..." He groaned, breathing deeply. "I could give you a bullet to the head, right now...but I have something far worse planned for you." His heavy spiked boots crunched on the ice as he wandered, aimlessly, limping heavily. "Look what you did..." he screamed, leaning across Thomas's face. Carried by the storm, there was a hint of the same distinctive mix of alcohol, sweat and old, damp wool Thomas remembered from the short, hazy encounter on *Terne*. "You'll die in fuckin' agony for this," Brann cried out, his face contorted in pain.

"And..." He lifted Thomas's rucksack and shook it. "I've got your gold. I knew it was you, I knew it. Now, you'll give me the rest. Understand? That's why you're still alive."

Lifting his head, Thomas tried to understand: the anchor, the rope, the fjord, the ice. Would this be what it was like? To die in the freezing water, bound and helpless, in pain, his legs probably shot to hell. "Not like this, please," he whispered. Shaking uncontrollably, he felt the noose being tightened further around his raw ankles and watched Brann preparing the ropes before setting off across the ice, into the bleak expanse of Hallangspollen, into the gathering dusk, the storm, the giant's huge frame lumbering and swaying, his injured leg dragging through the melting ice and snow. Beside him, Thomas heard the anchor scraping over the ice and through puddles of bloody water.

On and on Thomas was hauled, helpless and shivering, splashed in his face by icy water. His gloves were lost, his fingers intensely painful. But Brann was slowing, stopping time and again to gather his strength, holding his shattered leg and screaming in pain.

In despair, burning emotions flashed through Thomas's mind: a grinding frustration that he had been taken so easily; anger at having to die so young, so frighteningly and uselessly, before he had achieved a thing in life. The people who meant something to him flared up in his thoughts: most of all, inexplicably, Ingrid, with her beautiful smile and swaying hips. She, and Klara, his newly discovered parents, Agnes, Severin: all of them, they would all go from his life.

Brann stopped and turned, his head on one side, staring, the whole of his lower leg soaked in blood still seeping onto the wet ice. "Now," he said, pulling on the anchor rope, neatly coiling it in a series of well-practised swings of his arm. "Just tell me...where the fuckin' gold is hidden. Lorry 27..." He cried again in pain and despair. "I know it all, all of your sordid little story: the Lorry, the Merc, everything. Norway's greatest ever thief, eh? I figured it out..." He sighed. "Brann always figures it out." He then grunted and pulled out a long ice drill and a saw from his rucksack, dropping them, clattering, onto the ice.

"Here's a good place," he shouted, looking over his shoulder, staggering a few steps forward and holding ready the drill. It turned, biting into the ice, a horrible grinding sound. It finally broke through. Brann then grabbed the saw and, in small, sharp movements, began to cut the ice, groaning and breathing heavily as he worked.

Thomas finally grasped what was unfolding. Brann would dispose of him here, off Skarholmen, in the deep water under the ice...where his father went down. Exactly here. Unless...he released the secret of the gold. As his head settled back, he heard once again his father's cry for help: *'Jam the nets.'* He had watched as his father's hand sunk beneath the black water. Brann knew the story; he might even have heard it from his mother the day the farm was sold.

"Just the right size." Brann's voice sounded triumphant but barely audible as he stared at the hole in the ice. Then, taking a few steps, he squatted to readjust the noose around Thomas's ankles. Brann then placed the anchor next to the hole, his clothes flapping in the storm, his black hair flying loose beneath his hat.

"Well?" said Brann, his voice weak and in despair. "Last chance..."

"I'll tell you," shouted Thomas. "I'll take you to where the gold is buried. You can have it all."

A flurry of snow cut through Thomas's wet hair as he lay in a shallow, icy pool, his senses almost detached from his body. Coloured water lapped his mouth. Shuddering, he twitched at the taste of Brann's blood. His eyes opened briefly, taking in the swirling snow, the emptiness of the icy fjord, the almost-darkness. He knew his life was ebbing away. He could no longer feel anything, not even the cold. There was no light, no sound.

"You can have it. All of it," he shouted again, but his voice was no more than a whisper. Brann stood over him, swaying, waving a rifle in one hand, the Belgian .32 in the other, his eyes vacant; he no longer seemed to hear.

"It's too late," said Brann, his voice weak and broken by cries of pain. "I've had it. I'm as good as fuckin' dead." He held the two guns, trying to direct them at Thomas. "Both knees...that's what you'll get. And then the water...You'll fuckin' die...under the ice."

"You can have it all," Thomas shouted, a croaking, withered scream.

"Too late...too fuckin' late."

Brann stood, swaying, buffeted by the wind, his gaze unfocused. And then, as if in slow motion, the rifle slipped from his hand and tumbled across the ice. He groaned and lifted the revolver. There was a flash from the muzzle, a loud report, an agonising pain in Thomas's leg. Then, slowly, Brann started to crumble at the knees. For a moment he still stood, reeling, shaking. With a loud groan, he finally keeled over, crashing onto the ice. His head lifted momentarily, then fell back. He was breathing heavily, his fingers twitching.

Thomas, so weak he could barely move, forced himself to stay conscious, to not fade away. He dragged himself towards the fallen giant. Brann's eyes were pleading, his mouth opening and closing, wordlessly. Rivulets of pink water spread across the ice from his broken knee.

Thomas sat up, drawing the knife from the sheath on his lower left leg. Strand by strand, he cut the rope which bound his legs. Easing away the noose he was now free to move. He looked at Brann. Close to unconsciousness, he struggled to decide what he should do with the man who, moments ago, was set to kill him in the worst way imaginable. But if Brann were to survive...and he, Thomas, were to become unconscious....

Unsteady and shaking violently, he made a decision. He looped the rope around Brann's huge boots, tightening it as best he could. He then slid forward in a series of sharp pushes towards the ice hole. Looking back at Brann, prone and barely moving on the wet ice, he gave the anchor a final shove. It fell in with a dull splash. Through the wailing of the storm, Thomas shivered at Brann's scream. He dragged himself aside as the giant slid across the ice, his eyes bulging, his arms flailing. Then, suddenly, the rope jerked to a halt.

Half sitting, Thomas could see that Brann had stabbed a large hunting knife into the frozen surface, like an ice axe. Blood still poured from him, colouring a deep red the small pond in which he lay. Snow covered his body. His black hair was wet and plastered across his face. Thomas stood up, swaying and unsteady, looking down on Brann. All around the storm moaned and screamed, threatening to blow him over like a broken sapling.

"Cut the rope," whispered Brann, looking up, his voice gurgling as he clung on to the knife. "Save me, stop the blood. You're free now. Ya don't need t'do this. We can both come out of this alive."

Thomas waited, barely aware of the storm blowing with such awful violence, slicing through his wet clothes. He looked down at Brann's pleading eyes in the failing light, then again scanned the blur of the dark, frozen fjord. From far away, the death rattles of the breaking ice continued, carried by the storm. The coldest winter for a hundred years — its last gasp. He waited a moment and then...

"Sorry, Brann."

He swung his leg and gave Brann's hand a sharp kick. The knife clattered across the ice and Brann, writhing like a freshly caught fish, slithered again towards the ice hole, his mouth a silent scream, raw terror fixed on his face, his gloved hands scrabbling uselessly at the frozen surface. For a moment he lay spread-eagled across the ice hole, groaning, pleading, his arms flailing. Thomas shuffled towards him, looking down at the bulging eyes, feeling strangely calm, devoid of pity and unmoved by the squealing cries. Slowly, Brann was dragged into the ice hole, his hands frantically searching for a grip to save him, each desperate attempt to pull himself free cracking and breaking up the ice. His heavy winter coat floated for a moment and his long hair wafted in the reddened water. His mouth opened, taking in a huge gulp of air. Then the fjord closed slowly over him, a look of bewilderment and dread etched onto his pale grey face. A few bubbles rose and burst on the surface. Brann then sank, his ghostly face fading into the blackness of the deep water. A moment later, he was gone.

Stepping back from the ice hole, Thomas's legs gave way. The wind blew him aside and he felt himself fall, hitting wet snow and freezing water. As his eyes flickered, he knew his life was draining away and almost gone.

And then he heard...a voice, far away: a shout, fighting the thunder of the storm.

She was calling his name.

He turned.

A figure was running, faint in the gathering darkness.

PART FIVE
RESOLUTION

FIFTY-ONE

"A fine view," said Oberst Baumann gazing out from his first-floor office in Drøbak's Fjord Hotel. He turned to accept the day's briefing papers from his adjutant and then dismissed him. Not a lot had happened in the area since the 9th of April, which suited him well and, as he flicked through the reports, today was no different. He had established an efficient administrative team which had put in place food supplies, security and other essentials, and he could leave them to it. There was fighting in the north, but it was quiet enough in Drøbak.

He sat back in the chair and once again lifted his long legs onto the desk, crossing them at the ankles, then took a sip of dense black coffee from one of the hotel's bone-china cups. A supply ship trudged up the fjord towards Oslo, the dull thudding of its engine fading as it passed out of view. Closer by, a couple of boys were fishing from the quay, as if the invasion had never happened. His mind drifted back to a conundrum within which lay, he felt sure, an opportunity on the grand scale.

Baumann remained convinced that a hoard of Norway's central bank gold had ended up, in the panic of the 9th of April, not far from where he now sat. And now he had the time to do something about it. He lit a cigarette and ran through in his mind lines of evidence that had earer since he had first assembled the bare bones of the story in ays of the occupation.

ough liaising with Major Neef of the economic unit, the Wirtschaftstab, it had not been too difficult to discover that Matthias Holmbekk was not just a junior bank employee as some had said, but was, in fact, the senior clerk responsible for day-to-day management and record-keeping of Norges Bank's gold reserves: "a favoured employee of the Governor, no less," he whispered between long draws on his cigarette. Many local people were, it turned out, well aware of this, though Brann had decided to keep quiet on the matter. No, the big man could not be trusted. And, once again, he hadn't turned up for work.

Baumann swung out of his chair and pulled open the door. "Wagner!" The young corporal came running, fear etched onto his face.

"Sir?"

"Where's Brann?"

"Don't know, sir."

"Why not?" He let the fear linger. "Find him."

Brann knew more than he was letting on, that much was clear to Baumann. He would deal with him when they found him.

Matthias Holmbekk had also, of course, disappeared; he was dead in the view of local people, or had absconded to Sweden according to the Gestapo but, whatever the truth, it raised some interesting issues. Holmbekk had had a direct link to the gold, not just as the clerk responsible for the vault records, but through his likely actions on the 9th. The abandoned lorry found in forest, within walking distance of his own home, matched the description of the last vehicle seen leaving the bank on the day of the invasion. Lorry 27. And, by all accounts, it was Holmbekk who was at the wheel, the last to leave as the vaults were emptied, as befitted his job.

Under interrogation, several members of the Bank's audit team had eventually revealed to the Wirtschaftstab that everyone at the bank knew for sure this final load of gold had not made it to Lillehammer on the 9th and had been seized by the German army at a roadblock in central Oslo. But these people were not there at the time — they were on their way to Lillehammer — and they were simply parroting what Holmbekk had said in his report, which was now in his hands. However, Baumann knew from multiple army sources that no such lorry had been stopped in central Oslo. It was pure myth. And there was more. He pressed his thumb hard into his palm and turned it, like a screw. By the time Lorry 27 had left the bank, at around 1330 hours on the 9th, routes south out of Oslo had not yet been closed, as they had been to the north. Holmbekk could easily have driven the lorry down National Highway 1 and then turned off towards Drøbak.

For sure the bank clerk had been at the centre of the heist. But now he was dead.

Baumann let his legs fall off the desk and walked to the window. The kids had caught a small fish. His mind now drifted to Galtung and his likely role. Baumann opened the window and took in a long breath of cool Nordic air. Below lay the garages and inside the largest of these was the Bank Governor's Mercedes-Benz 540K. Several Wehrmacht soldiers on the day had confirmed that a fine Mercedes was seen behind the lorry as they left the bank and raced down Kirkegata. There are not many cars of this sort and colour in Norway, and it is logical to assume it must be the same car taken at the junction of the Ås road and Highway 1 on the evening of the 9th — approaching from Drøbak and just a mile or two further east from where the lorry was dumped. The soldiers closing the junction had been more interested in the car than its occupant, but it was telling that the description of the driver — tall, thin, fair-haired, early twenties — closely matched Galtung's appearance as recorded in the interrogation records of staff at the Castle on the night of the failed raid.

Baumann closed the window and paced the room, his boots heavy on the bare boards. Picturing the student as the second driver in the gold heist, his pulse quickened. Galtung must have been in on Holmbekk's plan. It made sense. The student, a family friend of the Holmbekks; the bank clerk in need of some reliable muscle and another driver. Two vehicles, both linked to Norges bank, both ending up in the Drøbak area. Two drivers known to each other, the best of friends. Holmbekk and Galtung. He thumped the table in triumph.

For sure, it was Galtung who had, once the gold was safely buried, killed Holmbekk. So only he now knows where Lorry 27's hoard is hidden.

"Zimmerman!" shouted Baumann.

His adjutant appeared at the door.

"I sent that fool Wagner to find Brann, the big Norwegian we use for information. Put a dozen men onto it. I want Brann in here now."

The door quietly closed and Baumann wandered across the room to a rather grand black and gilt mirror which had been moved to his office from the ballroom downstairs. He looked at himself and flicked at the first hints of greying hair around the ears. They gave him an air of gravitas, maturity; wisdom maybe. No one, he thought, not the Wirtschaftstab, not the Gestapo, no one else in the Wehrmacht, the local Police or the Bank knew the whole picture; no one could put all the pieces together to make the true story. Only him, Baumann. This was an opportunity of a lifetime to acquire wealth beyond anyone's imagination. The gold — half a truck of the stuff — had been off-loaded by Holmbekk and Galtung and hidden, most likely in the forest around Torsrud where the lorry had been abandoned. Torsrud: the home of Severin Nordby, the mad farmer, which Helgeland and Berg, Brann's men, had confirmed was regularly visited by Galtung. Where better for Galtung and Holmbekk to hide the gold than around the home of someone so stupid, apparently, that he would never be suspected of anything: *Mad Nordby*?

All that mattered was to get there first...before Brann. So it was vital to find out what the big man really knew.

FIFTY-TWO

Thomas waited at the bus-stop on the Ås road. He watched as a car passed by at speed, throwing dust up from the road. In the front seats were two Wehrmacht army officers, one with a cigarette with smoke trailing out of an open window. He saw them laugh as they passed by; and then they were gone, they and their joke. Minutes later the bus appeared, grinding noisily up the hill out of Drøbak. He climbed in, painfully, pushing on his stick and limping up the aisle, then slumping into a middle seat against the wide back window. He was lucky, he knew, to have survived his ordeal on the fjord, lucky his bullet had disabled Brann, lucky his own injury would one day heal...And lucky, most of all that Klara was the extraordinary woman she was.

The bus continued slowly up the hill, past the turning to the Bell House, then Frogn church and a series of small farms and isolated houses. For the first time in months he no longer found himself looking over his shoulder, listening at night for the sound of an intruder, feeling the steady rumble of fear in his gut.

The bus slowed as the junction with National Highway 1 came into view, then stopped. Ahead was a roadblock. He waited a while, then left the bus and watched it move slowly ahead, sat behind an aged black

Volvo, taking its turn in the queue. The soldiers at the roadblock glanced his way, but ignored him. Crossing the road, he headed for a track leading to a dense birchwood and mire. No one attempted to call him back. Looking up to the sun, his eyes closed and he breathed out a long, slow sigh.

Birds sang and he felt the warm breeze in his hair as he hobbled along the track. At the top of a steep rise, breathing heavily, he stood surveying the forest all around, shafts of sunlight cutting through the trees. Beyond the wood, the track passed through a jumble of grassy fields, one of which led his eye to the top of a rounded, rock-strewn hill. Above it rose a majestic white cloud towering into the rich blue sky as if to burst beyond it into space; a cloud so brilliant, so noble and sublime it seemed a tragedy it would not be there forever. Its finely-sculpted form, sharp against the heavens, would soon dissolve and fade away, its life ephemeral, its glory transient. He stood, planted, gazing at the cloud, overcome by a rush of melancholy. A tear formed in his eye and he brushed it away.

On through the landscape he walked until he found the abandoned roadworks. Pushing through an area of scrub and wet ground, he came upon a steep embankment, a layer of loose glacial till and, below, the dark colour of peat lying over a hard grey boulder clay. Below that, it seemed, was another organic layer: firm evidence of an earlier warmer climate. For a while he probed the deposits, then found a rock and sat with his lunch. It was time: he reached into his pocket and found his Petersen. Loading the bowl, he enjoyed his first smoke since arriving in Norway and, when he was done, he let the pipe cool and he cleaned it with a birch stick roughly fashioned with his whittling knife.

His mind drifted to the bus journey back and he thought again about the buried gold at Torsrud. It seemed unreal: the idea of hiding a fortune in gold beneath a pile of cow manure. Norway's gold had been saved and he smiled at the thought, but the question of his own one thousand sovereigns, if they really were his, had tested him for weeks. Pushing his hand into the rucksack, he touched the reassuring texture of canvas; his gold was still safe. He had thought to stop on the way back to Skarholmen and return it to the muckheap, but now he was not so sure. He thought about the roadblocks, the checks and searches, and the

Wehrmacht taking over in Drøbak; the Nazis commandeering the ground floor of the Castle and Klara's worries about the estate and whether it would survive and whether his own role for the British might one day be unmasked. An unknown future lay ahead. Gold could help his family; it could be his ticket to safety.

Again touching the canvas bag, feeling the coins inside, he covered it well with his anorak and drew tight the rucksack cord. He checked his watch. It was time to leave. He could join the Ås bus from Drøbak if he chose to hurry. If he caught that, he could visit the library. And if he visited the library, he could inquire about new research papers from Oslo, however unlikely the prospect. Perhaps he would see Ingrid again.

FIFTY-THREE

Baumann, satisfied that his responsibilities for the day were in good hands, headed out of town on the Ås road until he reached a turning into the forest heading towards higher land. Little used, potholed and largely grassed over, the track was ill-suited to his purloined Volvo PV51, but there was no rush and he took it slowly. Eventually, he passed an icy lake shaded by dense forest and drew his car to a halt by a log cabin sited on the upper part of a grassy clearing. An old man leaned against the door pillar.

"Herr Nordby, you come highly recommended," said Baumann. "I hope you will be able to help me."

"I doubt that."

"And why would that be?"

"Not much goes on here."

"But if you could help, you would?" Baumann smiled.

"Depends."

"Of course it depends, but let's see. I have a little problem I'd like to solve. I believe that somewhere in this vicinity there has been hidden some stolen goods. You'll no doubt know what I refer to."

"No idea," said Severin.

"Then you will have no objection if I were to look around your property? I come alone; it is quite safe. You have a cellar?"

Severin nodded towards a trap door in the floor.

"Show me."

A while later, Baumann was able to conclude that the cellar held little of interest. "You were quite right, Herr Nordby."

"And nothing upstairs, either," he lamented later on. "Nothing anywhere in the house. But I would not be doing my job, would I, if I were not to check? You do understand?"

Severin grunted.

"So, perhaps we can look outside. You see, after this winter — hellish it's been, yes? — the ground has been frozen and even now the frost is still deep in the shadows. Even your charming lake still has a layer of ice. Unbroken ice. And the rocks: so rocky up here, so little soil."

"Does me well enough."

"You have done well on it," said Baumann. "But there is one place, is there not, that is now ice-free, that could have been ice-free the whole terrible winter. Not your barns, which I have checked, or the pigsty. But there is one other place, yes?"

Severin offered no response, just some fidgeting and a shuffling of his feet.

"You see, before this terrible war I was a farmer myself. A noble way of life, wouldn't you agree? Now, all farms with animals — which includes most farms and many houses with gardens as we all know — have a muckheap, yes? Not at first sight the best place to hide stolen goods, I would concur, but they do tend not to freeze, even in a winter as cold as this one has been. Not that I have ever experienced a winter like this one, mind you. Perhaps it is because I have lived so much further south for most of my life. So, maybe, Herr Nordby, we could wander down to your muckheap, and you would do a little digging for me? You see, I did notice it has been disturbed recently."

"I've been spreading it, that's what we do. If you want good grass..."

"I am aware of that, Herr Nordby," said Baumann. "You only have a small amount left because most has been used, yes?"

As they walked towards the muckheap, Baumann felt a rising sense of anticipation, the more so as they came closer. He looked around at the forest. It was deserted. No one ever came here, except Galtung, but not today it seemed. Pity. He touched the pistol pressing against his right thigh. But there was no one to interrupt the discovery about to take place. The gold had to be here, under the muckheap, a place no one would ever think to search. He looked at Nordby, the old fool shuffling along, his boots already soiled with the freshly spread manure.

"Here? You want me to dig here?" said Severin. "Wasting your time, you are."

Baumann nodded. Severin thrust his spade into the muckheap, steam rising and dissipating into the warm air. He removed several spadefuls and looked at Baumann. "You sure?"

"Yes, quite sure. More, please," replied Baumann, smiling.

An hour later, with Severin's face running with sweat, the whole muckheap — the remains from the vast pile before it was spread — had been moved to one side. He had even skimmed the blackened grass and had thrown the turves aside.

"More," said Baumann, in rising frustration.

"God knows what you think is buried here," said Severin, wheezing. "See, nothing."

Baumann strode some distance back up the field, then returned, with great effort controlling his anger and frustration.

"Herr Nordby, I am very grateful for your efforts. But you leave me with a dilemma. You see, if you do not reveal what I am looking for I may be forced to, how shall we say it? Be a little more persuasive."

"And what are you looking for?"

"You know very well."

"No idea what you are talking about." Severin held out his arms. "Look wherever you want. There's nothing valuable here, except me grass."

"Herr Nordby," said Baumann, "there is a unit of Gestapo in town. You know, policemen, but not as you know them here in Norway."

"Ah."

"They can be, how shall we say, unforgiving at times. Vicious."

"Oh."

"I cannot be like this myself, but I can suggest to them methods of persuasion they are usually only too willing to use in situations like this."

"Sounds unpleasant."

"You understand my point."

Baumann took Severin by the arm and slowly walked him a few steps to take in the view over his land.

"You love your farm, I know that, and I have a kinder option for you to help with my search," said Baumann. "It would not involve the terrors of the Gestapo. You see, I believe you know what is hidden on this land. Buried by a bank clerk who is sadly no longer with us. Maybe with the help of an English student, hmm? Who seems to have disappeared too. What do you think?"

"You think I'd know a fancy bank clerk? Ha."

"I am giving you an option, Herr Nordby. This is between us, personally, you understand. I will use my authority to hold off the Gestapo and you will be left in peace with your farm. I guarantee this. In exchange, you will share with me your knowledge of where the valuable consignment is hidden. You know exactly what I refer to. You excavate it for me and shift it to a new location of my choosing using your horse and cart. We share it on a fifty-fifty basis. A happy outcome; we would both be winners."

Severin slapped his knee and burst out laughing. "Ah, the gold rumour. Lorry 27, they call it. No, Herr Baumann, you have the wrong end of the stick. If there were gold here, it would be better hidden than any place you have looked so far. But there ain't gold here, I can tell you that, and if there had been it would have been removed by now and safely locked away in a bank somewhere. Sweden maybe. And I would be a rich man. And I wouldn't be stood here talking t' you."

Later that day, as the sun began to drop below the top of the trees, and the shadows lengthened, and he had strained every sinew to contain the violence he felt exploding within him, Baumann felt an inescapable outcome weighing heavily on his shoulders. It would be impossible for a man so stupid as Nordby not to have given away the truth. Just a twitch of his hairy mouth would have revealed his deceit. But no, nothing. It could therefore, maddeningly, only be concluded that he was speaking the truth and that there was no gold hidden at Torsrud. It wasn't Nordby. And therefore it might not be Galtung, either. It was frustrating beyond belief. The gold could be anywhere, even lost entirely. It was impossible to know.

FIFTY-FOUR

Shortly after midnight, under the gaze of a half-moon, Severin left Torsrud and made his way on narrow paths down through the forest towards Skarholmen. He waited for a cloud to kill the silvery light before breaking cover to cross the causeway, arriving at the cabin a few minutes later. It appeared deserted, but a faint glow was visible through one of the windows and he tapped gently on the door.

The discussions that followed saw the short, dark summer night fade into a sun-filled new day. They all understood not one of them was safe, not completely. Not Severin, nor Thomas, nor Klara. Brann was gone, and Westervik, but the story of what had happened to the contents of Lorry 27 now resided solely with the three of them. Others would want that knowledge.

It was with some pride and glee that Severin told the story of how, a few days before Baumann's visit, he had decided to move the gold, using his horses, to a new location now that most of the muckheap had been spread.

"In the forest," he said, "a warm spot. I dug a pit and buried it there. Nicely lined and covered in spruce planking and bilberries and stones. You could stand on it and never know."

"Brilliant," said Thomas. "But Baumann won't give up. He might settle on any one of us now that Matthias has gone — almost certainly dead — and try to force the truth from us."

The cabin fell silent. From outside, a woodpecker tapped on an unseen tree and a beam of the early morning sun found a gap in the curtain, lighting up Severin's coffee cup as if it were a beacon. Next to the stove, a butterfly flapped between a couple of logs left over from the winter, trapped by a dusty cobweb. Klara freed it, releasing it through the window.

"I have an idea," she said, a smile spreading across her face. "We can stop Baumann's gold hunt in its tracks."

———

The following morning, Baumann sat at his desk at the Fjord Hotel, once again enjoying the view over the water. But the beauty of the Norwegian landscape would not solve the puzzle in front of him. A note had been found amongst the regular military post from Oslo HQ and addressed specifically to Oberst Baumann, marked 'Confidential' and dated today. A small dark-haired woman, a little bent with age and with a scarf over her head had been seen near the post-room that morning, but it was generally agreed she would not have been able to enter the building to deliver the letter into the official trays.

Baumann picked up the note, puffed at the poor German grammar and read it through for the tenth time. Brann, it would seem, had surfaced again and this time had something barely believable to say. The big man was now somewhere in Sweden, so the note said, sitting with half a ton of Norwegian gold coins which had previously been hidden, he said, in an area of state-owned forest somewhere between Drøbak and Ås. It obviously related to Lorry 27. The note concluded:

INVASION

IT WERE HOLMBEKK THE WEEDY CLERK WHAT HID THE
GOLD AND GALTUNG THE GLACIER STUDENT WHAT TOOK
THE MERCEDES. BOTH NOW DEAD.
YOU CAN THANK ME FOR THAT.
YOU WOULD LOVE TO KNOW WHERE THE GOLD IS NOW.
RIGHT? SAD FOR YOU ITS FAR AWAY. IN SWEDEN.
DON'T BELIEVE ME? EVER SEEN A TAG FROM A BAG OF
NORGES BANK GOLD COINS? HERE IS ONE, A SAMPLE FOR
YOU TO ADMIRE AND IMAGINE WHAT MIGHT HAVE BEEN.
HALF A BLOODY TON OF THE STUFF!
HOPE YOU GETTING ON ALL RIGHT WITHOUT ME.

Alexander Brann

FIFTY-FIVE

Alfred Johansen arrived outside the former Norwegian Police headquarters at Victoria Terrasse, Oslo. He had unfortunately been killed in the bombings of Oslo on the 9th, at least that was the sad tale that filtered its way back to Welhaven and the others. He was aware that, in accordance with protocol, the Monitoring Centre files had all been destroyed on the day of the invasion, together with a few notes he had left in the office, which would no doubt have been collected up by Welhaven's efficient secretary and disposed of too.

What none of them knew was that he had retained a folder of his most valuable and secret notes to await the attention of the German security services, once Oslo had been taken. He would hide these anonymous notes amongst out-of-date expenses records for the Oslo police, knowing there would be no chance of them being noticed or destroyed along with the Monitoring Centre files. Here, they could never be associated with him. And, if they were ever found — however unlikely that scenario — that would simply be the result of sloppy practice in the admin team.

Johansen waited near the main entrance, enjoying the clear Norwegian air. He glanced up at the vibrant blue of the sky, bespeckled with frothing white clouds, large and small, and he squinted in the sharp sun.

Across the road was a short queue lined up in the shade outside a bakery; the Norwegians were so orderly, like Germans. It had always struck him that occupying Norway made no sense, ideologically, and ideology was surely the fount of everything. There were plenty of Norwegians who supported the Nazi cause — there must have been an easier way.

He turned briskly around and entered the police headquarters, flashing a Gestapo identity card, which he would use for such day-to-day purposes. After a short wait he was taken by the guards down two flights of stairs and was given a key to basement room B24. He waited until he was alone and slid the key into the lock, then opened the door to reveal a small, windowless room lined with shelving, floor to ceiling, with files mostly dating back to the mid-thirties. He turned the switch and a single light flickered into life. Walking to the far side of the room, he quickly identified several thin files, which he placed on a heavy wood table occupying the centre of the room. The files he had selected were largely given over to the names, addresses and contact details of every one of the Monitoring Centre agents. These were not duplicates of the official files, which were heavily guarded, but information he had collected first-hand over the last three years, entrusted to memory and then recorded. In addition were a small number of secret files of special interest.

One was particularly satisfying. "Two for one," he whispered, rereading the brief note headed *Klara Holmbekk, 4th April 1940.* Klara would live — she did no real harm — but she would be taken in and questioned. Galtung, though, was for sure a dangerous British spy, an enemy of the Reich. This was the perfect material for passing onto Krimminalkommissar Huber, whom he would meet shortly.

So intent was Johansen on enjoying the evidence in front of him, he failed to hear a click of the door latch behind him.

Seconds later a female voice whispered: "Alfred, you're still alive. I'm very glad."

He turned, his hand sliding automatically towards the revolver hidden beneath his coat, to see a small woman push the door closed with a sharp but controlled backward kick of her boot. She wore a brown dress and dark-coloured cardigan, very feminine with bright red lipstick. Her hair was strikingly black, a wig, falling onto her shoulders; her nose elegantly turned up into a sharp point. She was armed with a silenced Luger, held in light grey kid gloves, the barrel pointed at his face. Despite the disguise, he knew instantly who she was.

For a few seconds the woman stood motionless, staring, her gun steady.

"Klara, this is a surprise," he said, calmly, so impossible it seemed that she should be pointing a German pistol at him.

"Checking your notes?" she said, quietly.

He squinted. "These were missed. They should have been destroyed."

"Only a traitor would make sure they weren't." Her arm stiffened, her finger tightening on the trigger.

"Klara..." he said, taking a half step back, his voice breaking. "Please, no."

There were the last spoken words of his life. A dull thud sounded from Klara's Luger, a puff of residue from the silencer, a moment of destruction between Alfred Johansen's eyes.

She picked up the files and pushed them into a smart document case after quickly reading Johansen's note of the 4th of April: her own and Thomas's death warrants. She then carefully positioned her gun a short distance in front of Johansen's body, from which was now spreading copious volumes of free-flowing blood. She quickly looked around, turned off the light and left the room. Locking the door, she slid the key through the gap at the bottom of the door and moved fast up a flight of stairs towards the exit.

At the top she slipped the case into the hands of Beate Torjesen, a middle-aged Norwegian administrator of exemplary ordinariness, who had worked for many years on the Holmbekk estate before taking a clerical job with the police when her husband had moved to a new job in Oslo in '37. Klara gave her a single instruction. "Destroy it immediately."

Klara tied a scarf over her hair, took a deep breath, and slowly walked out of the building, nodding to the guard on the way out after a cursory search.

FIFTY-SIX

The tops of the waves caught the glare of the afternoon sun, coalescing at the horizon far to the south to create a shimmering mass of light. Across a perfect dome of bright blue sky countless cotton-wool clouds lined up like giant sheep, each following an invisible leader to an unseen destination far beyond the distant mountains. A gull wheeled overhead, lifted in the updrafts, and disappeared over the treetops.

From the quay at Skarholmen, Thomas watched a coaster make its way up the fjord, nosing its way through the Narrows, its course exactly that taken by the tragic warship, *Blücher*, barely two months ago. The great fortress of Oscarsborg, where he had stood on that fateful day, lay silent, the violence of the invasion no more than a deep melancholic memory embedded in the great, curved ramparts and in the lives of those who were there. The swastika flew from the tall flagpole on the island's highpoint.

He picked up his rucksack and returned across the causeway, then turned to follow the eastern shoreline of Hallangspollen. Arriving at the old fisherman's path, he climbed up the fjord-side, then struck north into the forest.

Later that day, he arrived at the small settlement of Svestad. Houses large and small were scattered amongst rocky cliffs, forests and ice lakes. He found a steep, stony track, Gamlebryggevei, the Old Quay Road. It led past several fine villas to a path where heavy blocks of stone, placed every few yards, supported a roughly fixed railing which separated him from a long drop to the fjord below. Off this track, Toni had said he would find Knausen; a little, white-painted house set amongst the pine trees.

He climbed the steep, uneven steps. At the top, a low metal gate creaked as he pushed it open. The top step was slippery after a recent shower of rain. He scrubbed it with his foot, kicking away the moss.

Closing the gate behind him, he looked across a patch of lawn to a single-storey cabin of simple construction with a covered terrace, from which there must be long views across the fjord.

Sitting on the terrace was a small, neat woman with her hair tied up and held by a silver clasp. She rose to greet him.

"Thomas," she said. "I knew one day you would come."

THE END

AUTHOR'S NOTE

INVASION is a work of fiction, yet many of the events in the novel are, to the best of my knowledge, historically true and several of the characters really existed in the roles I describe.

A key thread in the story is the invasion of Norway by Nazi Germany on the 9th of April 1940 and the flight of Norway's gold reserves. These were true events and *The Bitter Years* by Richard Petrow and *Gold Run* by Robert Pearson provide good historical accounts. INVASION does not follow the flight of the gold north, although it is a thrilling and heroic story and one brilliantly told in *Flukten med Norges Gull* by Asbjørn Jaklin.

Several Norwegian cities were taken in Germany's coordinated invasion of Norway. The assault on Oslo was led by the new heavy cruiser, *Blücher*, which was hit by two massive shells and two torpedoes from the defences on Oscarsborg fortress. Lying on an island in the fjord off Drøbak, the fortress can be visited as a tourist and is a fascinating day out. Hit at short range, *Blücher* sunk, as Thomas witnesses in the novel. The wreck lies off the rocky islands of Askholmene.

An excellent source of information on *Blücher*, including extracts of its War Diary and other contemporary accounts, can be found in *Heavy Cruisers of the Admiral Hipper Class* by Gerhard Koop and Klaus-Peter

Schmolke. The flashes of light and booming sounds experienced by Thomas, under guard on the fortress, were real engagements although, of course, he would not have known what was happening far to the south down the fjord.

The repackaging of the gold reserves did take place as I describe and it was all taken to Lillehammer on the 9th of April 1940, just before German troops closed the escape routes out of Oslo. The Norges Bank headquarters, opened in 1906, was the scene of events played out in the novel. The fine building still exists, although it no longer functions as the bank HQ. I was lucky to be able to visit the original gold vaults in 2019, so although the character Matthias Holmbekk is entirely from my imagination, his place of work in the vaults is accurately described.

A number of characters were well-known figures in Norway at the time INVASION is set. Colonel Birger Eriksen was the commander of Oscarsborg fortress and gave the order to fire on *Blücher*, giving time for the King and government to escape north by train. Nicolai Rygg was the Governor of Norges Bank and Kristian Welhaven was the chief of Oslo police and the *Politiets Overvåkingssentral* (Police Surveillance Centre). Prime Minister Johan Nygardsvold and his two ministers were real figures too, as was Paul Sandvik and several other local policemen who feature in the story. A history of the Drøbak police can be found in *Politiet i Follo Gjennom 100 År* by Bjørn Lillestråtten and Ivar Simastuen.

Jon Sundby was a character who Thomas meets at the cocktail party at the Castle and who gives encouraging words to Matthias, before leaving to join government ministers at the railway station. Sundby was the grandfather of a friend of mine in Norway and I included him in the story in part for this reason, although he was a significant figure in Norwegian politics at the time, an expert agriculturalist and was on the board of Norges Bank, so his presence at the bank meeting in the early hours of the 9th of April 1940 is historically plausible.

The broad geography of the area is as I portray it, except for the island of Skarholmen and some features such as Steinborg, which I invented. I do, however, manipulate the scale and character of the landscape for dramatic effect and there are probably many who would not recognise Hallangspollen as the ominous place I make it out to be. The Castle and all the farms and cabins exist purely in my imagination, as are many of the characters who populate the novel. So, anyone searching for Torsrud or the Bell House, will be disappointed. Ivar Svensen, the shopkeeper, is a made-up character, although in 1940 there was a grocer's shop in just the location where I place his shop; it was run by Trygve Gulliksen and the building (though not the shop) is still there.

In 1939/40, Drøbak was a much smaller town and only the main street was named: Storgaten, which features frequently in the novel. After the war, new streets were built and Storgaten was renamed. The two quays, Sundbrygga and Lehmanns, still exist although features such as the harbourmaster's office and the boatshed where *Terne* was restored were invented.

To the best of my knowledge, the assassination attempt on Col. Eriksen and the killing of the gunners and the ferrymen never happened, and neither did the theft of the gold on Lorry 27. These events are not, however, entirely implausible, given the extent of Nazi Germany's commitment to covert operations in support of military objectives and the 'just in time' flight of the gold out of Oslo.

It's not out of the question, therefore, that a hoard of gold is still buried somewhere high in the forests above Drøbak, written off and lost from the records.

If you have enjoyed this book, please consider leaving an honest review.

You can also visit my website (roberttregay.com) to read my blog posts and learn more about my writing process.

ACKNOWLEDGMENTS

I am immensely grateful for the help and guidance I received from many people in Norway.

Trond Hugubakken of PST (Norwegian Police Security Service) gave me access to information on German spying activity prior to the invasion and helped me understand how *Politiets Overvåkingssentral* operated and disposed of its records in 1940.

Two local historians, Erik Askautrud and Solveig Krogsrud gave me insights into Drøbak in 1939/40, and Christian Hintz Holm guided me through events at the time of the invasion.

Bjørn Lilleslåtten is a former Drøbak policeman and identified who might have handled the investigations into the imagined events of the 8th and 9th of April 1940.

Staff at Fred Olsen Cruise Lines kindly researched and advised on *Black Prince* and her captain.

My brother, Graeme, came up with Matthias's killer plan in the gold vaults of Norges Bank and helped me with a number of ideas and technical points in the novel.

My old friend Professor John Lewin checked my work on Thomas's ice age research.

I am especially grateful to Rod Duncan, novelist and university teacher, for his unstinting support and inspiration, without whom, I am sure, I never would have written what I have.

Finally, I must acknowledge one writer whose most acclaimed book has captivated me and has been the primary inspiration for me becoming a novelist: Eric Newby's *Love and War in the Apennines*, published in 1971.

Printed in Great Britain
by Amazon

38425408R00219